American Casanova

American

Casanova

The Erotic Adventures of the Legendary Lover

a novel directed by
Maxim Jakubowski in collaboration with:

M. Christian, Michael Crawley,

Carol Anne Davis, O'Neil De Noux,

Stella Duffy, Sonia Florens,

John Grant, Michael Hemmingson,

Vicki Hendricks, Thomas S. Roche,

Mitzi Szereto, Lucy Taylor,

Matt Thorne, Mark Timlin,

Sage Vivant, and Molly Weatherfield.

AMERICAN CASANOVA

THE EROTIC ADVENTURE OF THE LEGENDARY LOVER

Published by
Thunder's Mouth Press
An Imprint of Avalon Publishing Group, Inc.
245 West 17th Street., 11th Floor
New York, NY 10011

AVALON
publishing group incorporated

Compilation copyright © 2006 by Maxim Jakubowski

Library of Congress Cataloging-in-Publication Data is available.

ISBN-10: 1-56025-766-0
ISBN-13: 978-1-56025-766-0

9 8 7 6 5 4 3 2 1

Book design by Susan Canavan
Printed in the United States of America
Distributed by Publishers Group West

Table of Contents

Chapter One

The shadow of the moon crossed the gleaming surface of the lagoon. Giacomo Casanova stirred in his sleep, his mind still exercised by the decrepitude that had overtaken his once valiant acrobat's body and increasingly blurred memories of women and matters past. He suffered from indigestion and was afraid he was going to get dropsy and had, in truth, become a thoroughly sedentary man as he worked his way through his still uncompleted memoirs. It was of course that special time of night, the three-in-the-morning abyss, when some men could not, with all the will in the world, prevent every single wave of remembrance from flooding back and banishing tranquil sleep to a distant and desolate prison. Pauline. Henriette. Cecilia. Madame F. Nanette. Faces. Bodies. Shards. But sharp stabs of pain were soon coursing yet again through his flesh and bones, banishing the indecent thoughts, and he somehow managed to fall asleep again.

When he awoke the next morning, the myriad pains had vanished altogether, and there was a distinct and different smell in the room, as if the waters of Venice had remained stagnant for a couple of centuries and the ensuing fragrance had floated through the air, a knitted patchwork of women's perfumes, incense, and rotten fish.

Casanova coughed, cleared his throat. Frowned. He opened his eyes. There were heavy drapes across the windows of the room. A vase filled with drooping winter flowers stood on the dresser that faced his bed. A half-empty glass of water sat on the bedside table to his left. He stretched his body, finding uncommon pleasure in the languorous action. And right then he knew. He was alive. ALIVE!

He violently pulled the bedcovers away from his body. Adrenaline was flowing through him at an incredible speed. He looked down at his chest, thin dark curls like a gentle carpet across his skin. No longer gray. He felt his cock and it stirred effortlessly. The constant ache from his prostate was gone. He was alive. He closed his eyes and reflected.

Yesterday, he had not just fallen asleep. He had died. It had been June 4, 1798. An honorable death, tempered only by the knowledge that the memoirs he had written did not span the whole arc of his life and had not progressed beyond 1774, when he was about to be pardoned by the Venetian Republic and allowed to return to Venice. Twelve volumes in all. When a correspondent had inquired why he had abruptly left matters in abeyance at the age of forty-seven, Casanova had told him that from fifty onward, he had nothing but sad things to talk about. He had begun writing with the notion of cheering himself up, and his readers with him. Had he continued beyond that point, he would have brought tears to the eyes of his readers, and he didn't think that was worth doing. At any rate, the memoirs had not even been published, although he had promised Canoness Cecile de Roggendorf he would gift her with the folios when the time would come.

There is an intense sadness about the dying of the light and the wilting of the body. Casanova was no mystic, despite his past dabbling in Kabbalah. But he knew this was magic of some sort. His body had been restored to its prime, and his mind felt serene and unclouded, if still burdened by the weight of his fruitful past. And he incontrovertibly knew that he was ready to accept this uncommon miracle. This second chance.

He swiftly rose from the bed, shedding the twisted shroud of white sheets in which his dying persona had accepted the inevitable veil of death. The furnishings of the room were tasteful, sleeker than the eighteenth-century ones he had grown accustomed to. The color scheme was pleasant and balanced. *So,* he deduced, *these are not my times any longer.* How could it be so if he had died and returned to the land of the living?

He walked to the window and pulled the drapes aside. It was a gray day, the color of early winter. The Grand Canal was visible in the distance, a line of delicate blue to the right of the balcony of his familiar apartment on the Calle dei Fabbri. There were subtle differences from the view he had known, but nothing major at first glance. In Venice, things seldom change. But by the hundred small details his eyes encompassed, Casanova also recognized that this was a whole new world and he would have to adapt. If he was here, in this present, it must be for a reason. He moved back into the room, crossed over to the adjoining bathroom, and ran himself a bath.

Lounging in the warm water, he reacquainted himself in curious fascination with his new body. His body of old had now been restored to its wonderful prime. He lazily spread the moist soap bar across his skin, cleansing himself, enjoying the pleasant fragrance of the green bath salts dissolving across him. The water seemed to be flowing freely through him, reinvigorating his muscles and sinews, as if they had lain dormant for too long during the course of that long sleep between the night of his quiet death and now. He stretched his hand down to his penis and held it between his fingers. It was thick, veiny, heavy with blood, and he felt it grow under his touch.

Casanova sighed. So the alluring pleasures of the flesh were now available to him again. As was love, although he instinctively also knew that his heart, on the other hand, had not grown younger like the rest of his anatomy. It still was bulging with the evanescent presence of countless passions as well as disappointments and was burdened with a longing even life eternal could not satisfy any longer.

He manipulated himself slowly, almost with a sense of distraction, while recalling at will all the smiles and faces of so many of those heavenly creatures he had known so intimately—the topography of their joyous bodies, their shapes, their sounds, the intimate secretions he had coaxed from them, the subtle palette of colors that female flesh could acquire in the throes of love. Therese, Lucrezia, the Marchioness, Bettina, the list was endless. He came silently. His seed scattered across the surface of the bathwater, white atolls floating a few inches from his body, drifting now, sinking there as he moved his limbs.

Casanova smiled.

He had been admiring his new wardrobe of clothes. They were all so much less elaborate, but the fabrics were smooth, often silky, and, after trying some on, he marveled at today's clothes makers and their wonderful sense of design. The suits were practical and effortlessly elegant, the shirts clung to the shape of his body, and the thin and light materials uncannily retained his body heat.

It was then he noticed the envelope propped up on the chimney ledge of the bricked-up fireplace in his study. "Au Chevalier de Seingalt" it read, using the title he had adopted when he lived in France. It was an invitation to a costumed ball being held at the Excelsior Hotel on Lido di Venezia. Casanova somehow guessed that the invitation was unlikely to be out of date and decided there and then that he would attend the function. What better opportunity could there be to reintegrate into the whirlpool of life and lust? He could think of no better occasion. It was as if his return had been carefully engineered by powers unknown and the ball was all part of the ritual, another episode in the great mystery. Was it Carnivale time, he wondered? It had always been his preferred time of year in the city of the doges, a week when all forms of decorum were set aside and the empire of the senses took hold for a while in all impudent impunity. Days summoned from the calendar for excess and pleasure.

His name had been penned, on both the envelope and the thick card within, in an elegant scroll of red ink. There was no indication of who was inviting him or what was actually being celebrated. It just said "the Excelsior Ball." No matter. It had been ages since he had participated in any kind of celebration. He was not about to turn the invitation down.

The chartered motorboat was speeding toward the Lido by the light of a full moon. Casanova stood on the wooden bridge, watching the city slowly shrink behind them, its familiar landscape receding, pinpricks of gentle fire against a shadow of darkness betraying all the secret lives unfolding behind scores of anonymous windows.

He felt wonderfully invigorated. This was a marvelous new world, full of wonders and decadence he could only guess at. He had spent a few days thoroughly exploring his new environment, gazing at the uncovered legs of so many women as they ran about the city of his youth, hypnotized by the shape of their bodies so barely protected by thin and flowing materials. This was a whole wide world of pleasure, of blessed innocence.

Women, girls of every conceivable nationality flittered across the Piazza San Marco at all hours, lithe, vivacious, enticingly wicked in their seeming availability, even out-crowding the overfed pigeons who had once shamelessly annexed these venerable stone pavements. At first it almost felt as if these assorted women all spoke in tongues, a veritable babble of voices, but Casanova soon sharpened his hearing and began to recognize a whole palette of foreign languages, where Italian and French were now in a distinct minority.

The new Venice he had miraculously awoken in was truly a garden of delights, a land of new opportunities. But he was in no hurry. First he must learn how to blend in, to adapt to these curious days.

As much as his primal instincts beckoned him to spend hour after indulgent hour gazing at the sheer amount of tantalizing beauty on constant display, his mind resolved to arm itself for the intellectual rigors this new century—as he had quickly established—would no doubt have him facing sooner rather than later. He found a library and spent a whole week educating himself afresh. There were plenty of surprises, things he still couldn't adequately grasp, but he had quickly absorbed the essential winds of change, he thought. He was now ready to become a full-fledged citizen of this new worldly order and already looked forward to the challenge. Not that this easily acquired knowledge could answer his essential question: why?

Surely there must be a reason for his return. His past life and his death were no dream. He had even found references to his previous persona in some of the books he had sped through, his eyes open wide with ever growing amazement. He just couldn't accept the theory of the intervention of some mysterious deity. He was too much of a sinner and a libertine at heart to believe in such superstitious excuses. But the fact was that he had been brought back, and his case was, it appeared, a totally isolated incident. Even in this twenty-first century so full of awe and wonders, there were no other reported instances of holy revenants that he could pinpoint. He was unique. But then, he had grinned, hadn't he always been so?

What the books couldn't supply, he cautiously learned from the sweet lips of Cristiana, who served behind the bar at the Caffe Cavour, a block or so from his apartment. She was a small blonde in her late twenties, with a strongly shaped nose and far from opulent breasts, but Casanova found her immensely desirable. Something about her mind as well as her face and body made her uncommon and fascinating. How typical she was of this modern world, he wasn't yet quite sure. She confessed to him that she wanted to be a writer and kept on insisting he should read some of her work, desperate as she was for reassurance about her worth. He told her he was still recovering from a bout of amnesia, following a bad illness. It was a perfect, and credible, excuse that allowed him to bombard her with a never-ending flurry of questions.

He had also discovered he was wealthy. There was enough gold stored in the old, battered, and still familiar leather case he had found in a corner of his closet to sustain him for years to come. Cristiana had introduced him to a local jeweler, who had been only too pleased to offer Casanova a fair price in modern currency for just a portion of his newfound wealth. He just hoped he had not been swindled.

It was all too good to be true, he felt. Surely the reckoning must come. Soon. Someone pulling unholy strings behind the metaphorical curtains would appear when he was least expecting it. Surely?

He had shown Cristiana the invitation to the party. They were sitting in a booth, sipping aromatic coffees shortly after she had completed her last shift. She had glanced at the thick card while Casanova once again peered down at her bare taut midriff. In his own century, a woman would have been thought a slut for such brazen exposure. Here, it was commonplace. And so damned seductive!

"This is amazing!" Cristiana said.

"Really?"

"Yes, it's a legendary ball. Very private. I'd heard only rumors of it before. I've never known anyone who has attended, let alone been officially invited. You must be a very important person."

"I think I was, once," he replied.

"Will you take me?" she asked, a glint of mischief in her eyes. "I'd behave. I would."

"Of course," he had said. It would be the perfect occasion to complete his seduction of the young woman. Her smile was slightly crooked, and for Casanova it was like a promise of wonderfully dirty sex.

"What do all the lights make you think of?" Cristiana now asked, slipping her hand under his arm as he watched Venice fade into the distance as the launch carved its way through the limpid waters toward the Lido island.

"Souls," he answered.

"How poetic, but then I would expect nothing less of you," she smiled, and cuddled up to him.

Night was falling. Other guests milled around the deck, absorbed in aimless conversation. The motorboat was shuttling people to and from the Excelsior's private beach, twenty or so at a time. Casanova towered over Cristiana, every glance downward revealing her dark brown nipples barely contained by the frills of her black strapless gown. "Goth fashion" was how she had described its style. Her straight ash-blonde hair fell softly against her shoulders.

Casanova himself was dressed in the manner of the eighteenth century, as if all those years had not really passed by in the blur of his death and reincarnation. Cristiana had introduced him to a small tailor's shop in a dark alley close to the Campo San Polo where he had been able to rent the outfit. It wasn't authentic, of course; no garment could have survived all these years. Just a clever replica, and on closer inspection the material was too heavy and clumsily sewn. But it felt natural to wear it.

Next to him, Cristiana shivered as a faint night breeze surrounded the fast-moving motor launch. Casanova looked down at her, admiring the way her dress constricted her minuscule waist. She was like a doll, albeit one whose past life was also betrayed by the pronounced darker shades of skin under her eyes and the pulpy vulgarity of her fleshy lower lip. Her small breasts floated inside the fabric of the gown, hard nipples jutting out and grazing the lining with every movement she made, all too visible from his natural vantage point.

"Cold?" he asked.

"Yes," she answered, "but very excited."

Casanova grinned and blew her a kiss.

The cavernous ballroom of the Excelsior was packed. Casanova uneasily tried to conceal his growing sense of wonder as the crowds circled him like a heaving maelstrom of human flesh, voices, and perfumes.

"Isn't this just awesome?" Cristiana said, her eyes darting across the busy room.

"Indeed, indeed," was all the wit Casanova could summon in response. His gaze was captured by every passing woman, couple, body, movement. For so many in the crowd were truly remarkable examples of modern humanity: splendid women clad in every conceivable fabric, many of which he could not even recognize or name, ranging from shiny leather to see-through crinolines and assorted opaque sheaths of rainbow colors, all outlining unmercifully the very shapes of their bodies as well as strategically uncovering flesh in the most impudent, if mischievous, manner. This animated spectacle left all the past Carnivales he had once attended well in the shade. Colorful was not the word, by far.

Cristiana noticed his fascination. "Not what you expected?" she queried.

"Not exactly," Casanova replied.

"It really is a celebration of the extreme," the young woman said. "For one night, anything is said to be allowed. It's very private. Now, I can understand why. I even feel somewhat overdressed myself," she pointed to a woman lounging on a red sofa a few yards away from them. "But I could never, really never, dare turn out in public like that."

Casanova glanced at the woman Cristiana was indicating. Her breasts were three-quarters exposed, held up in a vise by a curious open-fronted brassiere, while her lower parts were barely concealed by a thin undergarment made of shining threads of transparent silk. She also wore gartered white stockings. The ensuing vision was both quite obscene and strangely alluring.

His eyes moved along to another tall red-haired woman walking by arm in arm with a distinguished, aristocratic-looking older gentleman sporting the most exquisite velvet dinner jacket. Her voluminous breasts were cocooned in a green tank top that almost melted into her flesh, but it was what she wore below her waist that caught Casanova's eye. It was a black, lacy, flower-patterned undergarment that molded her exquisitely shaped rear, but only to halfway, as the globes of her ass were almost fully bared, as if the panties had been sectioned halfway down. And when the woman faced him, he saw a string of pearls connecting the front and back of the garment, cutting through the woman's cunt lips, slipping and sliding inside her with every, no doubt, lubricated movement. The fact that she had shaved her pudenda perfected the bizarre fashion.

"I've seen photos of those panties in magazines. They're from Myla in London," Cristiana remarked. "I would never dare wear that sort of thing, let alone in public, of course," she added.

"Surely," Casanova said, "they must prove . . . uncomfortable," and turned back to face the young Italian woman.

She looked him in the eye and blushed deeply.

It suited her.

"Shall we find our way to the refreshments?" Casanova suggested.

It took Casanova an hour or so to finally grow fully accustomed to the constant spectacle and sexual circus of the ball. There was no dancing, a notion he had dreaded, somehow guessing that such rituals would have much changed in the interim period spanning his death and his return to life. The open areas of the Excelsior had been crudely divided into self-contained sections, each of which appeared to follow an unspoken theme. Cristiana and Casanova had wandered across, timid explorers at first, shame-faced spectators and then supreme voyeurs later as the events on open display went from the mere provocative to the outrageous. It afforded them little conversation, just anecdotal asides that only served to betray their mutual embarrassment. He could easily imagine what was going through his escort's mind.

They had witnessed couples copulating wildly on an elevated stage, women with men, women with women, and men with men. Rutting like zoo animals in heat, while half the passers-by barely acknowledged the lusty activities on display and moved on to other parts with total indifference.

In one room, an Amazon-like woman, standing with legs wide apart over a gaggle of kneeling men, urinated straight into their open and grateful mouths. Others watched in silence, visibly playing with themselves. Elsewhere nude bodies were being caned and whipped while restrained or tied to crosses or the back of chairs. Men and women of every age, shape, and size, in varied states of undress serviced each other in every corner; a group of indeterminate gender writhed across a large king-size bed, limbs flaying, faces buried, rumps heaving, hair matted with sweat and whatever else was being conjured up by their lusty congresses. It was both hypnotic and repellent. In another room, a group of onlookers watched in religious silence as a small woman was being simultaneously mounted by three masked men just an arm's length from them, accepting her trio of suitors in all three of her openings. Casanova was briefly reminded of Bosch's "Garden of Earthly Delights." Cristiana's hand in his felt moist, shaky.

Was this hell he had traveled to?

Cristiana's exposed throat was flushed all the way down to the valley of her breasts. "I didn't know," she plaintively said. "I never realized it would be this way."

But Casanova could also read the lust in her eyes, the wanton need that was clearly taking hold of her. As much as she was ashamed of betraying her base feelings, her body was obviously excited. She looked up at him. Questioning. In search of release.

"Not here," he said, answering her silent request.

He was still a man of manners, even in the midst of an orgy; he had no wish to mount her in full public view, to offer the sordid spectacle of an anonymous coupling among this veritable sea of flesh.

"Come to the beach," he suggested, tugging her trembling hand.

Cristiana lowered her dark, tired eyes, acknowledging the fever spreading inside her. "I will," she meekly said. She followed him quietly through the maze of interlocked rooms onto the balcony that overlooked the waters of the lagoon, and they found the steps that led to the Excelsior's private beach, facing away from the city. Sharp spotlights illuminated the sand but there were still welcoming areas of semidarkness.

He had spread his dark cape across the humid sand, and Cristiana was now on her knees fellating him. They had initially embraced with hunger, and the crumpled top of her party dress had been lowered and pulled across her thin waist by his expert hands, with no objection on her part. Her mouth tasted of subtle spices, and Casanova had closed his eyes with undue pleasure as their tongues had endlessly explored each other and lazy waves of contentment began navigating through his limbs.

There was nothing shy about Cristiana's kisses. His mind had automatically conjured up the memory of all the other mouths, kisses, and tastes he had experienced in such a manner, and he had silently expressed his gratefulness to the unknown god who had made it all possible then and now again. Finally, he had opened his eyes and looked down with infinite gratitude at Cristiana's small but adorable breasts as her tongue explored inside his mouth. She had possibly taken it as a signal—which it wasn't—that he was tiring of her lips.

Silently, she had bent down and found her way to unlace the top of his trousers and swiftly uncovered his now engorged and heavy cock, which she took into her fiery mouth. It was a delight that women of his previous age had always been reluctant to offer and that he often had to coax out of them. Her hot, wet tongue lingered with deliberate slowness across the redder mushroom of his tip as she extracted it with a gentle sucking movement from his foreskin, which her tongue then peeled gently back. A strong, familiar tremor coursed through his whole body as she touched him there. Were all modern women this skilled in the art of cocksucking, he wondered?

Casanova then banished all thoughts and forced his consciousness to abandon itself to the moment. He could hear the gentle lapping of small waves on the shore, and every ebb and flow of the waters delightfully paralleled the systematic to and fro of Cristiana's lips across the girth of his captive cock.

"This is wonderful, thanks," he whispered, and placed his hands over her head, fingers digging into her thick blonde hair, marveling all along at the intuitive way the young woman punctuated every movement of her busy mouth to the rhythm of his rising pleasure.

It was an odd feeling. On one hand he reveled in the luxurious feeling of his hard cock being so assiduously serviced, while on the other he was also a detached spectator of the ongoing scene, carefully admiring the wonderfully obscene sight of the young woman's expert mouth stretched open by his still thickening member and a glaze of lust spreading across her eyes. This inseparable blend of vision and action only served to excite him more, and he knew that when the time was right he would take her from behind so he could watch with unending fascination as his mighty cock pushed its way past the pliant opening of her lower lips. He would enjoy the sight of her puckered anus winking at him with secret approval as he plunged deeper and deeper into her innards in search of la petite mort.

He instinctively took a harder grasp of the young woman's head and forced her mouth to impale itself deeper onto his cock. She did not resist. Didn't even gag. There was hunger and despair in her, he reckoned.

Out of the periphery of his vision came a quiet sound of steps. He turned his head in the direction of the movement. A gondola had beached on the shore to their right, and a couple had walked out onto the sand and were making their way toward the Excelsior. They were fully visible in the glare of the fierce spotlights and, likely, could not see Casanova and Cristiana, shrouded as they were in the darkness of the beach.

He was about to look away and busy himself with Cristiana's clever ministrations again when something about the couple caught his attention. The man was clad in black leather from head to boot and appeared to be connected to the dark silhouette of a tall, lithe woman. Casanova squinted and saw that the stranger was actually pulling on a thin metal leash, a golden chain that was attached to a collar tightly circling the woman's neck. Casanova held his breath.

The couple strolled across the beach with perfect assurance. The woman then moved into a pool of strong light, and Casanova's whole world toppled at that very instant.

She must have measured almost six feet, even without the high glass-heeled shoes she was wearing. Her hair was a whirlpool of blonde curls, a medusa-like array that spread with wild abandon like a crown. Could it be a wig? She was also absolutely naked but for the leather collar, a thin black mask through which dark brown eyes peered, and her glass shoes. Firm breasts swaying delicately in the gentle night breeze, flatter-than-flat stomach, pale alabaster skin, a high, majestic ass, and endless legs that recalled perfection. She was a vision of incomparable beauty.

She bathed in the circle of light for only a few seconds, as her master led her away toward the main festivities, but the image was already indelibly carved into Casanova's mind.

Her nipples had been provocatively rouged, and there were dark pink stripes generously adorning the delicate flesh of her regal ass. Her face also bore a sense of infinite sadness and nobility, which unbearably touched him in the very pit of his stomach.

Casanova gulped.

She walked away in slow motion, never looking into his direction, and just as she moved out of sight, a final beam of light lingered over her exposed genitalia. She had been carefully trimmed, and to his amazement he saw that small sequins had been intricately sewn into the many darker curls of her pubic hair, catching the light and shimmering wildly like the reflection of the moon over the waters of the lagoon. The view of her jeweled cunt was hypnotic. Her gash had also been exposed at the center of the glittering array of sequins, and the protruding inner lips were colored deep scarlet, matching her breasts' aureolas. There was a majestic pride about her posture and her steady, calculated movement across the wet sand.

"Is everything okay?" Cristiana asked, as she briefly neglected his cock and caught her breath, no doubt sensing his distraction.

"Yes, oh yes," he said. But his mouth was dry.

All he wanted now was to leave the beach and follow the mysterious couple into the ball and find out more about the woman. Meet her, even. He knew that task would now be his mission. There was no choice involved.

So the adventure begins.

Chapter Two

With his cock swollen and damp from Cristiana's ardent attentions, Casanova stared at the bright lights of the Excelsior's entrance.

"Did you want to go back inside?" she asked softly. A forlorn note of disappointment laced her voice.

He longed to say "yes, but not necessarily with you," but the gentleman in him censored such coarse instincts. He felt her pleading eyes on him but could not pull his gaze from the spot where he had just seen the most captivating female nature had ever fashioned. He forced himself to look down at Cristiana's lovely face and its roadmap of lipstick smears. She did look wonderfully disheveled with her hair tousled and her big brown eyes round with hunger and curiosity. Normally, he would have wanted nothing more than to release the full measure of her sexual aptitude and skill, to revel in the contrast of her silken, youthful skin against the rough and gritty sand, but that was before he had seen the masked and sequinned blonde.

"My wanton little angel," he said, quickly lapsing into the smooth, unflappable persona for which he liked to consider himself famous. "I find myself suddenly wanting to make love to you for all the world to see," he lied. "Your beauty is more than enough for one man, but when combined with your boundless sensuality and considerable carnal knowledge, I think it's nothing less than selfish to keep you here to myself. Can I convince you to return to the indecent fray inside?"

She tilted her head slightly, assessing him in the moonlight. Even with the passage of some two hundred years, women still apparently prided themselves on deciphering the emotional hieroglyphics of men, he thought. Though such a time-honored tradition was charming in its historical longevity, panic seared through him as he remembered how accurately most women guessed his motives. He continued to regard her as if she were the single most beautiful creature heaven deigned to set before him. Flattery, he had learned, was the best defense against women's intuition.

She gave him that delightfully crooked grin again, and Casanova immediately knew he had nothing to fear.

"I love it when you talk all formal like that. It suits your costume," she said, leaning back to rest her pert behind on her heels.

He made a mental note to watch more television to rid himself of what was clearly an antiquated speaking style.

"We can return to the party if you want. I guess I'm brave enough if you are," she said.

But the security staff would have none of it. The invitation had been collected when they had first arrived, and now there was no way to persuade the stone-faced gatekeeper to readmit them.

Casanova's cock ached as much as his soul. What travesty was this that would prevent him from possibly ever knowing the identity of that leashed and decorated goddess he had already dubbed Athena in his mind? Back in his time, he would have known who wielded influence enough to allow their reentry, but here, now, in twenty-first-century Italy, amid unfamiliar people and customs, he was as ineffectual as a pauper. The reality irritated him as much as Catherine of Russia's lukewarm welcome had back in 1765. He was as helpless to alter the course of events then as he was now, and the prospect frustrated him beyond measure.

"Bummer," Cristiana commented. "I guess we should have realized security would be this tight. What do you want to do now?"

His desire for Athena nearly blinded him to the delicious concoction of Cristiana in her slightly askew little black dress. The night air and sea breeze emphasized her dewy youthfulness, and he knew he would have been quite swept away by her beauty if not for the enduring image of Athena. He was hard, nearly mean with the need to feel feminine softness and heat in his arms, around his meat, on his tongue.

"Let us return to Venice," he said, taking Cristiana's hand and leading her to the motorboat that waited where they had left it.

Thinking only of Athena as he bent Cristiana over the railing of the boat, he pushed the hem of her dress up and over her darling derriere. Her nether lips were still slick from the encounter on the beach, but he stroked them nonetheless because they had become Athena's perfect pinkness, glistening with invitation under the lure of moonlight. The cheeks under his palms were fuller, more mature versions of the sweetly rounded morsels Cristiana offered. Had he bent Athena over the railing, the supreme length of her legs would have positioned her exquisitely proportioned ass to a higher, more regal height than what was before him now. His fingers trembled at the thought of the unknown woman's cunt creaming in his hand.

Yes, Cristiana's supple cheeks shook with magnificent gratitude with each of his thrusts. And it was true that her juicy cunt offered no end of succulence. Why, she even slammed herself against him to meet every push, a move that only the sauciest or most experienced women allowed themselves to make in his day. Her tiny waist was a marvel as it maneuvered her small hips into obscenely enticing gyrations. Her shouts resounded throughout the canals, assuring him of her pleasure, yet despite all of these attributes, when he emptied himself, it was into the transcendent depths of Athena.

When Cristiana turned around to face him, just as the boat approached Venice, the vision of her face instead of Athena's jarred him. It reminded him of his duty as her escort and as a gentleman. He smiled at her adorable, dreamy-eyed expression.

"Wow," she purred. "You are incredible."

As he looked down at her, becoming aware one by one of her assorted features as they replaced Athena's in his furtive imagination, he suddenly felt disgusted with himself for denying her the full attention he had given every woman he'd ever romanced. How dare he give her only a portion of himself when she deserved so much more? He glimpsed her diminutive brown nipples once again as his eyes grazed the top of her strapless dress, and he was as captivated as he had been before being smitten with the blonde Amazon.

As he walked Cristiana to her apartment, he held her small hand and silently chastised himself for his unforgivable behavior. She didn't seem to sense that anything was amiss—thanks to his being behind her when his thoughts had so fixated on Athena—but who knew what she would make of this evening tomorrow morning, after she'd had time to examine it, as women were wont to do?

He kissed her good night and made haste to his own quarters, where some serious thinking was on his agenda.

So discombobulated was Casanova by his complete obsession with Athena that he almost passed by the door to his building. Certainly he had had bouts of utter fascination with the fairer sex in his lifetime, but he had always found it distasteful to be thinking of one woman when he was in the arms of another (though many were the times he had engaged in such behavior). It was misspent ardor, which he abhorred, but it was also rude. He cared for Cristiana a great deal, even found her thoroughly desirable, which made his actions this evening feel like a horrible betrayal to his nature as well as to her. He resolved to rectify any misunderstandings the following day, but for now there was the matter of Athena to address.

Why hadn't he investigated the party more thoroughly before attending? He had been so caught up in acclimating to his new life that he hadn't paid adequate attention to details he never would have overlooked in the eighteenth century. Who, for instance, had hosted the soirée he had just enjoyed? For if he were to locate the incomparable Athena, he'd best inquire of the host about her identity. But his sloppy, self-absorbed behavior now made that quest impossible.

He shed himself of the historical garb he had worn to the party, grabbed a bottle of brandy, and wandered out in his underwear to the balcony. Lowering himself into one of the wrought-iron chairs there, he was unconcerned about who might view him in such a state of undress at this hour. Darkness still engulfed the city as far as the Grand Canal, and he knew, having experienced his share of twilights, that sunrise was still a good hour away. At least the light in Venice had not changed in all these years. Right now, that fact seemed the only thing he could count on, the only constant in an otherwise unpredictable world.

He rubbed his face with his palms as he wondered whether the party's host was the same person who left him the invitation. Surely it had to be, for who else would have had the authority to invite him? And if that were the case, then someone knew he was alive. For a second time. And they had access to his home.

Had his ego been so inflated by the invitation that he never paused to consider the implications of being known in this new century? Was the person who left the invitation responsible for bringing him back to life? Even in the likelihood of such an implausible fate, why would someone want him alive at this particular time in this particular place?

He took a swig of brandy to help him blot out such preposterous thoughts. Damn the beautiful Athena, for without her existence, perhaps he would never have stopped to consider how or why he was here. Instead, he could have merely existed, honing his hedonism in an age seemingly without boundaries.

He might have expected to sleep late due to his anxiety and depression, but after three solid hours of surprisingly tranquil rest, he arose to greet the day. He turned on the television Cristiana had given him (a small item that she claimed was so old, nobody would have bought it from her anyway) and listened to twenty-first-century Italian as he dressed, amazed by the idioms and words he did not recognize. Thanks to his innate intelligence and love of language, however, he was slowly putting many idioms into context to derive their meanings. He would never let a small obstacle such as language foil his efforts to live as fully as possible.

He waited until 10:00 before heading to the Caffe Cavour, because even in these modern times, no self-respecting Venetian began his day any earlier. Upon seeing Cristiana, he knew that she had been unaware of any strangeness or detached affections from him the night before. She smiled shyly, but with that undercurrent of corruption he so enjoyed.

"Good morning, my beauty," he said, truly happy to see her. "I had a wonderful time last night," he added in a quieter voice, mindful of protecting her reputation.

"I'm glad," she replied. "So did I. I'm afraid I didn't sleep very much."

"Oh?"

"Too excited," she growled, eyes sparkling.

With her words came his erection, which he tried to hide by sitting at the nearest table. She grinned, for his trousers hid little of his enthusiasm, and she immediately brought him a cappuccino.

"Are you able to join me?" He asked, looking around to note that only one other patron might require her services, and he was engrossed in a newspaper.

"Sure. For a little bit," she said, slipping into the seat across from him at the small round table.

"Do you happen to know who hosts the ball we attended last evening?"

She wore a clean white T-shirt that clung to her body with remarkable fortitude. She wore no bra and her nipples were clearly outlined. With her hair wrapped up in a makeshift twist at the back of her head, pieces of it escaped the barrette and softly brushed her flawless cheeks. She was positively enchanting, but not enough to erase the memory of Athena.

"Oh, nobody knows. I think that's the whole point. Whoever throws that bash loves the mystery of it all. Why do you ask?"

"I'm just terribly curious. Surely you've heard rumors?" Venice without unfounded gossip was a concept he could not even grasp.

"Of course," she grinned. "Most people say the host is a Frenchman, although I don't know why they say that. Maybe because of all the S and M stuff that goes on. Everybody likes to pin depravity on the French."

He chuckled knowingly, happy to know that the French claim to unfettered lust and debauchery had gone unabated in two hundred years. He was, however, unclear about something she said.

"S and M? What is that, exactly?"

"You know, bondage, stuff like that. Sadomasochism. Pain and pleasure." She blushed a bit. "You saw some of it last night."

"Saydo-massa-kism?" He pronounced it phonetically to be sure he got it right.

Surprise flashed across her face, but undoubtedly she attributed his lack of knowledge to his amnesia. She ripped a blank receipt out of her little book and wrote the word for him.

"It comes from Sade, as in Marquis de," she explained. "Marquis de Sade is the guy who made bondage and discipline a household word. Or concept. Whatever."

Casanova tried to recall a marquis in France by that name but failed. Cristiana must have mistaken his silence for continued confusion about sadomasochism, so she offered more information. "He wrote some books, if you want to read them. I don't remember the titles, because I'm not really into that scene, but I'm sure they're in the library. Even in bookstores."

"But could this marquis be the one who hosted the party last night?"

"Oh no!" She smiled. "He's been dead for a couple hundred years, I think."

Still, Casanova was so intrigued by sexual deviance having eponymous roots that he decided to spend the rest of the day at the library. After all, if this marquis could have activities named after him, perhaps there were sexual positions or even a lifestyle with his own name affixed to them. A man could dream, couldn't he? In the process, he would learn about something that Athena liked, which would ultimately bring him closer to her—of that he felt certain.

"I wonder, my love, if you could inquire about that party? It would mean so much to me to discover whose generosity I am indebted to," he implored the pretty blonde waitress. He let his eyes wander deliberately over her eyes, lips, neck, breasts, knowing that such a brazen inventory would cause her to imagine his hands and his mouth roaming the same terrain. Her eyes sparkled, and her color darkened just enough to let him know his intentions had taken effect.

"Yeah, sure, I can do that. But people are going to wonder why I care so much!" She laughed and looked at him as if she had questions, yet she didn't pose them.

"I don't mean to make things difficult for you."

"It's okay. Don't worry about it. I can probably find something out for you."

"Thank you. May I see you tonight?" His eyes bore into hers, and for a few seconds Athena disappeared. He saw—and wanted—only Cristiana's exuberant sexuality. Suckling at her impertinent little breasts sounded particularly appealing to him at that moment, and had he not already made a commitment to visit the library, he would have cajoled her away from her duties for a quick but satisfying romp in the storage room.

"Okay. I get off at six. Pick me up?"

"Yes, of course," he promised. He expected to have the majority of his research completed by then.

He learned a great deal about the man whose life missed his by a mere generation or so. He sat enraptured at a library table, devouring *Justine* as if it were the key to a magical world he longed to inhabit. In fact, the more he read, the more he believed he understood what might have motivated Athena to dress as she had. The more he read, the more he understood about why her costume excited him so.

And yet the passages dedicated to pain alarmed him, for they offended every sensibility he had come to cultivate and accept in himself. Women who desired pain, however, would be a different matter. Giving women what they most craved had always been one of his favorite pastimes. He had much to learn, he realized, and wondered whether Cristiana might be the right teacher for him. He suspected she would not, for hadn't she said she wasn't "into that scene"?

His reading had given him not only a lot to think about but also a slow and steady stirring of his privates. He doubted that libraries had changed much in the past couple of centuries and assumed that a librarian would not take kindly to readers who allowed literature to stimulate them in ways other than intellectually. To counter the effects of the marquis' writing, Casanova decided to conduct more research on the man himself. He found the following in the *Encyclopedia of Erotic Literature*:

> Born in Paris, 2 June 1740. Educated at Collège Louis-le-Grand, Paris, 1750–54; then attended a military school in 1754, becoming 2nd lieutenant in 1755. Served in the French army during the Seven Years War: Captain, 1759; resigned commission, 1763. Married Renée Pélagie Cordier de Launay de Montreuil in 1763 (separated 1790); two sons and one daughter. Succeeded to the title Comte, 1767; arrested and imprisoned briefly for sexual offences, but pardoned by the king, 1768; condemned to death for sex offences, 1772, but sentence commuted to imprisonment; held in Miolans, 1772–73 (escaped); convicted again and imprisoned in Vincennes, 1778–84, Bastille, Paris, 1784–89, and Charenton, 1789–90; liberated and joined Section des Picques, 1790: organized cavalry and served as hospital inspector; made a judge, 1793, but condemned for moderation and imprisoned, 1793–94; arrested for obscene work (*Justine*) and imprisoned in Sainte-Pélagie, 1801, and confined again in Charenton, from 1803 until his death on 2 December 1814.

Casanova quite liked the notion of being arrested for publishing books considered too risqué. He wondered whether his own memoirs had created a similar stir after his death. He returned to the device with the screen similar to that of the television Cristiana had given him and tapped the keys that spelled out C-A-S-A-N-O-V-A. His erection stiffened as he read the summation of his life.

> Born into a family of Venetian actors, Giacomo Casanova studied for the priesthood at a Seminary in Padua. Expelled for his salacious activities, he returned to Venice. Back in his hometown, Casanova made a living by conning the local nobility with a mixture of magic tricks, phoney alchemy, and vague occult mysticism. He was convicted of witchcraft by the Inquisition in 1755, and imprisoned in the Doge's palace.
>
> —The Biography Channel

Casanova took issue with the characterization of his talents, frowning at the writer's choice of words. One was truly at the mercy of ill-informed historians, he thought, mentally shrugging off the epithets and hoping to discover more complimentary descriptions as he continued to read.

> Styling himself "Jacques Casanova, the Chevalier de Seingalt," he then travelled to new countries, reinventing himself and his history, making and losing fortunes. In his time, he encountered such luminaries as Pope Clement XIII (1760), Voltaire (1760), Rousseau and Mozart (1787). His legacy was ensured by the publication of his "Histoire de Ma Vie"—a document better regarded for its portrait

of the social history of the Enlightenment period in conti-
nental Europe than for its strict biographical accuracy.

Well, then, he thought, *perhaps we are both guilty of revisionist history.*

Today, Casanova is best remembered as a symbol of prodigious sexual conquest. Despite his heterosexual reputation, however, Giacomo Casanova was blissfully bisexual
throughout his life.

Immense satisfaction coursed through him as he read and reread
the sentence, "Casanova is best remembered as a symbol of prodigious
sexual conquest." Not only had his book been published, but his name
had also endured to become associated with exactly what had made
him happiest in life: sex. He could barely wait to ask Cristiana what
she knew of the legend named Casanova.

Satisfied that he had made his mark on the world, and armed with
what he believed was adequate knowledge about the Marquis de Sade
and sadomasochism (he reminded himself to call it "S and M" as Cristiana did), he glanced at the clock and saw that it was already 3:00. He
wondered whether the library might have any information about the
party he attended last night.

As he sat mulling over his question, he felt a stare and turned to
meet the eyes of the librarian. This librarian was different from the
one he had seen at the desk earlier, however. This was a woman with
the alabaster creaminess, the dark, haunting eyes, and the sexual
ambiguity of his dear Teresa. What providence to find her here in this
place and time! She did not avert her stare when he caught her looking
at him, and so he stared back with equal intensity.

Surely this was indeed Teresa, for he could identify her singular beauty in a crowd of pale-skinned brunettes. Perhaps she stared because she recognized him, too, but could not speak from the shock of encountering him.

"Do you believe you know me?" he asked.

"Shhhhh!" came the hiss of fellow researchers. Casanova arose to bridge the two-table gap between him and the apparition he grew more certain by the second was Teresa. He stood before her desk. She wore a top of black ribbed fabric that clung to her curves, covering her neck almost completely but exposing her arms entirely. There was a sleekness about her that he had seen with some frequency among women and had come to appreciate in this new era. Still she stared at him, and in her expression was not the slightest compunction to turn away.

"I asked if you knew me," he insisted, as kindly as he knew how.

"I would have said hello, wouldn't I?"

"Then why do you stare at me?"

The beauty shrugged, but her eyes didn't return to her work.

"What is your name, if I may inquire?" he ventured.

"Bellino. Are you going to report my behavior to my boss or something?"

His heart leaped at her response. Bellino had been the name she had used when she was trying to pass as a castrato singer. She had insisted to all the world that she was a boy, but Casanova had known otherwise and went to great lengths to prove that his suspicions were correct. When she could no longer ignore her love for him, too, she had confessed her attempted deception and they became lovers.

Why was she playing this game with him now? In clothing that left little to the imagination, she could not be pretending to be a man, so why did she use the name Bellino? And why was she not as overjoyed as he to find them reunited in this time and place?

"Why do you use that name with me?" he whispered. "Is that ruse not behind you now?"

Nothing seemed to perturb this new incarnation of Teresa. "I use Bellino because that is my name."

He could see the exchange was destined for futility, so he tried a different line of questioning. "Why were you looking at me?"

"Why were you looking at me?" she replied.

How he longed to take her in his arms. He wanted to lavish her with the kisses he had stored since their final parting two centuries ago. He knew, however, how stubborn she could be, and if Bellino was the name she wished him to know, then that would be all he would know at this juncture.

"I thought I recognized you," he said sadly, "but the woman I knew abandoned the name Bellino long ago and used Teresa."

"I was looking at you because of what you're researching," she said, ignoring his comment. "I can monitor all of it from here." She gestured at her panel full of buttons and glowing screens.

"I see. In my experience, a man's browsing in a library was a matter requiring personal privacy."

"A lot has changed."

He paused, for this was the first sign she had given that she was aware that he had come from another time.

"Since terrorism has become so common," she added. Had there been a change in the depth of her eyes, or had he just imagined it?

"And my research has given you cause to believe I am a terrorist?" "Terrorism" was one of the words he had heard often since his arrival in 2005, and it hadn't taken him long to learn its definition in modern terms.

"No," she replied, with only a suggestion of a smirk. "I think it's more likely that you're just a horny bastard."

For the first time, her eyes traveled to his crotch, and stayed there far too long. He grew under her gaze, appalled and pleased by her boldness. Just recently, Cristiana had explained the word "horny" to him, so he understood Bellino's implication. He even agreed with it. He didn't mind giving credence to her brash assumption about him. If this lovely librarian who was Teresa, but denied all knowledge of her, thought he was an eager lothario, who was he to dispel her notions?

"You excel at your task of profiling library visitors," he said quietly. "I wonder, though, if you would be able to show me other items of interest to me?"

His question served a dual purpose, for if she took his question literally, he would be the recipient of more information to help him find Athena. If she chose to concentrate on his horny bastard persona instead, he could not help but feel he would benefit from those attentions as well.

"Follow me," she told him. When she rose, he took in the full effect of her height, form, and movement. Tight black pants emphasized the roundness of her bottom, which he knew beyond any doubt was the bottom of his beloved Teresa. Her slim but womanly hips swayed with a miraculous allure, punctuated by the powerful clacking of her black ankle boots. This was not Bellino pretending to be male—this was Bellino redefined as a woman without female pretenses. He had never before been in the presence of such powerful femininity. But she was a woman nonetheless, and so he vowed to rely on his prodigious seduction instincts should the need arise.

She led him through several hallways. He followed the mesmerizing rhythm of her solid high heels until she exited into the partial sunlight of a courtyard. They were alone with the explosive palette of colors in the small garden. The aroma of roses and jasmine seemed to soften her rough edges. Or perhaps it was just the dappled sunlight.

Either way, she had a less imposing air now that she was outside the confines of the library.

"I thought I had you figured out until you started researching Casanova," she said, eyeing him in a way that assumed some guilt on his part.

"What's wrong with Casanova?"

"You ought to know."

"How would I?" He inquired, hoping to break her of this ridiculous pretense, expecting that any moment she would melt into the sweet young woman who had stolen his heart and mind so many years before. She would say, "Who else but Casanova would know Casanova?" and they would laugh before he would ravish her in the flower beds beside them.

"You read about him long enough. You ought to be able to write a book about him."

Would it not have been redundant to remind her that he had already written such a book?

Her lips hovered near his as she stood far too close to him. She even smelled of the same *eau de mille fleurs* she had worn when they first met. Instead of the somewhat reticent maiden in his memory, however, the "new" Bellino cupped his crotch in her palm and palpitated him with the skill of a courtesan. The fleshiest part of her palm pressed firmly against the fleshiest part of his cock. She pressed, he pushed. She traced the bas relief of his arousal while he put his mouth to hers. The taste of her lips, even under the cloak of mass-produced cosmetics, was unmistakable to him, and he wanted to cry out from nostalgic frustration, even as she unzipped his trousers.

She then unbuckled his belt, whooshed it from its loops, and stepped back to taunt him with her prowess.

"Didn't see that coming, did you?"

He chuckled in spite of himself. It was just the sort of move he would expect from Teresa, that little sprite. "No," he confessed, "I did not."

"I have other surprises."

She approached him again, and before he knew what was happening, she tied his wrists behind him with his belt. He was mortified to discover he could not break free of the knot she created.

His hard cock protruded from his trousers with no way for him to protect it. She was no longer interested in kissing, despite his intense desire for her lips. She pressed her lithe, shapely body against his and spoke softly into his ear.

"This is how it feels to give up control. Do you like it?"

She massaged his cock, lingering every so often on the especially sensitive spot at his meaty tip. How would she know about that spot if she were not Teresa?

With her thumb, she spread the tiny drop of clear precum all over its swollen head. With her agile fingers, she worked his shaft, stimulating every vein until tiny lights sparked in his head.

"Do you want to come?" she asked. Her breath warmed his ear.

"Yes," he gasped, unable to think of anything else.

"Too bad. You'll come when I tell you."

He didn't ask why she saw fit to impose such a rule or why he ought to abide by it. When his balls tightened in response to the steady pumping from her fist, he thought about the garbage in the canals, the wonders of aerosol shaving cream, and whatever became of the lira in an attempt to comply with her request. His knees threatened to buckle and his balance wavered, but still he waited for her to give permission.

"Now," she said.

He spurt in a beautiful arc that landed squarely in the flower beds. While he tried to regulate his breathing, she untied him, freed his hands, and handed him his belt. She bent to extract something from her boot.

"Take this card," she said in a hoarse whisper. "Check it out on the Web and you may find what you're looking for."

"Thank you, Teresa."

She paused at the door and frowned at him. "Bellino." And she left him there in the courtyard, where he stared down at the card she had handed him:

The Power Company

www.powercompany.com

Perhaps he would require Cristiana's help in his search, after all. He looked at his watch, saw that it was five minutes past four o'clock, and made his way to the Caffe Cavour.

Chapter Three

On his way back to the café, the gray clouds above mirrored his suddenly overcast mind. Rain was threatening atmospherically, and a storm was similarly brewing up in his consciousness. Giddy at first from Teresa's—no, he corrected himself with a close of his eyes, an effort of will, not his beloved lover of centuries ago. Not Teresa. Bellino. An unearthly similarity. Pleasantly affected by *Bellino*'s skillful magic, he tried out the words, lips only, not giving them full voice so as not to appear mad to the hustling and bustling Venetians flowing by and around him: "S and M, sadomasochism." New terms, perhaps, but they were based on an idea as old as he was.

As he walked the undulating and weaving streets of his beloved city, the pleasure and excitement of Bellino's game flowed away, replaced by a powerful sense of uncertainty, an overwhelming feeling of doubt. *A new kind of game, yes,* he thought, coming to a stop in front of a small shop with lead glass windows. *As old as I am.* He wasn't even aware of what the shop was selling; his mind was elsewhere. A game was being played now; he was sure of it. But it wasn't just one of pain and pleasure, women at the end of jeweled chains, the taking and relinquishing of control or of power.

Throughout his former life, he had been very much in control of his destiny, aside from the times he'd spent within prison walls. Life had been his to relish and explore. Virgin as well as experienced flesh, fame as well as anonymity. Fortune and poverty. He'd been through it all. When one life had been exhausted, he had simply reinvented himself, a little sleight of hand and the man he had been became the man he wanted to be. His family had been on stage, performing roles for the crowd. His life was on a different kind of stage, his audience the entire world. The entire world had also become his boudoir.

Then he had died. Confessing to himself with a nod, he accepted that his magic had been merely tricks and illusion, calling attention to one hand while the other was performing in a theater no bigger than a card table. But he still knew real magic, real legerdemain when he experienced it—and he definitely had experienced it. He had expired, the chains that had bound his everlasting soul to the earth had been severed, and he had begun his last journey.

Heaven? Were his intentions better than his actions? His service to the Lord overriding his temptations and lapses? Or had he been bound to a lower dimension? Had his confessions and absolutions not been sufficient to spare him torment in the afterlife?

Two destinations had been before him—or so he'd thought on his deathbed. He never would have conceived of the third: Venice, in the year 2005. More pleasures of even more flesh, an introduction to a world he would never have conceived of. Women on the streets, exposing more flesh than in the lowest of common bordellos. Devices no larger than a snuff box, holding the sum of human knowledge, allowing instantaneous conversation with anyone, anywhere in the world. Pictures that moved, the death of theater, music like the braying of mules. It was so loud, this world. Even the formerly tranquil streets of Venice, La Serenissima, rang with the cacophony of it all.

Overwhelmed, he closed his eyes, breathing deep. There were similarities, of course. For all their revealing yet dull costumes, women of this year acted very much like those of his years. His enjoyments with the lithe and energetic Cristiana had been pleasurable, as had his experience with the manifestation of his beloved Teresa, but the true delight had been in only a glimpse of the woman he knew he must find.

He had felt this way before about the women—in his life—and even a few chosen men—but none of them had struck him with such force as the single sight he'd had of the woman—no, "lady," he corrected himself, for she seemed to his keen senses to be more than simply a female of the species—he called Athena. Was she the reason he had been resurrected to walk the world of 2005? Reason produced doubts, but his heart—ah, that spoke with a loud and definite voice of agreement.

But why? In all his years in the seminary and his preceding times dabbling with the occult, he had never heard of anything like this event. Something was happening. There was a cause.

The storm broke, water began tapping gently on the top of his head, dampening his hair and cooling the tips of his ears. Seeking shelter, he entered the shop, the door opening and then closing behind him, signaling his presence with the chiming of a miniature gold bell. Welcoming the distraction from his mental tempest, he joined the other customers in examining the store's wares.

Jet, turquoise, sapphire, gold, silver-painted dominoes; checkered half- or full-face harlequins; the crooked beaks of birds; the whiskers and feline deviltry of cats; the horns and mischievous moustaches of devils; the elegance of angelic purity, simple ivory faces; the swirls and ridges of scarred and tattooed Africans; the solemn tranquility of priestly appearance. *Carnivale.* A mask shop.

To give himself something to do, Casanova picked up a domino that twinkled with bright, yet clearly fake, jewels. Turning it over in his hands, his thoughts returned yet again to the question that was a gale in his mind: what was happening? Why was he here?

He knew one thing. It was all a masquerade. Behind the faces he had seen lurked something else, something making sport of him. A game of obstruction and desire. He just had to lift it all the way to see the real faces behind it all.

Purposed, he returned the mask to its display and left the shop with a polite touch of finger to eyebrow toward the proprietress, and stepped out into the rain.

Fortunately, the storm had turned hesitant and feeble, more a curtain of mist than a true downpour, so he was able to save himself from a soaking by making his way via careful darts to and from awnings and doorways. Seeing the protection other people sported, umbrellas and obviously costly coats and bright yellow capes they wrapped around themselves, Casanova at first thought about politely inquiring as to where he might purchase the same.

Then he noticed something else. As he made his way from awning to awning, doorway to doorway, he spontaneously turned—getting his bearings, nothing worse than losing your way in a rainstorm, no matter how feeble—and saw a shape dart toward the protection of a doorway. A shape dressed in a dark brown covering, a shoddy cape or long burlap shawl. A shape that was a man skillfully hiding his face. He knew now, with pure certainty: he was being followed.

Normally—he laughed at the thought of the word. *Normally?* What was normal about anything that was occurring to him? In his former life, he should say, he would have simply confronted the shadowy figure, demanding an explanation for the dogging of his footsteps. A cutpurse or thief, no doubt. A pathetic creature pushed into desperate violence by his body's demand for liquor, or opium. Nothing to worry about. A cuff to the ears or, had he a suitable blade, a scratch to the face or hand would have sent his stalker scurrying back into the sewers.

But this was not his old life, this was a new one. One with uncertain rules, and masks on many faces, dancing to a tune he did not understand in a masquerade of resurrection and no doubt powerful forces. So Casanova ran through the spitting rain, back to safety, to Cristiana.

"Well, it's a Web site," Cristiana said, turning the small rectangle of paper in her hand. "Aside from that I don't know anything. We can look it up in the morning."

"Of course, naturally. Foolish of me, really, to believe you might know more. Not that you haven't been an excellent guide," he said, smiling with more than his usual amount of charm, or so he hoped.

In Cristiana's little apartment, the shadowy figure he had glimpsed on the street almost forgotten, he sipped the tea she had prepared. In from the rain, he'd similarly sat in the café as she finished her shift for the evening, that time sampling a latte. The two drinks were a way of gathering his thoughts, stilling his restless spirit—an oddity, he observed with a chuckle to himself, after consuming well-known stimulants. In its own way, the café, with its chattering china and glassware ringing like bells, had been as relaxing as the sanctuary of her apartment. Its familiarity was comforting, the same kind of place from one century to the next.

After she finished work, he had walked with Cristiana back to her place, listening to her chat with youthful exuberance about her day, nodding, and tossing her a periodic pleasantry or compliment. When she finally asked, he responded that his day had been spent walking the streets of the city and doing "research" in the library. One a complete truth, the other only a partial one.

"I wish I had a computer here," she said, handing the card back. "But they are pretty expensive—even the cheapest ones." She sat down next to him on the edge of her too-soft bed. "Are you okay? You seem a bit distracted."

"Oh? Pardons. I guess I must be feeling a bit overwhelmed by my traveling. I shall endeavor to be much more attentive," he said, stroking the fine hairs on her lower arm. Her soft gasp and gentle shiver made him smile.

"I guess it's more of that kinky stuff," she said, drinking from her own cracked cup.

"I'm sorry, I'm confused."

A nod to the card, still in his hand. "That place. It doesn't sound like a simple sex site. Where did you get it?"

"Someone gave it to me," he said. "Someone who saw us at the party," he added, a complete lie this time. To cover himself, he drank some more. He was puzzled, though, by his untruthful words. What was this girl to him? Why did he feel the need to hide his afternoon with Teresa, with Bellino, from her? Cristiana was most certainly entertaining company, a lithe and vibrant young girl, an ardent and enthusiastic lover, but beyond that, what was she to him? He had always prided himself on his honesty with himself, always, and with his partners, when he could. Again, what was she to him?

"You certainly seem to be traveling in some pretty wild circles," she said with a smile, "for someone who's just arrived."

What was she to him? Enjoyable, most definitely, but when she said that, mentioning his so-recent arrival, his eyes grew wider, and he knew that she had a different quality than anyone else so far. He knew her. He trusted her.

"For which I am most grateful to be in the company of so excellent a guide," he said, honestly. "This has been an unusual and very pleasurable journey. Thank you for your company, your beauty—and especially your kindness."

"It's been fun for me as well. Educational, too."

"Oh, and what have you learned?" he said, grinning at the possibility that the girl who'd been his teacher of the twenty-first century still had knowledge to acquire, but also hopeful that she might have further information on the party, and from the party perhaps information that would lead him to some answers, and to Athena.

Unfortunately, in that regard she disappointed him: "About the party, nothing. Zilch."

"Zilch?" he said, like a parrot, the word unfamiliar.

"Nada. Nothing. I asked some people, even called the hotel. They said they couldn't tell me, and the people I talked to later, who *could* say something, wouldn't. Private group, very rich. Very exclusive. They said it takes a lot of connections just to learn the name of it. Sorry."

"Do not trouble yourself over it. You have performed a valuable service simply by asking. I appreciate it."

"There's something else, though. Something else I think I may have found out."

"Hum?"

She took a long moment to answer, then when she did, her voice dropped, almost to a whisper. "I thought I knew a lot about sex, I mean. I've done some pretty wild stuff. Some of it with you. But after that party, I started to think about other things. I thought it didn't work for me, that I wasn't interested. But I kept thinking about it, you know? All day at work. It wouldn't leave me alone. It took me awhile, but I realized that there might be something there, 'cause why else keep thinking about it, you know? But I just didn't trust anyone to go that way. But you're different. I want to find out with you."

"Find out? About what? My curiosity is intrigued. Tell me."

"I'd prefer it if you'd make me tell."

"Ah," was all he could say to that. The new game, a new person. The world seemed to shift and sway under him, but he managed to keep his balance. A new person to whom this way of play was seductive, a new path opening, perhaps, for her. For Casanova the door had been cracked, a new color of light emerging into the room of his previous life, by what he still suspected was a modern version of Teresa/Bellino.

Placing his cup down on the floor so it wouldn't get in the way, he leaned back—ever just so—and gestured for her to stand up. Unaware of what the details might be, or the rules, if there really were any, he took in a long, slow breath and tried to still his tapping heartbeat. Still, despite his unexpected nerves, he felt the first stirrings of real excitement. Sensitive to his body, aware of its every sensual tick and chime, his steady tumescence was welcoming. Youth, it seemed, or a second adolescence was part of his own resurrection—new things to learn in life. New things for Cristiana, too, for he would play the instructor this time.

Still in the dress of her profession, she stood. He had seen her before this way, of course, and removed it various times before enjoying her sensual pleasures, but as he assumed this new role, for some reason there was something almost virginal in her garments and stature. He felt his arousal become more severe, more insistent, and it took a slow intake of breath to steady his nerves and suppress the urge to simply rise and take her then and there. Instead: "Lovely. You are a very lovely young woman," he said to the small blonde. "I consider myself fortunate, very fortunate indeed, to be in your presence as well as being previously able to sample the sensuality of your body."

"Thanks," she said.

No, he thought, *this isn't quite right.* It may have been unfamiliar ground, but the soil under it yielded memories. There were times in his previous life, many times, when he had been in positions above or even below many lovers. He knew sex that brought bruises as well as orgasms, slaps as well as erections. But for some reason, starting firmly in the position of orchestrator had thrown him off his game. Erection still present, he knew he could always fall back on that form of entertainment for them, something coarse and rough, but he wanted something new, something different, something close to what Bellino had shown him.

Then he experienced a glow of inspiration. *You're a performer,* he recalled, remembering many a salon, an exhibition before nobles or even royalty. *This is just a different stage.*

Straightening his back, he flipped his wrists as if preparing to shuffle a deck of cards. *So,* he thought to himself in a mental approximation of his best exhibition voice, *let us begin.* "But now you are not just a beautiful woman, you are something else entirely. Do you know what that is?"

"No, sorry."

"Address me as Master. Do it now."

"Yes, Master."

"No, inadequate. Completely inadequate. Maybe you are unfamiliar with the situation, what is happening here. You think, perhaps, you are a woman, but that is an incorrect assumption. Shall I educate you?"

"Yes, Master," she said, some of her previous strength leaving her tone, a note of gentle fear invading her.

A shiver went from his lower back to the top of his shoulders. A performer, yes, but this role came much too naturally. A part, it frightened him to discover, he seemed a natural to play.

"You belong to me," he said. "You may appear to be a woman of great beauty, but that is not what you are, right now, in my presence." As he stood then, she took a tentative step back, and he could now look down into her upturned sheepish eyes and their dark surroundings of tiredness. Putting a finger under her chin, he lifted her head up even more, forcing her to arch her small feet and lengthen her back. "You are a thing, here solely for my pleasure. That is all. Now what do you call me? And this time I want to hear in your voice that you understand your position—and mine."

"Yes," she said, half closing her lovely eyes, her words saying more than simple agreement. "Master."

"Excellent. Defy or disappoint and there will be repercussions. Punishments." She was slim and shapely, but he still managed to expertly locate her hardened nipple through her clothing. A gentle caress was what he might have done, but now he wasn't just Casanova, but a new form of that person, a rebirth that pinched with cruel force. With a quick gasp, a frightened sound, her knees buckled and her hands rose but stopped short of touching him. That pleased him, a sign that despite the pain, the game hadn't ended.

"But please me and there will be rewards." This time he did give her a gentle caress, a simple gesture that he could have repeated endlessly.

"Yes, Master. I understand."

"This pleases me. Now, undress."

Reaching around to her back, she searched for a zipper. From there she continued: shoes and stockings. Dress and slip. Remaining, then also gone, dropped sensuously onto the floor: bra and panties. Not for the first time he could have applauded this modern age, this world of the future, for its simplicity of dress. Naked, she was a vision—maybe not quite the image of pure beauty that still haunted him, the erotic ghost of Athena—but she was still a supple and willing young woman. His ardor, if it was possible, became ever more insistent.

Like her, he realized that ever since this side of sex had emerged, he'd been thinking about it on some deeper level. Bellino hadn't unlocked a bolted door, she had just given him permission to enter. Now that he had begun the game, his head began to swim with possibilities. Like a director with the puppets of living actors, he sat down under the weight of too many possible performances. He had suspected, but now he knew, the power and seduction of this form of sex. Ah, what a world to be reborn into. So much to know, so much more to explore. But his manhood was ever more insistent, and he knew that for this time, this night, with this woman, simplicity would be the best course of action.

So, sitting on the bed to steady himself, he commanded her to do what she had not yet done in his presence: "Pleasure yourself."

That startled her.

"You wish to speak," he said, when she didn't. "Do so."

"I-I just have never done that in front of anyone, Master."

"Well, you shall do so now. Or this game is over and I am leaving."

"Yes, Master," she said, filling her lungs with the strength of air.

She began. Seeing the gentle quake in her fingers, he knew how far he had pushed her, but although he was aware and was in some way concerned, he also was enjoying the power he held. She was doing what he asked because *he* commanded it. It was a heady feeling, like a drug. Again he resisted the urge to go further. But it was difficult. He felt a cold shiver again: he was used to being the seducer, not being seduced by anyone or anything.

As he watched her hands, he could tell she was unfamiliar with the situation as well as the position. In a flash he imagined her on a bed, her long, thin legs spread wide, fingers urgently manipulating the pearl amid her folds. Now, though, she was standing, those same fingers gently stroking: circles, circles, circles as she took in deeper and deeper breaths. After a short—very short—time, her skin became softly reflective, the sweat of her excitement also bringing the smell of salt to the air of the apartment. Her nipples, how could he not have noticed their tension, their firmness? It was all he could do not to return his hands to them.

Her excitement was evident, as was her rapid escalation. Her body had been in his hands many times; he believed he knew how long her trips usually took. It amused him, and excited him, to see her approach so much faster. The game was good for her, and—his erection was demanding now—good for him as well.

Gleaming thighs. Ah, such a sight. Moisture so free and hot, dripping down her thighs from her melting quim. It was a magical moment—true magic—that mesmerized him. One hand, he noticed, had drifted up to her breasts and was feverishly tugging at the nipple, the force almost shocking.

Then, with a rattling moan, an aria of guttural, primordial bliss, she arrived. The trip had been fast and intense, brutally wonderful, so much so that her body deserted her and she sagged. It was only by his quick grasping of her narrow waist that he kept her from crashing to the floor.

After a time she had regained her strength, tension returning to her legs and her weight lifting off his. Back on her feet, she flicked back a few errant strands of blonde hair and absorbed a few deep breaths to further steady herself.

"An adequate performance," he said, stilling the reflex to compliment. He was still on stage, as well, after all. "But you're not finished. Not yet."

"Yes, Master, I understand," she said, her voice light if more than a bit exhausted.

"Good. Now I have a need that you will have to service," he said, reaching down and—as carefully and dramatically as possible—revealing his more than insistent erection. "Do a good job and there will be further rewards," he added, having no idea as to what those rewards could be, knowing only that it would be good for both of them.

"Definitely, Master," she said with a wry grin.

He thought he was prepared. He thought that by assuming the role he had taken on, he would be as in control as he pretended to be. The contact of her lips on his member was a shock, wet and tight and intense. It was all he could do to keep his own destination from arriving too quickly. Again, he thought about lessons, about all he had learned and would no doubt further learn in this new world.

Willing and passionate, she worked him. He thought he knew her abilities but was pleased to find that she had further talents to show him. And she did, with great vigor and delightful skill. Before too long he realized that there was no way he was going to be able to withhold his pleasurable release. At that instant, his own eruption began with a leaden rush from the base of his testicles and up—all the way to glorious heaven.

As exhaustion rolled over him and his own collapse threatened, he managed to regain a certain amount of composure, only to open his eyes to the sight of Cristiana wiping the excess from her lips with the back of a hand.

"Very good," he said, to both the girl and the new game they had played. "Very good indeed."

"Well," she said with exasperation, "that was a disappointment."

Casanova had to agree. Certainly the illustration there on the luminescent glass of the library device was provocative, and maybe even a bit exciting, but it didn't tell either him or Cristiana much of anything.

It was the night after. After a quick breakfast of latte and croissants, they had immediately gone to the library to consult with its machines on the Power Company. Although he'd had his concerns over balancing the two women, even going so far as to consider telling Cristiana that her help wasn't required at the library, Bellino was nowhere to be found. When he asked another member of the staff, he was told that the name was unknown.

For some reason this did not come as a surprise. Her appearance and performance had all the airs of an actress on the stage. He had been aware of this, but perhaps not conscious of it, for some time now. Whether she was part of his own resurrection or something else entirely, he did not know. The haunted feeling that had surrounded him the day before had not left, but perhaps because of its persistence the intensity seemed to be diminished. Was it that he was simply becoming inured to the unreality of what was occurring, that strangeness after strangeness had produced in this new life a form of commonality?

The image that appeared on the screen when they had sat themselves before the gently humming machine was simple and, according to Cristiana, who appeared to be knowledgeable about such things, not "clickable." All that was present was a headline, "The Power Company," in ornate white lettering on a black page. In the center of the darkness was a single illustration—no, *photograph* was the term. Captured from life, not interpreted by an artist. It was the image of a woman, naked and restrained by a complex web of ropes. She was lovely, with strong legs and thighs and with ample and uplifted breasts indicating youth and vigor, but he found himself less aroused by her beauty than disappointed that she was all there seemed to be on the page. The ropes, when he studied them, seemed to have no discernible pattern. Darkness, a title, and a photograph of a woman restrained was all there seemed to be.

"Curses," he mumbled to himself. "This is all?"

Cristiana ran the mouse in circles on the desk, clicking on everything. Nothing responded. "Sorry, it looks like that's it. Nothing's happening."

"How could that be it? It seems so pointless."

"But that's what it is. Getting angry won't make it any better."

"Apologies, my dear. I didn't mean to address my frustration toward you. It just seems that this whole world is somehow a game for which I have not been given the rules."

"Yeah, I feel the same way sometimes."

He appreciated her sympathy, but he knew there was no way she could understand his situation. In fact, the disparity between the two of them made him want to laugh. *If you only knew,* he thought, turning his eyes back to the image.

Games were one thing, but this was becoming ludicrous. His resurrection, the perfectly timed image of that other gentleman and the woman Athena—*yes, Athena*—and the appearance of Teresa's double in Bellino. A shadowy figure on Venice's drizzly streets. And now this image before him. There had to be a connection of some sort. There appeared to be some effort being made to lead him somewhere, for some purpose. For his next destination in this game to have just vanished didn't feel correct somehow. There had to be something he was not seeing, an element that was escaping his notice.

The woman on the screen was unfamiliar, though to be honest he had bedded so many in his previous life that he more than likely would not have been able to recognize her even if they had been intimate. Her posture was provocative but also meaningless. The ropes were in an asymmetrical pattern, but it also did not bring him any understanding.

"I have to get back to work soon," Cristiana said.

"Hmm? Ah, of course. I shall walk you there. Thank you for

coming with me, even if it has been a fool's errand." And there was no doubt in his mind who the fool was.

Then, before stepping out into a much clearer morning than the day before, he turned, seeing a splash of color on one wall of the ante-room. It had been there before, of course, the map of Venice. No doubt tacked up as an aid for those unfamiliar with its twisting courses and narrow streets. But now he looked at it with a fresh per-spective, one bound—so to speak—to recent experience. Very recent.

"Gods!" he found himself exclaiming as he grabbed her arm and pulled her back into the library. Luckily, the institution was practically empty in its first hour of being opened for the day, so their machine had not been claimed by another. On the screen was the same woman, the same pose, the same white lettering. The ropes,—he confirmed with an exuberant fist on the desk,—that were a good approximation of the lines and shapes on a map of Venice. Close to the glass, peering as he hadn't before, he saw that her right hand was pointing to one particular knot, a tangle of streets he knew all too well.

"Did you find out something?" Cristiana said, obviously not seeing the connection.

"Yes, my dear," he said. "I did indeed. Come, let's take a walk."

"A walk? But I have to get to the Caffe Cavour. I can't be late."

"It won't take more than a moment. It's not far."

Back into the streets, with the sun high in a cloud-interrupted blue sky, he felt lighter. He not only had a piece on this cryptic game board, but he also had a direction in which to move. Taking Cristiana's hand, he began to lead her along the stretches and knots of the city.

Then there was someone in front of them, someone in a tatty, brown hooded cloak. The figure from the day before, shadowy and pursuing. But this time he was not behind, ducking from one dark corner to another. This time he was blocking their way.

"Bastard!" The voice was cracked and broken, the single word present with distorted vowels and spat consonants. "You bastard!" the figure repeated, but this time the cloak parted, and a face was revealed. Filthy, mad, furious—and familiar.

Casanova cursed softly. Of all of them, of all the faces from those years in the past. Of all those names that should have been dead and at peace, he never would have expected to see him, to see François Marie Arouet de Voltaire.

Chapter Four

Casanova blurted, "François Marie? Is it really you?" The man had Voltaire's perfect aquiline nose, distinctive narrow jaw, and incongruously round dimpled chin, but on second look his eyes were too close together, and Voltaire had never acquired bad-tempered callipers around his mouth, even as an old man.

The ragged figure sneered. "I am Pierre Depuis, but I'm flattered to be taken for my illustrious ancestor, even by a traitorous dog like you!" His hand slid into a pocket, as if casually, but the muscles in his arm were tense.

Casanova had seen similar movements before. He swept Cristiana behind him and shrugged out of his jacket. Depuis' hand appeared to be empty when he withdrew it. For a second Casanova thought his alarm had been mistaken. Then Depuis' wrist flicked. A blade of gleaming steel sprouted from his fist, as if by magic. Of course, the tools of the assassin would have advanced along with all the other technological marvels Casanova had witnessed in this new age.

Casanova whipped his jacket around his left arm. He leaped forward, keeping his eyes on the knife and flailing at it. The blade slid through cloth and sliced Casanova's flesh, but it was a shallow wound and the weapon was entangled. A quick circular motion gave Depuis a choice between releasing his knife and suffering a sprained wrist.

Casanova's right hand came up, heel first, under Depuis' nose. The sole of Casanova's right shoe raked down the man's shin, from just below his knee to his instep. He fell backward and sprawled on the cobblestones, howling.

Cristiana was whimpering behind Casanova. Ignoring her, he stepped forward and stamped down on the man's belly. By the time Depuis could breathe again, Casanova had dragged him to his feet and had the point of the wicked blade at his eyeball.

"Why does he wish us harm?" Cristiana managed to get out.

"He's about to tell us."

Depuis winced, tears cutting furrows through the grime on his face. His head trembled as if he wanted to shake it but dared not, because of the knife. "Kill me if you will. I'll tell you nothing."

"Your resemblance to an old friend of mine moves me to show mercy."

The man seemed to grow inside his ragged clothes. "I have the honor to count François Marie de Voltaire among my ancestors."

"François' line? But he fathered no children."

"His daughter by the Marquise du Chatelet was never acknowledged."

"That explains the resemblance. It doesn't explain why you call me 'traitor' and wish to kill me."

"I have nothing to say, dog."

The knife flashed, sliced Depuis' left nostril, and was back at his eyeball before he could blink.

"That's for the 'dog.' Would you like to try a stronger epithet?"

Depuis' lips squeezed together, perhaps because blood was now flowing freely over his mouth.

"Let me guess. We seek a certain establishment. You appear, blocking our path. Could it be that you wish to prevent us from finding the Power Company?"

A crafty look came over Depuis' face. He squeezed, "You're looking for it?" between compressed lips.

"Yes."

"Then, with your permission, sir, I will happily be your guide."

Cristiana clutched Casanova's arm. "Don't trust him."

"But I do. I trust any man who can feel my blade against his skin." He spun the man around, caught his scruff, and pressed the knife's point to the base of his skull. "Lead on!"

Their limping, snuffling guide led them through lanes and alleys, each narrower than the one before, each twisted and shadowed. The stench of stagnant water became oppressive, relieved only by the sharper aroma of urine. Their footing became uncertain. Mostly, they trod crude cobbles, but sometimes they stumbled over blocks of tarred wood. For a stretch, many of those had been ripped up, no doubt to fuel some wretches' fires.

Cristiana shivered. "He's leading us into a trap."

"If he is, the last thing he'll hear is this knife's point scraping against the top of his skull, from the inside." Casanova pricked Depuis' skin in emphasis.

"I'll take you where you wish to go and deliver you there safely," Depuis assured them. "I swear it, on my honor."

Casanova's lip curled. "On your honor, you say? Then how can we doubt you?"

Cristiana tugged on Casanova's shirt. "What was all that about him looking like his ancestor who was your friend? It's not possible!"

"Hush, little one."

A right turn took them into a passage between two windowless stone buildings that were so close they had to go in single file. Casanova was just beginning to think Cristiana was right when it opened into an incongruously pleasant square, at the farthest point in

La Serenissima where you could be from the lagoon or the canals. It was evenly paved with flagstones and had a plot of hibiscus planted at its center. The facades surrounding it were grimy, with boarded-up windows, except for one narrow-shouldered building that had been restored to reveal intricately veined pale green marble. That building was just wide enough to accommodate a single carved oak door and one mullioned window, though it was five floors tall.

The keystone above the door bore a round black shield that bore a simple device—a wheel with three curved spokes. Casanova knew something of heraldry, as did any ambitious man of his day, but the insignia meant nothing to him.

"Here you are, safe and sound," the man announced, sounding suspiciously gleeful.

"Are we?" Casanova asked.

The man tugged on a simple brass ring. Somewhere inside, a deep bell sounded. In less than a minute, the door swung open.

The woman who appeared in the entrance was dressed in an eighteenth-century chambermaid's uniform—but adapted as it might have been for such events as the Excelsior Ball. Her full fuchsia skirt brushed the ground, but it was made of something gauzy so that, backlit as it was, it was translucent. Casanova raised an appreciative eyebrow at the long, slender legs that were silhouetted.

Her bodice was tightly laced to immediately below her breasts, forcing them to tilt upward. Those lush mounds were concealed in a froth of white lace that came no higher than the upper edges of her nipples' halos in front and rose to tiny cap sleeves on each side. Her snowy shoulders were bare. A black leather choker circled her throat. Her thin lips and lowered eyelids had been painted lavishly.

Without raising her eyes higher than Casanova's waist, she intoned, "Welcome to the Power Company, sir."

The scruffy man twisted aside with, "You see!" and hobbled away.

Casanova and Cristiana followed the woman into a marble lobby that was as wide as the house looked to be from the square but was lined on both sides with heavy doors. How big was the Power Company? Obviously, some, if not all, of the decrepit structures that formed the square were part of the same building.

"Your weapon, sir? They are forbidden within." She took the knife with distaste. "Your coat?"

Feeling a little ridiculous at entering so refined an establishment in his shirtsleeves and somewhat disheveled, Casanova unwound the slashed coat from his arm. Blood dripped from his fingertips to the tiled floor.

As coolly as if the arrival of wounded gentlemen were an everyday occurrence, she told him, "If you will come this way, I'll have your arm tended to." She opened a door for him. Cristiana moved to follow, but the woman stopped her with a single finger pressed to her chest. "Members only." To Casanova, she added, "The girl will be looked after until you require her."

Casanova opened his mouth to protest.

Cristiana said, "I'll be fine," and retreated.

The drawing room was two floors high and would have made a small ballroom. Its furniture was too spindly for his taste but obviously expensive. The woman led him to a striped chaise and bade him sit. He waited, clutching the cut in his forearm.

An impressively tall uniformed footman brought in a folding table and set it beside the chaise. He was followed by two pretty girls, garbed as the woman had been but one in lavender and the other in *eau de nile* green, bearing ornate silver trays laden with coffee, brandy, tiny cakes, and fruit. Casanova sipped coffee that was aromatic but a little bitter for his taste. How was he to explain himself? He could hardly say that he had sought out the Power Company in the hope of locating a woman whose name he didn't know but whom he'd seen once, naked, and was smitten with.

As if conjured by his thoughts, the woman Casanova had dubbed "Athena" entered the room through the farthest door. He inhaled sharply. His besotted mind had not exaggerated her ethereal beauty. She approached, carrying a white box marked with a red cross. For a heartbeat, he doubted his senses. It was that easy to find her?

She strode on stiletto heels, but slowly, as if in a procession. Her bearing was regal even though her eyes were downcast. Her costume was similar to those of the other women—long, full skirt and a tightly laced bodice—but had dramatic differences. It was made of dark green velvet. There were no flounces of lace rising up to veil her breasts. They were lifted and exposed, twin pink orbs, crimson tipped. Even more shocking, her skirts, though perfectly opaque, revealed more than the other women had displayed of their nether parts. It was formed of panels, gathered at her narrow waist and brushing the floor despite the elevation of her shoes. The central panel had been omitted. An opening, three inches wide at her waist and a foot across at her feet, exposed her naked sex. With each step she took, she flashed an incredible length of naked thigh.

Casanova waited, with his mouth dry and a growing discomfort in his trousers, until she came within six feet of where he sat. He rose and bowed with a flourish. "Madame."

Without raising her eyes, she gestured at the chaise. Casanova sat and patted the silk to his left. She sank to the chaise beside him, neither wanton nor ashamed. He found her matter-of-fact attitude perversely erotic. Being alone with a strange man, her breasts and now sequin-free delicate pubic curls blatantly displayed, seemed to her to be a casual event.

With cool efficiency, she cut his shirtsleeve away, cleaned his wound with a stinging liquid, patted a dressing in place, and secured it with strips of some adhesive material. Casanova felt a little dizzy. It wasn't from the trivial pain. Perhaps it was her presence, or her heady perfume.

His eyes misted. When he forced them to focus, they were directed at the neat pelt on her mound and the subtle crease below it. He lifted his eyes, to a pert nipple, then higher, to the scarlet cushion of her mouth.

"Is there anything else you require of me, sir?" she asked. Her voice was a soft ribbon of fur, dragged across his nape.

Her lips filled his vision. Did he require anything else? At that moment, his greatest desire was to sip the nectar her lips promised. He leaned closer. His mouth approached hers. Their lips touched.

Casanova slumped. His face fell into her lap, but his cheek took no pleasure from being pressed against her mound. The drug in his coffee had taken effect.

From time to time, he was vaguely aware that things were being done to him. Needles that he hardly felt were inserted into the veins of his arms. He was lifted and carried several times. Fingers raised his eyelids. Bloated and distorted faces loomed into sight and then disappeared. Once, he blinked his eyes open to stare straight up at a starry sky. He was on his back for a while, on something hard that rocked. There was a stench of fuel when he was in the dark, in the back of some vehicle. Time became distorted. He was in his stupor for hours, or days, or perhaps months.

His first thought, when he came to full consciousness, was of Athena and the kiss that he had failed to consummate. His second, guiltily, was of Cristiana. What had become of her?

He was in a bed, between crisp linen sheets. The room was small.

Sunlight dappled the ceiling. A subtle swaying told him he was on some type of ship. He turned a groggy head. The light that flooded through two brass-framed portholes was painfully bright.

He had been abducted. It didn't seem likely that his captors intended to consign him to the deeps. If they did, he would be in a weighted sack, not tucked up in bed. Casanova rolled, groaning, and was caught short. His right wrist was manacled to the bed. It, in turn, was bolted to the floor.

How long had he been comatose? The cut on his left arm was livid but closed. As well as he could judge, it had been healing for about a week. In seven days, with modern means of transportation, he could be anywhere in the world.

Frustrated, he jerked his chain. As if it were a signal, a girl entered with a tray. She was tiny. Jet-black hair and tilted almond eyes suggested the Far East, but her skin was the milk-and-roses complexion of an English maid. Her garb identified her as a servant of the Power Company. It was pale blue, gauzy, and frilled at the neckline with lace. She whispered, "Sir needs nourishment."

Casanova realized he was famished and thirsty. The exotic creature held a glass of water to his lips and then fed him spoons of hot beef broth. When he could, he demanded, "What's going on? Why am I being held prisoner?"

She shook her head, sadly.

"I insist you tell me!"

"Please, sir, I know nothing. Rest now, if you will."

The pressure of her hand on his bare chest was light, but he was weak. Casanova sank back and slept a deep but natural sleep.

There was a chamber pot beside his bed. It was emptied each time he used it, within minutes, so he was being observed. His meals graduated from broth to chopped meats, fruit, and cereals, and by the third day to chops and steaks. Each morning, his nursemaid shaved him and bathed him in his bed, sponging him with what she told him was surgical spirit. Her touch was efficient and impersonal, even when his staff rose as she lifted it on the backs of delicate fingers to wipe his groin and swab beneath his scrotum.

He learned that she was called "D," though she assured him that he need not name her when he addressed her, as she was the only servant who had contact with him.

On his fourth day, D brought him a full English breakfast, a treat that Voltaire, the real one, had described with relish. Casanova devoured bacon, eggs, a sliver of liver, a savory kidney, and a mountain of toast. D leaned across him to take his tray. He took her hair in one hand and burrowed the other into the top of her dress to grasp her delicate breast. Instead of struggling to escape his cruel grip, D relaxed across his lap on her back, arms to her sides.

His fingers dug into her flesh. "Where am I, and why am I a prisoner?" For emphasis, his hand crushed her until he felt the glandular masses in her breast compress and move under his fingers.

"What little I know, I'm forbidden to tell," she explained, sadly but calmly. She was wincing but made no protest.

There was a stirring at Casanova's groin. Damn! Didn't his cock know he was torturing the girl, not caressing her? He didn't want to enjoy inflicting pain. If he acknowledged the glee that sadism aroused in him, where would it lead?

The door opened. A tall, saturnine man, clad entirely in black, entered the cabin. His eyebrow lifted. "When you're done with the girl, perhaps you'd enjoy some outdoor exercise?"

Casanova released his victim, relieved that he hadn't had to test his own limits. D tumbled from the bed and crawled to the newcomer on her hands and knees. Her lips pressed to the toe of one black leather boot.

"You were careless," the man told her.

The flat of her tongue laved his glossy instep.

"Raise your skirts."

With her face pressed to his boot for support, D reached back and tucked her skirt up into her belt. Her deliciously rounded bottom bore half a dozen horizontal welts. She gripped the man's ankles in both hands. His hand rose with a leather riding crop in it. He slashed down. D jerked but didn't whimper. Five more blows followed the first, making a crosshatch on her taut pink skin.

Casanova felt he should have protested, but the scene was so bizarre he was at a loss for words. D was dismissed. The man released Casanova's manacle. "There are clothes in the closet. I'll wait outside."

Casanova dressed in khaki slacks and shirt, with espadrilles for his bare feet. They hadn't provided underwear, which was embarrassing. The erection that tormenting D had given him showed no sign of softening.

The dark stranger led Casanova along a gangway, up a flight of steps, another gangway, yet more steps, and out onto the deck. The ship was huge, by Casanova's standards. He estimated it was over one hundred yards from stem to stern. The decks were gleaming mahogany. The trim was bright brass. The officers he saw were in black, like his captor, but relieved by bright kerchiefs. Overmuscled deckhands went naked except for broad belts from which dangled ropes' ends and quirts. None of them were sweating. The actual work was performed by women and girls, half naked if they wore anything.

Keeping a craft and crew of this size had to cost a fortune. Just how rich and powerful was the Power Company?

"How should I address you?" Casanova inquired.

"On board, 'Captain' is appropriate."

They circled a gang of three naked women who were holy-stoning the deck. Their pendulous breasts swayed as they scrubbed. All were marked with welts, across their bottoms, their thighs, and even their tender bosoms. The massive creature who supervised them amused himself by tickling their buttocks with a three-stranded whip as they labored.

"Captain, may I ask why I am being held captive?"

"You may ask what you will, unless enjoined to silence. Your answers, however, must come from within."

"I don't understand."

"I didn't expect you to. Let us go forward. There's something I wish to show you."

A sprit jutted four yards ahead of the ship. Something dangled beneath it, suspended in a net that was attached at each end and hung free between. When they got closer, Casanova was horrified to see that a girl was so tightly confined in the mesh that squares of her flesh stood proud between the constricting strands. His horror grew when he recognized the prisoner as his Cristiana.

He rounded on the captain. "This is foul! Release her, immediately."

"She's there for but three hours a day, hostage to your good behavior. Annoy me in the slightest way, and her stint will be doubled."

Casanova made fists and then relaxed them. The captain was half a head taller and a good fifty pounds heavier. Brutish crewmen were within call. All an attack would achieve would be a beating for him and further torments for a girl he held high in his affections.

And it was he who had brought her to this.

"If you will give me your parole, I will grant you freedom of the ship. There will be no need for chains, except under special circumstances."

Casanova gave his word. It had been broken often enough before, and with less justification.

He took lunch in a spacious salon at the captain's table. The room contained a dozen tables, each with three or four occupants, mainly men dressed in severe black, though some were naked but for leather harnesses. Each man was attended by a girl or woman, variously garbed, but those whose sexual attributes were covered wore garments that allowed easy access to their female parts. A man with a scar above his left eye had his hand under a fragile brunette's brief skirt. Whatever he was doing was making her whimper, but no one seemed to pay any attention.

Casanova's and the captain's companions were a statuesque redhead and a voluptuous woman with raven hair, both dressed as his Athena had been when last he had seen her, bare breasted and open skirted, but in pink and yellow. The conversation was of art and the theater. The women were knowledgeable and witty, but they never raised their eyes and deferred to the captain in all things. Lobster and a salad were served by girls dressed as the maids had been.

The redhead, deliberately, to Casanova's eye, tipped a fork to the floor. A maid stooped to retrieve it. The redhead moved her foot and trapped the girl's hand under a viciously spiked heel.

"Naughty!" the captain reproved. "That merits a punishment."

"For me or for the girl?" the redhead asked.

"Both."

"Thank you, Captain."

The captain turned to Casanova. "She's a glutton, this one, but careful. Not a day passes but she provokes me in some minor, never major, way. Even a pain slut such as she knows better than to invite my more severe disciplines."

"Like being suspended in a net above the bow's spray?" Casanova dared ask, drily.

Both women suppressed giggles.

"That," the captain assured him, "is me at my most lenient." He dropped his napkin to the table. "I suggest you return to your cabin for a nap. There will be entertainment tonight that you will need to be well rested for."

It was dark outside when two burly crewmen came for Casanova. Despite his protests, his wrists were manacled behind him. "Captain's orders."

This time he was led down, not up, to a windowless chamber that was perhaps fifteen yards wide, thirty long, and too high for the illumination to reveal. It was hard to believe he was still at sea. The walls looked as if built from blocks of stone. The light was from torches that on closer inspection proved to be artificial. The furnishings could have been from the Inquisition's deepest dungeon. He recognized whipping posts, chained drums that might be variants of the dreaded rack, and a variety of wooden structures that seemed designed for binding victims to them in various uncomfortable positions. There were hooks and chains set into three walls. The fourth accommodated a St. Andrew's cross and an assortment of cog wheels that he dared not speculate on. Ropes and chains dangled from above.

A crowd was seated as if for entertainment. He recognized his dinner companions in the front row, on plush seats, flanked by a number of the ship's officers, several of whom had naked girls curled at their feet. Behind that row were wooden benches, occupied by the dominant men and submissive women he had seen in the salon.

His captors guided Casanova to a post and secured him to it with three broad leather straps; one each around his shoulders, abdomen, and thighs. His heart sank. Was he to provide the evening's entertainment? He had no doubt that the company was assembled to witness someone's torments.

D, stark naked now and flaunting her crosshatched hips, came to stand by him.

"Am I to be tortured?" he whispered to her.

"No, not physically, at least."

That was cold comfort. If he wasn't to be tortured "physically," then what? A terrible thought came to him. Being forced to watch Cristiana being abused would be a torture.

As if to confound his suspicions, she appeared, transformed yet again. When he had met her, she'd been a minx, lusty but seeming relatively innocent. Later, she had revealed a perverse taste for erotic servitude. Now she was something else, though he couldn't decide what. All she wore was a pair of plum velvet high-heeled boots that rose halfway up her slender thighs and matching gloves that covered her arms to her shoulders. Her body was stark white, as if powdered with snow.

Cristiana posed, arms held high, and turned. The left cheek of the bottom he had once showered with tender kisses was marked, perhaps tattooed, with the same insignia he had seen above the Power Company's door.

There was scattered applause. The audience approved.

Had she been drugged into compliance? It seemed not, for she gave him a saucy wink and a little wave. She appeared to be blissfully happy, as if she had found her true home aboard this floating sink of depravity. And he had been fretting about her safety! The girl he had considered naïve was proving to be as enigmatic as the most sophisticated courtesan he'd ever bedded.

The artificial torches dimmed. All chatter ceased. A powerful beam of light, directed from far above, created a brilliant circle on the floor. In that ring stood the captain, bare chested, his legs sheathed in black leather that divided to expose a matching codpiece.

Cristiana entered the circle and fell to her knees before him. A pang of envy twisted Casanova's gut. If Cristiana was to kneel in adoration, it should be he whom she worshipped.

Was this the torment that was planned for him—to witness Cristiana's betrayal? If so, it wouldn't be excruciating. She was obviously willing, and although he was fond of her, his true passion was reserved for Athena.

A second spotlight came on. It illuminated a pair of costumed girls. They had nodding plumes on their heads. Crisscrossed leather straps enhanced their nakedness. They were shod in boots that contrived to resemble horses' hooves. The pair of human ponies towed a flat cart that bore a coffin, bolted to stay upright.

A coffin? For him? For Cristiana?

As they came closer, followed by the light, he could see that it was no normal coffin. Its front—its lid—was made of horizontal bars, set a foot apart. Inside, the light made a chiaroscuro of a naked female body. Was a corpse to join this satanic revel?

The cart stopped. Two brutes, naked but for leather pouches over their genitals, opened the cage and with extreme deference, helped a woman alight.

Athena! She wore the same erotic garb as Cristiana, but in forest green, except that a spiked collar circled her pretty throat. When she turned, Casanova saw that her bottom was also marked by a well-healed branding with the initials "S H." Probably the initials of her erstwhile owner, he thought. The woman he was besotted with turned again, to stand with her legs spread. Casanova sucked a breath. Her sex was sealed between the teeth of a vicious jeweled clamp.

The light followed Athena's stride until it became a double pool, joining with the circle around Cristiana and the captain.

The captain nodded at Casanova. "For the benefit of our unwilling guest, sweet O, do you know what is to be done to you here?"

So "Athena" was "O"? Now he had a second sobriquet for the object of his passion.

"Pain," O replied. Her voice betrayed a hint of relish.

"And?"

"Humiliation."

"Do you deliver yourself willingly?"

"I do."

He came closer and rested a palm on her hip. "And who do you love?"

"You, my Master."

Casanova's heart sank.

"Why do you love me?"

She looked puzzled. "Why, because you are my everything, my all, my life."

"Even though I give you to others, to use and abuse?"

"I am yours. What comes from you, I embrace."

The captain looked at Casanova again. "Such love is beyond your comprehension, I'm sure. Perhaps you will learn to understand it."

Casanova shook his head. What the captain said was true. Even so, he envied the captain for being the recipient of such adoration. To be worshipped, without reason or limit, must feel glorious.

The captain pointed at the obscenity between O's thighs. "Remove that," he told Cristiana.

O spread her legs. Cristiana crawled to kneel between her feet. A squeeze released the clamp. Cristiana rose up and pressed her face to O's pudenda.

Casanova felt a sudden fever. In this modern world there were just two women he cared for. Now one of them was tonguing the other's sex. Had there been just the three of them there, it would have been the culmination of his erotic fantasies.

D's wet tongue was moving over his neck. She whispered, "This excites you, sir."

He couldn't deny it. She was fondling him through the fabric of his slacks. A lie would have been obvious.

The captain signaled to O to raise her hands before her. A chain descended, lowered by some mechanical device. As Cristiana slobbered lust between O's thighs, he wrapped leather straps around O's wrists. The chain pulled taut. O's hands were lifted above her head and higher. Suspended by her slender arms, the woman Casanova desired was lifted off her feet, to dangle with the toes of her boots inches above the floor. O spread wide, encouraging Cristiana, but without resting an ounce of weight on her.

The captain tapped Cristiana's shoulder with a long, vicious crop. She took it from him with obvious delight.

D drew the zipper of Casanova's fly down. A small hot hand worked into his slacks and drew his shaft and sac from them. Cristiana's hand drew back. Delicate fingers caressed Casanova's rigid length. The crop whistled. O jerked in her bonds. D's hand closed and slid slowly up, then down.

Casanova had endured extremes of lust before. There'd been the Moorish twins, with oiled bodies, who'd entwined like mating eels for an hour before inviting him to join their slippery conjunction. There'd been the fleshy English duchess who'd been blessed with an overlong tongue and a clitoris like a baby penis. Never before, in all his amorous adventures, had he suffered such lust.

He hissed, "Harder, D. Faster!"

She apologized, "I have been instructed, sir. The how and when of my services to you will be by the captain's prescription."

"The captain be damned!" Casanova tried to hump at D's hand, but the straps kept him immobile.

"Watch the entertainment, sir," D advised. "It's a rare privilege. O is seldom displayed in public."

Cristiana's blow sent O twirling on the end of her chain. The captain reached out, almost negligently, caught her ankle, and held it aside. Now that she was stilled and turned toward him, Casanova saw the marks Cristiana had inflicted. One oblique line marred the perfection of her thighs, above the tops of her boots. Two crossed the gentle swell of her belly, between her mound and her navel. Holding O's left leg high, the captain pointed to the inside of the thigh that was exposed.

Cristiana took careful aim.

D squatted and rubbed the head of Casanova's penis across her cheek.

The crop cracked down. O spasmed.

D took Casanova into her mouth. Her fingers played delicately with his dangling scrotum.

The captain dropped O's left ankle and raised her right. Cristiana's crop hesitated.

D's tongue made tiny tantalizing circles.

The crop hissed and cracked. O remained silent, but Casanova groaned.

At a signal from the captain, Cristiana threw the crop aside and rushed to lick O's welts with the flat of her tongue. It looked to Casanova that the girl had been weeping even as she had flogged O. Her face glistened with tears. How strange. She had been moved by the pain she herself had inflicted. What perverse conflict! He tried, and failed, to understand it.

D was stroking his shaft, pumping it, her lips working on him to the same rhythm.

There was activity under the spotlights. To his relief, or was it disappointment, O was being taken down. A muscled minion was wheeling a cart that was laden with objects, some bright steel, some glossy black, but Casanova couldn't discern their shapes. O was taken to one of the huge drums. Her wrists were shackled high on its rim. Her ankles were spread wide and strapped to ring bolts set in the floor.

D's tongue pressed his glans against the roof of her mouth.

A man cranked a wheel. The drum O was secured to turned. The tendons on the insides of her thighs stood proud. Her waist elongated. Her breasts lifted as she was arched backward. Her ribcage spread like a fan.

D bobbed, hard and fast.

The captain selected an instrument and approached O, lifting it to the junction of her thighs. Casanova knew that something terrible was about to be inflicted on the woman he adored. His insides knotted. Dread fought desire. O welcomed this horror, yet it was still horror. Her desire for pain was at once incomprehensible and shamefully exciting.

His compassion battled his lust. D's frantic suction tipped the scales. As he spurted his seed into D's willing mouth, O screamed.

The captain's back prevented Casanova from seeing how he was tormenting her sweet tender flesh. When the big man moved aside, Casanova screwed his eyes tight shut. Whatever was being done to his beloved, he dared not watch. His eyes remained closed through an eternity of O's whimpering and D's caresses. One so at odds with the other! And yet, to his shame, D's well-trained hands and avid mouth coaxed him into another erection. He refused to climax even when O's cries signaled the bliss of her orgasm. He would not take pleasure from her pain, even if she did, nor would he grace it with his glance.

It wasn't until he had been carried back to his cabin that he opened his eyes.

Come morning, Casanova lingered in his cabin until he felt he could contain his rage. When he made his way toward the salon, he passed his redheaded dining companion but almost didn't recognize her. She was sheathed in a green caftan, with a turban around her head.

"Good morning, Giacomo," she told him. "Try the scrambled eggs. They have truffles in them."

No one in the salon was dressed as before. The ship's officers were in crisp white uniforms. There were few waitresses, as it was a buffet. Those he saw were in demure black, with white aprons. He remembered one from the previous day, when a man had made her whimper in this same room. Cheery couples sat at the tables; the men in slacks and bright shirts, the women in holiday garb: sundresses, shorts, slacks that ended at their calves, brief skirts, and gay tops. It was noisy with the clatter of cutlery and inane chatter. Confused, he fled to the deck.

A woman he had last seen scrubbing planks slathered lotion over the back of a bikini-clad girl. A deckhand who had a scar above his eye, who wore white slacks and a striped jersey, was pointing out features of a distant coastline to a woman whose bare shoulders were covered in makeup. Casanova peered closer. The makeup almost concealed her bruises, but not quite. He hadn't woken from a nightmare. These were the same cold, sadistic masters and incomprehensibly willing slaves, but transformed.

Coastline? He rushed to the rail. A smeared glare of white sand was bordered by tall palm trees. Farther inland, pastel buildings reached for the azure sky.

"What land is that?" he croaked.

"Key West," the woman told him.

"Key West?"

"Florida."

"In the Americas?"

"Yes, the USA. Where else?"

Before thought could cloud his decision, Casanova threw himself overboard.

Chapter Five

As the choppy water closed over his head, Casanova dove deeply, swimming with long, powerful kicks intended to get him as far away from the ship as possible before he had to surface for air. At the same time an undercurrent of horror permeated his elation at having escaped. What in God's name was he doing? Fleeing the ship meant he was also leaving O. That thought brought despair and a surge of anguish. And what of Cristiana? Was he not abandoning her as well? But the truth was his loyalty to Cristiana was undercut entirely by his passion for and obsession with O.

He surfaced well away from the ship, gulping air before diving again, swimming in what he hoped was the direction of land. Either those on board the ship could not see him for the chop, or they elected to let him go, for no one pursued. What felt like hours passed, and Casanova's waterlogged clothing began weighing him down. Despite the warmth of the water, he was growing chilled, his strokes weaker and slower. When a wave momentarily buoyed him up, he tried to see how close he had swum to land. To his dismay, there was nothing on the horizon but a pale blue line. How could this be? Had he, in his confusion, swum away from the shore rather than toward it?

A roaring sound in the distance caught his attention. Zooming toward him was a small inflatable craft of the type he'd heard called a

Zodiac while on board the ship. A burly man wearing shorts and a pink shirt was at the controls, while a woman wearing a broad-brimmed hat and sunglasses occupied the seat in the bow. They pulled up a few feet from where Casanova was treading water, so exhausted now that he could barely keep his head up.

He dog-paddled to the Zodiac, where the muscular fellow at the tiller hoisted him over the side.

"You trying to swim to Cuba or what?" asked the boatman.

"I thought I was headed to Florida."

"Only place you were headed was into a shark's belly by nightfall," guffawed the other.

As his strength started to return, Casanova took in the woman. Although the towel covered her lower body, on top she wore the tiniest of black mesh bikinis, nipples jutting out against the nearly translucent fabric. He wished he could see her eyes and hair, but they were hidden behind the dark sunglasses and hat.

The boatman turned the Zodiac hard to starboard, and they roared off in the opposite direction from the one in which Casanova had been swimming. Trying to get his bearings, he hazarded to stand up and gaze toward the horizon. There was the unmistakable outline of land, and they were racing away from it.

"Wait, where are we going?" But he already knew. The boatman gave a harsh laugh and shrugged his wide shoulders.

"We're going back to the ship to see what the master has in store for you. And you'd better fucking behave or—" He reached down and flung the towel away from the woman's legs, revealing her tightly bound ankles "—she goes into the drink."

All thoughts of resistance fled Casanova's mind, for the woman now removed her hat and glasses, shaking out long black tresses and staring up at him with dark slanted eyes that beseeched him silently

73

not to further endanger her. Casanova recognized D, the Asian girl who had served him during his recovery on board the ship.

Despite her obvious terror, D, whose back was turned to the boatman, caught Casanova's eye. Her gaze slid to a pair of oars designed to be used in case of engine failure. Before he could even reflect upon the merit of what she proposed to do, D threw herself sideways, lifted one of the oars, and swung it in an arc that connected with a meaty thunk to the boatman's forehead.

He reeled backward, the Zodiac lurching off course as his hand left the tiller. A wave rammed the boat broadside. The Zodiac rocked wildly. Caught off balance, D tumbled over the side. The boatman, though dazed, kept his feet. Casanova grabbed the dropped oar and rammed the thin end into the fleshy mound of the man's solar plexus. He gave a high-pitched, wheezing sound and plopped backward into the water.

Casanova waited, but saw no sign of the boatman resurfacing. He turned in a circle, trying to spot D, whom he knew would drown in seconds with her legs bound. He glimpsed the gossamer ends of her jet hair slowly sinking below a wave crest, and for the second time that day, he threw himself into the sea.

D was limp and unresponsive when he hoisted her out of the water, shoved her over the side of the Zodiac, and climbed in himself. Her bikini top had come off when she toppled into the sea. Sunlight made the beads of water trickling between her breasts sparkle like gems. He knew she might be dying, yet at the sight of her he was abashed to feel his cock stiffening inside his sodden trousers. Lifting her, he cupped her breasts as he draped her over the side of the Zodiac and put hard, repeated pressure between her shoulder blades. After a few moments, she sputtered weakly and coughed up a great outpouring of water.

Knowing she was going to live freed Casanova from any

compunctions he might have had about satisfying his lust. Swiftly he bent down and freed her ankles, then removed the tiny triangle of cloth that covered the delectable curve of her pubic mound. He popped two fingers into his mouth, then slid them inside her while strumming and caressing her clitoris with his thumb. Her head tossed from side to side, and she gave a moan far different from the noise she had produced while regurgitating seawater.

Removing his fingers from inside her, Casanova freed his cock and penetrated her, not gently but in one long stroke that took in his entire length until he could feel the soft flesh of her rounded buttocks against his balls.

D's eyes opened sluggishly.

"We're alive?" she said. It was a question more than an observation.

"Yes, but five minutes ago I did not expect to be," said Casanova.

"Nor I. When I went over the side, I thought I was dead." She arched her back to meet his second, more energetic thrust. "You saved me. It's right that you should take me."

"Is it not your wish?"

She was silent a moment, regarding him with hungry eyes. Then he felt her inner muscles contract around him, squeezing and pulling, urging him into her ever more deeply. "No aphrodisiac is more powerful than a taste of death," she said.

It was as though the same feeling of relief and joy coursed through them both and translated into a fierce desire to celebrate the fact that they still breathed. Casanova found himself mentally paraphrasing the teaching of Descartes: *I fuck, therefore I am.* A certain truth to that, he thought. They made love as though it were the last time, because now each truly understood that it well might be. With every stroke inside D's supple body, Casanova felt like he was pushing away his own mortality.

Turning her over, he mounted her in the manner of dogs, cupping her breasts, sinking his teeth into the tender flesh at the back of her hair. He was alive and nothing else mattered.

When they finally lay exhausted in the bottom of the Zodiac, D with her head between Casanova's thighs, he felt physically sated but mentally more agitated than before. He craved more—and now—where only moments before had he craved nothing more than just to breathe air and pump his seed into the woman whose cheek now nuzzled his cock—his mind turned again to O. Surely she, of all women, could satisfy the desire that seemed only to increase each time he tried to satisfy it.

And if he never saw her again? The thought seared his soul. His only recourse was to direct his thoughts toward the land they were now heading for, hoping it would offer pleasures and diversions sufficient to distract him from his longing.

"Key West," he said, "is it as wanton a place as Venice?"

D's tongue reached out and languidly caressed his cock. "Much more so."

If Casanova had been shocked by the sights of modern-day Venice, he was even more dumbfounded by the relentless dedication to pleasure evidenced on Key West, where every inhabitant seemed bent on being happily inebriated and unabashedly aroused every possible second and where sunshine was soaked up like sweet wine.

Casanova and D strolled along Duval Street, past bars where throngs of skimpily clad young people raucously cavorted. At one such enterprise, Casanova beheld an ample-breasted young woman wearing nothing more than three tiny triangles of a see-through substance D said was called Saran Wrap covering her nether regions and nipples. A sign above the outdoor stage where she pranced and strutted read "Homemade Bikini Contest." At another bar, a pirate complete with eye patch and bottle of rum presided as judge of a dance contest in which young women attempted to shinny up a pole wearing nothing but the flimsiest of bathing suits and high heels.

Casanova was astonished and delighted at this unabashed display of lewdness. In his own time and place, not even whores comported themselves in such a way.

He was also keenly aware of the pairs of men who strolled unselfconsciously about the town, some gazing adoringly into each other's eyes, others meandering along the vibrant thoroughfares arm in arm, one partner sometimes reaching down to pinch or stroke the other's rear. There were pairs of women also, but these were more difficult for Casanova to discern, as here, as in his own time, it seemed that women of either sexual persuasion were permitted more freedom to show physical affection.

"This open displaying of lust between men," he said to D, "is that true throughout the Americas? I've witnessed it before, of course, but seldom in so public a fashion."

"People come here from all over the world," she replied, pausing to point out to him the crowd of tourists gathering to watch the sunset at Mallory Square. "I think when one is far from home, one's inhibitions lessen."

"I see," said Casanova, well aware that he of all people was far from home in every possible sense and considering the ramifications of her statement. "And is there entertainment geared to appeal to this 'less inhibited' audience?"

D slid her arm through his. "There's entertainment for every taste and predilection you can imagine. Did you have anything specific in mind?"

When Casanova told her what he wanted, they consulted a cheap-looking tabloid newspaper being given away free on the streets. Perusing the ads, D found a small, discreet one for a club called Domination.

"Even in Venice I've heard of this," she said. "It's part of the underground network of places where those so inclined can enjoy a multitude of debaucheries."

"You mean like the Power Company."

She smiled slyly. "The Power Company is in a class by itself."

Domination was located in the basement of an import/export warehouse north of Vermeer Street. After paying a fee to the doorman, they entered a dimly lit bar that reeked of tequila, cigarettes, and the hormonal stew of hot, rutting males. Pornographic images played on huge screens located around the room, and heavy metal music blared from speakers. Some of the men twisted around on their bar stools to openly appraise Casanova, who felt a surge of adrenaline-fueled anticipation. A few men glanced curiously at D, but no one seemed to consider her out of place. In fact, as she had earlier explained to Casanova, in this century it was not uncommon for people to elect to change genders—she might be any of an assortment of things, a boy in drag, a transsexual, or a hermaphrodite gifted with that rarest of treasures, an anatomy at once both male and female.

A second set of stairs led to a sub-basement level. Here a second doorman, this one immense and seemingly hairless, clad only in a leather loincloth, allowed admittance to this inner sanctuary. Casanova tipped the man a healthy sum, then doubled it when his inability to produce the required identification for either himself or D threatened to prevent their entering. Grunting, the man pocketed the money and indicated with a jerk of his bald pate that the two should proceed.

As his eyes adjusted to the lighting, Casanova beheld a stirring sight: a young man—hardly more than a boy, really—was affixed to a leather contraption that in most respects resembled a swing, except that in this case its occupant's wrists and ankles were bound with leather straps to the ropes that held the swing suspended from the ceiling. Several muscular men, all nude, surrounded the boy, who leaned back in the swing with his eyes shut as though close to a swoon. One by one the men stepped forward and pumped forth a stream of urine onto the boy's face, which he lapped up eagerly, opening his mouth wide to better receive their ablution.

As much as Casanova was repulsed by such unabashed perversion, he was transfixed by the look on the boy's face, an expression of rapturous bliss and ardent surrender. *What must it be like,* thought Casanova, *to thrill to such an extreme of submission? What must it feel like to be the one submitting and the one submitted to?*

"You're a new face," said an older man who had sidled up to Casanova and now regarded him with sharp, inquisitive eyes. He was lean, sinewy, every inch of his athletic body sun-baked to a deep and lustrous bronze. His eyes were a shocking shade of blue, the rich color of the finest Delft china, and his golden hair bore not a hint of graying or thinning. This, too, D had explained to Casanova—in this age many miracles were available to prolong the youthful vigor and appearance of those who were loathe to shrivel and crease unappealingly in the way Casanova recalled all too well from his own old age.

"The boy belongs to me," said the man, who introduced himself as Ronnie, "but I might be talked into lending him out for a few minutes, should that be your inclination." He eyed D with bemused curiosity. "Or hers."

D declined, and Casanova decided to postpone the decision. He saw the boy suddenly writhe and cry out as one of the men brutally penetrated him with a huge, lifelike black dildo. "A submissive's life must be painful," he commented. "Does the boy do this of his own free will?"

"What pleasure would I take from it if he did not?" said Ronnie.

"The amount of pain and humiliation he willingly elects to suffer is the measure of his adoration for me."

The skepticism must have shown in Casanova's face, because Ronnie went on. "I speak from my own experience that whatever discomfort he suffers is nothing compared to the pleasure of submitting to me or to those I give him to. As a young man, I was the most devoted of submissives. At that time I associated submission more with the feminine. I would dress in women's clothes—the frillier and more feminine, the better—and waylay sailors who frequented the downtown bars. I'd offer to suck their cocks for a ridiculously low wage. I would have paid for the privilege, of course, but I didn't dare reveal to them that I was, in truth, a man.

"Even now, as much as I enjoy dominating another sexually, I remember the exquisite thrill of submitting myself to another's will. There's such a freedom in it."

"Freedom?" said Casanova, who envisioned nothing of the kind.

"Of course. A submissive doesn't have to bother with all the messy choices and decisions that life offers. He or she only has to make one decision one time—to serve another's will entirely."

Casanova found himself at once repelled and fascinated. Everything in Ronnie's manner and appearance suggested a dominant, someone infinitely at ease when ordering another human being to submit to the most painful act or to perform the most degrading one. Yet here he was confessing, even boasting, that not so many years ago, he had played not only the role of a woman but an utterly submissive one as well. It was an avenue of pleasure Casanova had not entirely explored, which, like a woman whom he had not yet possessed, made it all the more alluring.

"Do you fancy the boy? I'm sure he would love any attentions you might wish to give him. In fact, I can guarantee it."

"May I whip him?"

"If I give him to you and instruct him to obey you, then I'm sure it would be his fondest wish. I know that in my own youth nothing would have pleased me more. I can only lend him to you for a short time, though. The slave auction is about to start, and I plan to get a princely sum for him."

Casanova was at once intrigued. "This slave auction, where is it held?"

As though he had expected the question, Ronnie beckoned him and D to follow.

Outside they came within sight of the ocean before descending a stone stairway and entering a long, low-ceilinged bar. In one corner a rock band produced a deafening cacophony, the sound reverberating through the small area like a series of explosions. So bludgeoningly loud was the music that Casanova wanted to press his hands to his ears, but didn't wish to appear rude or offend the musicians, who seemed as hirsute and savage as barbarians. The one who appeared to be the leader wielded an electric guitar as though it were an extension of his penis and thrust his hips in lewd, writhing gestures. His hair was a tumbled, black bird's nest framing a hooked nose and theatrically painted lips under incongruously small and elfin hazel eyes. Casanova found the performance compelling but distasteful, but he reminded himself that he was still a stranger here—both in Key West and in this century—and clearly he had much to learn.

He leaned toward Ronnie, whispering, "In here?" but Ronnie either didn't hear him or ignored him and continued to elbow his way through the crowd, men and women who ground their bodies together with lewd, copulating motions, some even going so far as to openly fornicate in the little grottoes that seemed to have been scooped out of the room's rock walls.

They moved quickly to a doorway on the far side of the room and pushed through it, entering what seemed to Casanova to be another world, a lush garden surrounded by high pink walls and decorated with an astonishing assortment of galvanizingly erotic statuary. Small lanterns lit the cobblestoned paths wending their way amid the profusion of greenery and titillating statues.

As Casanova was admiring a statue of a muscular youth with tight, well-rounded buttocks and a thick penis, pleasingly uncircumcised, he sensed that the man's dark eyes were following him. So taken aback was Casanova that he almost flinched, but he controlled his reaction for D's benefit, not wishing to seem jittery or easily surprised. In truth, however, he was quite flabbergasted to realize that what had appeared in the twilight to be stone sculpted to a lifelike form was actually real human flesh that subtly breathed and bent and cast furtive glances in his direction.

"Those on display here in the garden are the slaves waiting to be auctioned," Ronnie said, caressing the sleek flank of a languid-looking brunette, whose abundant curves reminded Casanova more of the body type in vogue during his own day. She shuddered visibly under his touch, but whether the reaction was from fear or from arousal was impossible to tell.

He felt D's hand on his back as she indicated a short, well-muscled blonde girl clad only in the flimsiest snippets of see-through gauze. Her body was a tapestry of color and design, with tattoos covering her breasts, arms, and shoulders. It occurred to Casanova that one could make love to her and at the same time read her like an illuminated manuscript.

There were several handsome men and boys as well, being scrutinized by potential buyers. Like docile horses, on command they turned this way and that, bent forward to display their muscular backsides, and allowed their penises to be caressed and commented on as to size and thickness. Then, once examined, they froze once again to became facsimiles of stone.

Casanova and D watched as several of the "statues" came to life and were led up onto a platform at the rear of the garden. Each slave had a different auctioneer, each inspired a plethora of lewd comments and gestures from the crowd. The excitement seemed to peak when a tall, muscular woman wearing thigh-high leather boots with three-inch heels, black gloves that extended up past her elbows, a leather mask, and nothing else came onto the platform. Her hair was a wild cascade of platinum flowing halfway down her back. Her scarlet mouth was painted the same vibrant shade as her nipples and her inch-long fingernails. In her hand she held a leather riding crop. Looking around the room, she sized up several likely candidates for her severe attentions before her eyes came to rest on a formidable man, a hirsute oaf who, in Casanova's estimations, with his swollen biceps and brutal, asymmetrical face that looked like it had been beaten with a board, resembled a gladiator out of ancient Rome.

Approaching the man, she said in a commanding voice, "Do you obey me?"

When he hesitated a fraction of a second, she cracked the whip across his meaty pectorals, leaving a thin pink line.

"Yes, Mistress, I obey you."

"Only me?"

"Only you."

The whip smacked resoundingly across his shoulders. "Say it respectfully."

His thick mouth twisted into a cruel smirk, but he managed to get out the words, "Yes, Mistress, only you."

"Anything I tell you, it is your privilege and pleasure to do?

"Anything."

She spun around on her towering heels, giving Casanova the impression she was forfeiting her command of the stage, but instead she used the whip to point out a second man, nude and almost as large and muscular as the first but stunningly blond, quite beautiful if Casanova could have applied such a description to a man.

"Him!" she said and whirled back on the dark-haired man she had beaten. As she did so, Casanova caught his breath and reached out a hand to D's arm to steady himself. On the dominatrix's nude flank was the unmistakable brand, the "S H" he had seen on the woman he adored back on the ship.

"O." The single syllable emerged from his throat like both an invocation and a prayer.

But this O was nothing like the submissive creature he had observed before. This version of his beloved strode in front of the gladiator, yanked his head back by a handful of hair, and indicating the blond man, said, "Suck his cock and make him come. Then let it run down your face so I can taste it in your hair when you fuck me."

"Yes, Mistress."

The gladiator's craggy, off-center features betrayed no emotion. He knelt before the other man, running his tongue over the thick, smooth head of his penis, then taking the length of it into his mouth until the entire shaft disappeared. The blond behemoth gripped the man's head, guiding it roughly back and forth until he baptized the other's face and hair with a silky jet of come.

While this was going on, O had relinquished her whip to an attendant, who helped her remove her boots and gloves. She stood completely nude now, the leather mask across her eyes all that remained of her dominatrix attire.

The spurt of come across his face seemed to revive the dark-haired man from a sort of trance. He straightened up and spun around, eyes falling immediately upon O. A look of such intense and cruel appetite transformed the man's already twisted features that Casanova found himself afraid for her.

The barbarian put his hand between O's shoulder blades and pushed her to her hands and knees. He spread her wide so her puckered asshole was on display for all to see, then penetrated her with no hesitation or preliminaries. Casanova could not see her face, but she made no sound of either passion or distress. For the next few minutes the dark-haired brute repaid her for the humiliations she had inflicted on him, taking her in every possible manner and position, inflicting on her a myriad of cruelties and indignations.

When he was done, an auburn-haired wench with a shaved pubic mound and painted nipples helped O to her feet. She snapped a pair of cufflinks attached to a chain around O's wrists and fastened her to a crossbeam at the front of the platform. She then retreated, head bent down submissively, to make way for the next auctioneer.

Transfixed and stupefied by the display, Casanova maneuvered his way through the crowd until he stood at the edge of the platform, gazing up at the woman who reigned over his thoughts and fantasies.

"I want her," Casanova said, surprised that he actually spoke the words out loud.

Ronnie was beside him. "Choose another one. She's not for you."

Casanova reacted predictably with outrage and hurt pride. What did this old queen, who had doubtlessly sucked more cocks than most whores, know of such things? Of who he was and of the fortune in gold at his command?

"You're wrong," he said coldly. "She's meant for me."

And indeed as soon as the words were said, he knew he meant them more literally than he had believed. In his own mind O had already attained an almost mythic status of perfection and sexual prowess, similar to the esteem in which he held his own endowments and abilities. Surely he would not have been brought to this time and place were it not to encounter and possess a woman whose erotic attributes matched his own.

A man wearing black jeans and a skimpy T-shirt with rips strategically placed to reveal a nipple and one side of his slablike abdomen came onto the platform. Casanova recognized him as the lout from the Zodiac, the one he had bashed in the head and whom he'd thought undoubtedly had drowned. Now he put his hands on O's hips and turned her so that the audience might have a different view. He then put a palm on the small of her back and bent her forward, so those in attendance had a view of her splendid flanks and buttocks.

Addressing the crowd, he said, "What will you give to possess this slave?"

Hands shot up and bids were shouted out, Casanova's voice among them.

The auctioneer took notice of him only long enough to sneer his contempt and then ignored him while nodding to someone in the back of the room. Casanova twisted around, but could see nothing of his rival. Several other hands went up. O's price increased to more than three times what had been paid for any other slave so far, but her expression never changed. She remained impassive, aloof, and unattainable. Casanova found himself both hating and admiring the man who could command this sort of absolute abandonment of her will for his. He tried to raise the bid again. This time the auctioneer's eye swept over him again. Casanova cursed and was about to leap upon the stage, having lost all rationality and intending to go for the man's throat, when D grabbed his arm and hissed into his ear. "Don't do it. You'll be making a mistake. Let her go for now. There'll be another chance."

The gavel banged down. O was wrapped in a black cloak and whisked outside.

Casanova elbowed his way through the crowd and out onto the street, but saw nothing other than a row of three flamboyantly painted trailers, each one more outlandish than the next. The guitarist whom he had seen before, all matted black hair and savage smile coupled with those incongruously innocent pale eyes, was guiding O into one of the trailers. Forgetting that there might be repercussions from such a rash act, Casanova screamed her name. O didn't turn around, but she froze for the briefest of instants, and in Casanova's fevered imagination it seemed a shudder traveled up her spine beneath the cloak, and her head tilted at the shouting of her name.

D was at his side. "Stop it," she said. "Do you know who that is that bought her? Do you want to die?"

But at that moment, so stricken with desire and longing was Casanova that he sincerely didn't care. All that held him back from flinging himself at the departing bus was D's promise that there would be another chance.

One by one, the garishly painted tour buses started up with a roar and an arrogant honking of horns. The convoy swept like an invading army out onto Duval Street, taking with it the woman of Casanova's dreams.

Chapter Six

With one shove to her back, O was propelled through the door of the trailer into its interior, where the air conditioning was turned up so high that her nipples, already hard, grew even harder. Despite the freezing temperature, the place stunk of sweat, sex, and dope. The guitarist followed her and slammed the door behind him. Inside it was dark and gloomy, the lights attached to the walls covered with filmy scarves, and it took a moment for O's eyes to become accustomed after the brightness of the Florida sunshine. But become accustomed they did, and she looked around her temporary prison.

The trailer was roughly forty feet long by twelve wide, and the ceiling was about eight feet above her. At the back end, beneath a picture window covered by a closed Venetian blind, was a double bed, unmade, the sheets a tangle. On it sat a young woman no more than seventeen it seemed, wearing just a pale blue chiffon blouse through which her tiny breasts tipped with pink nipples could be plainly seen. She was naked from the waist down, with her pubis waxed so smooth it seemed to shine even in the dim light. The girl looked up, grimaced, then returned to her task of rolling a joint on the cover of a vinyl copy of the Beatles' *Revolver* album. Next to the bed on a leather-upholstered captain's chair sat the biggest black man O had ever seen. His massive body was squeezed between the arms of the chair, and he sat impassively behind dark glasses, wearing a black suit, white dress shirt, and black tie. His massive feet, shod in dark brown leather boots, were flat on the floor, and he seemed to ignore both O and the guitarist as they entered, but she imagined his eyes moved behind the glasses. She also noticed a substantial bulge beneath his left shoulder, which showed he was armed and probably extremely dangerous.

The floor itself was ankle deep in the detritus of a rock band on tour. There was underwear and outerwear both male and female, socks, stockings, biker boots, and spike-heeled sling-back shoes. CD and DVD cases, loose CDs and DVDs, vinyl singles and albums in and out of their sleeves, pizza boxes, grease-stained hamburger and sandwich wrappings, beer and soda cans, liquor bottles, glasses, magazines, comic books, paperback novels, and the occasional tabloid newspaper. *The very stuff of life,* thought O as she turned her head and saw a pull-out bed, open in front of a giant TV with video, DVD, and satellite hook-up, a massive speaker system, and a CD player with a turntable skewed on top. Between the bed and the entertainment center was a coffee table with a mirrored surface upon which sat cigarettes, lighters, a pile of white powder, razor blades, credit cards, a crack pipe made from a Coke can and the barrel of a Bic pen, a pile of what had to be marijuana, cigarette papers, an automatic pistol, which she recognized as a Glock 9-millimeter, a huge Colt revolver probably chambered for .44 Magnum bullets, which looked capable of shooting through a bag of cement and still able to kill anything standing behind it, and a .38 Cooper Arms two-shot derringer, nickel plated with pearl handles. O's father, back in France, had been a gun freak, and he had taught her well. She could recognize most makes of guns and was herself a crack shot with small arms and long guns both. Many times he had taken her, while still in her teens, to practice in the nearby forest or at the semi-abandoned Foreign Legion training range that he had access to through his old military connections. It felt like a world away before her fall into submission.

The mirror itself was smeared and dirty, and O wrinkled her nose in disgust.

In the middle of the trailer was a small kitchen with stove, microwave, and a sink piled with dirty dishes. Beyond that was a door that appeared to hide a toilet and probably a shower, and beyond that again, a bedroom, and presumably up front the driver's cab.

All very comfy, thought O as she turned to see her new master and hoped that somehow Casanova, for it was his voice she had recognized calling to her back in the town, would have the balls and common sense to come to her rescue.

But how the hell had he got there?

As the trailer's engine sprang into life and the huge truck moved off, O's purchaser pushed her toward the bed where the young woman sat. "Welcome to my world," he said. "Meet Velma and Maurice," he said. His accent was a strange mix of London cockney and LA surfer. "And my name's Toby Faith, what's yours?"

"People call me O," replied O.

"That'll do, love," said Faith. "I kind of like it. Unusual, though. What do you reckon, Velma?"

The girl just shrugged and finished rolling the massive joint before searching for a book of matches and firing it up. Through a thick cloud of smoke she said, "What the fuck do you need her for? How much was she? I just knew going to a clandestine slave auction would see you getting up to no good—"

"Mind your own business, love," said Faith.

"You're crazy," she went on. "Why pay when you can get cunt for free any night of the week?"

"Not like this one," said Faith and tugged off O's cloak to display her lithe, undeniable assets. "This one will do absolutely anything. I own her now."

"Just another bitch in heat," said the girl, taking in the alabaster pallor of O's displayed body.

"You jealous?" asked Faith with a laugh. "Because she's got bigger tits than you?"

"Size isn't everything," replied the girl.

"That's not what you say when you've got my dick inside you, girl," said Faith.

"What do you reckon, Maurice?"

The black man had sat quietly throughout and just shrugged, picked up a Fantastic Five comic book from the stuff strewed around him, opened it, and began reading, deliberately ignoring the argument between his boss and the young girl.

"Maurice don't say much," said Faith to O. "But he thinks a lot. And he's my man. He looks after me. Ain't that right, Maurice?"

Maurice just shrugged again, but O got the feeling he didn't miss much. If she was going to get out of this, Maurice was the one to watch. *How could all this have come about?* she wondered. The Power Company authorities had surely not meant for her to be sold to this uncouth, malevolent musician.

But she also knew it was not her place to question her fate. Obedience was a must.

As the trailer picked up speed, O heard the sound of a police siren and looked at Faith. Was this her way out?

"Don't panic, darlin'," he said. "They ain't out to get us. People like me don't get nicked. That's our escort out of town, courtesy of the Key West police department."

Shit, thought O.

"Listen," said Faith after a moment to no one in particular. "Me and O got some things to talk about. What say we go down front and watch the world go by, darlin'?"

He grabbed O by her arm and hustled her past the kitchen and bathroom and through the door to the bedroom, slamming it behind them.

"Don't mind Velma," he said. "She's the jealous type. Gets the hump if I so much as look at another woman. Which is kind of tough on her, as I'm always looking. But she'll get over it. You two girls could get to become friends. Swap knitting patterns and recipes. That kind of thing."

From the look O had seen in Velma's eyes, she doubted that very much, but said nothing, and instead looked around the small bedroom.

Inside was a double bed that almost filled the room, sheets once again a mess. There was another covered window, and as the trailer ground on, Faith peered through the corner of the blind. "New Orleans," he said. "Ever been?"

O shook her head.

"What a fucking town. The Big Easy is right. Anything you want you get. Me and the boys anyway. He looked up at O standing by the door. "Got a big gig tomorrow night. Football stadium or some such. Big payday." Seeing the expression on her face, he said with a grin "Cheer up, darlin', you're along for the ride whether you like it or not. You cost me big-time; just couldn't resist that proud, ice-princess face of yours, and I know all too well how you'll melt once I've taken possession of your holes, and I expect to get a lot for my dough. Want a line?"

He rummaged around in the drawer of a minuscule bedside cabinet and came up with a clear plastic bag full of white powder. "The devil's dandruff," he said. "That's what me and the boys call it." He emptied a pile of the powder onto the shiny top of the cabinet and, pulling out his wallet, extracted a black American Express card and started cutting lines. Then he found a hundred-dollar bill, rolled it neatly, and snorted first one, then two, then three of the lines. "Fuckin' hell," he said, his eyes widening. "That's hit the spot. Now you."

O squeezed past the bed, knelt, accepted the note, and took one hit. The coke was as pure as she had ever known, and she felt the rush immediately. She swallowed the metallic taste and checked out Toby Faith sitting cross-legged on the bed and grinning fit to bust.

"It's good," she said.

"So it fucking well should be, the price of it these days."

"I thought you didn't care about cost," said O.

"At least I know you can speak. Well, that's a start. No, money don't matter. Not really. But where I came from money was tight. And you never forget."

"And where's that? Where you come from? Not from around here."

"No, not from around here. That's for sure. Canning Town, love. Good old lil' London."

"You're a long way from home."

"And so are you, darlin', ain't ya? Don't think I can't recognize that little Frenchie accent."

O nodded.

"But don't worry. You're with me now. I own you. Where I go, you go."

"And then?"

He smiled mischievously.

"Until I get tired of you, then I pass you on to the boys. Then when they're fed up, to the roadies. They're a rough bunch, so you'd better be good to me, and I may keep you around forever."

But somehow O doubted that. So if she was going to get away, it had better be soon.

"So, darlin'," said Faith. "I reckon it's about time I found if you're worth what I paid for you."

O looked at him properly for the first time then. Of course she had seen his face before on record sleeves, posters, and TV. But this close she could feel the charisma he exuded like musk. Thick black curls framed his half angel, half devil of a face. Green eyes that twinkled not just from the huge amount of cocaine he had ingested. Thick lips, brilliant white teeth, and a strong chin covered in a day or two's growth of beard. His body was thin and muscular, the skin pale white apart from reddening from the sun on his shoulders, which had been exposed by the black T-shirt he wore over tight, black leather trousers.

Faith saw her looking at him. "Like what you see?" he asked.

O said nothing, but thought, *Not bad. If I'm going to be used, at least its by someone with a decent body.*

"No answer, came the reply," said Faith. "Now what about this?"

He bounded from the bed and unzipped his trousers and pulled them off. He was wearing no underwear, and the cock he exposed was huge, half erect, the purple knob gorged with blood. Faith stroked himself and his penis grew longer. "Get on the bed," he said. "Face down."

O did as she was bidden, unquestioning, total obedience drummed into her by years of rigourous training. Toby Faith searched in the dresser drawer once again and came out with a tube of K-Y Jelly. "I bet you know what this is," he said.

She looked over her shoulder and nodded as he smeared the clear lubricant on his hands and cock, which seemed to be getting bigger by the second. Next, he forced her legs apart and gazed at her gorgeous ass. "Fantastic," he whispered as he pulled the twin globes apart to expose her anus. He said nothing about the initials branded into her skin. "I hope you like it up your jacksie," he said. "It's the English way. The third way, as our prime minister might say."

O had absolutely no idea what he was talking about.

First he inserted his little finger, smeared with K-Y, into her back passage. He was gentler than she had imagined he would be, and the experience was as pleasant as it always was. Then he pulled it out, sniffed it, and pushed in his middle finger, which made her wriggle with the start of the pain she knew she would feel before the sex was over.

Then, abruptly, he removed his digit, mounted her, and put his cock against the opening of the orifice. Suddenly savage, he shoved it into her hard, the lubricant allowing some ease of passage, but not enough to keep pain from running up her spine to her brain as his massive member invaded the tender opening.

"Jeeeez," she cried.

"No point in calling on Jesus," said Faith through gritted teeth. "It's his opposite number rules here," and he began to relentlessly pound his groin into her ass until she felt drops of sweat falling from his body onto the skin of her back.

"You fucking bitch," yelled Faith into her ear as he grabbed her hair and yanked her head back so hard she cried out again.

But suddenly, as she knew it would, the pain subsided and was replaced by the most exquisite pleasure as he fucked her even harder, and she spread her legs as wide as she could to allow his prick to fully enter her and his hairy balls to bang against her ass cheeks.

"You love it, you cunt," hissed Faith. "I knew it," and with an even louder shout he climaxed inside her, the hot spunk spurting up to complete the act for both of them as O came herself and bit hard down on the pillow beneath her face.

"So who are those people?" asked Casanova watching the departing convoy raise dust from the main street as they headed inland before a lone Key West police car took the lead, lights flashing and siren wailing.

"Don't you know anything?" said D. "That's Orange Sky. The biggest, baddest rock group in the world. English, of course. The bad boys always are. That guy was Toby Faith, the lead singer. Though what the hell they were doing playing in a dump like that, I don't know. Maybe he does."

She nodded over to the door of the club, where a young guy dressed in a checked shirt with pearl snap buttons, Levis, high-heeled boots, and a straw cowboy hat emerged blinking in the sun. He was handsome in a raffish way and grinned when he spotted D.

"Hey, Cowboy," she said. "What goes on?"

"That was awesome," he replied, pulling a pack of Marlboro Lights from the pocket of his shirt, fishing one out, and lighting it with a Zippo lighter. "Awesome. Orange Sky doing a gig down here." He laughed in delight. "Their road crew threw the house band off stage and they ripped. Orange Sky. Crazy motherfuckers. Make Guns and Roses look like school kids. Worse than The Who. Worse than Zeppelin. Worse than the fuckin' Stones. That Toby Faith. I heard he killed a guy. Shot him stone-cold dead and pissed on the body. Folks say he is the living reincarnation of Lucifer himself. They came for the auction, he picked up the best-looking woman there, and now they're off to the Big Easy for a concert tomorrow. Jesus, it would cost a couple of hundred bucks to see them there, and I saw them for free. Close enough to catch their spit. Awesome."

Casanova decided that the young man was rather wanting in the vocabulary department and wondered who or what were The Who and Zeppelin? And what did stones have to do with anything? But he made no comment.

"New Orleans, huh?" said D. Then to Casanova, "Fancy a road trip?"

He nodded. Anything to be close to O.

"You got wheels, Cowboy?" said D to the young man.

He pointed proudly to an open-top Jeep parked by the curb. It was pale blue with the decal of a shark in black across the hood. It stood high on chrome reverse wheels and giant all-terrain balloon tires. "That's my ride," he said. "Got a big-block Chevy under the hood. It'll do one-fifty no trouble."

D smiled at him seductively. "You busy today?"

He returned the smile, eyeing D's scantily clad body up and down, the bulge in the crotch of his faded jeans getting larger. "Not so's you'd notice."

"Fancy a trip to New Orleans?"

He thought about it, but only for a second. "Why the hell not? There's just one thing. You got gas money, baby? I'm kind of strapped right now."

D thought for a second, then tugged off the ring she wore on her pinky and tossed it to the boy. "Diamond," she said. "And platinum. Worth a thousand dollars. It's all yours."

The young man peered at the stone and rubbed it on his shirt. Then grinned. "You got yourself a deal. Let's go," he said, and headed for the Jeep.

"I may not know much," said Casanova to D. "But wasn't that rather over-generous?"

She grinned back at him. "Diamonique. Twenty-eight bucks from the Shopping Channel."

Casanova had no idea what either Diamonique or the Shopping Channel were, so he just shrugged and followed her to the vehicle, where he made himself comfortable on the narrow backseat as D climbed in next to the cowboy and patted him on the thigh.

Just as long as he could catch up with O.

"Hey, baby," said the cowboy to D. "I guess a blow job is out of the question once we hit New Orleans? I got friends there where we can crash."

D shrugged, and Casanova felt rather slighted that the cowboy had made so bold with his female companion. But after what he had seen of the morals in this strange new world, maybe that was the way people acted. Besides, D wasn't his concern. It was always O, always would be.

The Jeep started with a low rumble from its big V-8 engine, and the cowboy turned it in the direction that Orange Sky's convoy had headed, out of town toward the interstate, New Orleans, and whatever the future held.

"So what's the story?" he asked as they drove through the suburbs. "You two groupies?"

"He stole my woman," said Casanova, speaking to the cowboy for the first time.

"That fine-looking tall gal. She's yours?"

"That's correct," said Casanova. "And I intend to get her back."

"You're kidding," said the cowboy. "You got any idea how much Toby Faith paid for her?"

Casanova shrugged. "I don't care."

"So why the hell did you put her up for auction?" the young man asked Casanova.

"Gambling debt," D intervened, as Casanova searched for some explanation.

"Crazy," said the cowboy.

As they reached the outskirts of town, they passed the police car now parked at the side of the road, and the cowboy raised his hand in a salute to the cop. "Those guys in the band are armed to the teeth," said the cowboy. "You're looking at a world of pain."

"I'll do whatever it takes," said Casanova.

"Sounds fine to me," said the cowboy. "Just as well that I'm armed, too."

He pulled the Jeep off the road and out of sight of passing traffic and said to D, "Open up the glove compartment, little lady. Hey, what's your name, by the way?"

"They call me D."

"Fine." He turned in his seat. "And how about you, buddy?"

"Casanova."

"Casanova, huh. I'll just call you Cas if you don't mind."

Casanova shrugged again.

"My name's Brad," said the cowboy. "My mom was a big fan of the Magnificent Seven. She named me after Brad Dexter, the one no one ever remembers."

Meanwhile D had done as the young man had said and pulled out an old wooden case from its hiding place.

"Open her up," said the cowboy.

She unlocked the box and opened it. Inside was an ancient-looking long-barreled revolver, the bluing on the metal worn and faded.

"Army Colt," said Brad proudly. "Black powder. Makes enough noise to stampede a herd of buffalo. Belonged to my great-grandaddy. He was in the Seventh Cavalry. Fought with honor in the Civil War. And won. Cas, do me a favor and lift up that seat you're sitting on."

Awkwardly, Casanova maneuvered the seat from its fitting to discover a rifle and a shotgun neatly placed underneath it, complete with boxes of bullets and shells.

Casanova sighed. What was happening to him? He was pursuing the devil's spawn on an American road, which could likely lead to violent death, with enough weaponry under his feet to settle a small war.

He glanced at the curve of D's neck as she sat ahead of him in the vehicle's front seat. There was an exquisite delicacy to its shape. In days of old he would have loaned part of his soul to enjoy weeks of bliss with a creature of such beauty, let alone with the shy but worldly Cristiana, whose presence on the boat still confounded him. But today, all he could think of was O and the inner conviction that she was to be his salvation in this cruel, often beautiful but puzzling new world. And that he was fated to follow this dangerous road that must inevitably lead to her.

Life sometimes offers you no choices.

Chapter Seven

The blue Jeep sped down the interstate in pursuit of the rock band's caravan. A weighty silence descended on the ill-assorted trio as the uncommon landscape whizzed by, tropical and varied, and at times wondrous and bizarre, Casanova thought, as he observed the blend of poverty and affluence that characterized the South Florida hinterlands.

"So, what brings you folks to the US of A?" Brad suddenly asked.

Before Casanova could even formulate the shadow of an answer, D replied: "Adventure."

Brad burst out in laughter.

"Cool," he said. "I like me some adventure. Guns, gals, and adventure is my perfect recipe for a good day out. Puts sex, drugs, and rock 'n' roll in the shade." He paused, then chuckled as he reflected on what he had just said. "Mind you, I suppose sex and gals go together, too, don't they?"

He leered at D, sitting by his side at the front of the racing Jeep.

She looked over at him. "But guns don't, Cowboy," she said. "I'd prefer if you kept them out of sight. We won't have any use of them on this journey. I hope," she added.

"Better safe than sorry, my mama always said," Brad continued.

"Whatever you say, Cowboy," D said. "But what about hitting the gas a little harder? Don't want to fall behind too much, you know."

Casanova nodded in approval in the backseat.

In response, Brad deliberately slowed the vehicle down until they were just about crawling down the blacktop at 50 miles per hour. He took his eyes off the road and turned to D. "Yeah? So what about that blow job I asked you for?" he asked the young woman.

"You said when we get to New Orleans, Brad," she replied.

"I know. Well, I changed my mind," he said, "why put things off and all that, eh?"

D sighed.

The cowboy took this as a sign of assent and smiled broadly.

"That's a girl."

He hit the gas pedal harder, and they traveled in further silence another few miles down the road until they reached a rickety wooden bridge built over a now dried-out stream. Here, he braked violently and steered his screeching wheels onto a grassless ridge.

"Cas," Brad asked. "You did say the other gal we're chasing after, the tall one, was yours? So our young missus here is free, right? It's just that I don't like to use other men's women, especially if they're present . . . I'm a gentleman, you see."

Casanova was about to object to the man's manners and presumption, but D butted in first.

"Let's get it over with, Cowboy. We're just wasting time here. Unless you're all words and no action."

Brad chortled and opened the driver's door.

"Out you go then, girl," he said to D, as his feet hit the rocky ground.

She exited the vehicle from her side, her slim body vaulting elegantly down over the Jeep's running board.

"What about Cas?" the cowboy pointed out. "D'ya want him to watch, or should he stay in the car?"

"I have no modesty," D said. "But he's seen me before, so I reckon he can remain behind."

"Let's go then," Brad said as he grabbed D's hand and pulled her toward the small slope that led down to the base of the bridge, a mischievous grin spreading across his face.

As they disappeared from view, Casanova wondered why D had suddenly agreed to the man's demands. Although Brad had left the keys in the car's ignition, Casanova hadn't yet mastered the art of driving. All he knew was that the vulgar cowboy was unnecessary baggage, and quite likely a menace with his ambulant arsenal. Maybe this was an opportunity to do something about it.

He opened the car door as quietly as he could and tiptoed toward the incline below which the couple had disappeared. There was no sound coming from their direction. He should have picked up one of the weapons, he realized, but reckoned it was now too late to walk back to the Jeep.

D and the cowboy were right under the bridge, where a thin stream of water must once have run, before the summer heat had dissipated it away. Weeds grew weakly through the riverbed strewn with rocks of all shapes and colors. Brad stood with his head held high, gazing in the distance of the sheer blue sky, oblivious to the surroundings. His jeans were crumpled around his ankles and boots, and his short but uncommonly thick cock was thrusting in and out D's mouth as she kneeled at his feet. He firmly held her hair in one hand, directing her whole head onto his member, impaling her as far as he could go. His other hand was far from inactive, having brutally torn her T-shirt away from her body, and he was pinching her dark nipples with sadistic glee while he enjoyed the ministrations of her hot mouth.

Casanova could not help finding the spectacle arousing.

Without interrupting the steady movements of her lips around the cowboy's engorged penis, D looked sideways and saw Casanova. She nodded ever so slightly in his direction, without being distracted her from her task, and Casanova understood what she wanted him to do.

Brad moaned as his breathing became shorter.

Casanova bent over and picked up the heaviest stone he could lift from the deserted riverbed. He stealthily moved close to the busy couple and took aim. The gray stone made perfect contact with the back of Brad's head, and without a sound, he slid like a a puppet to the ground, his still wet cock shriveling as he collapsed, the purple glans retreating like a snail into his loose, pink foreskin.

"What took you so long?" D asked Casanova, pulling the torn halves of her shirt together and rising to her feet. "A few more seconds and he would have come. And I just know he wouldn't have tasted nice at all."

Casanova apologized. "I wasn't quite sure what you were expecting me to do."

"I thought that was obvious, no?"

"How was I to know? Life in these parts is so full of surprises. Sexual favors as currency and all that."

"At any rate, your timely intervention was better late than never," D said. She leaned over the cowboy's prostrate body, checked his pockets, and retrieved her ring.

"Is he still alive?" Casanova inquired.

"Of course," D replied. "It will just be an unpleasant bump and a headache in the morning. His type always survive. Let's hit the road and see where those devils are taking O."

"Can you drive?" Casanova asked.

"Of course," D said. "Doesn't everyone?"

Casanova had always found traveling monotonous, and modern days were no exception as the landscape roared by in a daze of light and blurry movement. For the first time since his return to life, he felt tired. Mentally as well as physically. But he could not find the solace of sleep, too many questions and wonders jostling around frantically inside his brain, and not an answer in sight.

D's eyes were focused on the highway ahead.

"Who are you?" Casanova asked the young woman.

"D."

"What is your real name?"

"That's not important." She didn't look over at him as she answered his questions.

"I'd like to know," he insisted.

"It's Sarah," she said.

"So why not call yourself S?"

"Power Company whores are named by the letters of the alphabet. I had no choice in the matter."

"Is O a Power Company whore?"

"Yes and no, "she hesitated. "O is the prime letter. I am not the only D; there are others with whom I share the letter, the name. But there is only ever one O at a given time. She is the chosen one."

Casanova digested the bizarre morsel of information. It still made no sense.

"Why are you with me? Are you still in the employ of the Power Company?"

"Yes."

"Why?"

"I'm instructed to remain with you until further notice, help you where I can, and offer gratification of any kind."

"Why?" he asked again.

"Because those are my orders," she said.

"What about the young girl I came across in Venice, Cristiana? Is she also one of your group of holy whores?"

"No," D replied.

"So why was she on the boat?" he continued.

"One of the shareholders thought she had the potential to be useful to us."

"I see. So a whore in waiting, then?"

"That's one way of putting it."

"Would you accept any form of order from them?" Casanova asked her.

"Yes."

"Any?"

"Unconditionally," she confirmed. "I am owned."

"What about O? Does she also belong to them?"

"She is different. She transcends ownership."

"Can you be more explicit," he requested.

"I can't, Giacomo. I do not know the way they think." She sighed softly. "You wish to see O again, and I will do my utmost to get you to her. That is my role."

The torn front halves of her white shirt had flapped open, and Casanova could not help feasting his eyes on the dark, hard nipples of her compact breasts.

"And allowing that uncouth man to violate you in any way, had I not intervened, would have been part of your duties?"

"Yes," D said. "My body no longer belongs to me. I am holes, I am fuck meat."

Casanova frowned at her directness and repressed a terrible wave of sadness rising inside his heart. How could it be that a beautiful young woman could speak of herself in such crude and degrading terms?

He extended his hand toward her and gently caressed her right knee.

"Sarah?" he ventured.

"I am D," she answered.

"Sarah," Casanova insisted. "Tell me about yourself, your life before you were called D."

"Must I?" she queried, a look of profound despair sweeping across her pale features.

"Consider it part of your orders to keep me satisfied," he argued.

There was a moment of silence as the Jeep overtook a long trailer loaded high with heavy, wooden logs.

"Once I was Sarah," she finally said, her voice a full degree lower than previously. "My father was of Irish extraction and my mother was half Vietnamese. Something of a melting pot. I can't even pretend I had an unhappy childhood. A little boring maybe, traditional, but both my parents loved me and I wanted for nothing. I had a good education, friends, social graces, but . . . to cut a long story short, I ended up damaged."

Casanova parted his lips to say something, but D beat him to it.

"If you want to hear my story, just let me talk. No interruptions, Giacomo, please."

He nodded.

"There were boys, then there were men, of course. I could even take my pick. Some tweaked a chord in my heart and others in my loins only. But at the end of the day, the sex always felt hollow, invariably incomplete. And at the back of my mind, I always knew there must be something more, even if I couldn't seize its essence, analyze this sense of dread, of emptiness. Sure, I'd sometimes come, but even at that very moment when all inside me melted and I was supposed to experience joy unbound, there was always that specter that kept on questioning the whole experience somehow. I wanted more. But for quite some years I never knew what the 'more' could be. So I forged a career, worked in the advertising trade. I painlessly rose through the echelons to middle management. It was easy. It's not that I was particularly bright, more like the competition was dumber. Some might say I lacked self-belief, but it was all like a second-class life, going through the motions.

"One day I was introduced to a man. I'd vaguely heard of him before in the circles I was moving in. It was at a media party of some sort. He wasn't particularly good looking, but he had wit and a sense of danger. I went back to his place on the first night we met. I didn't feel it was worth wasting time and delaying the obvious with aimless small talk and puerile flirtation. We kissed from the moment the door to his apartment closed behind us. He tasted of strong alcohol. His hands slipped under my clothing as we embraced, assessing my skin and its pliancy, its softness, calmly fingering my parts like an explorer taking possession of new lands. So far, everything seemed normal. I liked the fact that he was taking command, not meekly asking for my approval, the way he assumed I was already his. He was a man of few words, I remember.

"We fucked. Later that evening, he ordered me on all fours and took me roughly from behind, ploughing repeatedly into me as he forced me to arch my back so that my rump was better offered, open to him. I felt his hands move across my shoulders to my neck and stretch across my skin as he took a grip of me, pressing against my throat until I gasped; then he took hold of my hair and pulled hard, using my head as leverage for his thrusting. It hurt; it was scary, but it made me feel alive.

"He withdrew savagely from my cunt, leaving me hungry for more and without a word of warning also slipped out his finger from my anus, where it had been lingering, pinching my skin, widening me, and violently breached my sphincter with his still wet cock. I had only once been sodomized before, and it had neither proved successful nor pleasurable. The young man with whom I had agreed to try it out had been too hesitant, while I had been too nervous and too tight. I screamed, but he recognized that there was also pleasure involved beyond that initial barrier of pain. He didn't come inside me, but after a prolonged period of investing my ass, he finally pulled out, leaving me gaping like I never had before.

"Every new instruction that night, every further defilement took place in utter silence. His and mine. My muteness was my way of approving the violation that was taking place, not just physically but also in my mind. He was testing my limits, and I was already looking forward to every journey we were about to take into the darkness.

"I became his. I came alive.

"And when in the morning he asked me if I liked it that way, all I could say, avoiding his eyes, was yes and yes again. I was bruised all over, from the slaps, from his large hands, from his belt, from his punches even, the skin on my wrists and ankles was raw from the rope he had secured me with when he had bound me in increasingly awkward if not utterly obscene positions while he used me again and again.

"I was standing in the bathroom, washing my face for the first time since I had entered the apartment, my makeup had run badly because of the tears of pain I could not avoid at times in the midst of the sex, and he watched me, impassive and imperious. I needed to pee, and I gestured toward the door so he might close it and allow me some necessary privacy. 'No,' he said, and indicated the toilet. I understood right there and then that privacy was the last thing I was to be given. I sat down. At first I thought I would not be able to 'perform' with a man looking at me, but the need was too strong and eventually I did so. 'Open your legs more,' he ordered me. I did. I'm sure my face was bright red already.

"Then he moved closer to me and put his hard cock alongside my mouth. He intimated that I should part my lips and then penetrated me to the throat. I gagged, but he did not stop, and I had to gasp for breath. The stream of urine from my cunt dribbled to a stop, but he kept on fucking my mouth, each time digging deeper and deeper until once again my eyes were full of tears. Somehow it felt as if his cock was growing thicker and thicker, longer and longer inside my mouth, and I knew I couldn't take it anymore. Sensing this, he cruelly took hold of my head and impaled me just an inch or so further onto his cock, and I was violently sick. He made me lick him clean. I had become his bitch."

Casanova gulped.

D continued her tale.

"I was with him for nearly two years, and never once did I disobey an order. The experience was humiliating, frightening, but it brought my senses alight, and I knew very quickly I could not go back to my old life—the 'vanilla life,' as he affectionately called it. I dressed the way he wanted me to; I even quit my job and he installed me in his apartment. I wasn't his mistress—just his 'thing,' his toy, his piece of fuck meat. But that was fine with me.

"I looked forward to our encounters, never knowing what subtle new variation he would bring into play, what exquisite torture he would inflict on me. I was displayed publicly. I was shared with others. I was filmed. I was whored. I was given away as a prize at poker games. I was chained and spread-eagled and left as prey for strangers to abuse me. I had my parts clamped and stretched until I fainted. I was made to crawl naked on all fours and was mounted like a dog. I was trained in the art of pleasing men and women and groups.

"And in his own way, I think my first master loved me. He never said so, but there were times when after the most excruciating scenes, he would allow me to curl against him, find shelter in the cradle of his arms, and I would find solace, peace, innocence again. Whenever I had been marked too badly, he would console me by insisting it was only my body and that my soul was untouched.

"That was life with him, and I am not seeking for you or anyone to understand. It's just something you experience. I need no justification for what I have done."

"I do not judge you," Casanova said. The first sign for New Orleans had just appeared on the roadside. They should be there within an hour or two, he estimated from the speed their vehicle was now traveling. "When did all this occur?"

"Some years back," D said.

"What happened?" Casanova asked.

"I don't know," she said, still focused on the road. "Maybe he tired of me. Maybe I wasn't good enough. . . ." Her voice trailed away as the memories came flooding back inside her.

"The day he told me I was no longer required felt as if it was the very end of the world," she finally continued. "I could see no reason left to live. I begged him not to let me go, and he informed me that he was moving overseas for a prolonged period and that after due consideration he had decided he could not take me with him. I cried, and I argued with all the energy of despair for him to change his mind. That I would be good, better than I had been, that I would do anything, as if I hadn't done so most abjectly in the times we had been together. What further degradation had I not already experienced? I'm sure I was pitiful. But he was unswerving. Finally, he agreed to sell me.

"Which is how I became property of the Power Company. I had heard of the organization before, vaguely. I knew they had sponsored or, at any rate, been involved in the planning of some of the more extreme private parties my master and I had attended. Apparently my docility or willingness had been noted, and I had been deemed to be an acceptable acquisition.

"The day he left for the airport, I was abandoned, stripped naked, kneeling in a position of submission on the varnished wooden floor of my master's apartment. There was just me, the place having been rid of all furniture, and the sound of my breath echoed gently through the empty rooms. Half an hour after his departure, the Power Company came for me. I signed my slavery papers without even reading through the six-page document I was presented with. I have been their property ever since. They own my body, my holes, my free will. It's not the life I would have wished for, but I find pride in serving. It gives some form of meaning to my life."

"But, Sarah, what . . . ?" Casanova interjected.

"I am no longer Sarah. She was another person who no longer exists," the young woman said with a voice full of muted sadness. "I am now D. I will always be D. Accept that."

There were so many other questions he wanted to ask D, but he knew he would learn no more from her today. Maybe another time?

She was just another melancholy woman in a chain that now trailed back through the centuries. He now felt ashamed of the way he had taken her on the Zodiac, as if she were an animal, a body, a piece of meat through which he had channeled his aggressive needs. Yet again, names of beauties past crowded his mind—Teresa, Allessandra, Bellino, and all of the other names, faces, souls. He sighed.

Silence fell.

O was handcuffed to the bed's headboard in the bedroom of the suite that Toby Faith now occupied at the Royal Bourbon Hotel. The band's convoy had reached the Crescent City, and their technical crew was already busy down at the House of Blues setting up the gear for the small-scale gig they would be playing there the following night. The show would be a form of rehearsal for the major concert booked for later in the week at local stadium.

Faith and his fellow musicians were out exploring the Creole neighborhood of the Vieux Carré, revisiting old haunts and dives. New Orleans had always been the place of choice for rock bands on national tours, and the members of Orange Sky had arranged to spend some free time in the city both before and after their performances.

Before he had gone out, Faith had used O's mouth. She could still taste him in her throat. Every man's come tasted different, she knew from sad experience, and his was unique—bitter, fiery, twisted. There was something of the night in Toby Faith, and she dreaded the likely days to come in his company. As if sensing her apprehension, he had immobilized her and also warned her that the fearsome Maurice would be sitting on the other side of the door, which was no doubt locked, cutting off any likely escape route. He had made it clear that he intended to use her most thoroughly and beyond, and was not about to waste a penny of his new investment. The sex and the abuse did not bother O too much; she had experienced most things. She was well trained. But the sense of absolute evil that floated like an invisible aura around the lanky English singer distinctly worried her. As did his obvious unpredictability.

She had almost drifted off into a lazy twilight zone between sleep and consciousness when her reverie was interrupted by the sound of voices in the suite's other room. She quickly recognized Toby Faith's tone and accent. The other man with him was evidently a local, from the sound of his extended drawl. She strained to listen to their conversation above the hissing drone of the air conditioning.

" . . . been much too long, Mr. Faith, much too long. . . ."

O could almost hear the sly smile spreading across the singer's aquiline face as he spoke. "Too right," he agreed with his interlocutor.

"But it's nice to see you again. I must confess that the place has been much too quiet since you were last here. A touch of havoc is always welcome in my books."

O heard Toby chortle. Then the sound of drinks being poured.

Several floors below, a new band began a set at one of the many open-windowed Bourbon Street bars, and O struggled to follow more of the conversation. Immediately, the zydeco outfit performing for the massed drinkers in the bar on the opposite side of the street pushed up the volume, and the dueling strains of music quickly drowned out any further attempt to listen to the two men on the other side of the door.

The soul shouters took a break some ten minutes later, and O was once again able to eavesdrop.

There now appeared to be a third voice.

" . . . at the Pavilion this weekend. Something more refined . . . ," one of the men said.

"I think I have just the right gal for you," Toby said. "Picked her up in the Florida Keys. Classy but proud. Paid a lot for her . . . I think she'll be just perfect . . ." His voice again faded away.

O shivered. She had heard of the Pavilion. It was reputedly a notorious underground club where the worst excesses occurred. So this is what the British musician had in mind for her, was it?

During her training period at Roissy, she had heard other submissives talk of the Pavilion. Not that any had ever been or taken there. It was even said that no slaves ever returned from a sojourn at the Pavilion. Whenever things at Roissy, or wherever in their travails, took a harsh turn for the worse, it was a truism that at least they were being spared the Pavilion. It was reputed to be the stuff of living nightmares.

O suddenly remembered Kate, a woman she had come across briefly during the course of earlier adventures of the flesh. She had been on the run from a marriage that had turned sour following an affair gone wrong with the wrong man at the wrong time. She wasn't truly a submissive at heart, although she responded strongly to the dominant men with whom they were both familiar. Kate accepted the sexual abuse of her willing slavery as a form of self-punishment, forever seeking to debase herself in search of some unattainable form of redemption from imagined sins. She navigated the tides of lust with both indifference and fervor, taking every new punishment and form of servitude in her stride, remote, accepting, resigned. Even when she submitted, there was a core at her center that others could not reach, a coldness of the heart that O understood and at the same time pitied.

One day Kate had moved on. Over the following months, O had heard of Kate being in Los Angeles involved in a porn shoot, and later in Miami desultorily whoring. The last place she had been seen was in New Orleans, where rumor had it she had ended up at the Pavilion, where she had finally committed suicide. She had hanged herself. O was told that the room in which this had taken place had been renamed "Kate's Room," whether as warning or entertainment, no one knew. Even the Power Company had no control or influence over the owners of the Pavilion.

Whether the story was true, O didn't know. There had been a lot of pain in Kate's heart, but O had never thought the young English woman would one day take her own life. Maybe what happened at the Pavilion had pushed her over the edge.

Once, a man had even looked at the two of them as they stood naked in a lineup, ready to be chosen, similar blonde hair and pale alabaster skin, their nipples and shaven gashes rouged, and asked whether they were sisters, twins even.

Now, O knew that she did not wish to be taken to the Pavilion.

Whatever the circumstances. And what was being planned for her on the other side of that door, she sensed, would have nothing to do with sex, lust, or even entertainment as she knew it. It would be another version of hell.

They stopped at a gas station on a strip mall just fifteen minutes from the New Orleans city limits.

D had handed Casanova a bunch of ten-dollar bills and asked him to find her a cheap sweatshirt to wear.

"Can't land in the Big Easy with my tits on show for free," she said, pointing at her torn shirt and the cheeky globes on open display.

It was the first time she had spoken to him since telling him her story earlier today. Or at least as much of her story as she had been willing to reveal for now. Casanova still remained intensely curious about the Power Company, its possible role in his resurrection, and the reasons he had been allowed to escape—for he knew this was the case—and why D had been assigned to escort him here.

If he was a pawn in a larger game, he was willing to remain so for now. For Athena, or O as he now knew her to be. That sheer exquisite image of womanly perfection. And mystery.

Apart from his manly desires, something undeniably linked him and O together, and he was determined to pursue her until he discovered the truth. Until the end of the world if he had to.

D shrugged off her torn top and slipped on the shapeless gray sweatshirt he had acquired and drove off toward the city.

"So," she said, with a faint smile, "I suppose you've heard a lot of stories about New Orleans?"

"Actually, no," Casanova replied truthfully. He had never evinced much interest in the Americas in his original incarnation. Europe was so full of beautiful women already, and his eyes had always been bigger than his stomach. Let alone his cock. He watched as D's stiff, dark nipples scratched softly against the fabric of the garment as she rolled it down over her chest.

Damn, he was getting hard again . . .

"Well, I am sure there are going to be many surprises . . . It's a curious place, I am told. It'll be my first time, too. A city where the senses take precedence."

For Casanova, who found this modern world a veritable maelstrom of decadence and once forbidden delights, it was an invitation he knew he could not turn down.

Even more so with O at the other end of the rainbow.

Chapter Eight

"I'm no architectural expert," Casanova told D, "but this French Quarter looks more like Spanish architecture." They parked the Jeep in an parking lot on a street called Chartres.

"It is. The Spanish ruled Louisiana after the French. When most of the city burned down, the Spanish rebuilt it their way." D took Casanova's hand and led him down the narrow street, walking beneath lacework balconies of black wrought iron. The city did look almost European. In the distance a calliope echoed.

"Riverboat," D explained. "Steamboat. Tourist attraction these days."

"You seem to know a lot about New Orleans."

She shrugged. "I've read a lot about the place. Mardi Gras is a silly time. People get polluted on liquor and drugs. Women bare their breasts for decorative beads. Ordinary woman, not just whores."

"My kind of town," Casanova said. The pungent aroma of cooking drew him to stop outside a small café. He felt his stomach churn and looked at D, who grinned.

"Smells delicious," he said.

D announced, "You're in the culinary capital of North America."

The sign outside declared this was the Napoleon House, a national historic landmark. A brass plaque next to the front door declared how one of the mayors of New Orleans prepared an elaborate apartment atop his three-story building as a refuge for Emperor Napoleon Bona-parte, should he escape imprisonment by the British at St. Helena, as he had escaped from the island of Elba. In fact, a rescue mission was planned by a group of New Orleans Frenchmen. Sadly, Napoleon died before he could be rescued.

"Bad form. He should have had the decency to live longer," declared Casanova. "I've read up on this Napoleon. Fine general. A political leader of great controversy."

D opened the café door. "Let's eat."

A prim waiter, who introduced himself as Alvin, led them though the bar area, past a large, brooding gray bust of Napoleon, dark walls adorned with paintings of the emperor, and out to a patio with a table next to a banana tree.

"What is that wonderful scent?" Casanova asked as the waiter passed them menus.

"You got me," said Alvin. "Could be the gumbo. Could be the shrimp Creole. Could be the cook's cigar breath. Take your choice."

D ordered something called étoufée for both of them, which the waiter wrote down before asking, "And to drink?"

Such casual phrasing still caught Casanova unawares. He looked at D, who said she would have iced tea. Casanova asked for the wine list.

Alvin laughed. "We got red and we got white. Both go with étoufée."

"And what is the vintage?"

"Recent," said the waiter. "Nothing too old."

Casanova ordered the red, which, when he tasted it, wasn't bad at all. He examined the bottle. Cabernet Sauvignon from California. Pleasantly dry. "I'd prefer Valpolicella, but Verona's Bolla vineyards are a distance away, are they not?"

Bright sunlight filtered into the patio, giving it a warm afternoon glow. As they sat there awaiting their food, Casanova's mind flashed back to other patios, some where he had had to climb down from balconies, much like these, to escape the untimely arrival of a husband. He smiled to himself, drawing a curious stare from D.

The étoufée arrived, smelling wonderful and tasting even better. D dipped a slice of French bread into her bowl as Casanova studied the food, noting the chunks of what appeared to be seafood floating in the thick broth, which lay on a bed of white rice. Not quite a soup, with heavy brownish-red gravy flavored with onions and garlic and several types of peppers. The combination of spices and meat was delightful.

"What is the meat?" he asked D.

"Crawfish."

"As in crayfish?"

"In Louisiana, it's crawfish. Same creature. A freshwater mini-lobster with a bad attitude and delicious tail meat. A speciality around these parts."

"This is absolutely delicious."

D smiled warmly for the first time in a while. She looked a little weary. "We'll try the crawfish bisque tomorrow."

"Bisque?"

"It has gravy, too, and is served over rice, only they chop the meat into a paste with more spices, then stuff it into the shells and you have to dig it out."

Casanova poured her a second glass of wine just as a loud group of five young women came barreling into the courtyard, each carrying a tall glass containing bright red liquid.

They were young, in their twenties, all wearing tight jeans and skimpy blouses. All were blonde or, more likely, dyed blonde. Two of them cast Casanova a lingering stare as they passed. One carried a CD player (Casanova recognized the appliance), which she cranked up as she wiggled her butt while a different prim waiter tried to steer the women to the table at the far end of the patio.

"What is that racket?" Casanova asked D.

"Music. That's Orange Sky, the band that snatched O."

"They earn a living from that?"

"Very much so."

Casanova listened a few seconds longer before asking, "I assume those are musical instruments, but why is he screeching?"

"They all screech." D nodded, laughing now. "Nobody plays the harpsichord anymore, not since Simon and Garfunkel, anyway."

The waiter asked the women to turn down the music.

The butt wiggler stood up and screamed, "Orange . . . Sky . . . They rock . . . and rule, man!"

The waiter waited patiently. The girl's friend, thankfully, turned down the volume before he said, "Turn it off, please, or I might accidentally spill a glass of iced tea on it." He left menus.

One of the women called him a faggot, another winked at Casanova and licked her lips. He smiled back before refocusing his attention on the étouffée, which was spicier and infinitely more pleasurable, he was certain.

Finishing their meal, they left a decent tip. Casanova noticed the waiter hadn't returned to the loud women, who seemed content to drink their red drinks.

"Hurricanes," D said. "They're drinking hurricanes. Potent liquors mixed with fruit juices."

As they moved back into the main café, one of the women rushed past them, asking for the ladies room.

"Good idea," D said, following the woman into the ladies room. Casanova availed himself of the men's facility and urinated while staring at a picture of Napoleon on a rearing white steed.

D came out with a bounce in her step, took his hand, and led him outside. She stopped and pointed across the street. "That big hotel." It was five stories tall and ran the length of the entire block. "It's where Orange Sky is staying. Toby Faith. The big black guy. O is there."

Casanova was taken aback and opened his mouth to ask how she knew, but D beat him to it with, "Woman in the bathroom told me. They're band groupies. In town for the concert tomorrow night. They've been trying to worm their way into Faith's room all day."

They took a room at the Royal Bourbon Hotel.

"We're rolling in luck," D said. "Orange Sky is in a suite on the floor above us. And the parking lot where we stashed the Jeep is owned by the hotel."

"Should we try the direct approach? Confront them?" Casanova felt his blood rising, wishing he had a decent rapier. Maybe D would know where to locate one.

"No. No." D opened their room using a strange card given to her by the concierge when she paid for the room with one of several credit cards she had found and taken from the Jeep. "We'll use an indirect path to get O away from them."

"How?"

"I'm working on it."

The room was smallish with a double bed and bathroom. D stripped immediately and climbed into the shower. Casanova, knowing O was on the floor above, had a hard time controlling himself. He wanted to thrash this Toby Faith within an inch of his life. The nerve of the bastard, purchasing O right from under him.

Eventually he joined D in the shower, and they washed each other thoroughly, shampooing each other's hair, toweling off their water-slicked bodies before tumbling naked into bed.

"Now, tell me your plan," he said, secretly resenting the fact that he had no plan of his own. Not that he disliked having a woman come up with a plan; he had learned long ago that the fairer sex were the most wily creatures on earth. He'd always been drawn to smart women, as well as the good-looking sort. When they were both, that was the real pleasure.

He just wanted to be able to put his mind to a problem and solve it. But it was D who knew this city and what she described as the "nocturnal ways" of rock bands.

"They're probably not even awake right now."

"Then we should go at them when they are at rest," Casanova said. The cooling effect of the ceiling fan above the bed, matched with the air conditioning, made him drowsy, although he felt his cock stirring as he looked at D's body.

"They'll come out tonight," D said confidently. "The concert isn't until tomorrow night, so tonight they'll go out with O. They'll want to share her, or show her off. They won't stay cooped up in their hotel room. Trust me on this."

Casanova felt himself drifting until D laid a hand on his cock. It throbbed in response and she stroked it gently, her eyes closed, her lips pursed. He was breathing heavily by the time she wrapped those lips around his cock and bobbed her head up and down, tongue working him until he came in long, violent spurts.

She lay back down next to him, wiping her mouth with the back of her hand as Casanova's breathing evened out and he drifted to sleep.

At nine o'clock that evening, not a half hour after D had positioned herself and Casanova on a concrete bench across the street from the Royal Bourbon Hotel, big bad Maurice stepped out of the hotel, followed immediately by Toby Faith and O. Toby was dressed in all black;

O wore a diaphanous white dress that the evening breeze pressed against her perfect form. Her nipples were aroused, pointed against the silky dress, her blonde hair hanging in long curls, her face angelic with only a hint of rouge, her lips painted a fiery red. In the tall high-heeled shoes that made a modern woman's leg look ravishing, she towered over Toby and was as tall as ugly Maurice.

"She's going with them willingly," Casanova whispered to D as they followed the three, staying across the street, keeping the passing tourists between them and the street. Not that Toby or even Maurice were looking around.

"If they jump into a taxi," D said nervously, "we'll lose them." She looked gorgeous herself that evening in a short, navy blue strapless dress that barely covered her sleek body. Passers-by certainly took note, a couple of men whistling at D, who remained focused on O's group.

"Maybe you should get the Jeep," Casanova speculated.

"Too far to go," she said as the three crossed Royal Street and continued on, moving purposefully.

"They're not taking a cab," D concluded when they reached the next corner and kept going. They crossed a street jammed with people, loud music echoing, cars having a hard time getting through the crowd.

"Bourbon Street," D said as they crossed, still pacing the three. "Never closes. A street of sin."

Casanova took a quick look at the happy faces of uninhibited people having a good time. Somewhere a woman laughed hysterically. Looking back as D pulled his hand, he saw Toby and Maurice picking up the pace with O sandwiched between them now.

Three blocks later they reached a boulevard. Across the street was a large park with a lighted archway with the words "Armstrong Park" emblazoned in multi-colors. Toby led the way across the street and the three walked alongside the park. D and Casanova stayed on the other side of the wide street and paralleled them, easily hidden behind parked cars and groups of passing tourists.

"The park's named for Louis Armstrong," D said with a nervous hint to her voice. "He was a great musician from here, a jazz man. That used to be called Congo Square. Voodoo rituals were held there."

"Voodoo?"

As they continued pacing the group across the street, D explained as much as she could about voodoo, a quasi religion imported from Haiti by slaves, of spells and curses and sex rituals and the active laying-on of hands. Casanova was intrigued, especially with the last part.

"There's talk that some of the spells really work," D said as O and company reached the end of the park and turned down a dark street. Crossing the boulevard, Casanova and D reached the corner and spotted O standing with Toby Faith across the street from a brightly lit three-story building. A commotion outside had stopped Toby and O, drawing Maurice into the crowd, probably to ascertain what was happening.

"Police," D said, pressing against Casanova.

The crowd in front of the building parted somewhat, and several men in blue uniforms led a half-naked man from the building, while other men in uniforms led women wrapped in robes, some with capes over their heads. A line of cars and vans across the street were opened and the escorted individuals unceremoniously shoved inside.

A gasp from D drew Casanova's attention.

"It's the Pavilion. I've heard of it." D wrapped her arms around Casanova's right arm. The girl shivered. "It's a place of unspeakable pleasure and . . . pain. Where the worst excesses occur. It's the stuff of nightmares."

Sirens echoed behind Casanova, adding to the rising hysteria in the air. The noise seemed to cut right through them.

"If O had gone in there, she may have never come out." D's voice quivered. "Not alive."

Just then a large black man, naked except for a codpiece around his member, was dragged from the place. He screamed, and Casanova saw blood splattered over his face and arms.

The crowd wavered and suddenly O was there, her high heels in her left hand, a determined look on her face as she stared right at Casanova and hurried toward him.

"She got away," D stammered. Casanova saw Maurice's angry face across the street. The big man was pointing at O, who hurried up to Casanova and grabbed his hand.

"Hurry!" She pulled them away, back toward the park and around it, away from the crowd and the sirens. He caught a whiff of her perfume and felt excitement growing in his loins as they raced away from Toby Faith and the hulking Maurice.

They kept looking over their shoulders and thought they saw someone following, but lost him around the next corner. They turned another corner. Finally, O slowed as they drew alongside a white cement wall, which ran the length of another wide boulevard.

It took a few moments for them to catch their breath as O continued leading them away. Running his hand along the wall as he moved, Casanova felt something, a sudden coolness. What was this place? His answer came a half minute later as they passed the locked gate of a cemetery. Casanova stopped and looked inside, at sepulchres and crypts, all built aboveground.

"St. Louis Cemetery. The oldest in the city," D said, finally catching her breath.

"Let's hide inside," O said as she tossed her high heels over the gate and scaled the wrought-iron gate as easily as a cat. D went right behind, and Casanova was next, a memory flashing in his mind.

How many gates, how many fences had he scaled in those stolen nights of bliss?

The air was thicker in the cemetery, hotter, more humid, and the sounds outside, the echo of sirens, the hum of passing cars, faded as they moved along the brick walkways and narrow passageways in this little city of the dead. It smelled musty, it smelled damp and sickly sweet.

O led the way past rows of crypts, past walled tombs, like little apartments for coffins. She didn't stop until she reached a white marble crypt near the center of the cemetery next to a tall mausoleum of dead French sailors.

She opened her arms, threw back her head, and closed her eyes as she turned slowly, ever so slowly. Casanova felt his breath slip away as he watched her in the pale moonlight. She was angelic, a goddess, a face of such beauty that he felt he could hear the beat of his heart.

O stopped and focused her luminous brown eyes at him and smiled seductively. She unfastened her dress and let it fall to her feet. She wasn't Athena. She wasn't even Aphrodite, goddess of beauty. *They* paled in comparison to this naked beauty with her full breasts, round hips, and buff of soft, silky hair between her long, shapely legs.

She reached her arms for him but he couldn't move. The great lover stood frozen, watching her, drinking in the vision, savoring the image . . . until he felt hands on his belt buckle, hands pulling off his shirt. He realized, as he watched O, that D was undressing him.

He finally glanced at D and saw the pleasure on her face as she smiled up at him. She was already naked and had him naked a moment later, pulling away to let him go to O.

He did, purposefully, patiently, moving to her, his fingers gently caressing her fingers as they drew together and kissed softly, ever so softly. Their lips embraced and the kiss lingered, increasing in strength until her tongue flicked inside his mouth and their tongues worked together. He felt her pointed nipples pressing against his chest like hot coals.

His throbbing cock brushed her sparse pubic bush as she pulled him to her. The kiss continued as she drew him down to the cold marble. She lay beneath him. He hovered over her, their bodies barely touching, until he felt her hand grab his cock and guide it to her opening. She gasped as he sank into the velveteen walls of her cunt, and they began to move in unison, fucking atop the tomb. Stroke after stroke, heart stammering, he pulled his lips away from hers and looked at her gorgeous face enraptured in pleasure.

There was a sound, behind him. A gasp. D gasped and then he heard footsteps and a loud voice. "What the fuck is this?!"

Casanova looked up at a snarling face as dark as Maurice's but not Maurice's. He was aware of another face behind the dark one, a paler face with a similar snarl on it. The second man was shorter and broader.

"I don't fuckin' believe this," said the second face as two men stepped up, both in dark clothing, both with pistols in their hands. "These aren't our thieves. They're fucking!"

"I know that." The black man looked at the pale man and said, "Can you believe this shit?"

The pale man began to laugh and kicked at the ground as he slipped his gun back into a holster. It was then Casanova saw the badge clipped to the man's belt. The other man had a badge, too.

"Get the fuck up," snarled the dark man. "Fuckin' on a grave. You should be ashamed of yourself."

Casanova's erection was gone by the time he was standing with O, facing the two angry policemen. The pale man waved D over to stand with them. The men examined the naked women, leering at them.

The dark man finally slid his gun into its holster, then huffed loudly before leaning forward, addressing O. "Two women for this skinny guy? What's he supposed to be, some sorta Casanova?"

"Actually, I am," said Casanova proudly. He extended his right hand to shake, and the cops stepped back as if he had the plague.

"Fucker thinks he's a Spanish lover," said the dark cop.

"Casanova was Italian," said his partner.

"You mean like *you*—a fuckin' wop!"

Casanova waited a moment before stating the obvious. "I say. This is a strange city. You have cemetery police?"

"No, you dumb wop," said the white cop. "We're the *real* police. People been stealing statues from these graves. Angels. Marble hearts. Even tombstones. We got a tip tonight."

The black cop slapped his partner's shoulder. "Why you explaining to them? They're the ones caught with their drawers down." His voice was still angry, but there was something else in it, something deeper, something more elemental. He stared at O as she stood before him in her naked glory, and Casanova could see the lust in his eyes.

The seconds crept past. Casanova felt perspiration working its way down his back in the steamy cemetery atmosphere. O and D were breathing heavier now, and the two policemen were beginning to breathe deeper, both staring at the women as if finally seeing what stood before them.

Casanova broke the silence. "What is a wop?"

"You," said the whiter cop. "And me. If you're Italian."

"Ah," Casanova crossed his arms. "A term of endearment."

O smiled at him, then turned the smile to the dark detective. The smile turned wicked as she took a step toward him. He took in a deep breath and put his hands on his hips.

His partner spoke as D stepped toward him. "Mine looks Japanese or . . ."

"Try Vietnamese," D said huskily as she moved up to the man, went up on her toes, and brushed her lips across his. O took the other man's hand and drew him atop the tomb and slowly undressed him. D helped the other policeman out of his clothes as Casanova took a few steps back and leaned against a concrete crypt to watch.

"Condom," said the dark detective as he passed his partner a wrapped plasticine packet.

"You don't need those with us," D said.

"Yeah. Right. We're cops. We're always careful." Looking back at Casanova, the dark cop pointed to his gun, still within easy reach, and said sarcastically, "Don't try anything foolish, Casanova."

"Wouldn't dream of it."

O moved as in a dance, a waltz of pure sexuality, moving with the dark-skinned man as they stood there kissing and fondling each other. She grabbed his thick cock and stroked it as he fondled her perfect breasts. Casanova was mesmerized by the scene, the two couples moving in the moonlight, saying nothing, just groping and kissing and sucking each other. D wrapped her experienced lips around her mate's cock, her head bobbing up and down as he moaned. O, too, bent over and wrapped her mouth around the thick cock that filled her mouth.

Both men gasped and pumped their hips as they fucked the women's mouths, until the big man drew O up and shoved his tongue into her mouth. The women dressed the cocks with the condoms, then lay back on the tomb, side by side, legs open, knees up.

The men climbed atop the women and wormed their cocks into the respective vaginas. Casanova moved to one side to see O more clearly, his own cock throbbing again, thickening, hardening, wanting her so desperately and yet . . . drawn to watch her as she was fucked, like a moth drawn to a brilliant light.

The lusty black man worked O, pumping her gently at first in long, deep strokes, curling her back, making her gasp with pleasure with each stroke. Then the pumping increased as he slammed her ass against the marble. Casanova could see the man's cock moving in and out of her as they fucked. It became furious and O cried out in pleasure, the man grunting.

The air seemed thicker now, heavier with humidity, closing around Casanova, driven by a warm breeze that was almost hot. The atmosphere caressed him, making his own cock quiver and constrict. It was . . . for lack of a better word . . . otherworldly. In this den of death there seemed to be so much life, as if a thousand eyes were peering at them, whispering in the wall tombs.

His breathing was labored and he felt as if, no, he did feel a squirt and looked down as his cock ejaculated, shooting steady spurts of seed into the air. Amazed, he just watched. Casanova could not recall the last time he'd had a spontaneous ejaculation. Not since he was a teenager at least.

The man atop D grunted loudly and began pounding her. She cried out and hung to his shoulders, wrapping her legs around his waist. He was the first to finish and climbed off D almost too quickly. He peeled off his condom as she lay there catching her breath. The condom was filled. Obviously the man had been hoarding ejaculate. Most likely a married man.

O screeched with pleasure as her fucker hit his stride, fucking her furiously and yelling, "Yeah! Yeah! Yeah!" as he obviously came. Rolling off to catch his breath, sweat dripped from his face and chest.

Casanova stared at O as she lay spread-eagle before him. He moved to her. The white cop, already dressed, told the other cop something in code and the big man started dressing.

O peeked up at Casanova as he stood between her legs, his cock once again sticking straight up again like a flagpole. She smiled wickedly.

"No time for that, lover boy," said the big cop. He nodded across the cemetery. "See those buildings?" He pointed to red brick buildings just beyond the far wall. "That's the Iberville Housing Project. The home boys are probably watching us right now. We leave and they'll come eat you alive. Gobble up these white women."

The men dressed quickly. Casanova's cock still throbbed as he watched O stand on shaky legs. He helped her into her dress, and D helped him into his clothes, as she had dressed already.

O brushed his crotch with her hand, which made his dick swell even more. He was still amazed at how excited he became watching her get fucked, seeing this gorgeous woman ravished by the dark stranger, feeling his heart race as this woman he had cherished, for centuries, got pleasured.

"This cemetery has magical properties," Casanova said. "I hear talk of voodoo here.

"Yeah," the shorter policeman said with a snarl. "We got a couple voodoo queens buried in here."

The policemen had a key to the front gate of the cemetery and led them out, the women straightening their dresses as they stepped out on the sidewalk.

"Hey!" a loud voice boomed. "Over here!"

Casanova saw Toby Faith hustling their way, with Maurice behind him. The policemen moved in front of the rushing men.

"Get the fuck out of my way!" Toby snapped as he tried to shove past the big copper, who grabbed him by the neck and slammed him against the cemetery wall.

Maurice raised a fist and the white policeman raised his pistol. "Police! Up against the wall, motherfucker!"

They shoved Maurice against the wall and searched both men, manacling them with handcuffs in a few seconds.

"Wait! Wait!" Toby wailed. "I'm a rock star. We're Orange Sky."

"You're our prisoners, is what you are." The big, dark cop pulled Toby away from the wall.

"I'm arrested?" wailed Faith. "What for?"

"Pissing off the police. Never put your hand on a cop. Especially in New Orleans, you cocksucker."

"I want to speak with the British Counsel!"

"Yeah. Yeah. You can call him from the parish prison."

"Wait! The blonde," Toby went on, "she's mine. I bought her!"

The big cop yanked Toby around and pressed his face close. "Man, slavery went out with Abe Lincoln." He led Toby past Casanova, the smaller cop shoving Maurice by. The cops turned to the women and said, "Ladies. Thanks for the memories."

Casanova watched the two police detectives lead the rock star and his bodyguard toward a dark sedan parked against the curb, then shove them inside. He felt a hand on his shoulder and turned to see D looking over her shoulder at O, who was getting in a taxi. She must have hailed it silently while their attention was elsewhere

"Good. We'll go back to the hotel then."

But O precipitously shut the door of the cab, and the taxi pulled away from the curb, leaving a stunned Casanova standing there with D. As the taxi quickly darted away, O rolled the window down, leaned out, and waved back to them, an enigmatic smile spreading across her pale but beautiful face. Casanova sighed. This was no longer a game. Would she ever be his fully?

"What now?" D asked. "I just cannot understand that woman."

Casanova answered, "We find her."

Chapter Nine

Since it was now early morning, Casanova and D decided to go back and have a snack of beignets and orange juice at the Café du Monde, by Jackson Square, where they hoped to find some inspiration. They lingered over their food longer than necessary, neither eating with much enthusiasm, returning to the Royal Bourbon Hotel in defeat. O could have gone anywhere in that taxi, be anywhere by now, perhaps even well on her way out of New Orleans. A wise move, in Casanova's sage opinion. He had already had enough of New Orleans himself, good gumbo or not. The crawfish had reawakened his old nemesis: indigestion. He imagined them seeking revenge in his belly, gnawing away at his innards until the blood ran. All that spicy Cajun food gave him wind. Not exactly a condition befitting a gentleman of his standing. Indeed, he couldn't wait to get out of there—with O in tow. He wasn't about to leave without her.

Upon reaching their floor, he heard a horrendous din thundering through the ceiling. His heart sank. Orange Sky. Surely those scoundrels could not have been released from jail! Yet the awful truth was right there above his head. By now he knew their distinctive wails; they were probably in their suite listening to their own recordings and clapping one another on the back with pride at creating such sublime artistry. *The proverbial dog returning to its vomit,* mused Casanova sourly, feeling the insides of his ears blistering in agony. How he pined for the rich melodies of his old cohort Mozart, a fellow nearly as debauched as himself. Ahhh, that was music!

Using the strange plastic card, D unlocked the door to their room. An envelope embossed with the hotel's name lay on the carpet just inside. A delicately swirled "G" had been written across the front in black ink. Casanova bent down to retrieve it, feeling every year of his life screaming along his spinal column. The pain worried him. This wasn't the first time he had felt it. Could it be he might return to the husk of the man he was as he'd lingered on the threshold of death, the smell of his white face powder mingling with that of the Grim Reaper? To think he had come this far, only to reach so pathetic an end—and just when he was on the verge of achieving the bliss he had spent a lifetime searching for—the bliss he knew could only be provided by O. He had loved and lost many women in his life. Would she be added to the list as well?

He tore open the envelope. Inside was a note in the same delicate hand as the one that had penned the "G" of his Christian name—Giacomo. Whenever she would say it, one day soon he hoped, he imagined he would hear the fluttering of birds' wings, a musical tinkling of notes far superior to anything Mozart could have concocted in that deranged brain of his.

Casanova felt a stirring in his trousers—a powerful, relentless stirring that could only have been inspired by one woman. From beside him D strained to read the note. For some reason he could not fathom, he stuffed the paper into his trouser pocket. D had been a good companion to him, a good lover. Why should he behave thus? Yet perhaps it was time to part company. Although the thought saddened him, it exhilarated him, too. He wished he could have known her when she was still Sarah—in the days before she had a master. It would have been fascinating to know her taste, her scent, before they had been corrupted by those who sought to dominate her body and mind. Yes, he'd had many women in his time, though most of them had long since become dust. Remaining with one eternally—that was something he couldn't grasp. Except when it came to O.

"I must rest," he replied, his recently acquired vigor waning. "It has been an extremely trying day."

D leaned in close, allowing her hand to brush against the front of Casanova's trousers. Apparently she was encouraged by what she felt there, for she continued to sweep the back of her hand to and fro along the fabric, reminding Casanova of a metronome. "Do you not wish for me to help you relax?" she queried with a raised eyebrow, grinning suggestively. This time such feminine wiles had no effect. Casanova's thoughts were focused squarely on O and the curious message she had left for him.

A new destination. Far away from Orange Sky and the Royal Bourbon Hotel.

Far away from D.

In recent days O had experienced a sort of epiphany. Her body had been used and abused for as long as she could remember. Was she truly this passive, submissive creature whose orifices were available for any transgression man or woman could perpetrate? The marks and brandings on her flesh were permanent; she would never be able to erase them, nor would they ever fade. If her skull were broken open to see inside, her brain would bear the welts and burns of her degradation as well. They had become part of her, in her blood, her soul, the scent of her sex. Venice. The Power Company. Orange Sky. Was it too late to take control of her destiny? The taste of pain and humiliation was no longer so sweet on her tongue. It hadn't been for some time.

It was good to be alone, to have a moment to pause and reflect. From the cemetery, the cab had let her off in an industrial part of town, where she had ducked into an alleyway behind a disused warehouse, hoping she hadn't been followed by those police officers, or even Casanova and D. She couldn't deal with them right now. She didn't want anyone to lead her away from her thoughts—the future she might have.

With the dawning of a new hot and damp Louisiana day, the distinctive bouquet of the river grew stronger, earthier, more menacing. O could smell herself, the sweat of the steamy New Orleans day combining with the scent of the previous night's sex. She thought back on her innumerable violations, from the first to the most recent in the cemetery. So many men, violating her in so many ways. Had it been possible to rent more openings in her body for them to use, they would have.

She felt a frisson of excitement at the memory of the many public displays of her intimate flesh, the keening song of the crop as it had come down upon her flesh, and more recently, of Toby Faith plunging roughly into her backside. The insides of her thighs grew sticky and she squeezed them together, only to quickly open them. Such closing off of her parts was forbidden, as it had been since that long ago day she had first crossed Roissy's threshold.

O's first instinct was to touch herself. She knew she would be wet, that her clitoris would be erect and demanding release. Her finger moved of its own will, rubbing hard, cruelly. She wasn't used to a gentle touch. She pinched at the delicate flesh, lights flashing in her eyes, blood pounding in her ears. Her heartbeat speeded up and she pinched harder, twisting, pulling, tears streaming down her cheeks at the exquisite pain, the torture. And then she stopped. This wasn't how it was supposed to be. Not anymore.

Her fingers clawed at the leather collar around her neck in desperation to remove it, only to discover it was a phantom collar. She had grown so accustomed to her bindings that even when she went without she still felt as if she were wearing them. Whimpering like a sick animal, she continued to scratch at her neck, her nails scoring red trails into the flesh. She would be a slave no longer.

She needed to get away. By herself. To find something that had meaning. She knew it existed; during her brief captivity, she had heard Toby and the other band members talk about a place called Seattle. "Mecca," they called it, nodding knowingly. O had heard about Mecca on television—every year thousands of pilgrims went there, seeking out something bigger than themselves, something holy. According to Toby and the band, this Mecca-Seattle was where God had dwelled. Kurt Cobain had been His name. She wanted to find out more. Not that she had any strong religious convictions, but her years of indoctrination into sexual pain had given her a sort of spiritual awakening on many levels. Maybe the time had come for O to seek out something beyond herself. Beyond the pain. It made no sense, but something was drawing her toward Seattle. Damn the logic!

And then she had been given a sign.

The previous morning, when she had been held in Toby's room, she'd found a rock 'n' roller's guidebook on Seattle. While he sat on the toilet reading a back issue of *Rolling Stone* and singing the band's latest hit, she leafed through the guide, hoping she might find a landmark, a place to start on her quest, her mission, to find Him. As luck would have it, she heard the sound of the toilet flushing all too soon, so she scribbled down the first place she saw listed. Only now she wondered whether she had done the right thing in leaving the note for Casanova, which would enable him to follow her. Because follow her he would, she knew deep inside. Well, she would leave it to fate, to the gods—or in this case "God"—as to their meeting up again.

. . .

Casanova did not sleep that night. Instead he watched stealthily as D slept, her body naked and available to him, should he desire it. The gentle rise and fall of her breasts, so lovely, so lush. The moonlight streaming through the partially opened draperies illuminated the pale mound of her sex, a spotlight placing her clitoris on center stage. Although the tip always had a habit of peeking out from her hairless vulva, tonight it seemed especially prominent. Perhaps she was dreaming of O, mused the once legendary lover, experiencing his own increasing prominence. He fought the instinct to reach out and touch her, to give her a friendly twiddle, a teasing lick. Alas, there was no place for such luxuries now. He had to meet O, and he had very little time to do so!

When he was certain D was in the deepest part of her slumber, he slipped out of bed. Dressing hurriedly, he collected some belongings and crept from the room, O's note a burning ember in his trouser pocket. As he made his way to the hotel lobby, he prayed he would not encounter any of those uncouth English ruffians from Orange Sky. Had there been time, he might have challenged Toby Faith to a duel. But then, duels were for gentlemen. And Toby Faith was no gentleman.

A cab waited outside the hotel. Casanova jumped into it, his movements less dignified than usual. "To the airport, my good man," he directed, leaning back in the torn plastic seat. There was a distinctive odor of urine in the car, and he wrinkled his nose, trying to close off his nostrils. The smell reminded him of when the rains caused the water level to rise in the canals of his beloved Venice. How he missed Venice, the elegance of his former life. O would have enjoyed living then, of that he was certain. During the journey he sat quietly, reading and rereading the note she had left for him, his fingers trembling with excitement as he struggled to make sense of it.

. . .

Gone to Seattle to find Kurt Cobain.

Meet me at Starbucks. Broadway Ave. Capitol Hill.

Tomorrow. 4:00 P.M.

God bless!

O checked into a cheap residential hotel near the Seattle Space Needle. The taxi driver had said it was a "good place" and "centrally located." Central to what, she wasn't sure. But she was tired from the flight and needed sleep and a shower before she set off on her pilgrimage to find Kurt Cobain. The driver appeared not to know who He was when she had asked, though she attributed this to the fact that the man was from India and probably prayed to his own gods.

When she finally stretched out on the lumpy bed, sleep eluded her. She was too excited, too wired, for anything as pedestrian as sleep. Instead she took a quick shower and put on the same clothes she had been wearing since St. Louis Cemetery. They smelled a bit and were stained with the fluids of sex, but He would not mind. They were earthly things, of little consequence.

It was already past lunchtime, but O didn't care about food. In between her escape from the cemetery in New Orleans and her arrival in Seattle, the seam of her dress had become ripped on one side, revealing the fact that she wasn't wearing any undergarments. But O didn't care about that either. She had work to do. She needed to get started, so she began to trek up and down the hilly streets of Queen Anne Hill, asking anyone who showed a willingness to stop where Kurt Cobain might be found. Most everyone was very friendly and seemed to take a great deal of time with her, although no one could give her a specific answer as to His whereabouts. What O did not realize was that most of her interlocutors thought her crazy, unaware as she was that Kurt Cobain died in 1994.

By mid-afternoon she was exhausted. She returned to her hotel to freshen up, only to dash back out again when she saw on the bedside clock that it was 3:45 P.M. She felt terribly guilty. Giacomo would be so disappointed that she had failed in her mission. She believed that he, too, needed meaning in his life, spiritual guidance. He needed to find God just as she did.

Instead she found Dwayne Deacon.

Casanova arrived on Seattle's Capitol Hill an hour before the appointed time. He had dressed carefully for the occasion, in a white linen suit of summer weight, a red bow tie, and white patent leather shoes. He had even taken time to powder his face in the old manner, except he couldn't find any of the fine white powder he was accustomed to. He'd had to settle on some abominable flesh-toned concoction compressed into a clamlike device he had purchased at a large shop called a "drug store." Nevertheless, he looked quite the gentleman. O would surely be unable to resist him now!

Too excited to wait for the appointed hour, Casanova traversed the streets searching for O. Every moment without her was a knife in his gut (unless that seafood gumbo he had eaten yesterday was still plaguing him); he couldn't afford to waste another precious second. As he familiarized himself with the terrain, he began to wonder if this city called Seattle suffered from inbreeding. He remembered from his travels that this was not unusual in some parts of the world. Why, he'd been guilty of perpetuating the phenomenon himself! Almost everyone he encountered looked the same: long greasy hair, dirty denim jeans, tattered T-shirt, the swagger of youth that would leave them soon enough. He remembered well his own youthful swagger and its potent effect on the women and men of his day. How could he forget that aging Viennese countess with the peculiar dog? But no, this was not the time for fond reminiscences. He would make new memories with O.

Not seeing anyone who even remotely resembled his beloved, he decided to change his tactics. "I am Giacomo Casanova, the Chevalier de Seingalt, and I am seeking Kurt Cobain," he stated with authority to all who passed. The usual response he received was a baffled stare or a look of uncomprehension. But no one dared to tell him the truth about the rock god's passing. He then proceeded to describe O as best he could, asking if anyone had seen her. After all, she couldn't be far. Could she?

"Got any change, man?" slurred a youth with a dilapidated backpack slung across one shoulder and a sweetish-smelling cigarette dangling from his lower lip. He clearly wasn't interested in Casanova's rapturous description of the delicious O. Moved by his shabby appearance, Casanova pulled out his billfold and handed the boy a dollar, only to be rewarded by a dark scowl. "Whoa, big spender," the youth tossed over his shoulder as he slunk off, only to stop the next pedestrian, whom Casanova noted, was female. "Got any change, man?"

It started to rain. Since it was almost time for his appointment with O, Casanova enlisted the aid of two fellows of a persuasion not altogether unknown to him, receiving a merry escort to the Starbucks specified in O's note. He hastened inside with relief. Not seeing her at any of the tables, he headed up to the counter, intent on refreshment. Alas, he couldn't make hide nor hair of the strange assortment of beverages on offer. However, the comforting smell of coffee did go some way toward reassuring him that he was indeed on familiar territory.

He noticed that the other patrons were staring pointedly at him, as was the young woman behind the counter with a tiny silver dagger piercing the septum of her nose. His heart thundered in his chest. Sweat dripped from his armpits, collecting in the waistband of his trousers. Somehow, the prospect of meeting O again was disturbing him, upsetting the equilibrium of his mind and body. At that moment he did not feel like the elegant and refined nobleman he had once been and was hoping to become again, but rather like some illiterate oaf who had blundered into a royal garden party. "What do you recommend, my good woman?" he queried, unable to look away from the gruesome sight of the nasal dagger.

"Dunno. Whatcha want?" she retorted.

Casanova perused the wall menu again, his ears roaring with white noise. He began to panic. He couldn't very well stand at the counter all afternoon. A crowd was forming behind him, obscuring his line of sight to the door. What if O came in and, thinking he wasn't there, left? The smell of coffee was making his mouth water. Only which of the items on the menu contained coffee? He couldn't be certain. Many of them had names he didn't recognize. The dagger-nosed girl narrowed her eyes, seeming to intimidate him into making a decision. Well, so be it. He would throw caution to the wind. "I will have a mocha latte, please."

"Tall?"

"Pardon me?"

Sigh. "TALL?"

"Yes, thank you." Tall? Did it not come in a cup?

After he paid, Casanova was directed to wait at another section of the counter. Thankfully, he was now better able to watch the door and anyone either coming in or going out. His refreshment arrived within five minutes, and he went to sit on a chair piled with newspapers. He was too nervous to remove them.

The clock on the wall indicated 4:00 P.M. The door opened and Casanova's heart stopped. Instinctively he reached up to check that his hair was in order, his bow tie straight. A young couple with matching long greasy hair came in, a thick plume of cigarette smoke following them.

"Hey, no smoking, man!" yelled Dagger Nose from behind the counter.

"Fuck you, man!" they yelled back, beating a hasty retreat back out the door and into the pouring rain.

Four fifteen. No sign of O.

Casanova fidgeted on the chair, taking sips from his mocha latte, TALL, which was surprisingly tasty.

Four thirty. Still no sign of O.

He dug into his pocket, retrieving the note written on Royal Bourbon Hotel stationery. Yes, he had gotten the time correct—4:00 P.M. Surely O would not intentionally mislead him, would she?

At 4:45 P.M. a young man in the customary uniform of the neighborhood—dirty denim jeans, tattered T-shirt, long greasy hair—came loping over to Casanova. "Hey, you—the Chevalier de—the Chevalier de—de—ahh, fuck it!"

Casanova stood bolt upright and puffed out his chest. "Yes. I am the Chevalier de Seingalt."

"Someone wants to see you, man. C'mon."

"But to where are we going?"

"It ain't far, man. It ain't far."

He duly followed his messenger outside, the seat of his once pristine white linen trousers now wet and stained with newsprint.

Dwayne Deacon had a beatific smile, showing off front teeth that sat crookedly in his gums. Barely twenty, he sported a slew of pimples across his forehead, some of which oozed slightly. O had been rushing out of her hotel when they collided on the sidewalk. It was 3:45 P.M.; she had to be on Capitol Hill at 4:00 to meet Casanova. That is, if he had decided to pursue her here in America's northwestern reaches. How could she presume that he would, though? But if he had made the journey toward the appointed meeting spot, she would never make it now!

The stack of pamphlets in Dwayne's hands went flying in all directions, the cold Seattle rain drenching them instantly as they landed on the sidewalk and in the gutter. "I'm so sorry!" O stopped, bending to retrieve what she could of them. Her years of training had not prepared her for modesty. Rather than squatting with knees together in a ladylike fashion, she bent fully forward from the waist, thighs parted (she had been forbidden to keep her legs together or cross them), the torn skirt of her dress opening to display a rear view of her pudenda to anyone who happened to be in the vicinity, which now included a flushed Dwayne Deacon. He moved his hands, which had been dangling at his sides, in front of him at crotch line, then cleared his throat.

"There's no need for that," he stammered, the tips of his ears beet red.

"But your papers—they're ruined!" O stood up, the soggy pamphlets in her hand testifying to their pathetic state. Her skirt continued to gape open at the rear, revealing her crop-conditioned buttocks. Dwayne's breathing had become labored, and she feared he might collapse. To think her clumsiness had caused him such consternation!

His voice came out a strangled croak. "I can always get more back at the mission."

"The mission?"

"Yes. It is where we assemble to do the Lord's work." Dwayne offered O one of his innocent crooked-toothed smiles, no doubt sensing that he might have a new recruit to aid in God's work. "Would you like to come back with me? There are many there who would like to meet you. Come," he placed a hand alongside her shoulder, not quite touching it. "Warm yourself with a cup of soup and with the love of the Lord, for he dwells where we dwell."

"But I can't! I'm on a mission to find Kurt Cobain!" cried O, panicking. By now she had forgotten all about her appointment with Casanova.

Dwayne nodded, a shadow of sadness passing across his eyes. "Yes, there are many here like yourself. Do not worry. He is with us. Come." And this time he allowed his hand to make contact with O's shoulder, the pimples on his forehead glowing bright red as a gust of wind off Puget Sound provided everyone on Queen Anne Hill with a panoramic view of O's naked lower half.

The scruffy youth led Casanova through the rain to an old wood-frame house. His white linen suit was by now completely ruined, and he loitered miserably on the sidewalk, not certain he wished to venture inside, let alone step foot on the periphery of the shabby dwelling. The postage-stamp front lawn was choked with weeds and strewn with bits of rubbish, including a small pipe and several discarded pieces of silver foil. The house had an unlived-in air, the paint—or what remained of it—having peeled away, revealing a moldy underside. A commune of fire ants appeared to be making a happy home in the damp flesh of the structure, causing Casanova to instinctively scratch at himself.

"Hey, you coming or what, man?"

Taking a fortifying breath, Casanova followed his guide up some cracked steps to the front door. A dreadful noise was coming from beyond—a sound reminiscent of the cacophony perpetrated by Orange Sky. No. Impossible!

"Go in, man. He's expecting you."

"Who is expecting me?" asked Casanova, suddenly wary.

"Him." The boy swiped at his nose with a forearm. As he turned to go, he froze as if he had forgotten something. "Oh, yeah," he sniffed. "Got any change, man?"

"But I am not worthy of Him!" protested O between sips of watery chicken broth. She sat at attention in her chair, her legs parted as training dictated. The others at the mission had gathered closely around, smiling with encouragement, some even seating themselves at her knee. How kind everyone had been since her arrival!

Dwayne patted her bare thigh reassuringly, allowing his fingers to linger. The skirt of O's dress had pulled completely open in front, placing every detail of her femininity on display. "The Lord loves all sinners. And we are sinners all," he replied, urging a stack of pamphlets toward her.

She began to tremble, knowing that this might be the moment of truth—the moment she had been waiting for her entire life. The answer to the reason she had been brought to America. Yes, she would do Kurt Cobain's work. And she would never look back. The old O was gone.

Accepting the pamphlets from Dwayne, O followed in the wake of her fellow missionaries, going from door to door, spreading His word.

The house on Capitol Hill stank of rotting meat, old wine, and cigarette smoke. There was little in the way of décor, save for a stained sofa with the stuffing oozing out. Several guitars had been propped against the wall, some plugged into amplifiers. A pallid young woman with bleached blonde hair the texture of straw half sat, half lay in a corner, arms and legs strewn wide, as though someone had tossed her there like a rag doll. Her features appeared out of kilter, one eye half closed, the red color painted on her lips smeared to her chin. She might have been pretty, except for the fact that she looked as if she had been dragged along the roadside. "They killed him," she kept repeating in a gravelly voice, blood trickling from a vein in her bruised left arm. "They fuckin' killed him, man."

Lying amid the litter of dirty plates and cigarette ends, Casanova watched as a needle penetrated the bulging blue vein in his arm, his breath catching in his throat at the sight of his blood spurting back into the syringe like seed into a woman's quim. The ghostly young man who held the device smiled a death mask's smile, as if the act of smiling were too painful. Casanova smelled the grease from the youth's lank blond hair. He wore dirty denim jeans and an old yellow cardigan, the yarns unraveling at the cuffs. There was a beauty to this ephemeral creature before him—a languid apathy that reached into his very soul.

Casanova remembered with fondness his many dalliances with young men. How delightful were their bodies! They possessed a hard sweetness when he penetrated them, their passages seeming to reject yet receive at the same time. He wanted to reach out to touch this young man's whiskered cheek, to slip his fingers inside the fly of his filthy jeans, but he could not move his other arm. The one with the hypodermic continued to be held by his administering blond angel, who'd begun to loosen the rubber tie from Casanova's biceps.

The last thing Giacomo Casanova would hear before he lost consciousness was a tormented male voice singing something about Polly wanting a cracker.

Chapter Ten

When D woke up in the New Orleans hotel room, Casanova was not there. She thought he might be taking a bath, or had gone out to get some breakfast for the two of them. But after an hour went by, watching television to keep herself distracted, she feared that Toby Faith and Maurice may have broken in while she was asleep and taken Casanova, to get O back into their possession. But if this were the case, wouldn't they have taken her as well?

Then, in the wastebasket, she found the note O had left for "G." Seattle? Starbucks? Kurt Cobain?

"What the fuck," she mumbled.

She sat on the bed and realized she had been abandoned in Louisiana. The bastard didn't even leave her a note or an explanation!

"What a jerk," she said to herself.

But wasn't this what she was used to? Like the day her first master left her alone and naked in that empty apartment? The pain of it all returned and it excited her. D lay back on the bed and reached between her legs. Her pussy was wet, wetter than it'd been in a while, even during all the sexual exploits she had recently had with Giacomo Casanova. She began to pleasure herself, starting off with a circular caress of her index finger around her clit, and then inserting that finger into her musky cunt . . . and a second finger. She wished she had a dildo in the room, something long and thick and black. She imagined Maurice breaking into the room, holding her down, demanding to know where O went, and when she refused to speak, he penetrated her with an enormous cock, so big that it felt like it was ripping her in two. She imagined that in the background was Toby Faith, watching, saying, "That's it, Maurice, fuck that whore good, fuck that slut, shove it up that trollop's ass," and that when Maurice flipped her over, one hand on her head and another on her back, and forced himself into her rear end, her entire body went limp while Toby Faith laughed and laughed.

The fantasy made her come pretty hard.

She caught her breath and picked up the hotel phone. She made a long distance call to the Power Company. She was put on hold and switched to other lines twice. A deep male voice said, "Yes?"

That voice caused shivers to go up and down her spine, like it always had. She had never seen the face attached to the voice, nor had she ever pleasured the body; all she knew was that she belonged completely the voice; she was the voice's property.

"This is D, sir."

"Yes?"

She told the voice what had happened.

There was a long pause.

"I'm sorry, sir," she said.

"Wait there for further instructions."

The line went dead.

She took a quick shower and almost masturbated again under the water; but if she missed the call, she would be in terrible trouble. She sat, naked, on the bed. The phone didn't ring until two hours later.

"Hello?"

"D."

"Yes, sir."

"You have a new assignment."

"I'm not coming back?"

"No," said the voice. "You are going to Los Angeles. There is a ticket at the airport waiting for you, American Airlines, direct to LAX. A limo driver will meet you and take you to your next job."

"I understand."

The line went dead.

"What's your name, baby?" asked the young lady with long, dirty red hair and illustrations all over her arms and back.

"Giacomo Casanova," he said, groggy and slow. "Some have called me Jacques."

"You're funny, Jack," she said, and giggled.

She wore only sheer panties and a grin. She was also injecting a needle into her arm. Casanova remembered that such a needle had gone into his own arm earlier. How long had he been unconscious?

"What is that you're doing?" he asked the girl. "What have you people done to me?"

"How do you feel, baby? Do you like it? Isn't this shit rad?"

"Rad?" he retorted with sluggish curiosity.

"Dude," she said, crawling into his lap, "this is God's Magic Mixture."

Her skin and hair smelled like sweat, dirt, sex, and urine. Oddly, this aroused Casanova. He felt a surge of delight go through his body. He had never felt anything like this before.

"A blend of Ecstasy, heroin, and cocaine, with a touch, a splash, of psilocybin," the girl whispered in his ear, "and it takes you to heaven. Only God can take you to heaven. Do you feel it, baby? Dude, are you with me?"

"Yes . . . I feel it."

"Touch me. Touch me all over."

O was hanging around in the mission with Dwayne Deacon, waiting to get more flyers about the Divine One. Dwayne was looking at her with eyes she knew too well. She thought he was some kind of angel. "You," she started to say, but he shook his head.

"You're so beautiful," he said.

She just smiled.

"I know what you want, I know what you need," said O, moving close to him. She sat him down on a metal chair. She knelt down before him, like she was about to pray. She touched the zipper of his baggy pants. She could tell he was getting hard, but he was also blushing and looking away.

"What's wrong?" she asked.

He shrugged.

She grabbed his erection and said, "Don't you like this?"

His body shuddered.

"Y-yes," he said.

She unzipped him and started fishing around in his pants.

"Wait," he said, touching her arm.

"What is it?" she said. "Don't you like your cock to be sucked? I'm very, very good. I was trained well. I trained on hundreds of men to be the best cocksucker in the world."

"What about . . . ," and he gestured to the other people in the mission, men and women (but mostly men), who were taking notice of what he and O were doing.

"I don't care," she said, "do you?"

"I guess not. It's the sort of thing He would approve of."

"I know," she said, feeling better about this, almost as if Kurt Cobain were watching her and nodding his head and giving the thumbs up. She pulled Dwayne's cock out of his pants. It was long and maybe a little too thin for her liking, but he did have a big bulb of a head, and she knew that it would feel good if he ever fucked her, which she was sure he would sometime in the near future. She stroked his dick and took the head in her mouth. She worked her way down, trying to get as much of it into her mouth as she could and show Dwayne just how good she was.

"Oh, that's damn fine," Dwayne moaned, placing both hands on her head and making her swallow him to the hilt.

Casanova was enjoying touching the girl in his lap all over. She seemed to be having orgasms with each caress—from her neck to her belly, she would smile and sigh and her eyes would get big and she would say, "Oh, that's damn fine, baby."

"What's your name, dear sweet girl?"

"JoAnne. But people call me JoJo."

"JoJo . . . you're so nice . . ."

"You're pretty nice, too, for an older dude."

"Tell me the meaning of all these illustrations on your skin."

"The meaning of my tats? That's pretty funny. Does there have to be a meaning for everything?"

"I find them uncanny."

"I find them pretty cool."

"Why do you have them?"

"Why not?" she said. "You talk too much." And with that, she removed her panties and put one of his hands between her legs. Her pubic hair was wispy, wiry, and red—Casanova liked it a lot.

"Finger-fuck me," JoJo said, "hell, fist-fuck me . . . get your whole hand up there if you can, baby."

"I will do my best, my dear," he replied.

On the 747 to Los Angeles, D had an interesting sexual encounter.

One for the books, she thought. She was waiting in line to use the restroom, after having two vodka and tonics off the flight attendant's tray. There was a tall man with a deep tan standing in front of her. She liked the cologne he was wearing; it reminded her of something . . . what, she didn't know. Another man? A forgotten place? Where had she smelled this cologne before?

The more the scent entered her nostrils, the more aroused she became. The man was handsome, too, with quite a chiseled profile. He kept turning around and looking at her, smiling with perfectly even white teeth and glittering blue eyes. What the hell was going on here? She felt like she was under some kind of spell, like she was enchanted and inspired by unseen forces to do something dirty and nasty. So why fight it? A plan formed in her slave-whore mind.

As the man's turn came to go into the lavatory, she pushed him in and followed, quickly closing and locking the door. They were cramped in the small space but fit well enough. The man turned around and started to say something, but she put two fingers to his lips and shook her head. She saw that he understood. He leaned against the mirror at the small basin as D got on her knees, unzipped the man's trousers, and pulled out his flaccid dick. Soft, it was big; she took the thing in her mouth and it soon grew even bigger. She always liked the way a limp dick would strengthen inside her mouth.

The cologne, mixed with the pungent scent of this stranger's crotch, made her scalp tingle. She sucked him hard and good and fast, because there wasn't time to really enjoy this act. She wanted him to come fast, and he did, shooting three thick bursts of semen to the back of her throat and down into her stomach, where it settled with the tonic water, vodka, and complimentary peanuts.

She stood up and wiped her mouth with the back of her hand.

He zipped up.

"That was pleasant and unexpected," he said.

"You're telling me," she said, licking the back of her hand. "What's that cologne you're wearing?"

"I don't know. My wife got it for me."

"Smart woman."

"If she could only see me now," he said, and chuckled.

"I need to . . ."

"Please."

He looked away as she lifted her dress, pulled down her panties, and sat on the toilet.

"You can watch if you want," she told him, "I don't mind."

"It's okay."

"I know you want to."

Indeed he did, because he turned his head and watched her sitting there, letting loose a stream.

"You're quite the item," he said.

"Thanks."

She was done. She wiped, then stood and said, "I don't need to watch you. I'll be going now."

"Thanks for . . . the encounter," he said.

"Thanks for the sperm," D said.

She walked out of the restroom. There were three people in line—two men and one woman. They didn't look at her; they seemed embarrassed, having seen a man and a woman go in there together and knowing what must have happened. D squeezed past the three with a devious grin on her face. She didn't care what they knew or thought.

Away from the man, she was surprised herself, for taking such an initiative when she was used to men taking the reins. That damn cologne! She needed another vodka and tonic to get the stranger's taste out of her mouth.

Dwayne sucked in a long breath of air and then blew his wad into O's mouth. There was a lot, more than O was ready for; she couldn't swallow it all, and strands of semen poured out of her mouth and down Dwayne's shaft and into his pants. "You emptied my nuts," Dwayne said in a small voice.

Then came the applause.

O had completely forgotten about the other people in the mission, and that they had been watching her suck Dwayne off. But she was used to having an audience.

A man with a shaved head and goatee and a tattoo of a snake on his neck stepped forward and said, "So am I next?"

"If you must," O said.

"Oh, I must," he said.

He stood in front of her and whipped his cock out.

There were about eight other men standing around, and O knew she would have to blow them all.

Again, nothing she wasn't used to.

"Oh yeah, Jack, stuff me all the way," cried JoJo.

Casanova had the pale, tattooed young woman on the ratty, stained sofa, on her back, her legs lifted high. He had four fingers inside her cunt and was attempting to get his thumb in there, too. His whole body was on fire from the mixture that was put into his arm, and he knew her body was the same. The only thing was, he didn't seem to have an erection and that confused him. There was certainly a lot of mental desire, and just touching the girl and her touching him back was fantastic. But what was going on with his trusty member? Why was it failing the usually hard Casanova?

The pallid young woman with the bleached blonde hair still sat in her corner, oblivious to what Casanova and JoJo were doing; she was mumbling to herself: "Killed him . . . killed him . . . the bastards . . ."

Just as he was about to get his hand all the way inside JoJo, a group of people burst into the living room. A dozen young men and women, greasy, unwashed, tattooed, and enraptured by the man they were following: the beautiful man with blond hair, dirty jeans, and the yellow cardigan sweater.

"Come as you are," he said, holding his arms out. He noticed Casanova and JoJo and said, "What do we have here? Well, what do we have here? Very nice."

The entourage giggled and pointed at where Casanova's hand now was.

"Don't stop now!" said JoJo, annoyed.

"Yeah, yeah," said the cardigan-adorned angel, "don't stop on account of us. In fact . . ."

He turned to his entourage and clapped his hands three times. Immediately, the young men and women undressed and began to grope and kiss each other.

The angel nodded and smiled. "I'm so happy," he said, "because today I found my friends."

After the eighth cock, O wasn't sure if she could swallow any more man seed. Her stomach was getting full. Every man at the mission was pleased with her, though, especially Dwayne. The few women, standing in the corners, eyed her with envy. She started to wonder if she would have to somehow please them, too. She was ready, if necessary.

"You are worthy of Him," Dwayne said. "Yes, you are."

"I can only hope," O replied, softly, as semen dribbled out of her mouth and dangled off her chin.

"Stand up."

She was happy to get back on her feet; her knees were starting to get cramped and uncomfortable.

"Let's go."

"Where are we going?" asked O.

"To meet Him, of course."

"Oh!" said O.

"He'll be pleased with you."

"Who?" she asked.

"Who do you think?" returned Dwayne Deacon, winking.

D's flight landed on time at LAX. Near the baggage claim was a woman in a driver's uniform holding a placard that said "SARAH." Odd. She didn't see any other drivers with signs. D approached the woman and asked, "Are you here for me?"

"I guess that depends if you're Sarah," said the driver, her voice like ice.

"I used to be. Now I'm D."

"Of course. I'm your driver. Let's go."

"Where are we going?"

"To the office. Don't ask me questions, okay? I just drive. I don't have the answers."

The driver led D outside and to a black stretch limo. Nice. There was a wet bar and a TV inside. D made herself a vodka and tonic. There were many questions she wanted to ask the driver, but she knew to keep her mouth shut. The Power Company would have told her more if they thought she needed to know. She would take her orders and do whatever was required.

The driver was eyeing D in the rearview mirror.

D held up her glass and raised a brow.

"You're one hot bitch," said the driver.

"Why, thank you."

"I'd pull over and have a go with you whether you like doing women or not," said the driver, "but I've been instructed not to touch the goods."

"Well," D said, "that's too bad, isn't it?"

"I just drive. I don't get to have any fun."

Holding her hand, Dwayne led O to the decrepit house on Capitol Hill. It was late and drizzling outside. O told herself she was ready for anything. The inside smelled like dead fish, stale merlot, and fuck. Probably because there was a lot of fucking gong on. There were naked bodies all over the floor, bumping and grinding, kissing and licking, humping and jumping. Sitting on the floor, holding a paint-chipped Fender Mustang with a worn-down fret board, plugged into a 60-watt, two-speaker Carver guitar amp, was Him. That was definitely Him. She had seen his pictures, she knew his face. He looked at her with mild amusement.

"Dwayne Deacon, my brother in the Cause," said He, "what is it here that you have brought into my house?"

"A wonderful gift," said Dwayne, "one of the finest sluts I've ever come across."

He stood up and held out his arm, expecting her to go to Him. Of course, she would have, if her attention hadn't been diverted by what she saw on a grimy, ugly couch—a naked man whose body she knew: a naked man who was on his hands and knees, a funny expression on his face. A skinny, naked redheaded woman with tattoos all over her body was behind him, holding a tube of K-Y Jelly in one hand; her other hand was between the man's buttocks.

"Casanova!" she cried.

He looked up and appeared surprised. "O, my dear . . . fancy meeting you here."

"Indeed."

"Seems you have found me in a predicament."

"So it seems, Giacomo!"

"Well, I got three fingers up there!" exclaimed the naked redhead with pride. "Wanna go for more, Jack?"

"Why not," said Casanova, "why stop the fun?"

"May I help?" asked O.

"Hey," Dwayne interrupted, "He is here. You wanted to meet Him!"

"Who?" said O.

The limousine entered the underground parking lot of a fifteen-story building in downtown Los Angeles that was shaped like a phallus—its design was round with a bulb at the top. She had seen pictures of this building before. On the top, in red and blue lights, were the words FULL MOON RECORDS. The limo stopped and the driver turned and looked at D.

"Okay, sexy bitch. The elevator is over there. Take it to the top floor, the boss's penthouse suite and office. He's waiting for you."

D finished her drink and got out of the limo. Why didn't the driver open the door for her? Isn't that what drivers are supposed to do?

She knew the driver was watching her, so she put some extra sway into her walk as she made her way toward the elevator. In the elevator, she pressed 15. It was a swift ride up.

The top floor was large, circular, dark, and empty. There was a waterbed against the wall, and across the room stood a large glass desk. A man sat in the chair; he had a drink in his hand. D could smell the alcohol—Chivas Regal. She knew that smell. The smell took her back to . . .

"Come closer," the man said.

She took two steps forward.

"Closer."

She was shaking.

"What's the matter with you, wench?"

That voice . . . she knew that voice . . . didn't she?

She said, "I'm scared."

"Why?"

"I don't know."

He stood up. The lights from downtown LA glared across his face, and she saw who he was! Her first master! The one and only. D gasped and started to rush toward him—she was ready to jump over the desk—but he held up a hand and said, "Stop. Stay right there, right where you are."

Shaking, she stood still. She tried not to cry.

"Take off your clothes," he said, "now."

She didn't hesitate to get naked.

Once again, on display . . . for him.

"Very nice," he said, "your body is just as I remember it."

"I missed you so," said D.

"Get on the floor," he told her, "get on your hands and knees, with your sweet, round ass facing me."

She did as he commanded. She heard him walk toward her, then heard him loosening his belt and dropping his pants. She felt him positioning himself behind her, on his knees, his hands on her hips. She could feel the heat coming off his body and what she knew was his hard prick. He rubbed her pussy, but she was already dripping wet with the anticipation of this reconnection with her former master. When he entered her, she whispered, "Yes."

The limo driver was in the basement, listening to Orange Sky on the

CD player. She loved this evil band! She could only imagine what was being done to that hot bitch on the top floor. The driver opened up her pants and reached inside. She wasn't wearing panties. She imagined herself licking that hot bitch all over . . .

"Oh, yes! At last!" said Casanova, as his member finally became hard from O's oral administrations, while JoJo continued to slide three fingers in and out of his tender rear end.

Her former master vigorously fucked her; one hand pulled her hair, another explored her asshole. It was just like that first time, years ago, especially when he pulled out of her pussy and sodomized her.

They both fell to the floor, and he rapidly went in and out her. "It's so good to have you inside me again," she said, but he wasn't listening to her, he was only enjoying her, and that's all D ever wanted: to please him for the rest of her life and any other lives to follow.

After he spent himself, he got up to make himself another drink and sat at his desk. "Just stay there," he told her.

D remained on the floor and relished the sensation of his semen slowly leaking out of her ass.

"I never thought I'd see you again," she said.

"It was bound to happen," he said.

"How—," she started to say, but he told her to be quiet.

She lay on the floor. She was quiet.

He sipped his Chivas Regal and then told her how when he had left her at the apartment, naked and alone, he'd gone to London and started Full Moon Records with two partners. It was a small company, but they signed and distributed albums from a couple of new bands that had made it big, very big . . . and made him rich. "Including Orange Sky," he added, "have you heard of that band?"

"The name sounds familiar," D said, a little grin on her face.

"I have a new star, a potential star, a solo artist that I'll have to handpick a band for. Rocking Robby is what he calls himself, but we'll find a better name. I found him on a street corner, strumming an old acoustic guitar and singing out some very . . . interesting songs. Songs that I know will become top-ten hits if done right. Problem is, Robby isn't all that right in the head. But what rock star ever is?

"What Robby needs is a muse, a wanton whore, a woman who will be there for him and do anything he wants, sexually or otherwise, as he gets his first album done. Every woman he's known has broken his heart; he needs a woman who will heal him. There are plenty of women I could hire in Los Angeles to do this, but it would be artificial; it would merely be a job. I needed a woman who would take pleasure in such a thing, and who would do it for a purpose. Who would do it for me. And I thought of you. My sweet slave. So I put a phone call in to the Power Company."

"And here I am," said D.

"Here you are, dirty and willing as ever."

"I will do whatever you want."

"Of course you will."

She was allowed to wear only her shoes. Otherwise naked, still leaking cum, she was led by her former master back down to the basement. The limo driver didn't register any surprise. D and her former master entered the limousine. He gave the driver an address in Santa Monica.

The limo got on to the 10 West freeway. It was a little after midnight. "Traffic is light tonight," said her former master, looking out the window, one hand on her leg.

"Is there anything I can do for you?" D asked.

"You can suck my prick," he said.

That's what she wanted to hear! She curled up into his lap and took his cock out.

The limo driver watched in the rearview mirror.

The limo got off the freeway in Santa Monica, and drove to a set of bungalows near Pico Boulevard and Centinela Avenue. They passed a number of Oriental massage parlors, stripper bars, and prostitutes walking up and down the street. The area where the bungalows stood was dark and serene. The limo stopped, and the driver got out and opened the door.

"Move your ass," D's former master said. She did. She stepped out of the limo. She was cold. Her nipples were hard.

He got out after her and led her to one of the little bungalows. He knocked on the door. "Robby, it's me."

"Door's unlocked," a male voice inside said. "Come in, bro."

D and her former master walked into the bungalow. It was small and smelled like incense and marijuana. There were a lot of beanbags on the floor, and three TV sets, each tuned to a different channel, no sound. The only other light came from two white candles. Sitting on a beanbag, with an acoustic guitar, was a man in his mid-twenties, thin, shirtless, wearing boxers; he had long black hair and several days' growth of beard. He was handsome, but there was something about his eyes—they were crazy eyes. Green, but crazy.

"Is this her?" the man asked.

"As promised," said D's former master. "She will help you."

"She looks like she can help. Thanks, bro. You're the best."

"Now get to work. Good-bye for now," D's former master said, kissing her on the forehead.

She wanted to ask when she would next see him, but she knew better. Her former master left. She heard him get into the limo and leave. She stood naked in front of Rocking Robby.

"Come here," Robby told her, "sit next to me," and he patted one of the beanbags.

She went to him.

"Nice, very nice," he said, looking her body over.

"Do you want to fuck me now?" she asked. "I'm here to do whatever you want. Use me whatever way you need."

"I'll fuck you later," he said, "but right now I want you to hear one of my songs. I need your ear, and your opinion. Okay?"

"All right."

He strummed the guitar. "Ideally this will be loud, full of feedback, and then something like the James Bond theme song comes on, then stops, and then something very grungy or metal."

Then he sang his song, what he called "Bad Girlfriend."

> *Bad girlfriend*
> *She always tells me lies*
> *Bad girlfriend*
> *I think she sleeps with spies*
>
> *So she's walking down the street*
> *Late at night, she's such a treat*
> *She walks into any bar*
> *Leaves with strange men in their car*
> *She walks into a saloon*
> *With a smile like a balloon*
> *She puts her hands on her hips*
> *And says, "Baby, let's turn some tricks"*
>
> *Bad girlfriend*
> *She never tells the truth*

Bad girlfriend
Her head's a-bobbing in a booth

"And that's the song so far," Robby said.

She clapped. What else could she do?

"It's the first song in an album I want to call *Sad Ballads about Cocks and Cunts*. Mostly rock and blues, with one real ballad called 'She Wants to Marry Every Man but Me.' Other songs will be called 'Metaphysical Bitch' and 'Pan-dimensional Itch.' Just before you came over, I was working on what will be a twelve-bar blues diddy called 'Cocksucker.' "

"How about 'Cocksucker Blues'?" D suggested.

"Hey, I like that. Yeah, I like that. I can change the lyrics better. Do you want to hear what I have?"

"Of course."

Robby started in on a blues riff in G and F, then sang more obscene doggerel. D's mind wandered until Robby's song came to its natural end.

"Yeah," D finally said, clapping her hands.

"What do you think?" Robby said.

"I think your cock needs to get out of the blues and get sucked," D said, still swishing some of her former master's semen in her mouth.

She needed more, and Robby needed what she had to offer.

"That's a great idea," Robby said, pulling off his boxer shorts.

It was past noon when Casanova and O woke up. They were still naked and in each other's arms on the stained couch. It was raining hard outside. The house smelled something awful, worse than before. All the fucking people who were here last night, having fun, were gone.

Casanova had a bad taste in his mouth. The blond man in the cardigan sweater was sitting on the floor, playing an acoustic guitar, mumbling something about being on a plain and not complaining.

"Oh," said O, and hugged Casanova.

"Why are you always slipping away from my grasp?" he asked her, softly.

"It's simply in her nature," the blond man in the cardigan sweater said.

"Who are you, sir?" asked Casanova. "I never did get your name."

"You can call me K."

"K?"

"K, okay?"

"If you insist."

"It's Him," O said, getting off the couch and bowing, as if in prayer.

"Not quite, but close," said K. "I don't know about you two, but I'm starving. Let's go get some lunch and have a chat about the nature of everything and the meaning of nothing."

Chapter Eleven

Though the sky was overcast, the light seared Casanova's eyes like a white-hot blade. Somehow stepping into the day was a shock, but he pushed himself along, wanting to get as far from the putrid couch and possible return of peasants as possible. He was tired of an audience and other participants, no matter what they had to offer. He just wanted O to himself again, so he could get to know her and understand his feelings more fully, what he might even have called love. K was an irritation and an impediment.

"Starbucks will do us," said K. "Your girlfriend needs some strong coffee."

My girlfriend, Casanova thought, such a modest expression for the feelings overwhelming his life, yet it implied that K understood something of their attachment. He held O's limp hand as they followed K down the wet sidewalk. She walked with her usual sensuous sway, the ripped skirt occasionally allowing a glimpse of glorious cunt, which he tried to cover from passing children, but her face conveyed no feeling, and the dark pupils of her eyes were huge, giving her an innocence he wanted to protect, especially from K. It wouldn't be easy. He himself felt detached from his body, fatigued, and had to stop again and again from grinding his molars.

He thought he remembered the way to Starbucks, but so much of

the new world looked exactly the same that when K took an unexpected turn, he was not surprised to see the café at his side, as if it had
been moved there in one piece. The green placard above the door was
the same—the tables, the list of beverages—yet there were subtle differences in the brickwork. Another Starbucks. Why?

K held the door, and Casanova passed him and pulled out a chair
for O. He wasn't hungry, and K, His Godliness, did not impress him.
All he really wanted was to get O away to a private hotel room for a
nap, but that might take some convincing.

K went to the counter for mocha lattes and Casanova patted O's
hand. She gazed out the window. He glanced across the street. There
was a Body Shop and a Gap. He had seen those shops before, too, several times. The peek into a Body Shop window had been a colossal
disappointment—bath salts and soaps, when he had expected a display of the lovely body parts that women could now purchase to
enhance themselves.

He continued to be wrong about so many things, and there was
much he didn't understand. What was the purpose of making everything the same? Were there so few good things in existence that they
all must be repeated? No difference in taste? He had always considered his ability to adapt to every circumstance as a virtue, but he
wasn't sure he wanted to adapt anymore. There were ideas and pleasures from his era worth saving. Of course, there was no way of doing
so. These people were so deprived of the individuality and leisure he
had known that they would never understand the concepts. Everything was a swirling blend, a single mixture of culture, race—and sex.
Often he even failed to identify the men from the women, especially
in Key West, where things seemed to have progressed more swiftly.
Not only the attire, but the minds and bodies underneath were often
indistinguishable. Changing one's sex was still unusual, but now with

the ability to choose, why not choose both? It was just a matter of time till that became popular, and although the occasional fling with a talented hermaphrodite was stimulating, he envisioned a world of hermaphrodites as tiring beyond even his capacity.

He glanced at the shoppers and their children strolling by and felt sorry for them. No one was special, and all was communicated publicly and instantly. He felt sorry for himself, too, merely ordinary in a world where no type of consensual sex was forbidden. Wilt Chamberlain—a ball player by trade—had surpassed his number of sexual conquests two hundred times over and published a book about it. According to the Internet, Casanova's legend "paled by comparison" to the seven-foot giant's, and he knew there was no chance for his writing or his life to shine forth in the present flood of information. He had gleaned this staggering information while still in Venice when sweet Cristiana had been teaching him the ways of this brave, if hardy new world.

K brought the lattes to the table on a tray with pastries and sandwiches. "Help yourself," he said. Casanova nodded. K was generous to people he barely knew, perhaps because he could see they were like everybody else. Casanova supposed this was the bright side. In some future century with all people the same and nothing to desire, wars would cease, and life would be easy.

He selected a dark chocolate square, heavy and moist, and decided that the experience of Starbucks, as much else, was indeed worth repeating. He was adept at hedonistic enjoyment, and the new array of substances to ingest and the freedom of sexual indulgence, without the responsibility of begetting a child, were obviously the keys to life as it had evolved. Perhaps this was why he had been resurrected and transported to this particular time, where he fit the mold, unlike the era in which he had been born. His gloom lifted further as he drank his latte and sipped at the vision of O's cleavage, which was taking on a healthy color. Her breasts were perfect, as were all the breasts he'd encountered so far, some of them possibly purchased, but all of them undeniably satisfying to suck and palm. He had found her, and she was all that mattered to him.

As K discussed his popularity and outlined the plans for his next recording, Casanova only hoped that O was with him in her thoughts, eager to detach from her "God" and find the hotel. She nodded occasionally but said nothing, and he wasn't sure if she was still in a drug-induced state or entranced with K.

At some point the silence alerted Casanova that K had finished speaking. O was taking her last sip of latte. Casanova stood and gathered their napkins and cups onto the trays as he had observed others doing. O wiped her lips and stood up.

"We thank you heartily for the delights, good sir," said Casanova. "I hope one day to repay the favor." He took the trays and remains to the proper bins, then took O's hand and bowed as he moved her toward the door.

K stood and followed. "You're welcome. Let's go to my place. I have anything you want."

Casanova put his arm around O's waist. "Another time, good sir. We really must go. Many appointments to keep."

K took O's hand to his mouth and sucked her middle finger. "What about you, baby girl? My place?"

She laughed and the rip in her skirt widened as her legs moved apart. K's eyes flicked downward and his mouth opened.

Casanova could feel his cock swell and heat rush to his head. He grabbed O's wrist, worried that she would object, but unable to stop himself. He pulled her closer to his side and positioned his body, chest up, in a wide stance that was immediately and correctly interpreted

171

by K, no matter that it was centuries old. K took a step back. He looked at O.

"All righty then, if that's your plan. But you might not get another chance with me."

Casanova knew that he would have to give in to O's wishes, but he stood his ground, waiting for her verdict.

O made a face. "We're outta here," she said, her eyes finally now focused and clear as the drugs began to loosen their hold on her will. She passed K, who was still following the slit in her skirt with his eyes.

As they stepped outside, Casanova took the direction opposite K and moved O swiftly along beside him.

"I'm doing so well with the American language, yes?" O said. She looked back over her shoulder. "What a bore! I don't care if he *is* God. He's too fucking full of himself. Yucko."

"I agree," said Casanova, "Yucko." Being "full of himself" seemed paradoxical, and "fucking full" did nothing to clarify the expression, but all he wanted was distance from the man. O seemed to brighten with the exercise, so he kept up the pace and hoped he would soon see a street he recognized in order to find his hotel.

"Yes!" said O, halting before a shop window of pink and white lace undergarments. "Victoria's Secret. I am sick of every idiot in town staring into my crotch. This isn't New Orleans or Key West, baby. Do you have some money?"

"Certainly," he said, and pulled out a large roll from his money belt, pushing it all into her delicate fingers. Luckily, he had learned the use of the always-available ATM. He was surprised at her desire for undergarments. Apparently there were some boundaries that he didn't understand. He had seen the looks from some unshaven street fellows, and could tell that there were levels of pain in the new world that went beyond recovery. Being unarmed, he would truly feel better if she were to cover up. This was a grand opportunity to show his worth as a gentleman.

"My dear," she said, "you wait here. I want to surprise you later."

He was stung with the fear that he might lose her again, but he had no choice, being uninvited. He stepped back as she opened the door. An atmosphere heavy with flowery scents engulfed him, making his eyes water. He snuffled. "I'll explore the shops nearby while you talk with Victoria. Just wait here if you don't see me."

O frowned and then wrinkled up her nose in a girlish snort. Then she kissed him on the cheek and dashed inside. He was left to ponder the direction of his hotel, and to worry about O.

He looked left and right, but nothing was familiar. Two doors down the name of a shop, "Something Wicked . . ." caught his attention. It was a phrase from the famous playwright Shakespeare, a bit before his own time—uncanny how many of his lines remained in the language. Casanova had a continued interest in activities others deemed "wicked," such as magic and the occult, and although he had landed in prison in his first lifetime for being involved in such activities, here, in an age of free thinking, he was not surprised that magic would be openly promoted. A potion or spell to assure O's fidelity was just what he needed.

As usual, the name of the shop was misleading. The window contained small painted figures, "Bart Simpson," "Spiderman," many strange creatures sprouting fiery hair or other frightening features, and among them, erotically dressed women figures, reminding him of the Power Company females. "Collectibles," the sign said. Tall, skeletal figures beckoned him inside, and he could see shelves of books, jewelry made of bones, and bins of colorful items. Magic, after all, perhaps.

He looked back at the door of Madam Victoria's. Some things

hadn't changed over the centuries, and he felt he had plenty of time before O would emerge with her purchases. The thought of her swollen pink vulva, slippery and hot under loose white lace, engorged his cock, and his erection pressed against the stiff fabric of his trousers. At any second he might ejaculate in his pants like a schoolboy, standing on the street. Oh, to move the lace aside with one finger and lick the drops of salty sauce from just inside her honey cunt, hardening her clit, and dragging his tongue from her delicate slot to the rosy, bittersweet hole of her ass . . .

He paused in the doorway and quieted his breath. He would hire a taxi to find the hotel. It wouldn't be long until he stroked her silken lips with velvet-headed flesh and plunged himself, hard and eager, inside her meaty, gripping walls. . . . *Stop.* Patience was not often required in this world, but he had practiced it successfully in the past, and was often rewarded. He remembered an orgasm of such hot, tight release that it had drained him and laid him flat. He was unable to move or care that the candle had fallen and caught one corner of the bedclothes on fire, though the servant was slow in putting it out.

He glanced back—still no O—and stepped into the collectible shop. It smelled of incense, and the quantity of goods was dizzying. A woman of regal proportions raised her head above a counter. "Can I help you?"

"I . . . yes. Do you have love potions available?"

"Real potions? No, but I have books that tell you how to make them."

"That would be helpful," he said.

She pointed to a shelf on the left and he started toward it, but there on a round rack was a figure that made him gasp. "It is me!"

" 'Scuse me?"

"Nothing," he said.

He stooped down to pull the package from its hook. The word

Casanova was printed in big letters and *Giovanni Giacomo* in smaller print. Impossible! He was a collectible? What did it mean?

The hair was somewhat more reddish than his own, but the nose was perfect, and his eyes had the devilish stare that he had often been accused of. Amazing. The small figure held a black mask and wore a bright blue coat over an ugly green vest and a silver ascot. Truly a gaudy imitation of the finery he once wore, but nevertheless, his face was handsome and his body well formed. *Action Figure.* The arms were hinged to move. He turned over the package and found his history printed on the back in four sections: *Lover, Adventurer, Author, and Legend.*

Joyous spirits filled his chest and his laughter bubbled out, surprising him. The woman stretched her neck to squint at him over her counter. Ha! To be remembered and collected, more than two hundred years after his death, in all his glory! He looked at the other figures nearby, no Wilt Chamberlain, but there was the irritating Mozart—a bit disturbing—and some other fellows of action, Sigmund Freud, Edgar Allan Poe, Albert Einstein. He would have to find out about them on the Internet when he had time.

He turned over his own package and read. Mostly accurate. Damnation! An "Interesting Fact" reported that he had been expelled from the seminary for scandalous conduct. Did the whole world know of that? And there it was, "sentenced to five years in prison for his involvement in occult activities . . . escaped on Halloween a year later." No doubt this was the reason his action figure held a mask.

"Ah." He read the last line of his legend aloud, "a caring and thoughtful lover who had honest feelings for many of the women he had relations with."

The woman looked up, but he shook his head and smiled down at himself. It was a triumph—to be judged well by enlightened generations after his, remembered, molded, cast into eternal form, and distributed to the masses. "Caution: Small parts not suitable for children under 36 months." Certainly not.

He took his prize and approached the woman. This was amusing; he had to acquire the figure almost as a matter of pride.

"Eight fifty, plus tax."

He handed over Brad's credit card, remembering he had given all his money to O. He was now beginning to understand fully the virtue of having deposited his funds in a bank back in Italy at Cristiana's insistence. *O!,* he suddenly remembered. He had no idea how long he had been standing in the shop.

As the woman completed the charge, he ran to the door and looked down the street at Victoria's. No O. He signed quickly and took his package. As he turned, he saw a quizzical expression on the woman's face, and he knew he had been recognized.

He dashed outside and strode into Victoria's, looking around for O, praying that she hadn't left him. The scents clogged his nose, and his eyes burned as he searched up one rack of corsets and garters and down another of sheer silk dressing gowns. His feeling of triumph dissolved into pity, then anger, as he berated himself for his vanity and inconsideration. Or perhaps this had been her plan all along?

But there she was! Sliding pink paper bags from the counter, talking to a petite blonde nearly hidden by the pile of merchandise. He rushed up to O. "Sweet love! I thought I'd missed you!"

"I have a big surprise for you," she said. She held out her hand to present the blonde, who was now peering around the bags.

"Cristiana! I've been so worried!" In truth, she had been in his thoughts just a moment ago.

"Really?"

"I . . . yes. I didn't know how to find you." He took her hand and kissed it.

"I recognized her instantly," said O. "She hooked up with a guy in Key West, after the boat boarded."

"A skydiver in Sugarloaf Key. He taught me how to skydive—I have twenty jumps in my logbook already. We came here to escape the heat. I'm doing some part-time work here to earn some extra cash."

"That's wonderful," said Casanova. We must meet for dinner." He turned to O.

"We need to find a taxi to my hotel."

"No, no! Cristiana and I have a plan that's much more exciting! But you go on."

He couldn't think of anything more exciting than getting her into a soft bed, fucking and napping, but he could tell by her voice that he must take part in whatever they had decided. He dare not let O out of his sight again.

"Cristiana is finished working in half an hour. She's going to take us skydiving."

"Skydiving?" asked Casanova. "What exactly is that?"

"You will love it," O said. "But first we have to stop at the Gap."

The weather had cleared in late afternoon. Strapped naked to Jason, the rugged, dark tandem master whom she had selected, O viewed pure blue sky from the window of the small Cessna. His hands rested on her thighs, his tan, slender fingers once touching her pubic hair, but innocently, with no other place to go, since she was attached to him by short nylon straps and perched half on his lap by necessity, his muscular legs spread under hers, thighs supporting her bare ass in comfort. He had been gentle as he hooked her up, not touching her bare skin except where necessary—but necessary often—and his eyes floated over her as he pulled her close to carefully clip her harness to his and inspect the connections.

She had been told the ride to altitude would be chilly in the nude, but well worth the cold for the extreme "airgasm" on the fast trip down. Nudity was a common skydiving practice to increase the thrill. Right now, her thoughts were hot enough to keep her body warm. She could feel an erection jabbing between her cheeks through Jason's cotton jump suit, and she felt the slipperiness in her vagina, a trickle of juice, at the thought of maybe fucking him later.

As the plane ascended toward twelve thousand feet, the air cooled and dried, and she found she had to lick her teeth to keep her lips from sticking to them, unable to remove the wide grin from her face. She couldn't remember a feeling like this, both wonderful and terrifying, acceptance of the universe, to live or die!

The sexual heights she had reached, the repeated instruction and practice of her past, enabled her to call up a hot ripple of pleasure through her body anytime she wanted, when alone, or to relieve boring activity, and she would never have given that up, but her choices and abilities were ready to expand. So many feelings to explore, new avenues of challenge. The sky was not the limit.

Cristiana was seated nude, except for the rig on her back, with her legs crossed, her smooth, compact figure close to the door, ready to jump alone. She winked back at O, grinned wide, and reached to stroke O's palm with two fingers, a seeming good-luck gesture. Then she flicked her tongue and pulled her knees toward her chest so O could see the shaved pink pouch of her lips, giving O's cunt a surge of memory of their last contact. A delicate silver post through Cristiana's clit sparkled in O's direction, a piercing to be gently tongued or tugged.

If O hadn't been strapped to Jason, she would have crawled between Cristiana's thighs, to return the earlier favor, working her clit until she gushed onto the floor of the plane. None of the men would mind. She was irresistible, dark brown nipples hard with the chill and tits pushed up by the chest strap. O licked her lips. She wanted to taste all of her, suck her mouth, and breathe in the flowery, musk-tinged scent that followed Cristiana from the lingerie shop. The girl was amazing, rigged up in her own parachute, secure in her ability to survive, and eager to take the plunge. They would become good friends if the future allowed.

O turned to Casanova seated beside her. He was clothed and strapped to another male skydiver, and his eyes were frozen on the window across from him. He seemed to lack interest in Cristiana's beautiful display of cunt. From his face, it seemed that he'd never been in a plane before. Decidedly, this was much more a test of his devotion than O had realized.

"Isn't this great?" she asked him. "Fantastic?"

He was pale, and his lips were tight. To get his attention over the engine roar, she tapped his thigh. "Great, no?"

He jumped, then nodded and smiled with fake enthusiasm.

"Sick?"

"No. Fine."

She patted his hand. For a second, she felt guilty for dragging him, using his obvious obsession and his credit card to fuel her expensive fun. But then again, he seemed to pride himself on having an adventurous spirit. He should appreciate the chance to gain the understanding of self that is only discovered in extremes. She had learned that through the hands of others, and it was a good lesson. But from now on, O would do things her way.

"Door!" the pilot yelled.

Cristiana pushed up the clear panel. The wind outroared the engine as she knelt on her hands and knees, looking down at the far-off ground, unaware of the tantalizing back view of the split of her ass. "Cut!" she yelled. The engine slowed, and in a blink she had tossed herself out and disappeared, her wild yell, "Yahoo!" ripped away by the wind.

Jason gave O a "thumbs up," and they edged toward the open square of blue. With the air whipping between her thighs, her wet opening was instantly dry. But she was hot as well as cold. She crossed her arms over her breasts as instructed. Sitting at the edge of the door, with her legs dangling in the wind, she felt stimulated but alone, despite Jason's presence four inches behind her, ready to push. Her chest heaved with the recognition that she was about to let herself drop, loose, toward the distant earth. And then . . . before thought came feeling . . . a smooth blast into nothing . . . all speed . . . no bonds . . . a semiconscious flickering—which way was down? No worries.

Jason gave her a tap. It meant to open up and fly. She flung her arms wide. She was a bird! Her eyes focused and her head cleared. Mountains and the Puget Sound, misty silver lakes and deep blue forests, the edge of the city—the beautiful sight was inspiring. She gulped in the vision like it all belonged to her, and felt her body, every inch. She set her thoughts on the wind searing her cunt, reaming her asshole, the invisible strength compressing her breasts, playing with her nipples, stimulating all her skin at once.

The skydiver on her back was necessary equipment, but the experience was all hers. She let herself go deeply into the flood of natural ecstasy, a long, cleansing rush that rolled from head to toe, leaving a tight tingle in her cunt, energizing her with a hard, true feeling of survival and delight. The ground was still far below, but she was confident that the parachute would open when it was time. She could do anything. She had found her god. She was filled with him!

Cristiana had told O that the skydivers often built a bonfire at the airport at night, drinking, smoking dope, playing with fire. They had adopted favorite pastimes like "Clits and Dicks," where everyone took turns flaunting their wares in the firelight, and "Monkey See, Monkey

Do," a game two women would start by kissing each other, daring a pair of heterosexual men to repeat their actions as they intensified. Sometimes a skydiver trained to do piercings would invite an audience as he did free work on a tongue, nipples, clitoris, or penis. This was how, Casanova learned, Cristiana had obtained hers. He still recalled the natural look of her abundant pubic hair and thick labia.

However, rain was predicted for that evening, so Cristiana had given directions for O and Casanova to join the skydiving crowd at a bar near the drop zone owned by one of the skydivers, where beer was cheap and skydive videos played all night. Rules were nonexistent. "No adult supervision," Cristiana had said, laughing.

Arriving at the bar, it was soon obvious to O that quantities of alcohol and drugs were the next order of adventure for skydivers. Surely sex would soon follow. She glanced around for Jason, but he wasn't in sight. The men outnumbered the women by more than double, so each woman had as many flirting admirers as she could handle. A petite girl with pierced nipples had her shirt off and seemed about to demonstrate a jump from the bar, helpful hands offering to catch her. Cristiana, wearing a thin half T-shirt and cutoff jeans, stood in a circle with four men and seemed to be involved in some choreography related to skydiving that required repeated touching under the edges of her cutoffs and between her breasts.

O took a table where she could watch the door for her jump master. She was still high from the jump, and when Casanova brought her a Corona with lime, she took a gulp and felt she had never tasted anything better.

He sat next to her and massaged her thigh through her new Gap jeans. His eyes were bright and his face animated. "They tell me orgasms are extraordinary after an adrenaline rush."

"I certainly believe it," she said. Her head turned involuntarily as

Jason came through the door, clean shaven, hair damp, wearing a fresh white T-shirt and jeans. He had sleepy eyes and long lashes she had been too excited to notice before. He looked around as he headed to the bar.

"Jason!" She waved her arm and his face opened into a wicked grin, his earrings catching light as if to dazzle O further. She had formed an instant bond with him, as if they had done X together.

He came to the table. She jumped from her chair and flung her arms around him in a hug. Her breasts were loose inside her T-shirt, and she pressed them into his ribs, standing on her toes as she kissed his smooth tan cheek. "Thank you so much for the jump," she said.

"Any time." His eyes fell downward to the peaks of her nipples, body language O understood.

He pointed at her beer. "Ah, the next step after a skydive."

She nodded and smiled slowly, running her fingers down his firm chest as she freed him from the hug. "I plan to make it a long evening."

"Can I get you a beverage, Jason?" Casanova asked.

"Sure, Corona. Thank you, Cas."

They drank a few, and then Casanova wandered over to watch what Cristiana was doing on the bar. He already knew inside his heart that O had drifted away from him, for tonight at least. But somehow, he was also aware that fate had brought them together for a reason and that he must be magnanimous and patient and wait for the right time and place.

O could see in glimpses between the crowd that Cristiana had unzipped her jeans down to the start of her pubic hair, and men and women were lined up taking turns doing tequila shots from her navel. Her arms were bent at the elbows, hands cushioning her head, legs spread wide, relaxed in pleasure. The preliminary lime bite was accompanied by a finger or two down her crotch from one fellow, as another pulled up her T-shirt and sucked her nipples. They were an enthusiastic group, and O expected they could hold their alcohol as well as keep Cristiana busy for a while. Casanova moved closer to the bar. How could she have changed so much since Venice? How could women be so fickle in this damn century?

O visualized Cristiana's pierced clit, and her cunt started to ache with a need to come. She looked at Jason, biting her bottom lip.

His white teeth gleamed back. "Leave your friend?" He motioned toward Casanova.

O shrugged. "He'll be okay. He's enjoying himself, I think."

Jason's small trailer was mostly taken up by a huge bed under a jumble of blankets. As they stepped inside, he pointed at the refrigerator. "Beer?"

"No."

He started to reach for one, but she leaped on him, flinging the door shut and tumbling his muscular body into the bed. She sprawled over his hips, breathless, pressing his chest to keep him down. A brown and white puppy that had been sleeping on the pillows lifted its head.

"I can't wait to get inside your pants," she said. "I felt your big cock against my ass."

"You can feel my big cock wherever you want," he said, and the rock-hard crotch of his jeans backed up his words. He lifted her T-shirt over her head and cupped her breasts to rub his nose and lips over them, rubbing, sucking, licking, good hard stimulation that didn't hurt but brought saliva to her mouth, craving his cock.

She unzipped him and pulled down his jeans, and he kicked them off into a corner. His smooth cock rose, stiff, in front of her, and she saw that it was adorned with a row of six fine rings from the edge of the head in a straight line down the shaft. She took him to the root, working her lips up and down, sliding over the rings that she knew would give her pleasure, shielding him from her teeth, except for a gentle nip, grazing his thighs, lifting his balls, and tracing the cracks that sometimes get neglected. He kept his hands tight at his sides so she was free to move her head as she pleased, but his groans and taut position told her that he was near bursting.

She stripped off her jeans and straddled him in a deep squat, slipping down his hard shaft, then up and down, able to balance on her feet without touching any other part of his body. The rings rippled like keys on a piano, against the outer edges of her cunt as she gripped and released with her sensitive, trained muscles, intense waves of pleasure spreading upward, hot juice running down to his groin. She pivoted slowly, without lifting herself, until she faced his legs and could squeeze his balls as she squatted up and down. He hardened even more, as she knew he would, with the view of her beautiful ass.

She leaned forward and let the rings catch on her clit one by one as she descended, putting her over the last edge, so she had to put her hands on his thighs to hold herself steady. A roar in her head, like the engine of the plane, blotted the world out of existence.

She concentrated all feeling into her cunt and rode him out, peaking in short bursts as she slid over the rings, until he gave a long, low groan and she joined him in one hard, final orgasm, letting herself empty completely.

Her legs shook and she dropped down on his chest, panting and sweaty, kissing a nipple the best she could without raising her head. She reached up her hand to pet the dog still on the upper corner of the pillow, undoubtedly used to sharing Jason's bed. He licked her hand with his soft warm tongue. She drifted off.

Chapter Twelve

After her experience with Jason, O slept hard, succumbing to a sleep without dreams. Nonetheless, the feel of a needle sliding into her vein woke her with a start. Her eyes wide, she went to sit up—but was held down by Jason's strong arm across her shoulders as he depressed the plunger of the syringe in her forearm.

With her eyes still blurred by sleep, she looked up into Jason's face and saw a smile marred by cruelty and a hint of sadness.

"What," she began, but her tongue already felt thick in her mouth, the drugs in the syringe already affecting her. She struggled briefly, then went slack as she began to lose consciousness again.

The last thing she heard before returning to unconsciousness was Jason's voice: "Sorry, baby. You were great. But you belong to someone else. He paid good money for you."

Then she was gone, lost in blackness.

Occupied as he was by a petite girl with pierced nipples whose mouth rose and fell rhythmically on his cock, Casanova took quite some time to realize that O had departed. She had not just drifted away from him—she had left the bar altogether. Though the petite girl showed great skill with his member, he felt a sudden longing for O and found himself unable to reach his completion. He gently eased the girl's mouth off of his cock, her face out of his crotch.

"Don't you like what I'm doing?" she said with a smile.

"Very much," lied Casanova. While it had been quite an enthusiastic ministration, inwardly he cursed himself for having lost track of O again. "But I need to find my companion."

"She's on the bar," said the girl, whose name Casanova had forgotten almost the moment she had told it to him.

Casanova looked over to where Cristiana sat on the edge of the bar, having long since lost the skin-tight cutoff jeans she wore. Her legs were spread, and one of the men who'd earlier been crowded around her was applying his mouth to her exposed sex. Another man, positioned behind the bar, was kissing Cristiana deeply and fondling her small breasts, one hand tucked firmly under the tight half T-shirt she wore.

"Not that one," he said.

"Oh," replied the petite girl, seemingly disinterested in Casanova's problems. She placed a series of kisses down Casanova's belly and let her tongue draw a circle around the glistening head of his prick. "She left with Jason." She then returned her attentions to Casanova's cock and began to suck him eagerly.

"I need to find her," said Casanova with a sigh as the slender girl swallowed his cock to the hilt. She ignored his entreaty, and Casanova let her keep sucking him, soothed by the knowledge that at least O was somewhere she could be found. His sigh turned into a moan, and despite his worry he allowed the small girl to finish him off.

Meanwhile, Cristiana kept occupied on the bar, leaning well back so she could take the man's cock in her mouth. She, like Casanova, had forgotten her partner's name almost as soon as it was told to her. Of course, he was only one of her partners, as the man between her legs was still expertly tonguing her clit—and her hand, almost of its own volition, had reached out and found an anonymous cock, hard and already oozing precum, belonging to a man whose name she had never known in the first place. She began stroking it firmly, her mouth full of cock and the skillful tongue on her clit driving her urgently toward an orgasm.

It was true what they said, she decided. Sex really *was* better after an adrenaline rush.

D sprawled face down over the beanbag chair, leaking Robby's come not only from her sex but from her rear entrance, which he had used quite as urgently even after orgasming in her cunt.

After using her, Robby put to good use the three-foot-tall skull-shaped bong in one corner of the room and was now sprawled nearby on the floor, stoned out of his gourd. D had accepted a hit or two before he fucked her, and was still pleasantly high. Robby had fucked her enthusiastically enough to leave her a little sore, however—fueled, no doubt, by the three lines of cocaine he'd snorted off her ass. Dimly, D heard the door opening.

"Come with me," came the voice of D's first master.

She knew better than to disobey that voice—in fact, it was utterly beyond her nature to do so. She rose painfully from the beanbag chair and began to look around for her clothes.

"Don't get dressed," growled her master, with obvious annoyance. "Come as you are."

Some distant part of D was surprised that she could still blush. Then again, it had been quite some time since she had regularly received such orders from her master. Nonetheless, she obeyed, lowering her eyes and saying softly, "Yes, sir."

Robby took a deep drag on his cigarette and called after them:

"Sure you don't want to leave her for a while longer? I wouldn't mind giving her another go."

Master chuckled. "I'm afraid we've got business up north," he said, and D followed him out the door. Following her master at a respectful distance—three steps behind—she walked naked down the long, cold corridor of the office building, only once passing a man in jeans and a T-shirt, who ogled her shamelessly. She saw her master turn his head, and for a moment she thought he was going to give her to the stranger. But there was evidently no time for that. Instead, he led his slave down a corridor. Now barefoot, she noticed the rough carpet abrading the soles of her feet. She was led to an elevator, which descended the dozen-plus stories to the basement parking garage.

Though D, as a slave, was well acquainted with the sensation of being naked before others, she was still relieved that they passed only a few people walking to their cars—all of them men. Each time, she felt a quiver between her legs as her master made eye contact with the strangers, and she wondered if he might require her to service the stranger. She could still feel Robby's come dripping down the insides and the backs of her thighs, and if she had needed any reminder of her status, that would have provided it in spades.

The limousine was waiting at the end of a long line of parked cars; the black-suited driver held the door, his eyes openly appraising D's naked body. Her master climbed into the back of the limousine, and she followed, well aware that her soiled bottom would leave a streak of come on the plush seats. The driver closed the door. Behind the shaded windows, D felt safe from inquisitive eyes—but the disapproving look her master gave her was enough to strip her to the bone.

She knew better than to ask her master where precisely they were going or what business they might have "up north"—but he volunteered all the information she needed.

"You were assigned a simple task," he said. "Serve him in every way possible. Do whatever he required. I would have thought you would be well acquainted with that task and would be able to fulfill it with no trouble."

D's throat felt tight, constricted,—and not just because of the thorough plumbing it had gotten from Robby's cock. She finally managed to speak.

"I'm sorry, Master. He's . . . an unusual man."

"To say the least," growled the master. "Your excuses are meaningless. You're being returned to the Power Company for punishment."

Despite the shiver of fear that went through D's naked body, she felt a heat growing between her legs. She had failed at serving Casanova,—had not even stayed with him. Whatever was to be done to her, she deserved it. But what could be done to her that hadn't been done before? Lashings, canings, cuttings, sexual violation, utter humiliation—she had endured all those and more, hungering for greater degradation with each ordeal she suffered. What punishment had not been visited upon her?

D knew the Power Company well,—as well as she knew her first master. She had confidence that they would find something.

By the time Casanova convinced the petite girl to take him to Jason's trailer, he had lost track of time.—O might have been gone for two hours, or six, or twelve. What he did know is that it was still dark, but he could smell and see the pregnant promise of dawn swelling just over the horizon. Before leaving the mostly depleted orgy, he found out for the second time—and this time did not immediately forget— that the slender girl's name was Lilah. Though with her small size and elfin looks she could have passed for nineteen, the slight lines around her eyes told Casanova that she was at least in her mid-twenties. Her hair was clipped close, and an array of silver earrings depended from her ears. She was quite beautiful,—the sort of woman that Casanova, in other circumstances, would have focused all his attentions—for a time—on bedding. The circumstances in this case, however, were somewhat different.

Cristiana, having satisfied herself—and a number of the men present—had agreed to come along, though after her performance on the bar (and the barstools, and several tables), she languished in the backseat of Lilah's old Volkswagen, lolling in and out of sleep.

How long ago it seemed that Casanova had encountered Cristiana in Venice—and found her a naïve ingénue, hungry to learn the ways of the flesh. She had learned, all right, and in contrast to many of his long-ago liaisons, Casanova had not been the one to teach her. Or at least not the only one.

Lilah pulled off the street onto a dirt road marked Windy Pines Trailer Park. She drove down endless lines of small, dilapidated metal buildings, some of them with wheels and others propped up on short stalks. Though the park was mostly quiet, a couple of the trailers had people out front, drinking beer. They gave Lilah's car suspicious looks as it passed.

"Here it is," said Lilah, pulling up in front of one of the trailers near the back of the park. It abutted a thick copse of trees. "I gotta tell you, though, I'd bet they're still busy in there." She smiled mischievously and giggled a little. "Jason, he kinda . . . goes all night." The giggle, combined with the expression on her face, made it quite clear to Casanova that Lilah knew firsthand how long Jason tended to "go."

"Don't worry," said Casanova coldly. "I'll knock first."

As Casanova went to get out of the VW, Lilah reached out and grabbed his arm.

"You're not, like, her husband, are you? Are you gonna go all Jerry Springer?"

Casanova frowned; he wasn't familiar with Jerry Springer, but assumed he was some kind of famous murderer.

"No, of course not," said Casanova. "It's nothing like that." Lilah didn't seem convinced, so he added: "It's well behind my nature to hurt her. And I certainly have no grievance with him."

He left the car and approached the trailer. The place seemed deserted—the lights were out, and not a sound came from inside—even after Casanova had knocked several times on the door.

Lilah got out of the VW, leaving Cristiana dozing in the back. "Maybe they went out for something to eat?"

Casanova tried the door and found it open. Entering the dark trailer, he smelled the telltale aroma of recent sex—male come, female juices, and the sweat of both sexes. Somewhere in the mélange he could recognize O's scent, which had indelibly impressed itself on his brain once and for all. He felt around in the dark for a light switch and found one.

The trailer was indeed deserted. Even Jason's dog was gone. Its tiny bed was in disarray, the sheets tangled and stained. But one pillow had been placed in the center, fluffed neatly, and on it rested an ivory-colored card.

Retrieving it, Casanova noticed that the card was imprinted with the telltale signet of the Power Company, along with an address and a date and time. And the words "ADMIT ONE. PLUS GUEST(S)." The address was on Harrison Street in San Francisco; the date and time was the midnight after next.

Scattered over the floor near the bed were the undergarments that O had purchased at Victoria's Secret. Casanova lifted the discarded panties to his face and slowly inhaled of her scent. He sighed deeply.

Tucking the panties into his pocket, he exited the trailer with the card in his hand. The door swung open, and Casanova did not bother to close it.

He returned to the car.

"We need to go to San Francisco," he told Lilah.

"No shit? I've been wanting to go there."

"I'll pay you well if you'll drive us."

"What's in San Francisco?"

"O," said Casanova. "And some others, to whom I owe a visit."

In the backseat, Cristiana stirred and murmured in her sleep. And she smiled, Casanova noticed briefly, as if all along she had subconsciously known the trailer would be found empty.

Though the windows of the limousine were darkened, as the sun rose D could see the hills of the California coast rolling by in their glorious splendor. Her first master had her service him twice orally before he allowed her to doze. The feel of his cock in her mouth induced a sort of rapture in D's body. She was soothed by the familiarity of the texture and the taste, of the way his hands gripped her hair while she bobbed up and down on his organ. She knew better than to beg him to fuck her,—but by the time she felt his second load erupt into her mouth, that is what she so desperately wanted.

But her master did nothing of the sort. Instead, when she had satisfied him orally for the second time, he merely said: "You may sleep now."

Also knowing better than to argue with such a command, D, who long ago had been Sarah, crawled to the cushy seat opposite her master. She curled herself up into a ball and shut her eyes. Though she was far from comfortable—not least because of the burning hunger in her loins, a hunger to be taken again by her first master—she felt herself slipping away.

"Soon," she heard her master saying. "Soon, slave, you'll receive your punishment—that which you so richly deserve. The Power Company sees to such things quite effectively, as you know."

"Yes, Master," she murmured sleepily.

Room 13B of the Willamette Motel was the only available room with a king-size bed; it was a smoking room, and it smelled stale and sharp. The scent brought back a variety of sordid memories for Casanova, but then he anticipated sordid goings-on in the place, so it only seemed appropriate.

Lilah insisted on taking a shower before going to bed. Cristiana, however, had no such needs. Casanova drew her to him and kissed her deeply the moment the bathroom door was closed, and within seconds he found himself sprawled on the bed with his trousers open and Cristiana's mouth on his cock, hungrily servicing him. The two of them wriggled out of their clothes, and Casanova thrilled to the feel of Cristiana's slim, nude body against him, undaunted by the slickness of her thighs and her sex after her performance at the bar in Seattle.

He entered her smoothly, loving the poetry of her moans as his cock slid rhythmically in and out of her pussy. By the time Lilah came out of the bathroom, freshly scrubbed, Casanova had flipped Cristiana over and lifted her hips to meet his thrust, entering her from behind. When he reached under to touch her adorned clitoris, it brought still louder moans from the Italian girl's lips. She had been so much more tentative back in Venice, but that now felt like years ago.

"Well, well," smiled Lilah. "You two don't waste any time."

Now that she was naked, Casanova could see that she was not only splendid in her nudity, but was adorned far more than just with rings through her nipples. Several abstract tattoos danced across her slim belly, caressing her hips. An archaic symbol was etched just above her shaved sex, in the spot where her pubic hair might have been. Casanova recognized the symbol as one with occult meaning—a sign of sexual potency. With her sex shorn, it was also quite evident that her nether lips were pierced with several shimmering silver rings—more, even, than on her ears. Her clitoral bud also bore a ring, this one jeweled.

Still mounting Cristiana from behind, Casanova beckoned to Lilah with his eyes. With a flirtatious smile, she chose to mount the king-size bed closer to the head of it, spreading her legs wide and drawing Cristiana's face between her open thighs.

"Did I mention that I swing both ways?" smiled Lilah, winking at Casanova over Cristiana's undulating back.

Cristiana's nude body gave a shiver;—though she had certainly shown enthusiasm for it while on the yacht, servicing women was still relatively new to her. Nonetheless, as Lilah guided Cristiana's face into her sex, the Italian girl overcame her momentary hesitation and applied her mouth to Lilah's pierced sex. Casanova drove his cock deeper into Cristiana from behind, feeling the great shudder that her body gave as, with newfound enthusiasm, she addressed the task of orally pleasuring Lilah.

Lilah moaned softly, her eyes meeting Casanova's as she sank into her pleasure. Gazing at each other over Cristiana's back, the two of them smiled.

Lilah let out a sudden gasp as Cristiana's tongue applied firmer pressure to her pierced clit. Lilah reached over Cristiana and grasped Casanova's hand—and Casanova, with a burst of energy flowing into him despite his growing exhaustion—drove into Cristiana's cunt with ever increasing ardor.

O came to her senses in a cage the size of a single bed. The room she was in seemed large, but since it was lit only by candles burning some distance away, at first she could not see much. As her eyes grew accustomed to the half light, she recognized the structure of the room, though not the room itself. She had been in many such rooms during her training and service. She knew them intimately, as she knew the things that would doubtless be done to her here.

It was a dungeon.

But this was no typical dungeon. It had been built in to a small nightclub, perhaps a converted warehouse space, with small cocktail tables scattered among bondage equipment and a small stage at the far end of the room. Though the club was no larger than a smallish jazz club, it had been packed full with tables and implements of torment.

O squinted into the darkness, letting her eyes acclimate further. A few feet from her cage, she could see a rack, intended to painfully stretch out a victim so that she could be punished. Beyond that were several benches, built from sawhorses and reinforced with metal struts, obviously used for spankings and whippings. Beyond that, on the stage was the familiar X-shape of a St. Andrew's cross—no, two of them. Two St. Andrew's crosses, side by side onstage. The walls of the club were adorned with racks that held whips, canes, manacles, and other devices—even, she was quite sure, a cattle prod.

She shivered as she regarded each implement. Like all slaves, O had been disobedient many times during her training; it scarcely would have been training otherwise. Beyond this, she knew it was the privilege of her owners to punish her as they saw fit, for their own amusement or the amusement of others. But this time she had committed a transgression so extreme that, perhaps for the first time, she truly feared the punishment that awaited her. She had run away from a legitimate buyer—asserting her own will over that of a man who had paid good money for her. What horrible torments would she reap from the sowing of such total disobedience?

She heard heavy footsteps approaching; there in the semidarkness she could see heavy boots in front of her cage and a shadowy male figure towering over her. She heard the rattle of keys. The padlock that secured her cage was unfastened, and the door slid open.

"Crawl," was the only command.

As if finally comprehending what sort of trouble she was in, O instantly complied, crawling out of the cage and planting her lips on the man's boots. For her show of devotion, she received a slap across the face.

"It's too late for that," came a growl from overhead. "You'll get what's coming to you, little slave. But first we've got to pretty you up for the proceedings. The salon is waiting."

"Yes, sir," whispered O.

She received another slap. The man snapped his fingers and pointed into the darkness. With her thighs trembling and the rough carpet abrading the flesh of her knees, O began to crawl in the direction indicated.

The thrust of a boot into her bare buttocks, still sore from Jason's attentions, brought a whimper from O's mouth. She was thrust forward into the darkness and crawled as fast as she could. Tears welled in her eyes.

Though Casanova wished he could dally longer with these two beautiful women, there was important business in San Francisco. According to Lilah, they still had quite a long drive ahead of them. By the time the three lovers had slaked their lusts and dozed pleasantly for a while, only a little more than fifteen hours remained until the event. They all showered, freshened up as well as they could without a change of clothes, and dined in the small, seedy restaurant adjacent to the motel. Casanova found the food sorely lacking, but as none of them had eaten in some hours, they nonetheless made quite a meal of it under the disapproving stares of a crotchety, elderly waitress who clearly didn't think much of Cristiana's and Lilah's revealing clothes. After that, they gassed up Lilah's ancient Volkswagen and returned to the freeway.

"If it's the kind of party I suspect it will be," said Lilah as she drove, "we can't show up dressed like this. I know a place where we can stop and buy something to wear."

Lost in the sights of Northern California's hills, Cristiana perked up—whether at the mention a fetish party or of shopping, Casanova wasn't sure. She certainly had changed. It was if he had missed out on an important chapter in Cristiana's life while he was following O's elusive trail. He knew he should ask her, hear her story, an explanation, but then again maybe it was better to let their destiny unfold. There were too many unanswered questions in his new life already.

Their route took them from the valleys north of Sacramento through the agricultural regions of the Central Valley, the smell of which—fertilizer and other rotting matter—caused Casanova to wrinkle his nose and roll up the creaking window of the VW. By mid-afternoon they had reached the maze of freeways that led through Berkeley and Oakland to San Francisco. Traffic slowed to a crawl as they approached the Golden Gate Bridge, and it was late in the afternoon when Lilah nosed the VW into the South of Market district.

Casanova recognized the name of Folsom Street; in his research on the Internet, he had run across it several times. It was reputed to be a place where, three decades before, the culture of pleasure and pain had developed in the darkened bars frequented by men for whom the rough touch of other men brought the greatest form of ecstasy. That culture had since been challenged by an illness that greatly damaged the community, but remained a thriving underground with great pride in its history. Nonetheless, the district still promised much of the debauchery it had in previous years, and the store to which Lilah took them was located there—as was the address on the mysterious card, just a block off the legendary Folsom Street.

The store was known as Stormy Leather. "Stormy Leather, get it?

Like the song," Lilah told Casanova as they parked, but both he and Cristiana looked at Lilah blankly.

The place was packed full of revealing women's garments, fashioned of different varieties of leather and synthetic fabrics, the likes of which Casanova had never seen in his time. There was a large array of corsets, however, which Casanova approved of. Both Lilah and Cristiana looked quite fetching as they tried on the restrictive garments, laced tightly into them with the assistance of the pierced and tattooed salesgirl.

With the salesgirl's help, and that of his two female companions, Casanova found himself purchasing a pair of skin-tight pants of shimmering material. The discomfort their tightness caused was nothing compared to the clothing of years past, and both Lilah and Cristiana approved of the way they accented his lithe, muscled form. The same was true of the black leather vest they selected for him, which they insisted he wear without a shirt.

Lilah and Cristiana, for their part, had each selected a tightly fitting leather corset adorned with different brocaded patterns, matched, for Lilah, with a skin-tight pair of shiny short pants and stockings that resembled black fishnet. Cristina took a short leather skirt and black stockings, and each selected a pair of high heels.

Their purchases made, the three of them found a nearby hotel to freshen up and get dressed for the evening. As Cristiana and Lilah fretted over their outfits and the makeup they had purchased in a drugstore along the way, Casanova watched them, disturbed that the half-clothed women did not stir his lust. As the moment approached when—he hoped—he would once again meet O, his thoughts were entirely with her. The Power Company had thus far showed no compunctions about employing kidnapping, extortion, and physical violence to further their mysterious ends—whatever those ends might be. And wherever he was in the world. Who was behind this Power Company?

Were they responsible for his mysterious appearance in this century? Clearly the invitation had been left in Jason's trailer for Casanova to find. It went without saying that the dark architects of the Power Company knew where he was and, if pressed, how to get to him. Was there some wicked design in his being lured to this San Francisco club for his expected reunion with O?

Once the garments were zipped and laced and buckled, the makeup applied, the trio made their way down Harrison Street to the address given on the "invitation." They arrived at a simple steel door in what appeared to be an abandoned warehouse. Lilah pressed the doorbell. A moment later, the steel door was opened by an enormous, muscled man in tight leather pants and a black tank top.

Casanova presented the card he had retrieved from Jason's trailer. The doorman studied it for a moment, then fixed Casanova with a cold glare.

"These are your guests?"

"They are," he said.

"Your female guests are your responsibility," said the doorman as he stepped aside, holding the door open. "On the right you'll find the stairs."

Casanova led the way into the darkened warehouse.

The scent of sex was in the air as the trio descended into the basement. At the foot of the stairs there was a red velvet curtain; Casanova swept it aside and the three proceeded inside.

The nightclub was already filled with guests wearing clothes much the same as those they had bought at Stormy Leather. The exception was that many of the female guests were in considerably greater stages of undress; many of them, in fact, were nude except for high-heeled shoes and stockings. It was not a large club, but Casanova estimated that at least a hundred people had been packed into it, some seated at cocktail tables waiting for the show to begin, others making use of the bondage equipment. Throughout, only the female guests were bound. Casanova listened to the cries of ecstatic pain as leather-clad men applied paddles, whips, and bare hands to the exposed bottoms of nude women bent over spanking benches and strapped to tables. A woman in a leather bra and G-string, standing gracefully on impossibly high heels, stepped in front of Casanova.

"Your table," she said, indicating the only cocktail table that had no one sitting at it. In the center of the table was a sign reading RESERVED.

Casanova's eyes narrowed as he looked at the woman, beautiful beyond compare, with long black hair and eyes that sparkled green even in the dim light of the club. Her gaze offered him no clue as to the purpose for which he had been lured here, or what he could expect.

Threading their way through the crowd toward the empty table, Casanova's blood suddenly ran cold as he saw a face he recognized: Toby Faith, the man who had made off with his beloved O so long ago in Florida. Casanova's eyes narrowed as he stared at Faith, but the rock star was obviously more occupied with a slim girl sitting on his lap and gave no indication of having recognized him. Beside Faith sat a large black man in a black suit and tie, looking bored and reading a comic book.

Casanova brushed past Faith, and the trio took their seats at the empty table. Almost before they had sat down, a slender blonde girl in a G-string, high heels, and nothing else appeared with a tray of champagne. She deposited the drinks on the table.

"Wow," said Lilah, grasping her champagne flute nervously as her eyes roved all over the club. "This is really extreme."

Casanova took a sip of the champagne; it tasted more like fizzy wine, and cheap, not at all to his taste.

Within moments, the lights dimmed and the revelers making use of the bondage equipment politely stopped their ministrations. The moans of pained pleasure dwindled to the whimpers of afterglow.

"Please take your seats," announced a voice from unseen speakers. "Tonight we have two women very much in need of correction, and we'd like all our guests to witness their punishment."

Lilah and Cristiana craned their necks as two women, nude except for collars and leashes were led through the crowd by two women in skin-tight, shimmering body suits. Casanova did not crane his neck, because he had guessed already what was coming. As O passed him, he caught her eyes, ripe with shame and haunted by the overwhelming sadness that had first drawn him to her.

O's eyes locked with Casanova's for just a moment, and in that instant it seemed eternity passed. Casanova saw the sparkle of recognition, but then, like a blazing coal going suddenly to a smoking ember, he saw the message of dismissal.

Casanova did not expect to recognize the woman who passed behind O. It was D, equally naked, equally cowed and submissive. She, too, looked into Casanova's eyes as she passed, but there was no sense of dismissal about her, just mute acceptance that he should be here to witness her punishment, for he was the one she had abandoned, thus sealing her fate.

O and D were led onstage, and their leashes were unhitched. Casanova watched as the two nude, collared women were shackled to X-shaped crosses on the stage, their backsides presented to the crowd. He realized for the first time that twin video monitors hung from the ceilings over the stage, one at each corner. They flickered to life, each monitor showing the face of the woman about to be punished.

Casanova looked away. He had seen O punished before, but now, after his long chase, his mysterious ordeal, this seemed too much to bear.

"And now, we shall all witness and enjoy the punishment of rebellious women. Administered by those they have wronged."

Casanova's pulse quickened as he saw the woman in the leather bikini—the one who had directed them to their table—approach the table where Toby Faith sat with a blonde on his lap. She held out an implement, which Faith snatched with a cruel, barbarous laugh.

As Faith mounted the stage, Casanova saw that it was a leather flogger, an enormous whip of the sort that would administer terribly punishing blows. He caught his breath.

The leather-clad woman was walking toward his table.

She stopped before Casanova, and held it out—another flogger, heavy and cruel and savage.

"Your whip, Chevalier. She has wronged you. She is yours to punish."

Casanova's eyes narrowed and his lips tightened as he looked into the woman's cold green eyes. Inexplicably, the woman smiled.

Casanova reached up and accepted the whip.

Chapter Thirteen

D's turn came first. A procession of unknown men took ritual turns whipping her until the skin on her back was the sheer color of blood. From his vantage point, Casanova could not keep his eyes away from the young woman's calvary. At one point she fainted. Within a few seconds the women in attendance had thrown cold water over her face to revive her. Unconsciousness was no safety. It seemed to go on forever, although D kept silent throughout her ordeal, through the torrent of tears pearling down her face and onto her martyred body.

When the time finally came to unshackle her, she could not stand up on her own and she was dragged off the stage. Casanova noticed that she had lost control of her bowels, and urine and feces dripped from her openings as she was pulled into the darkness.

There was a lull.

The time then came for O to be punished.

Toby Faith moved toward the cross.

Casanova sighed. What could he punish her for? *He* wasn't her master; she hadn't disobeyed *him*. No matter. He would punish her for making him want her so dreadfully. In the last instance, he suspected that was why everybody punished her.

He was still a novice when it came to this sort of thing; the little bit of play he had indulged in with Cristiana was like an eleven-year-old's furtive groping. *I know nothing,* he told himself, *except what* she's *taught me.* She. O. Difficult to give voice to the single, pure, perfect syllable—more than a name and less than one at the same time.

Simply by watching her, he had become cognizant of the distance he would have to go to catch up with her. And yet he was perfectly confident that he would get there.

Odd—given the single-mindedness of this new passion—how scrupulously he had avoided it back in his old life. He'd rather had to work, in fact, to stay clear of it. Every brothel in Venice, and all the other cities as well, had had its red-painted torture room. But as "a caring and thoughtful lover" he simply hadn't been interested. Probably simply the blind luck of his *destiny* (as he'd called it in his memoirs) had kept him away. His destiny, his fate, and his genius had been a willingness to learn from women: his earliest teachers had been lusty girls who'd taken for granted their right to gratification. They had set him to work; he had obeyed, all enthusiasm and innocent good faith. Caring, thoughtful, dutiful even. They should have added "dutiful" to his action figure biography, the text on the back of the box.

Well, it was time to start thinking (as they might say here) outside the box.

I'll punish you, bella, *not only for my own desire, but for making everyone else want you, too.*

At the moment, though, he found himself utterly captivated by the video monitors. He suspected that he was enjoying them more than anyone in the room, because they were so new, so mysterious to him. Flesh simultaneous with the ghost of flesh—the solidity of her face somehow transmuted to light. Unmediated, there were glimpses of the leather flogger cutting into the skin of her ass (too bad he couldn't see more of it; nobody could, with Toby-fucking-Faith blocking their view). After which, you could quickly cut back to the ghost of her face on the monitors. He liked the tension, the movement, the constant, delightful frustration of not being able to see everything at once and the endless, tantalizing promise that perhaps one could figure out a way to do it.

She was weeping, biting her lips, holding back. Toby Faith hadn't begun to plumb the depths of what she was capable of.

Is she waiting for me? he asked himself. Of course she was.

Whimpering now, moaning a bit, from the look of her. The pompous little rock star—skinny ass in leather pants, strutting, pathetic—hadn't yet drawn a full scream.

But even if he had, would one be able to hear her? Not from where he was sitting,—as the audience was drowning her out with their own noise. *Woo-woo yup-yup-yup-yup.* And then there was the music coming from those boxes up there. A whole massive bank of them. To flatter the man of the hour, they had caught and played Toby Faith's voice; it wailed out from the . . . speakers, they called them.

If I were proprietor of this place . . . Why not? He could afford to buy the business, the building, the whole city block. In this new world he could buy anything he wanted. His eighteenth-century gold coins were priceless; what he had been paid for the few of them he'd sold was an absurdity.

Even then, bewildered as he had been by his resurrection, he'd been wary enough to entertain the possibility that he was being cheated. He had been *smart,* as they seemed to like to say here. In any case, he had been *clever* with his old gold coins, only sold a few of them in exchange for modern-day cash. Most were still in a bank, a safe-deposit box, in Venice.

If he were proprietor of this place, there would be different music playing.

He glanced up at the other screen, where D's earlier ordeal was being shown on a loop. D in excruciating agony. All very nice to see; lovely girl; he didn't care in the slightest. It was the taller, sad woman he wanted, the pale flickering ghost of a pure oval face washed in tears.

He tightened his fingers around the handle of the flogger he'd been given. Splendid heft to it. He balanced it in his palm. A craftsman had made it. He corrected himself—a crafts*person,* they would say. Really, they were so amusing, the citizens of this new world, their little sensibilities so tender, even as they played with the talismans of pain and power. Still, it was nice to hold an object that had the mark of a human hand in its making. What magic did they employ to create the artifacts they surrounded themselves with? And why wasn't it a better magic? Why wasn't there more beauty?

Her eyes were shut. She was groaning now—you couldn't hear it, but he could tell from the shape of her mouth. He chided himself for his excess of sensibility. It was magical and miraculous that he was alive, splendid and dazzling that he had found her. Anyway, there was ugliness in every time and place. One took beauty where one could find it.

Which made it no less true that he and the whip maker must be on a . . . wavelength, perhaps they would say, or a vibe that transcended physical proximity. The object was patterned—patiently and lovingly, fearfully and respectfully—after the sort of thing the British navy had used to punish sailors. His mates on the docks at Wapping, where he had once worked, their backs . . . no one sitting in this club could begin to understand what could happen to a man's back, flogged in all due deference and subjugation to His Majesty George III—the one who'd lost the American colonies, as it happened. But the craftsperson—no, it had been a craftswoman; somehow he was sure of it—must have had some serious intuitions of all that.

Of course, this was far less vicious an implement than an

eighteenth-century British boatswain would use. But the knots (he twirled one through his fingers) were a nice facsimile. He balanced the handle on his open palm—not bad. Tame, a bit of a toy, but no, not bad. He was sure a woman had made it, because he could feel himself learning something, simply from holding it. Because he was the kind of man who learned things from women.

Just as well, really, that she hadn't made it more authentic—for he was sure she would have known how to. But she knew her patrons; she wasn't a fool. Whoever she was, she had known better than to supply Toby Faith with the sort of thing His Majesty's Royal Navy had had at their disposal.

And as for O? He had been watching her, raptly, delightedly, through his idle meditations. He had to admit that he was rather enjoying watching Toby Faith lay his whip on her. O was screaming now. Her eyes were huge; the video monitor registered them as black voids.

The announcer had said that each of the men punishing her would get twelve minutes. Eight or so must have passed. He felt his cock swelling against the Stormy Leather trousers he was beginning to realize he rather despised. Why? He had liked them well enough when he'd bought them. He wasn't sure. Something to do with the feel of the whip handle, the craft of it, the sharp and obvious contrast to the lack of craft devoted to what he was wearing.

Why did they give me a whip? The question wouldn't go away. For certainly they knew he had no claim on her except his desire. *And who were they, anyway?* The Power Company that owned her: did they also own the oil, the electricity? He had skimmed through enough newspapers to understand something about the simultaneous flows—of physical energy and political control—in this new world.

It wasn't out of kindness and generosity that they were giving him a crack at her. He winced at his own diction; you could sound remarkably foolish in the language of Shakespeare. You could use a stale old expression—"yeah, and if you think they're doing this out of kindness, I've got a bridge I could sell you . . ." No one could possibly believe they were doing this out of kindness.

Why then?

He was getting tired of little Toby Faith, the self-satisfaction, the lack of focus or finesse. The whoops and the starstruck applause were getting old. As was not being able to get a clearer view of the spreading bruises and rising welts on her ass. Clumsily staged, no sense of pomp, of propriety.

Sell the whole enterprise to me, and I'll *give you a show. I'd change everything, when . . . if . . .*

Hold on, he told himself, *don't cash out yet.*

All right, so they were fools here. Their costumes (he was coming to understand) were no more than humiliating motley, their music less attuned to the modalities of force than the lightest of Mozart's sonatas, the wittiest of his overtures. But they must understand *something,* because they had given him a flogger. They knew how much he wanted her. They knew him.

Unpleasant but arousing, good to feel the old instincts, nerves like gold wire spun from the base of his spine. He smelled metal, sweat, the chill wet paving stones and filthy human refuse of a blind alley at the end of a canal, just before dawn on the day after Carnivale.

Leaving his table, he made his way to the side of the room. If he pressed himself against the wall, he could see a bit more; the angle was better, you barely had to watch the rock singer at all. Oh yes, the ropy welts were darkening now, sublimity of abused flesh.

You could see the audience better from here, too. Most of them costumed as foolishly as he was. But he had caught sight of two tables whose occupants were dressed more somberly, in very fine black wool.

A red-haired woman sat at one of those tables, her black suit open in a deep V—no shirt underneath, just pale naked skin. Surrounded by solicitous companions, she was weeping silently, ecstatically, her eyes never leaving the stage.

He sniffed. The wet, cold, fascinating smell of power came drifting across the room. From her table. But it came far stronger from the other table, where they were all men and no one was weeping.

Later, he would have to think more about the people at those tables. Right now he had no choice but to watch the face on the monitor. The tears coming quickly, transmuted into diamonds and pearls on the video screen. Almost choking her. Ah yes, good. That's how she would look when she took his cock into her mouth.

But she was beginning to catch her breath now. Toby Faith was prancing about as he administered the punishment so gracelessly, wiggling his ass and grandstanding. The rock singer was losing focus on her, taking all the attention for himself. Fools in the audience going wild—more profoundly aroused by the triviality of his fame than by the beauty of her suffering.

Still, it gave her a little respite. She would need it, he assured himself. Even if it did make his attention wander. Back to the Power Company—well, to whatever powered this place—somehow he was sure these things were related. He wished he could understand how the sound and light worked. He understood a bit about electricity—*fascinating,* he had read as much as he could about the American Benjamin Franklin and his experiments. Electronics, on the other hand, meant absolutely nothing to him.

What about the ear-splitting sound from the speakers? He didn't want to ask; it was something you were supposed to know. Well, you'd have to know it in a club, a nation—a world, more likely—that was ruled by the Power Company.

Perhaps . . . yes, against the opposite wall over there, on a platform. The man looked like a musician, though Casanova didn't recognize his instrument. Still, he wove his way across the room. "Hey."

A nod, a furrowed brow. Attention reluctantly turned away from the black knobs—no instrument he had ever seen.

"Hey," the musician said.

"Can you play anything by Mozart?" He had expected ridicule, but the man was, as they liked to say, cool. Not a man, though. A boy? A girl? A European or a Moor? A mixture of all of those things, it seemed.

"No Mozart, sorry." A friendly grin. A girl, most likely—if one must have some point of reference. People here said they had gotten past needing such signposts, but he didn't believe them.

"Anything written for the harpsichord . . . clavichord . . . even the pianoforte?"

"You're up next, right?" She winked. "Yeah, I got something for you. Classical. Well, a classic, anyhow. It'll create a nice change of pace and atmosphere."

"Thanks."

"Right. The name's Croy, by the way. And I've read your *Memoirs,* well, a lot of it. Very excellent."

He nodded, returning her grin, allowing himself a moment of indulgence, pure self-absorbed infallible pleasure that there was one person in the place, at least, who had almost read his too-long book.

Just a moment's time out. From his Venetian alertness, his painful enthralment with the woman onstage.

What was she saying now? "You'll be safe, if you stay with the Association . . ."

Was that like "get with the program"?

He was about to ask her, when Faith's twelve minutes came to an end.

The fool was waving his whip in the air, doing a little victory dance . . . TOW-BEE-FAITH . . . TOW-BEE-FAITH . . . the audience was cheering and chanting now. The rock star pranced back to his seat, amid stomping so loud that the volume of the speakers must have been unearthly. Because everybody sat up and took clear notice of the loud, dissonant scratching suddenly flooding the air like the smell of a coming thunderstorm.

A fanfare, an overture—a gentleman of the eighteenth century could recognize one when he heard it, even one with no discernible melody or harmony. The musician seemed to have made it by wiggling her finger.

Silence now. A very thin slice of it. And yes, Croy did have something for him.

A child's voice, almost, wafting out of the speakers. Wistful, eager to please.

"It is the evening of the day-ay-ay-ay . . ." Harpsichord.

The crowd wasn't sure they liked it.

A spotlight caught Casanova on his way up to the stage to take his turn. The crowd wasn't sure they liked *him* either. Well, he would like himself quite a bit more if he weren't wearing this clownish vest and pants. Which didn't mean that he wouldn't take his time, sauntering up between the tables.

Vaulting onto the platform now. Quickly. He slapped her punished ass with the flat of his hand.

The crowd roared. He hardly noticed the sound, so enchanted was he by the way her flesh rose to meet him. Exquisite, the way it spread and curled below his palm. A flower opening.

He laid the flogger on her softly, lightly at first, just to get the feel of it. Just to see how the thongs would spread themselves over the flesh. Like the fingers of a skeleton hand, the knots biting into her. The white globes of her ass were mottled, marbled—the colors ran from palest blue to darkest mulberry. He wanted to worship it, even if he didn't believe in the divine.

(Oh, of course he had professed to believe, in his memoirs. Well, wouldn't you if you'd been denounced by the Inquisition for practicing magic and sentenced to five years in lead chambers in the doge's palace? He had thought about this a lot while he scanned the newspapers in this new world. Before they were finished, a lot of people might have to learn his skills of religious double-talk, to please the people in charge—the Power Company? Still, at the moment, he could almost believe that the ass he was punishing had been divinely created to receive the strokes of a whip.)

The only bad thing about being up on stage was that you couldn't see the video monitor from here. But he had to give the producers of this entertainment *some* credit—there was a mirror. You couldn't see it from the audience, but up here, on the stage, he and she could both watch themselves.

He walked up to her, whispered in her ear. "I want you to keep your eyes open. I want you to watch yourself suffering at my hands."

He thought that she might have smiled, if she'd had the strength to waste on a smile. "Oui, monsieur," she whispered.

He had his bearings now. He drew back his arm—a perfect arc from shoulder to wrist to fingers around the wooden handle. The scream he drew from her was so loud, so pure, that he was sure the audience could hear it as well. But perhaps that was only because the musical accompaniment was so soft, the harpsichord moving so confidently from dominant to tonic.

Another blow. Quickly. He couldn't lose his balance or his center. And yes, her eyes were wide open, enthralled, even through her pain, by the rhythm he had struck, the clarity and authority with which he wielded the flogger.

No more harpsichord. He didn't recognize what the little her-maphrodite musician Croy was playing, but it was both tasteful and apposite. What bothered him was that his time was running out so quickly. Twelve minutes would be far too short.

He—and his whip, too—needed to know her entire body. A pity her breasts weren't available. He envied her for a moment, simply for living inside her own beautiful skin in a way that he could only approach through force and imagination.

Ah, he hadn't thought he could hit her any harder. But it seemed he could. Envy had been the spark. She almost had to shut her eyes against the last blow he had given her.

He didn't credit the divine, but he had never stopped believing in sin, and the mortal ones in particular. Lust. Envy. And when you crossed lust with envy? Of course he was no mathematician. Nor a metaphysician, and—Inquisition aside—not much of a magician either. But he liked to contemplate the magnitude of it. Lust crossed with envy: power beyond his imagining.

"You disobeyed me, you betrayed me, you abandoned me, lured by the tides of lust," he whispered. "I'm disappointed in you."

Her eyes flew open. Her lips trembled. She was ashamed, for failing him.

At this moment, at least he could plumb the depths of her shame. Later, he would find a way to touch every part of her body. Perhaps he could add a second act to this show.

Right now—a few welts on her upper back. With respect for the beauty of the scapulae, her shoulder blades. Her wings. *Take flight, angel.* She almost did, her body rippling from his blows, ass bouncing, soles and toes of her feet quivering.

Not so good, though, below her ass.

"You're hiding from me," he told her. "You're holding back." With the butt end of the whip, he forced her thighs farther apart. Was she wet between her legs? He hoped not. This wasn't about her pleasure. A quick finger to check. No, not at all. Good.

Underhand, now. A more difficult angle, where the round globes of her ass met the tops of her thighs.

"Please!" she screamed. "Please, no more, monsieur!"

Did she dare to tell him what he might do? He reached farther, twisted his wrist and arm to get to the place she didn't like to be touched.

"Arrête!"

But he wouldn't stop.

Later, he would realize that it was at this moment that he had begun to wander across the line. While it was happening, though, he didn't understand anything, except that he needed to make her give herself in a way that she didn't want to do. Not because it would hurt more than the blows she had already endured, but because part of her wanted to keep it from him.

Suddenly, she stopped resisting and found a way to let go. He sighed with delight, ached with pleasure. She was giving him what he wanted, simply because he wanted it. She was writhing, arching, scraping her front, her neck, and her beautiful breasts against the cross to give him more access to that strip of flesh that she had wanted to protect from him.

A pity it was so difficult, the cross so crude, really. *Stop,* he wanted to say. *Stop, we need a different piece of equipment.*

Stop, darling, we'll do it later.

Her face in the mirror, mobile, ecstatic—arpeggios of emotion: pleasure, desire, pity. Pity. Because he was as much a fool as anyone in the place, dull eyed, mugging from under their little leather motorcycle caps. He had lost. They could do anything to him now. Though in fact, at that moment, he had only felt the faintest intuition, a whiff of the power smell. He would only know it for certain later.

Right now, his attention was monopolized by the task at hand. Her long, unmarked thighs, silk and cream. Faith had barely touched them. And once again the harpsichord, the waif child, the tears going by. It was kind of his little musician to play it again, warn him that he had only two minutes left. He ran his fingers, even his nails, over the marks he had made on O's body. To show her, *Look, these are my marks; I've left them on you. You gave me yourself and I took it.*

And then, even worse (*stop, darling*—the moment of love, of sympathy), he had given himself back to her.

Everyone had seen it. He and she had committed theft together. In front of a room full of witnesses, he had stolen her fealty from the men who rightly owned her. And then he had given it back to her— wrapped, like a birthday present, in himself. The second transgression, he suspected, was so much worse than the first that he could hardly guess what would happen to either of them.

The music stopped. He was almost paralyzed by the knowledge of what he had done. Hell, he couldn't have done anything else. And wouldn't, if he'd had it to do over again. Which was what they had known when they'd given him the whip.

The women in body suits had mounted the stage to undo the shackles. He pushed them away. He would do it himself. But she would fall . . . no, she was used to this. She slid down to her hands and knees. He looped his finger through the ring in her collar. She kneeled up on her haunches, face swollen and choked with tears.

"You know what I want," he told her. The audience was quiet.

"Well?" he slapped her face. They liked that; they cheered.

He backed away a few steps so that she would have to crawl toward him. Something about the way her breasts swung from her chest made him want to gasp, to weep; beautiful as she was, when she crawled there was something bestial about her.

Someone was training bright white light down from the ceiling, at her flesh.

She dipped her head down, to kiss his shoes, her breasts crushed beneath her, on the dirty floor. She knelt up now, sat back on her haunches. He could tell that it hurt, the stripes he had put on the back of her thighs.

"Your mouth. Come on."

She licked her lips while she unzipped his fly. He was glad, in any case, that he wasn't wearing anything under the stupid tight pantaloons. A few whistles from the audience at the size and angle of his erection.

She was still weeping, but serenely, her attention focused on taking as much of him as she could into her mouth.

The audience was quiet, almost humming. He turned toward the table where the red-haired woman was sitting. He hoped he might be giving her some pleasure. But then he saw that he was in serious trouble.

Some of the people at her table had their little telephones out; all of them looked alert and worried. Scanning the house . . . waiting for . . . something. A thin, rather patrician-looking man was staring at Croy, still seated at her instrument.

Casanova peered down at O, working him so beautifully, elegantly, and now, just beginning to notice that his attention had wandered. Her large eyes. He wasn't sure in these lights—looking troubled, guilty: *why,* she was clearly thinking, *hadn't she pleased him?*

He put a hand to her cheek to stop her. The crowd didn't like that. He reached for her hand, to help her to her feet. There had to be an escape route.

The music stopped. The lights went out. Screams. Her hand was still in his. Perhaps they could make it to that door to the right.

"Come on," he told her.

"I'm yours," she said. "I'm yours, Giacomo."

"Moi aussi, bella."

A loud, leaden, but distinctly nonelectronic sound now. More lights went out. In the darkness Casanova felt O's hand torn from his, brutally. He grasped and she was gone. He stepped forward, hands searching for her, and stumbled. His head hit the stage floor with a thump. He blacked out, darkness merging into an ebony shade of night.

They were walking together, by a river. No, it was the Grand Canal; he was helping her into a large, graceful gondola. But they didn't make that particular craft anymore, stopped during the 1750s perhaps . . . which was his first signal that this wasn't real, this was a delirious fantasy, sent because his brain couldn't bear the unbearable reality.

"Thank you, Giacomo," she said.

Another signal. She would have said Signore.

He pushed the thought away. She smiled up at him. She was dressed in sea green, blonde lace like seafoam surrounding her breasts, the nipples exposed, like a Venetian courtesan of his time. A small star at the corner of her mouth, just a touch of black court plaster. Her hair was a pale chestnut—sunbleached; she had sat on the roof for days to get it to look like that. Lovely hair, scooped away from a high, ethereal forehead, pearls and sequins woven through it.—Under her skirt, her cunt was sequined as well. Yes, he had put his hand over it, he could feel it. She smiled at him, a bit naughtily now. Her eyes tilted upward at their corners when she smiled like that;—he hadn't had a chance to notice that before. She was daring him to allow her to stare at him so boldly, lustily, admiring his body in somber, tailored black. She was . . .

Gone. And he was sprawled in the backseat of a big automobile.

Conscious. No, spiraling downward into darkness, as though he'd been knifed and tossed into the canal. But he hadn't been knifed. The darkness came from the pain in his head—and from the knowledge that he'd lost her. Again.

How long had it been before he had surfaced, swum back to consciousness? He guessed it had been awhile. He thought they might be crossing one of those huge bridges that connected San Francisco to the other cities. His legs looked very long to him, sprawled out in front of him. He felt clumsy, embarrassed, and only then, fearful.

The fear subsided, though, when he realized that his head was lolling on a woman's shoulder. The weeping red-haired woman from the club, sitting next to him, to his right, on the very soft leather seat.

Not weeping anymore, though. Smiling at him. Large, pale, sea green eyes, carefully outlined in what must have been very good waterproof, tear-proof black paint. He hadn't considered how beautiful she was. She kissed his forehead gently and stroked his hair.

"You're safe with us. And I'm Kate. Welcome, Signore."

"Call me Jack." He'd had friends on the London docks who had called him that. These people looked like they could be his friends.

"Jack Newhouse, sure." A chuckle from the older gentleman seated on his left. Sixty perhaps, suave, well groomed, of diminutive stature—the sort of man with the wits to survive in the papal court.

"My most grateful thanks, to all of you." But now came the more difficult part. The questions—so many of them, "How? . . . Why?" And best to know, even if dangerous to ask. "Are you the . . . Association?"

The woman seated next to the driver turned around. "Yes," she said, "we are from the association." She shrugged. "Small 'a.' Somehow, that affects how you pronounce it. And as for why the small 'a,' well, that's a long story, or perhaps a bad joke."

She had dark blue eyes, slightly too close together in a narrow face the color of skimmed milk. Nervous energy, high-strung, sexy in a way he wasn't sure he liked.

"Not funny, Ariel." The older man spoke wearily. "No," he added, "we are actually, and I hope it's not confusing you now, from the Order." He shrugged. "Different name, different aims."

"But Ariel's right, in a sense." That was Croy, cuddled up with Ariel in the front passenger seat. She was small; he hadn't noticed her until now, but he was glad she was here. "Because, you know, the Order's like the good guys, in this fight. The Power Company's like . . ."

The driver's voice was dry. Casanova could see from the back of his head that he was the thin, elegant-looking man who'd sat next to Kate, holding her hand at the club. "Jesus, Kate, did we have to bring the peanut gallery along? Give the poor guy a break, Croy, he's from the eighteenth . . ."

Casanova raised a hand. "That's all right, I keep up . . ."

"Hey, it was Croy, you know," Ariel said, "who cut the power at just the right moment, Jonathan, so you and I could grab him."

"And anyway," Croy was speaking at the same time, "what's so great about the situation?"

Each of them had something to say, it seemed, except Kate, who looked as though she were going to cry again.

"Quiet!" Casanova—Jack—surprised himself, shouting at his benefactors. "Just shut the hell up!" he added, though the babbling had already subsided.

"Thanks," Kate whispered.

"Dear friends," he told them. "I'm sure you are brave, and I know you're not fools. So I must surmise that O is in danger, and that you'd rather say anything than tell me that."

The look on Kate's face told him he was right.

Chapter Fourteen

"Where are we going?" said Casanova after a long while. The car was still speeding through the darkness. The lights of San Francisco had faded from view behind them to be replaced by those of the freeway. To Casanova, peering through the glass, the cars ahead were scurrying spiders watching him with hostile red eyes.

It was the driver, Jonathan, who responded to the question, his eyes still fixed on the highway in front of him. "To New York, in the longer term," he said. "More immediately, to a private airstrip we own about a hundred miles north of SF."

" 'SF'?"

"San Francisco." Jonathan gave a chuckle.

"Another plane ride?" said Casanova. He had very little idea where the two cities were in relation to each other. He wondered if San Francisco had even existed back in his own time.

"You got it." The driver lifted his right hand from the wheel and made it swoop around like a gliding hawk, banking this way and that. "Five hours—maybe four if we're lucky with the wind." He made a whooshing noise that Casanova guessed was supposed to be the whine of a high-powered machine.

Casanova's stomach sank. He had been on a plane precisely twice now, and neither time had he much enjoyed the experience. In retrospect, the long flight from swampy New Orleans to Seattle had not been too bad. One of the flight attendants had been rather pretty, although she had rejected his amatory suggestions with the kind of glazed smile that told him she hadn't been listening to them, a suspicion confirmed when she reappeared at his elbow a couple of minutes later to give him a second bag of pretzels. After that he had laid into the in-flight alcohol with a will, so that he'd arrived in Seattle with his mind muzzily happy and his innards less so. The shorter flight for that foolhardy skydiving exercise had been far worse. Even now, the thought of jumping out of the plane into emptiness made his heart seem to clamor at the back of his throat.

He wondered what it was that kept planes in the air. Did they have huge hot air sacs hidden inside them?

"Why New York?" he asked, just for something to take his mind off the impending voyage through the clouds.

He was startled when Kate spoke in his ear. He thought she had fallen asleep.

"Because that's where the Order's headquarters are. And it's also where we think they've taken O."

"Why?"

She shrugged, a movement that squashed her breast against his shoulder in a way he ordinarily would have found delicious. "Because it was what we were hoping they wouldn't do."

That didn't seem like much of an answer.

Croy must have sensed his dissatisfaction, because once more she swiveled around to look at him over the seat back.

"You've got to understand one thing, Jack. It wasn't you we were in the club to seize. It was O. And D. We got D all right—when she was carried off the stage, it was straight to an ambulance driven by one of our people, and she should be at the airstrip by now, waiting for us.

But in the dark and confusion, numb nuts here"—she twitched her head toward Jonathan, who just grinned—"grabbed the wrong body. By the time we realized what had happened, O was gone and we were left with you as the next best thing. I mean"—she turned her face fully toward Jonathan—"you must have something seriously wrong with your sex hormones, you asshole, if you couldn't tell a gorgeous bare-assed female from Jack here, even in the gloom."

Jonathan continued grinning. Although Casanova could see just the side of the man's face, he could tell the grin was a deliberately maintained mask to hide stark embarrassment.

"Why did you want to seize the two women?" said Casanova.

Croy returned her attention fully to him. He looked into her eyes, which were such a deep brown that they seemed as black as her skin. She was, he realized in a way that he had not back in the crowded environment of the Power Company's arena, quite unconscionably lovely. Her face was almost elfin with its high, fine cheekbones in a strange but wonderfully balanced contrast with the fullness of her lips. She had set loose the bushy jet-black hair that had been tied back earlier, and now it hung to her shoulders in a thick, crinkly cascade.

She held his gaze for a long moment, then her eyes flickered toward the elderly man at his side. "How much can I tell him, George?"

George gave a dry cough. "Just enough to satisfy his curiosity at the moment, my dear. We'll be at the strip in less than ten minutes. You can tell him the full story on the plane."

"Okay." Croy's lips quirked as she looked back to Casanova. "You heard the man."

Just ten minutes? thought the primitive being within the Chevalier. *That means that in as little as fifteen minutes we could be off the ground. And we're going to stay that way for a whole five hours.* His primitive self sounded even more frightened as it added, *If we're lucky...*

Croy had begun speaking. In his trepidation he had missed her first few words.

". . . like Kate here. Kate was in exactly the same situation once, before she came to us. She was even a friend of O's, back in her earlier life. In Roissy days. They went around together. Sometimes they were actually mistaken for sisters, would you believe it? I don't think they look remotely like each other, but there you are."

Trying not to turn and peer rudely at the redheaded woman, Casanova realized that even in the first moment he had seen her weeping at her table in the Power Company's cellar, there had been something tantalizingly familiar about her, but he had been far too engrossed in his own self-aggrandizement and the prospect of imminent sadism to register the fact.

Remembering the way he had been then, he wanted to shrivel up like a salted slug. What could have possessed him? He had inflicted pain upon the woman he adored more than anything in this vexing new world. He had inflicted pain, full stop. Ever since he had arrived in this strangely alienating century, he had been behaving strangely. He had come from a brutal age whose brutality he himself had not shared. In some ways he found this brash new era even more brutal for all its veneer of compassion and tolerance.

"I think they look a little alike," he murmured softly, his throat dry, his voice barely audible above the quiet hum of the car's powerful engine.

Kate squeezed his arm as if to tell him he'd said the right thing.

Croy rolled her eyes. "You like 'em statuesque, eh?"

"That's not what I meant," Casanova protested, but with depleted passion. He was exhausted from the rigors of the day, and the wooziness had still not dissipated from the blow on the head and whatever drug they'd given him to keep him under long enough to spirit him from the club.

The dark woman giggled. "I know. I was just winding you up. Anyway, there was a time when Kate was like O, someone else's property, someone else's fuck meat, someone else's whipping post. She sank as low as she could sink. One day she was at her master's behest eating raw sewage while he was trying to maneuver a donkey's penis into her ass—just one of his cute little games, you know?—when the stranglehold of submissiveness he had locked around her mind just shattered. She couldn't take it anymore. She had been kidding herself that it was his way of expressing his love for her, or at least that she was proving to him how much she loved him by making herself entirely his plaything, and suddenly she knew it was all plain shit—as plain as the shit she was eating. So she stood up and rammed a fistful of the stuff right down his throat, and then she turned on her heel and ran. Isn't that right, Kate?"

This time Casanova chanced a longer glance in the redheaded woman's direction. He had been expecting her to be showing some signs of shame or humiliation, but instead she was just nodding her head benignly, a slight smile on her lips, like a wife at the dinner table hearing for the hundredth time an anecdote of her husband's that hadn't been particularly funny in the first place.

She has come to terms with herself, Casanova suddenly realized, astonished at his own unexpected level of insight. *That was something in her past that she would never do again, but it isn't anything she can change, so she's not going to let herself be ruled by it any more than she's going to let herself be ruled by another master. She has accepted her past as something neither good nor bad, merely a part of who she is now.*

"I'd advise you against eating raw sewage," said Kate, feeling his gaze upon her and broadening her smile. She might have been warning him at a formal party that the vol-au-vents were suspect. "It really does taste pretty disgusting."

"Ma'am," said Casanova politely, bowing his head in respect, "you are speaking to one who has more than once been compelled to swim in the canals of Venice. I need no explanation."

"She was lucky, of course," said Croy with a malicious little grin, showing her white canines. "The bastard would have caught her if the donkey, terrified by what was going on, hadn't lashed out with its back legs and kicked him with pinpoint accuracy smack in the nuts. My guess is he's still got three Adam's apples. She was able to evade his servants and make good her escape. Somehow she found her way to us, to the Order."

Casanova was beginning to put two and two together. "Is that another name for what people call the Pavilion?"

"You're smarter than you look," said Croy.

Casanova didn't know whether to feel complimented or stung.

"Yes," Croy continued. "That's us. The Power Company can't bear the thought of our existence, and it certainly doesn't want its slaves to know of our true nature, so it puts out the rumor that we're an organization even more sadistic than it is itself. We're like hell, in a way—the place where you're warned you'll go if you don't obey every last instruction, the place where people sometimes go but they never, ever come back. Going to the Pavilion's like being given to the bogey-man, who eats naughty children for his supper. We've heard that the Power Company tells a lurid tale of how Kate was driven so far into despair at the Pavilion that she killed herself. That's fine by us. It means no one comes looking for her. And it's true the part about no slave ever coming back from the Pavilion if she goes there. They arrive as slaves, and the slave is never seen again. Only the woman."

"What about you?" said Casanova, regretting the question even as he spoke it.

"Not me," said Croy, unfazed. "I'm one of the lucky ones. I'm just an employee—hired help."

George snorted.

Casanova glanced at him questioningly.

"Croy practically runs the Order," said George. "She approached us, offering her services. Her elder sister fell in with the Power Company and lost her life to a master who flogged her to within an inch of her life, and then just that one fatal inch more. Ever since then, Croy's been wanting to destroy the Company and every male in it. It was something she knew she couldn't do on her own. So . . . she came to us."

"And one day I'll—we'll—succeed," said Croy in a low voice. Her guise of casual lightheartedness slipped from her for a moment, and Casanova was aware of the naked ferocity dwelling behind it.

And then she was smiling easily again.

"We're here," she said, glancing back over her shoulder through the car window to where bright lights made a severe tableau out of low buildings and some scattered vehicles, among them a couple of small planes and one not so small one. "Did you pack your baggage yourself, sir?" she asked Casanova, raising an eyebrow at him.

He laughed. "I haven't got any baggage," he said. "Just the clothes I stand up in."

Croy sniffed in perfect mimicry of a bored check-in clerk. "We all have baggage. Now, would sir like a window seat or an aisle seat?"

"A seat beside you, please, so you can tell me the rest of the story."

Casanova leaned his head against the window of the Lear jet, feeling the chill of the toughened glass against his temple. Outside there was a blackness unrelieved by stars.

He sighed. "But I'm as guilty as any of those you hate so much," he said. "You saw me with your own eyes, back there at the club. I even made special efforts to hurt her as much as possible."

It was hard to believe he had done that, had spread her legs and angled the blows so that he could . . .

Croy had been holding his hand these past few minutes, paradoxically extending her comfort to him. Now she pressed the back of it to her heart. He could feel her small breast against his knuckles, and despite the dreadful sense of remorse that was seeping through him, leavening his soul, he could sense his blood begin to quicken.

"It's not your fault," she said quietly, her breath warm in his ear. "Didn't you think it was strange that in an exclusive club run by the Power Company the champagne tasted so cheap?"

Now that he reflected on it, that *had* seemed odd. The label had been Dom Perignon, but the taste was Lancers.

"Your two woman friends who shared the wine with you," continued Croy, "were they not cheering you on as the lashes cut into O's tenderest flesh?"

He hadn't noticed. How would he? He had been strutting proudly amid the bright lights, his mind full of schemes for another's pain, his erection guiding his consciousness.

"There was something in the wine?" he hazarded.

She chuckled. It was a sensuous, confidential sound. "Oh, you better believe there was something in the wine, pal."

He sighed again, his breath steaming the black glass. "Why is it that everyone in this accursed century seems to want to pour drugs into me?"

"Not just any old drug, this one," said Croy. "The rumor goes there's a tribe in the Amazon jungle that extracts it from the bark of one of the trees there. They give it to their warriors before they attack the neighboring tribes, and it arouses them to unspeakable cruelties. What you drank, Jack, turned you temporarily into a sadistic psychopath. You're not to blame for what you did."

"It's not that easy." It would be a long time before the guilt left him, he knew. Perhaps forever. "It's not that easy to forgive myself. I cannot hide the fact that whatever I was intoxicated with awoke something dormant in me. Something real. A part of me that had always been there."

"For what it's worth," she said, "I forgive you."

A few seconds passed. The vibrations of the jet engines drummed against his skull.

"And," she added, "I don't offer forgiveness easily."

He turned to look at her then. The feral light he'd seen so briefly back in the car had returned to her eyes. Once again it vanished almost as soon as it had arrived.

"You're very kind," he said.

She choked back laughter. "I wouldn't say that."

"Even so."

He resumed staring out the window, watching the nothingness beyond the pale shadow of the wing.

The custom-fitted jet was filled with polished-bronze-and-black-leather luxury. There was a central cabin where he and Croy sat in low lounge chairs. Up near the cockpit was a small bedroom with a single bed. Behind them a galley was dominated by a refrigerator stocked with fine foods, liquors, wines, and beers. Beyond that was a washroom, which he had used as soon as he'd come aboard to clean himself up, trying to shower away the toxins that seemed to him to be greasing his skin like a second coat of sweat. He had known even as he'd scrubbed that the toxins were of the mind, not the body, but he had needed the symbol of cleansing himself of them anyway. The rear of the plane was occupied by a generous bedroom, where on a king-size bed D now lay. She was being tended by Kate, who had shooed Croy and Casanova away and shut the door firmly on them. D had indeed been waiting with the ambulance at the airstrip, and had raised her head long enough to speak a weak greeting to them before faintness drew curtains across her eyes once more. George and Ariel had said their farewells to the others at the foot of the steps leading up to the plane; they were returning to San Francisco to "try to clear up some of the mess we left behind." Jonathan, versatile in his choice of vehicles, was piloting the plane.

As George and Ariel had walked slowly back to the car, their arms around each other's waist, the slender young woman towering over the stooped older man, Casanova had murmured something to Croy about how they made an odd couple—was Ariel the old man's daughter?

"His wife."

"I can hardly . . ."

"They adore each other. They have eyes for no one else. She guards him as fiercely as a wildcat."

He had taken Croy's small hand impulsively as he remembered the chill that had run through him when Ariel had sized him up in the car. Croy had started to tug her hand away, then relented and let her fingers lie loosely in his grip.

With his head still against the cold window of the plane, Casanova shifted in his seat. After he had showered, Croy had given him a loose white togalike robe to wear in place of the clothes he had bought for the damned ritual of cruelty he now despised. She was still in her all-black costume: the thin black silk shirt through which could be seen alluringly vague shapes that moved when she did, and the black needle-cord jeans that fitted her like an extra skin.

Another silence had fallen now between Casanova and Croy, and yet he sensed the silence was not empty. Despite the gloomy turn of his thoughts, he was becoming increasingly aware of her physical presence next to him. He moved again, hoping the folds of the toga would hide the evidence of his reflexive arousal. If these people, the Order, were dedicated to rescuing sado-sexual slaves from the clutches of the Power Company and other, similar organizations around the world, as Croy had later explained to him in more detail, they must presumably observe a traditional morality themselves. This was more than a guess on his part. George and Ariel were married, Croy had told him, and were apparently zealously faithful to each other. Croy was overtly friendly to him, and yet it seemed to him to be largely a professional friendliness: he was a bird with a broken wing, and she had been assigned to care for him. He wasn't going to pretend to himself that it was otherwise. Ordinarily, the distance she was keeping would have represented a challenge to him, making him even more eager to seduce her, to enjoy the conquest of her, but tonight his spirits were too low to engage in the chase, and besides, he'd had his fill, back at the club, of notions of conquest, of subjugation.

"Are you falling asleep?" she said, disturbing the morose shadows of his thoughts.

"No. I'm so, so tired, but I feel that I'll never fall asleep again."

He was surprised by his own honesty. His past was made up of dissimulation in front of women, of concealment of all of his true feelings except his desire for them. Yet, at Croy's question, he had without thinking let her glimpse into his soul.

She was tugging at his hand.

"Come with me."

He turned and looked up at her where she stood in the aisle.

"Come on," she said, adding her other hand to the first and yanking hard, so that he almost fell across the seat she had vacated.

He resisted the pull. If he stood up, there was no way the folds of his robe would . . .

Croy read his mind.

"Don't worry. I've already noticed that."

Still reluctant, he let her haul him to his feet and followed her down the aisle. For the first two or three yards there were seat backs he could reach out to with his free hand for balance; after that his progress was a slow, lurching waltz. His erection, jutting up beneath the thin material of the robe, jigged from side to side in a slightly different cadence from his stagger, seeming to mock him. When he glanced down at Croy's exquisitely rounded little rump, the globes separated by the tight jeans, the size of his erection seemed to leap by an extra inch. Part of him was desperate to allow it release; part of him was saying that this wasn't the right time—that he should instead be on his knees praying for forgiveness from the God he knew didn't exist for the cruelties he had inflicted upon his beloved.

In a way he hoped that it was the plane's little forward bedroom Croy was leading him to; yet in a far more profound way he hoped it was not.

Casanova shook his head in half-angry confusion. This wasn't like him. He couldn't ever remember feeling reluctant about the prospect of lovemaking with a beautiful woman, and rarely with a plain or even downright ugly one. There had been plenty of those in his long career—and men, too, although they were less to his taste. Yet now he was like an adolescent eager to lose his virginity, but somehow at the same time fearful lest he make himself an object of ridicule.

It was indeed to the cramped extra bedroom that Croy led him. There was hardly space in there for the two of them in addition to the narrow single bed. Clearly the room was intended only for people in search of a quick nap, not for serious sleeping . . . and certainly not for lovemaking.

Croy shoved him ahead of her, turning him so that the hard edge of the mattress pressed behind his knees.

233

He kept his balance with difficulty.

"Sit," she said firmly.

He sat, and Croy sat down beside him. She reached out with her black-slippered foot and pushed the door closed.

"It's too bright in here," she said mainly to herself. "Hang on a moment."

She stretched across him, her breasts playing against his chest, and turned a dimmer over the headboard until the room was filled with a twilight gray.

Oh, well, thought Casanova. *To hell with all this rue and remorse . . .*

As she straightened again, he thrust his hand up under her shirt to grab at the nearest breast.

The slap across his face, though not overly hard, momentarily stunned him.

"This is for me to give, not for you to take," Croy hissed. Yet again there was that wild ferocity in her eyes. They seemed to glow with warning in the dusk. "Just bide your time. Wait. Be patient. Or, so help me, I'll stuff your head so far down the toilet, the treetops will be hitting you in the face. Got that?"

She fluttered her long, silver-painted fingernails in front of him like a fan, and he realized there were even worse threats she could have made.

Then Croy was grinning cockily at him again. "Just so we understand each other."

Casanova nodded, not daring to speak in case he said something stupid. This was too strange for him. He was accustomed to being the one in control. Now here was this slight, seemingly frail woman controlling *him* with what appeared to be perfect ease. *Maybe it's just because my spirits are so low,* he tried to reassure himself, but he knew the thought was a lie. Even had his morale been at its most rampant, he would still have been under Croy's thrall.

She caressed his cheek with her palm, the grin fading as she looked earnestly into his eyes.

"Why are you doing this?" he said, raising the courage to speak at last.

"Because I want to," she said, the rhythm of her stroking not varying an iota. "If it were just you who wanted to, you wouldn't be here and neither would I."

"But why do you want to?"

"Because you're wounded and you need healing, and it's in my power to heal you. Because I've decided I like you. Because you're quite a good-looking man when you forget about wanting to fuck everything that moves. And"—she shrugged—"because, to be honest, I'm a little horny anyway. Even though all the flogging at the club was a hell of a turnoff, O has . . . an effect on women as well as men."

None of this was the answer Casanova had wanted. Usually, if any woman had said this to him, he would have either thrown her aside or forced himself on her in a way that made clear who was fucking who. It sounded all too much as if Croy were seducing him out of pity, nothing more, and the last thing he needed was to be fucked because someone felt sorry for him. And yet . . . and yet there was some aura around her that made everything seem all right, somehow. Yes, it was strange to be seduced rather than do the seducing, but it was also deeply relaxing, as if he could simply lean back into the situation like settling himself into a favorite chair.

He gave her a watery smile.

"I *do* like you, you know," she said. "This isn't something I normally even think of doing as . . . as part of the healing process."

A sop to his pride that she needn't have offered. He was grateful for it anyhow.

"Kiss me," she said, half closing her eyes.

He put his arm around her back and pulled her to him. The first kiss they shared was tentative, a mere touching of the lips, but then she slid her hands up to the sides of his head and held him tightly as her tongue forced its way between his teeth, flicking hotly from side to side like a flame. He felt his will drain away from him, and succumbed to the sensation of her long, slow embrace.

His entire skin seemed to have become highly susceptible to sensation. He could feel every stitch of the robe he wore, most especially where it was bunched against his painfully straining erection, but not only there. It was as if having Croy in his arms had made the whole of his body as sensitive to touch as the tenderest part of that organ. Even through the silk of her shirt and the fabric of his robe, the light brush of her nipples against his chest sparked off traces of desire that ran like electrical charges all through him.

Earlier Casanova had whimsically thought of himself as being like a virgin. Now he knew that he was. He had never felt like this before, had never been so completely lost in the intimate presence of a woman, so filled with the scent and touch and taste of her, that his lust became a secondary thing, subservient to the yearning—to the *need*—to let himself become a part of her. Always there had been a part of him that observed his ecstasies from a distance, commenting wryly on them, congratulating him as he reached each new pitch of sensation.

Not now. Now he just *was*.

"Please . . ." he said, drawing back from her for a moment, then realized he didn't know what he'd been about to ask for.

She ran the tip of one of her silvery claws down the bony length of his nose.

"The buttons are at the back," she said.

Blindly he fumbled with them, undoing them one by one. His clumsiness didn't matter. Virgins were always clumsy.

At last the task was done. She leaned away from him and extended her arms so that he could tug the shirt off her. Her breasts were small, in keeping with the rest of her—but he had known that, of course. They were two adorably round black apples, crested by dark pink little knots. He put up a hand to cup one of them, rubbing his thumb over the hardness of the nipple.

Croy moaned, her eyes now completely closed.

With his free hand he probed at the back of her jeans until at last he was able to slip a finger down past the tight waistband to rest in the crease of her rear.

She was kissing him again. Covering his face in a storm of kisses. Nipping at his earlobes with her sharp teeth. Moaning. Moving her hips so that his trapped finger rubbed up and down within its niche in imitation of coitus.

And then she was pushing herself away again.

"Hold back," she said. "Wait."

Still not opening her eyes, she stood up from the bed, stood with the spiral of her navel directly in front of his flushed face, and pushed hard against the clasp at the waist of her jeans. Her hand was trembling as she pulled carefully, carefully down on the zip to reveal a densely packed bush of hair. He put his face forward to kiss the top of the tangle, feeling the coarse strands between his teeth and against his tongue, only vaguely conscious of her struggling to push the garment down over her hips. The first he knew that she had succeeded was when she took a half step back to rest her rear against the door as she kicked the leather slippers from her feet and the jeans from her ankles.

At last she was completely naked to his view.

Casanova sucked in his breath. Her body was perfect. All female bodies were perfect in his eyes—big, small, rounded, bony, fleshy, thin—because what he saw were not the bodies but the different women who dwelled within each of them. But even so, Croy's body was possessed of a loveliness of form unsurpassed by any he had ever seen before. He felt almost ashamed as he admitted to himself that O's body, too, was among that multitude.

The indentations left on her hips and waist by the seams of her jeans only made Croy's body yet lovelier.

He began to wrestle himself out of his robe, but was halted by a little clucking noise Croy made at the base of her throat. She was squinting at him through the narrowest slits of her eyes.

"Not yet," she whispered.

She moved forward and slowly raised her right leg to put her foot on the bed beside him, her hands on his shoulders. Accepting the offer she was making him, Casanova slid down until he could see the pink of her wet sex peeping at him through the crowded zigzagging curls of black hair. He put out his tongue and, the musk of her filling his nostrils—seemingly filling his entire awareness—touched the very tip to the top of her opening. At the contact, she rammed her mound against him, gliding his tongue down over the glossy slick flesh. With his hands holding her smooth buttocks, he clutched her even more firmly to him as he probed his tongue in between the folds of her, feeling her little nub pressing on his lip.

Croy squirmed in his grasp, twisting him around until she was able to fall back onto the bed, her knees raised, so that he could push his face even closer against her. She must have come already, because the hair around her sex was awash with fluid. Straining against her fierce grip, he held his lips half an inch from her wetness and gently blew on it, cooling it, sending her into spasms of sensation. Then his mouth was covering her again, his tongue delving deeply into her, pushing in and out of her with a slowly increasing rhythm until . . .

He felt the little butterfly pulses that presaged another climax for her, and built up the speed of his movements as her own became uncoordinated.

This time Croy shrieked as she came, flooding his face with an outpouring of sweet honey. She rubbed herself up and down against his mouth and nose as if somehow she might make her orgasm go on forever.

At last her hips slowed and she lay on her back staring at the ceiling, her fingers toying idly with Casanova's hair, her breathing profoundly deep.

Casanova had no idea how long he knelt there by the side of the bed before he became aware of the ache in his knee—the one he had sprained escaping from a Marseilles mob long ago and had troubled him ever since. He moved uncomfortably to try to take the weight off it, and Croy took this as a signal to release his head. Gratefully, he stood, looking down on her. Her breasts and torso were a sheen of sweat. She grinned up at him impishly, not in the least concerned that her sex was wide open to his gaze.

"I could," she said, her breathing still unsteady, "come to be far fonder of you than it would be wise for me to be, Giacomo."

She pronounced his name so tenderly—so different from the harsh straightforwardness of "Jack"—that he felt the sounds burrow into him, curling up there somewhere near the very core of him. He knew they would be with him for all time.

"But I'm not going to let myself do that," she continued, her voice dreamy. "I can't. Just for a short while, though, just until we get to La Guardia, I can pretend . . ."

Casanova pulled his robe over his head. Following the line of her gaze, he let his own fall to his erection, still rigid in front of him. The single eye staring back up at him seemed to be filled with tears. His penis felt bigger and heavier than surely it could feasibly be. His balls seemed twice their normal size, dragging down on an impossibly stretched sac. Yet, where before he had been on the brink of climax, now the unrelenting pressure of his arousal had numbed him.

"Be inside me, Casanova," murmured Croy, taking his hand in both of hers.

He climbed onto the bed between her outstretched legs and slowly lowered himself to her. She reached down past her flat belly and her soaking thatch of pubic hair and took his shaft in her hand, holding it as delicately as if it were a champagne flute, then she guided him to her opening.

As he made to lunge into her she halted him.

"Wait," she said yet again.

For over a minute they stayed motionless, only the bulb of his penis within her. Casanova could scarcely believe the sensations darting through him as Croy flexed her muscles so that her quim was kissing the engorged glans. Then at last she drew the full length of him inside her until she had swallowed him to the root.

Without words, he understood what she wanted of him. He drew himself in and out of her in slow, languorous, unhurried strokes, experiencing each sensation to the fullest, savoring it, drawing it out until the moment came when he made the smooth transition to the next. The touch of his balls against the smooth flesh of her rear. The warm, damp pressure of her internal walls against his shaft. The taste of her mouth against his as he bent his back to kiss her. There was no question of rushing himself to orgasm, as he so often did. Instead, he dreaded the prospect of climaxing, because it would bring an end to this gentle ecstasy.

When he felt the first pangs of culmination begin, he pulled himself out of her, kissed his way all down over her breasts and stomach until he reached her ready cleft, and licked until his own fever had passed. With her acquiescence, he turned her around so that she was on her hands and knees, the gloriously feminine swell of her rear in front of him. For a long time he simply caressed that twin roundness, sometimes letting his hand stray to where her wetness welcomed him, sometimes dipping his head to run his tongue up the crease between her buttocks to reach the dimpled cavity above the base of her spine that he had discovered was especially sensitive to her.

He no longer knew how often she had lost herself in orgasm when he lifted her hips into his lap and pushed the length of his erection into her again.

Now he moved in her more swiftly, anticipating that her wish for gentleness was past. Her hand cupped his balls and pulled on them insistently as he drove himself repeatedly into her. His long-delayed climax was building once more. He couldn't hold it back any longer.

Except that—

Croy wriggled out of his hold and, before he knew quite what was happening, had flipped him over onto his back.

"I want us to be able to see each other," she said quietly, wistfully, as she straddled him, her fingers lingering on his soaking cock before she gradually impaled herself on him. She reared back, pulling his hands to her breasts, arching her spine, beginning to ride him more and more swiftly. He raised his head, saw the white shaft of his penis appearing and disappearing repeatedly as her darkness withdrew from it and engulfed it, felt the stuff of his soul gathering itself as his sac tightened.

"Now!" Croy screamed, shooting her head forward, her hair whiplashing in a frenzy between their faces. "Now! *Now!*"

The walls of her sex were knotting themselves around him with greater and greater urgency, and it was this that finally drew him past the point of no return. He felt the surge of his elixir push itself in strong, irresistible, heavy pulses up the length of him until at last they burst into her. He bucked his pelvis up beneath her, his rear clear of the bed, twisting his penis as if it could somehow be driven any further into her, feeling even more release as yet another current of his thick fluid erupted inside her. It was not just his seed he was giving to her, he knew, but the self of him. Wherever the future took the two of them, Croy would always possess the essence of Giacomo Casanova. And she, too, would dwell within him.

For a long time afterward they lay on the bed without words, pooled in each other's sweat, just holding on to each other as if each were the other's life raft in a stormy sea. Then at last they began to speak, exchanging little fragments of sentences that weren't really jokes but were funny anyway, and in the end they found themselves making love again, very tenderly, as if this were merely a continuation of the conversation.

Last of all they slept briefly in each other's arms, exhausted, until Jonathan's incongruously unruffled voice over the plane's intercom woke them to announce that they would be arriving at La Guardia in fifteen minutes.

"Thank you," said Casanova as they hastily showered together. "You've healed me. Healed me, I think," he added, "for the rest of my life."

Croy grinned. "Yeah. Right. You think you've been healed. I think I've been just about crippled . . ."

Chapter Fifteen

Another city, another luxurious vehicle, another finely threaded pattern of bridges and tunnels and roads, trucks and cars expelling their fumes and noise to the front, behind and on either side, all of them churning onwards, barreling toward an individual—and yet in their speed and direction—united destination. The city. If there was one thing Casanova would never have expected from this century's travel, it was that it could be more exhausting to traverse a continent these days than it would have been in his own time. The coming and going, the air travel, the road journeys, the never-stopping force of what appeared to be progress clearly had a draining effect, not only on the people in the car with him, but also on those who traveled alongside them. Not one of the drivers in the cars they passed was smiling, every one of them intent on the road, intent on the forward point. Casanova thought longingly of a slow boat trip, a gentle walk, a quiet bed.

And yet, even as he imagined falling back into smooth sheets and soft down, something else took hold. Another feeling, another imagining. Casanova smiled to himself, even now, after all this time, all these times, he could still feel the thrill of a new sensation. Tired as he was—no doubt from his exertions with Croy, or his earlier efforts at the club, or merely from what these people called jet lag—there was something else stirring within. Something wild, energized.

The car had traversed the Triboro Bridge, and as he looked through the window at the savagely pinnacled sweep of Manhattan reaching far to the south, Casanova recognized a sense of excitement he had not felt for years. Not only these years, the years he'd been sleeping—or dead—whatever he had been, but also his own adult years, the lived years. His time past and his time now, an excitement that the adult Casanova had yearned for every day and had tried in so many ways to recapture. Something of the first blush of desire, the initial stirring of passion that had infected him as a youth and on which he'd fed for so long afterward. He had been a youth—and a man—who loved new adventure, fresh joys, who could never bear the same routine for any length of time, no matter what promises a deeper knowing might have held.

Sitting in the back of the car, traveling at speed into the city, Casanova was excited. Purely excited. Like a little boy, a child, thrill surging up from the pit of his stomach to his face, forcing his neck slightly forward, arcing his eyebrows, opening his eyes wide, and finally curling his lips into a grin of anticipation. This was birthday enjoyment, feast day excitement, the thrill of a purloined coin from an open purse.

For fifteen minutes he sat transfixed, staring out of the window, until eventually the car began to slow, caught in traffic and also nearing their destination, turning from the wider roads to narrower, and then narrower still.

Croy looked questioningly at Casanova. "What is it? People generally have something to say the first time they see Manhattan."

She reached out a hand to him and Casanova felt the warmth of her skin on his, rippling through his body from the light touch on his arm, all the way down his torso. They had left Kate at La Guardia, waiting for the privately staffed ambulance that had been ordered for

D, but Jonathan, too, was interested in Casanova's reaction, dividing his attention between the road in front of them and the rearview mirror in which he watched his passenger's face.

Casanova leaned farther forward, craning his neck through the darkened window, staring up and up and up at the buildings that now loomed above the vehicle, making a narrow canyon of the street, and he nodded, grinned, broke into a smile, and then into a laugh.

"It's this place, this city. It's incredible. It feels . . . there's a feeling . . . I can't . . . it's so . . ."

Casanova, the man who understood the weapon of words as well as he knew his own passions, was stunned at his inability to articulate his feelings. He felt Croy smile almost indulgently at him as Jonathan pulled up at a traffic light and twisted in his seat to nod back at the two of them. "This is the city that doesn't sleep, man. The Big Apple. This is it."

"Big apple?"

And even as he repeated the phrase, Casanova acknowledged a new feeling creeping in, another knowing perhaps, partially hidden by the excitement, but there all the same.

"The Big Apple," Jonathan repeated. "It's what they call New York."

"Among other things," Croy said quietly, almost to herself.

Jonathan took another corner and then brought the car to a smooth halt.

"Here we are, folks."

Sitting there, as they arrived at yet another unknown venue, in yet another unknown city, despite the excitement he now felt surging through his veins and the pleasure of Croy's soft hand on his arm, an unbidden and unwanted image came to Casanova. It was the picture of a worm, hidden in crisp and cool white flesh, burrowing its way to the core of an apple so fresh it still hung on the tree. A worm slowly turning inside.

An hour later Casanova was resting on the guest bed in Jonathan's apartment. Or at least he assumed it was Jonathan's apartment; they had been welcomed by the doorman, and Jonathan had led them to an elevator that, fifteen stories up, opened directly into the entrance hall of this cool and quiet home. He had told Casanova it was one of the better converted lofts Manhattan had to offer, certainly in this up-and-coming part of town. Casanova didn't know what he was talking about. The street below had seemed dark and dingy, poor almost, the building—from the steps to the entrance hall to the apartment itself—anything but. Jonathan had shown both Casanova and Croy to this spacious guest room, opening a door to a dressing room with a wide range of men's attire, any of which Casanova was welcome to try for himself.

After a quick bout of lovemaking on the bed, immeasurably enhanced by being on terra firma—even many stories above the ground—Croy was now in the shower, her small and lithe body pummeled by four differently angled shower heads, singing quietly to herself as she soaped and rinsed her willing flesh. She came back into the bedroom, draped in a wide white towel, the contrast between her black skin and the abundant fabric stirring Casanova all over again.

"Oh no you don't," she said, smiling at his rising cock. "We have work to do. You wash, I'll talk to Jonathan. Come join us for food when you're done." She leaned down, placing a soft kiss on each of his balls, another just skimming the rise of his pubic hair. "There'll be time enough for more of this . . . later."

It was nine in the evening. Casanova, Jonathan, Croy, and Kate sat on the terrace of the apartment, looking north over the Bowery and up to the tall buildings beyond. Casanova was finding it hard to pull his attention back from the view to the matter at hand. Kate had just given them a rundown on D's current state—"She'll live. And be glad to"—and they were now discussing how best to learn more about O's whereabouts. They had listed the likely people and places who might have information and kept coming back to one name, one location. Mr. Miller's bar.

"This Mr. Miller, who is he?" Casanova asked.

"More a place than a person," Kate answered.

"Though a person as well," Croy added.

Jonathan smiled, "Yes, definitely a person as well."

The three of them were quiet then as far below car horns beeped and people hurried about their evening's business. Casanova felt they were all waiting for him to speak. "Should we all go then? To this Mr. Miller's?" He nodded his head in as deferential and gentlemanly a fashion as he could while wearing the tight white T-shirt he'd found in the dressing room. "Or just Croy and myself, if Kate needs to return to D?"

"I can't go there, Jack." Croy spoke clearly into the semidarkness. "Neither can Kate."

"Why ever not?"

Jonathan answered, "Mr. Miller's is a gay bar. Men only."

Casanova nodded, "Oh. I see. Gay as in homosexual?"

"You got it."

"In that case, we'll go together, you and I."

Jonathan hesitated.

"What?" Casanova asked.

"Well, I do need you to come with me. They only allow men in as couples. Once we're inside it's fine, but that's their door policy. No single men."

"Fine."

"But you should know . . . it's quite . . . hardcore. You can't just go there to . . . view."

Casanova realized they were all watching him intently. At first he didn't understand why, then slowly it dawned on him that they weren't sure how he would react to the suggestion of homosexual activity. "Oh, I see. You think that's a problem for me? Sex with a man?" He burst out laughing. "Really, it's very strange how sanitized my reputation has become while I've been away."

They walked into the bar and almost immediately Casanova felt another old flame reignite. Not the sex flame, that one never went out, no more than had his ardent desire for O, that impossible, will-o'-the-wisp of passion that had drawn him on for what felt like an age now. This, though, was an altogether different burning. Rampant lust. He looked around the room. Men, boys, male figures caught in the turn from youth to adult, old men, young men. So very many young men. All heights and widths and colors of skin, the variety before him should have been incredible, at least three hundred male bodies packed into one welcoming place. And yet, regardless of the basic differences to do with genetics, every man he laid eyes on—was even tempted to lay hands on, fingers on, mouth on, cock on—every one of them was also fit and strong and smooth.

Casanova stood in the center of a room full of seminaked hairless bodies, toned and glistening with their own and each other's sweat. All around him there were bodies being pummeled and pushed and beaten in a glorious submission to the demands of the time, of this time, serried ranks of self-created Adonises, lined up and standing and staring and dancing and undulating. Every single one a perfect body, all of them bodies forged in sweat and pain. Bodies built in a way he knew—as a man himself, a man who fully understood his own flesh, he intimately knew—that no woman of this century, or any other, could achieve. These were the bodies that only diligence and attention to detail and pure testosterone could create.

Casanova knew himself to be a highly sexed man. How could he not know this most basic of his own truths? He also knew himself to be primarily a heterosexual man. But he had always, for centuries it would now appear, felt sorry for the traditional hetero man. The kind of man who believed himself capable of taking any woman to the heights of fucking orgasm, and yet who had never indulged, never dared to indulge, in the joy of being fucked himself. Casanova considered himself a fully rounded man. Proud to call himself giver and receiver. Yes, he and Jonathan were here on the search for O. Of course they were. He could not forget that, would not forget that—though his dalliance with Croy had made him aware of other possibilities—but he was here after all. Here and now. And while he was atoning for his sins in San Francisco, doing what he could to make things right, surely it couldn't be too wicked to take a bite of this fresh apple so generously laid out before him? In Casanova's day the homosex he'd enjoyed had, perforce, been furtive and hurried, as often as not with a priest or monk who had entered holy orders only to enter other men with less likelihood of being found out. And tried. And killed. Hung drawn and quartered, beaten, savaged, broken, abused, and finally, killed. A corpse thrown to the unhallowed earth. Casanova knew, Jonathan had explained on the way here, that there remained parts of even this delicious, if troubling, new world that didn't approve of homosexuality, still wanted it banned and broken, derided and denied, but right now, looking at the cavalcade of willing flesh all around him, he didn't think it could be all that bad for these young—and older—men.

Discreetly crossing himself in sorrow and sympathy and the remembrance of things long passed, Casanova thought back to his own first homosexual experiences. Those long summer nights with the willing and generous Friar Lawrence and, many years later, the friar's condemnation and agonizing death—a death made all the more painful by the holy man's certainty of the eternal hellfire awaiting him. The friar had been a fine teacher, in both the alchemical arts and the sexual ones. Tutoring the young Casanova in the art of giving to and receiving from another man.

Casanova watched as two young men pranced across a raised dais in small leather thongs, slapping each other playfully on their bare buttocks, to the joyous whoops of the assembled crowd. In fact, he thought Friar Lawrence might well have been appalled at the licentiousness in this long, narrow, spotlit room. The friar's death had been another martyrdom in religion's long—and surely, ultimately pointless—fight against the primal in man. In men. Looking about him, he couldn't imagine any of these youths getting on their knees in the morning and giving thanks for the martyrs who had paved their way to this carnival of carnal freedom. But maybe they did, and more than that, maybe he had no right to judge.

They squeezed past another trio of beautiful young men, Jonathan leading him on and farther into the room, and Casanova checked himself, chastized himself. For even if in his past life he had created his own legend, become the man every woman wanted, the one every man wanted to be, he knew for a heart-stopping fact that in his current regeneration he was also the Casanova who had been willing to beat his adored O within an inch of her life. The Casanova who had been drawn into—surprised by, certainly, but utterly absorbed in—the delights of pain, the entertainment of dominance.

Giacomo Casanova, Chevalier de Seingalt, the man who had fucked more women than he could possibly count, who had been fucked almost as many times in return, lifted a hand as if to slap himself. And he would have done so had he not known it would create a revolt in the building, an orgy of flagellation. One he would rather not see right now, not yet at least. He followed Jonathan and knew he had no right to judge. He was human, and so he did judge, but he knew he had no right to do so. These men were no different from himself. They paid no more obeisance in the dark to their antecedents, to the people who made their current joy possible, than he did to the Eve who had once persuaded Adam of the joys of her flesh. Not now anyway, not in the heat and the strobe and the pumping, thumping, chest-beating possibilities of the music that seemed to rise from the floor and fall from the ceiling to meet in his heart.

A young man stopped before him, offering a vial from which he inhaled deeply, and then another proffered a small tablet, which he took on his tongue as willingly and delicately as he might have taken the host. And then it was all joy, and only joy, it was pumping and fast and impossibly possible, this public exultation in the thrill of another man, this legal indulgence of the male body. Casanova flung back his head, raised his arms, let out a whoop of bliss, and felt his groin move, his lips open, and his torso and heart and blood pump to the resounding rhythm of the room. He grinned and smiled and kissed a stranger and then another, pushing his tongue far into the young man's mouth, tasting the boy's otherness and his sameness. Where was the god to strike him down, the law to condemn his action? What a century, what a life, what limitless possibilities . . .

Casanova was deep in the whirl of dance and desire when he heard Jonathan shouting at him, pointing to the back of the room.

"I'm going to talk to Mr. Miller, okay? I don't know how long it will take. Here—," Jonathan held out a card. "In case I don't find you later. It's got the address of the apartment on it. Come back there. Yes?"

Casanova took the card from him and put it in his pocket without even looking as he nodded in agreement. He didn't care at all how long Jonathan would be, didn't care in the least. Jonathan smiled approval and edged away, and Casanova was carried along on a wave of hard bodies dancing as one. And then, in a movement that must have been practiced, had to have been rehearsed and re-created so many times before, and yet seemed impulsive, felt immensely flattering (as it was no doubt meant to do), one of the bodies pulled itself away from the crowd, detached, became deliciously singular, and presented itself in front of Casanova.

"You're beautiful."

Casanova stopped, looked, and smiled. The young man came into focus. Eighteen, maybe nineteen, maybe twenty-five in daylight. "I'm sorry? The music's very loud." He had heard. He wanted to hear again.

"I said . . . ," the young man leaned in, his sweet minted breath closer to Casanova's ear, warm on his cheek, and a well-intentioned hand hot on his cock. "I said, you're beautiful."

Casanova looked at the green eyes that were staring at him. Same height green eyes. Same level wide mouth. The bright, white teeth of this wealthy nation. The warm, welcoming body of this willing man.

"We both are."

"I'm Adrian."

"Jack."

"Do you want to fuck, Jack?"

"Yes. I do."

And now they are in a cab on the way to the Meatpacking District. And when Adrian directs the driver and tells him their destination, he names it with his hand firmly on Casanova and every intention of single innuendo. His home is not far, Adrian has said, but he wants to get there as quickly as they can, wants Jack in bed as quickly as they can.

And the cab driver is not much interested in them, as he is listening to the radio, there are people shouting at each other in some language

Casanova does not know but thinks must be of Asian origin. The people's voices are rising and falling in impassioned speed as the cab moves on through one-way roads, lights, and buildings and a drumming of engines. Casanova is bent down across the backseat of the cab and has opened the three metal clasps on Adrian's old, soft denim jeans, and now he has Adrian's cock in his mouth, Adrian's fingers in his hair, and this is New York and the twenty-first century, and the cab driver turns to Adrian and says he will have to charge another five bucks if there is any mess, and Adrian looks down at his crotch with a question on his lips, and the immensely skilled Jack smiles with a mouth full of this other, this other yet same, this man, and Jack smiles, and speaking with his mouth full and his body eager, promises there will be no mess. Adrian laughs and his hand massages the back of Casanova's neck, and the driver turns up the sound of the shouting people, and now Casanova has all of Adrian in his mouth, and his tongue works the shaft as his lips pulsate his cock, and now he has freed a hand to gently, fiercely, gently cup Adrian's balls, and now that hand has freed a finger to smoothly, carefully find its way to Adrian's ass, and then slowly, with infinite care and absolute knowledge of its goal, to his prostate, and there to stop and stay and keep on, keep on with the intimate massage and the eager mouth that give Adrian the internal and external orgasm he so desires.

The backseat is clean.

Adrian is delighted, "God, Jack, you're good."

Casanova considers, nods. "Yes, I am."

At Adrian's apartment there is cold beer, and there is sparkling water for good health, and there is sharp white cocaine passed on the tongue, tongue to tongue, tongue to nipple, tongue to tingling cock tip, tongue to willing, wanting rim. Adrian may be young, is certainly not centuries old, but he knows what to do, is accustomed and accomplished, and Casanova has been fucking for so long now, then and now, all of this time now, taking the lead of fucking, the in charge of fucking, and he wants a rest, he wants to be taken care of, be laid down, satisfied, fucked. Adrian is more than happy to oblige. But not before he has rolled on a bright pink, and ribbed, condom.

"Ah . . . what? Why?" Casanova asks.

"Come on, Jack. Standard procedure, right?"

"But the women I . . . they haven't . . . they didn't . . ."

Adrian sneers, "Straight girls? Yeah, well, I don't want to sound sexist or anything, but they can be a little dumb about taking care of themselves. See a nice bit of cock and just don't know how to take it slow. You want to take care there, man, no idea what they're giving you."

Casanova has no idea what "sexist" means; he does not know how to say this is the first time he's come across this particular modern practice, nor does he understand why this "standard procedure" has not been standard until now, with this man, in this room. It's not as if they need to worry about making a child. And he would say, would ask, but Adrian is holding him, and readying him, and now Adrian is fucking him, whispering himself into Casanova's body, one arm wrapped around and across his chest, the other hand to work in front, so slow, so easy, until the switch, the click, the point when the rhythm is all, and it is no longer easy or slow, it is all there is.

From a high bed on the tenth story, looking out beyond the West Side Highway, as Lady Liberty's tiny red torchlight fights for the West against the rising sun, Casanova opens his body to another man, this other man, creating a joint rhythm, their two taut, fine-made bodies coming together in a moment of conjoined orgasm that is pure testosterone. And Casanova recollects, for the first time in more than two hundred years, how very much he enjoys the company of men.

"Almost as good as the Mets winning the World Series, huh Jack?" Adrian grins, as they part their single, sweated body to lie separate and together in the early light.

Casanova has no idea what Adrian is talking about. And he sleeps.

When Casanova awoke, it was ten in the morning and Adrian was still sleeping beside him, wrapped into the stained and sweated sheets. Casanova lifted himself from the bed, careful not to wake his companion. He looked down at the young man's hard body, fresh passion rising within—and without—the twist of Adrian's naked torso delineating each hard-won muscle and sinew. But it was already late. And, he smiled at himself in the floor-to-ceiling mirror that reflected the river, he had been well serviced; it was time to play the gentleman again.

O was still out there somewhere in this teeming city, waiting no doubt for rescue, for sanctuary. Even with the connection he felt now to Croy, Casanova understood there to be something that ran very deep between O and himself, something vital. Not least the amends he had yet to make. Jonathan had assured him that the conversation with Mr. Miller, somewhere in that mêlée of men, would lead them today to O.

As Casanova pulled on the clothes he had discarded so feverishly not four hours before, he shook his head at his own impetuousness. Perhaps he should have stayed with Jonathan last night; then he, too, could have spoken to this Mr. Miller, known what Jonathan, Croy, and the others no doubt now knew. But, as always, his cock had led him on, led him astray.

Ever since he'd woken up that morning in Venice, since whoever or whatever had returned him to this world, he had so often nearly understood why he was here, felt tantalizingly close to the truth, and yet each time, just at the point when he might have asked the question that could only result in an answer of total truth, he had been taken back—or taken himself—to—the realm of the physical. Allowing his body to take precedence where answers might have been preferable. Casanova sighed, and then he smiled. It was something, at least, to know himself. To know himself in this body, in his prime, rather than as an old man, looking back. Now all he had to do was turn that knowledge to his own use. And maybe to O's as well.

Out on the street, Casanova hailed a cab and, giving the driver the address from Jonathan's card, made his way back to the apartment, where the doorman welcomed him with the same disinterested smile he had offered the day before. The open elevator took him up the fifteen stories, and he walked into the apartment feeling just a little shame-faced that the others had no doubt spent the night working on a way to help O, while he'd been working on his own desires. He shouted out a greeting and heard nothing in reply.

There was no one there. Nothing there. The kitchen, the sitting room, terrace, bedrooms, dressing room, were all empty. Not a stick of furniture, no sign that anyone had ever been there at all. The rooms were bright and shiny and bare, the fixtures and fittings looked brand-new, the shower where Croy had lathered herself so luxuriously was clean and dry and seemingly untouched. Casanova stared around him in disbelief. And not a little fear.

And then the door to the elevator opened behind him, and a man stepped out. It was the black man he had seen with Toby Faith. The comic-reading bodyguard. He was holding a comic book now, rolled up in his left hand, tapping it quietly against his massive thigh.

"Hello, Jack."

"Maurice?"

The man was smiling at him. "Have you come to view the apartment?"

"I'm sorry?"

Maurice stepped a little closer. "The apartment. It's for sale."

"Oh, I see, this is Toby Faith's home?"

The man stepped closer still. Casanova wanted to move away, but he knew to do so would look like giving in, giving ground. He stood firm in the center of the empty room.

"No. This is my apartment."

"Yours . . . but how?"

Maurice sighed. "Toby Faith works for me. So does Jonathan. And Kate. And Croy."

And now Casanova did step back. It was that or allow his knees to buckle beneath him. "I don't understand."

"I don't suppose you do. You saw a black guy—a big, black guy— sitting next to Toby Faith, and like any other white man, you made your assumptions. You're always so ready to believe the black man in a subservient role, aren't you? You never even think the guy behind the dark glasses might be watching you. As far as you're concerned, he's just doing a job. Whatever you ask of him, nothing too hard, nothing too taxing. Bouncer, bodyguard, janitor. Which does make sense, in a way, because I am here to clean up."

"But where are the others? We were supposed to meet. They were going to . . . I was . . . I . . ."

Maurice shook his head. "You're amazing, man. You really do think it's all about you, don't you?"

"I don't . . ." Casanova felt his energy slip from him, the buildings outside on the skyline seemed to sway. "I don't know. Just tell me what's going on. Please, Maurice."

"Maurice? Nah, I don't think so. The name's Mr. Miller to you, Jack."

Chapter Sixteen

For a long time O had been staring into the darkness, using the faint candlelight to try to make out the letters scraped into the brickwork. GOD. Did they expect her to find religion? Surely not. After everything she had experienced, the answer couldn't be redemption, could it? Then, last night it finally came to her. She saw the small dots between the letters. It wasn't GOD; it was G.O.D. G. Giacomo. O. And D. Even in her diminished circumstances, the thought of soon being reunited with her half-Vietnamese, half-Irish friend was exciting to her. She was no longer afraid; she had come so far since her days at Roissy. In many ways, she often considered, the brand that she would have burnt into the flesh of her scarred bottom forever was no longer a symbol of Sir Stephen's eternal ownership of her, but a reminder of the beginning of a process that over more than one lifetime had taken her from being a Justine to a Juliette, a heroine even the Divine Marquis would have trouble understanding. She had never been a victim, but she was now furious with the Power Company, because she believed they had reneged on their deal.

Casanova was unable to move. At first he thought he had been drugged yet again—he had long since grown tired of being a pawn in the struggle between the Order and the Power Company, but as long

as O's well-being was at stake, he knew he had no choice but to continue with the game—but a sudden starburst of horrible head pain
reminded him of the blow from Mr. Miller's minion's blackjack. He
was terrified by the blackness, worried that his second life had been
terminated before he had the chance to complete his mission. But
slowly he worked out his situation. He realized his arms were bound,
the cords pulled so tight that there was an almost pleasant pain in his
taut muscles. His feet were strapped together, but free—it was possible to move both of them together. He had some kind of hood over
his face, heavy, presumably black, but made of material that felt soft
against his skin. His abductors had some mercy then. The next thing
he registered was that he was in a car, and that it was being driven at
considerable speed. Finally he realized that his fly was open and his
penis was exposed.

In different circumstances, this would've excited him. But tonight
he found it contemptible. It felt at best like a deliberate attempt to
unman him; at worse an implicit threat. It seemed so cruel for his tormentors to mock him in this way. He thought of some of the women
he had seen naked recently, remembering D, collared and shackled to
her X-shaped cross. Even when she had been whipped so violently
that she had lost control of her bladder and bowels, she had a dignity
that he didn't have now. He remembered Lilah's defiant nudity. With
her tattooed vagina and the multiple silver rings decorating her clitoral bud and labia, it was as if she was protected from ever being
properly naked.

He thought of the different attitude women had about their genitals now than they did when he was first alive. It pleased him that any
sense of shame seemed to have disappeared, and he couldn't imagine
any modern woman feeling as exposed as he did now. He found himself considering what it might be like if he were forced to become a

slave himself; if that was the destination he was being driven to now. He could imagine taking pleasure in fucking to order; in many ways it would only be a ritualized form of something he had experienced throughout his life. He didn't see himself as a slave to women. But a slave to his libido? Maybe.

He felt a hand around his cock. It came as a relief. He was unable to tell whether it was male or female, but the smaller width of the hand suggested a woman. Casanova had experienced more hands around his penis than he would ever be able to count, but whoever was manipulating him now had the technique down to perfection. It was only when his masturbator stopped, pressing down on the especially sensitive spot on the tip, that he knew who it was. Teresa. Or rather, Bellino. It had to be her. She was using her thumb to spread the precum over the tip in exactly the same way as she had before.

"Bellino?" he whispered.

She laughed. He was certain it must be her. No longer so irritated, he allowed himself to relax and enjoy the experience as she brought him closer and closer to orgasm. But it was just a tease, and every time he got close, she squeezed him so tightly that the sensation would all but vanish and she would have to start again.

"Please," he muttered, "let me come."

"Okay," she laughed again, and as if it were all just a joke, she quickly masturbated him until he came. There was something wonderful about his orgasm, and he heard her voice saying, "Oh, it's all over the back of the seat. Never mind, it's leather." He felt her small breasts brush lightly against him as she leaned forward. Then she said, "Mmm, you have such delicious sperm, Giacomo."

"I don't understand," he said, thinking back to his meeting with Bellino, shortly after his rebirth. "You were the one who introduced me to the Power Company. If you're part of the Order, then . . ."

"Darling Giacomo, remember how it used to be, when you were the only one who knew my secret? Well, this is the same thing, just on a larger scale. Think about what you know already."

"I feel like I don't know anything anymore."

"Well, that's perfect. Look, it's really not that hard. Let me test some theories out on you and see which one you believe. Let's try this first: I'm a double agent. I work for the Order, but the Power Company believes I work for them. And they have no reason to believe that I would betray them; after all, they were the ones responsible for bringing me back."

"And me, too?" Casanova asked, feeling frustratingly close to being able to resolve a mystery.

"Everyone alive or who has ever lived has at one time or other either wittingly or unwittingly aided the Power Company. In which case, maybe the Order is part of the Power Company. There have been rumors about that for years. So what is the purpose of the Order? To aid the Power Company by working against them? Maybe that seems too paranoid for you. There has to be at least the possibility of resistance, don't you think? In life, in religion, in existence itself? Life and death. Good and evil. Black and white. But what if all of these divisions are false?

"Okay, this may be too much for you. Let's assume, for the moment, that the Power Company and the Order are separate organizations. Of course, there is also 'the association,' with a small 'a,' naturally. I'm sure you've heard of them. But they're small fry compared to these two big guys. Let's assume that you have become unwittingly involved in an epic battle between two ancient sects, locked in mutual antagonism. And this is a situation that will continue forever, unless the Power Company is destroyed from within.

"Let me explain. You are being delivered to the Power Company as a prisoner. This could turn out to be a deeply unpleasant experience for you. Although I have worked for them for many years, I have no idea of their intentions for you. But once you are there, you will have opportunities that no one else has ever had. You can play Superman, Casanova."

"And O? Is she involved with this?"

"Of course. The Power Company already has her."

"But Croy told me that O had been taken to the headquarters of the Order."

"You mustn't trust Croy. She is playing a role. We all are, in a manner of speaking, but Croy is particularly good at hers. It's not about sex for her. She is . . . well, let's just say that her perversions aren't strictly speaking sexual. Try this one for size, Giacomo. You can tell Croy was lying to you, because the Order doesn't have a headquarters; they're a much more flexible organization than that.

"The Power Company can have headquarters, because as far as everyone else is concerned their role is a benign one. Everyone trusts the Power Company. But only those at the highest level understand what's really going on. Croy gave you this misinformation because she needed to get you here. Right from the very beginning you've been a pawn, Giacomo. Now we need you to complete your mission."

"But I don't understand. Are you working for the Order, or the Power Company, or both?"

"You choose, Giacomo."

"I'm fed up with your riddling. How do I know whether I can trust a word you say?"

"What other choice do you have?"

"True," he admitted, "but it makes no sense to me. Why go through this charade if you're working for the Order? Tying me up, scaring me . . . couldn't you have just told me about my mission and let me go myself?"

"So you have to believe my other hypothesis? That there is no difference between the two organizations? Or could it be," her voice took on a withering tone, "that you do not understand the Power Company? Could it be the case that if we delivered you to them and you hadn't actually been scared, at least for a while, they would know that it's a setup?

"How about this? They have machines that can measure your emotional mood, and if you didn't at least look roughed up, there's no way they would let you in. Sure they want you there, but you're not *that* important. They're going to enjoy torturing you, but if they had any suspicions that you were going in there to make mayhem, well, I think they would find it simpler to have you thrown to the metaphorical lions."

Without warning, Casanova received another heavy blow to the back of the head.

Of course, it wasn't the first time that O had been taken to the headquarters of the Power Company, but there had been many changes while she had been away, and she was worried that whoever was now in power didn't know what he was doing. He certainly had an imagination, she would give him that much. When they wheeled her in here on a hospital bed, the flight and everything that had happened to her in the past few days had left her delirious. And although she had by no means explored all of the enormous building, she knew that the wing she was being taken into was new. There was the smell of fresh paint everywhere, and the doors and corridors had a strangely artificial look to them, like a fake house in a do-it-yourself store or a new attraction at Disneyland.

The wing was full of small rooms, or cells. Above each room was an ornate letter, running from A to Z. As she was wheeled down the corridor, she saw that some doors were open, revealing women chained to beds; others were closed, but the doors were not sufficiently sound-proofed to muffle the cries of the women inside. Others revealed couples making love in the most tender fashion, or women being violently sodomized, or whipped, or about to have their bodies branded or burned with hot wax. In one or two rooms she could see men rather than women, and there was one homosexual couple making love who were so beautiful that she wished she could stay and watch. Room D was empty, as was G. H had a kneeling woman surrounded by six Japanese men gathered around, jostling for position in a no doubt doomed attempt to simultaneously ejaculate onto her face.

When O reached her room, she at first felt relieved that she would be left alone, even if she remained chained to her bed. But after several hours she began to grow frustrated, especially by the poor light in the room. It was ridiculous—they were the Power Company, and given the legitimate disguise under which they operated when not involved in their clandestine libertine operation, it seemed perverse that they should force her to remain in such dim light. She screamed until she was hoarse, but the only response she received was a few answering screams from some of the other rooms.

Her body was still so raw from the flogging that Casanova had given her at the Power Company's club on Harrison Street in San Francisco that even if she weren't restrained, it would be difficult to lie in any position that wouldn't chafe one of her many wounds.

The human body was so strange, O thought. Maybe it was just hers—she was certainly different from most women, other than the few she had persuaded to join her, almost always with a guilty conscience, either at the Chateau or later with the Power Company (and her brief, traitorous period with the Order)—but although she had been whipped so many times in her life, her skin had never managed more than the most superficial toughening. With every rebirth, in fact, it was as if she were losing another skin, like the lives of a cat. What was that song they had played at one of the many ceremonies? Ah, yes, that was it: "Rebirth of the Flesh." She had no idea who recorded it, but whoever had must have understood something of what she had been through. Each time she was brought back, she felt rawer, more alive; sometimes in dreams she wished she could be flayed to the bone.

But in many ways, Casanova's punishment of her had been the most severe she had ever received. Even the brief tickle he had given her with the thongs of the flogger had carried a charge to her inner being. Various factors had made her fear much greater than normal— the smell of shit and piss from D's flogging beside her, and the worry that although it had never happened before, she might also betray herself in this manner; the liquored-up audience and the video cameras that transformed the sacred rituals she had enjoyed at Roissy into an X-rated MTV extravaganza (she was so glad to be rid of Toby Faith and those wannabe libertines in Orange Sky). But most of all it was the sense that Casanova would do something to her that no one before, not Rene, not Sir Stephen, nor any of the countless others that had come after him, had managed.

It wasn't anything to do with physical force. Casanova was powerfully built, but he was nothing compared to some of the flagellators she had faced before—men chosen purely for their strength and skills with a whip. Her ass had already been raw when he started, that was true, but that wasn't it either. She had felt so relieved that he wasn't able to get to her breasts with his whip, at least at first, but the damage he did to the rest of her body was punishment enough. And then later, when she had given in, she'd twisted so that he could mark the flesh there and sensed how much he had enjoyed this. Knowing he only had twelve minutes to go to work on her was some relief, but when you were being flogged by someone who knew what they were doing, that time could stretch to an eternity. A true whip artist could make you inhabit your pain so fully that you feared you would never escape it. Other men had left lashes on the surface of her brain; Casanova had whipped through to her heart.

Sucking his cock afterward had come as sweet relief, but then he had stopped her before his ejaculate had filled her mouth. Why? She had no idea, but it made it all the more painful when she was torn from him. She had tasted his spunk before, of course, most plentifully when JoJo's digital probing into his asshole had massaged his prostate and helped him truly unload into her mouth. But there was something terribly upsetting to her about this interrupted blow job, and it somehow blanked her memory of the flavor of Casanova's sperm.

The door to her room opened and a woman in a white lab coat came in. She had blonde hair tied back in a tight bun and a pair of black glasses. O could tell she was either naked or wearing only underwear beneath the coat. The only other item she was wearing was a pair of black high heels. She didn't say anything as she carefully unchained O. She briefly ducked back outside and wheeled in a white trolley on which was placed a small plastic bowl of water, a yellow sponge, and various bottles of ointments. The woman carefully washed O's body, administering lotion to the nastiest cuts. Then she turned O onto her belly and carefully stretched open her bottom. O protested, but the woman shook her off. She went over and picked up one of the candles from the floor of the room. O worried the woman was going to drip wax onto her anus, but she only seemed to want to use it to get a better view. She leaned in very close and stared at O's asshole for what felt like an incredibly long period of time. O was more used to her ass being the subject of a whip's attentions than a woman's gaze, especially in such close proximity, and it made her feel awkward and embarrassed.

"Is something wrong?" O asked, trying to turn around.

"No," said the woman, raising her glasses, "nothing's wrong."

The woman slid her tongue up inside O's asshole. O quivered with pleasure. She wondered who this woman was and whether she was now acting under the commands of the Power Company or doing this purely for her own amusement. Maybe she felt that after everything O had been through, she deserved this relief. O arched her haunches up as the white-coated woman slowly, and with the utmost sensitivity, reached up inside O's vagina to the most sensitive spot and began gently stroking against the inner wall there. She released O's buttocks, her face now buried deep enough, and O loose enough, for her to be able to carry on licking without impediment. With this hand, she now began to stroke O's clitoris. These new pleasures combined with the physical pain from her recently washed wounds into a kind of delicious neuralgia, the kind of ice-cream headache that many people hated but, as the masochist inside her would never fully vanish, she had always secretly relished.

The blonde-haired woman brought forth from O the most enjoyable orgasm she could remember having in a long time. She was so used to pain that she sometimes worried she no longer knew how to enjoy simple pleasures, and she was so relieved to discover that this wasn't the case that she cried tears of real gratitude.

"Thank you," she said.

"No," said the blonde-haired woman, "thank you. It's something I'll be able to tell my grandchildren."

O laughed. Although she was grateful for what had just happened, she couldn't help thinking there was something untrustworthy about this woman. Testing this theory, she said, "And now you must let me return the favor."

"No," said the woman, "you are in pain. It's not right for you to pleasure me."

"I want to," said O, "please let me."

"No."

"Are you not allowed? Is that your instruction?"

"I can do as I please. I came to you as a doctor, and that is how I examined your wounds, but what I just did, that was for me."

"Can I at least kiss your breasts? Just for a moment?"

The woman hesitated for a moment, and the way she looked up at the corner of the ceiling made O wonder if there was a secret camera hidden there. She quickly unbuttoned her coat and dropped it to the floor. As O had suspected, she was naked underneath. Her pubic hair was surprisingly thick and dark, which made O suspect that her blonde hair was dyed. She moved back closer to O's bed and proffered her breasts to her. They were beautiful breasts, clearly real, and although they suited her, just a little too heavy for the woman's frame. O gently took the woman's left nipple into her mouth. She nuzzled for a short while there and then did the same thing to the woman's right breast. O put her hand between the blonde woman's thighs, and she immediately jumped back.

"I told you no," she said, kneeling to the floor to pick up her white coat. O stared at the woman's ass, wondering why she was so reluctant to let O pleasure her. O realized the woman was crying.

"What's wrong?" she asked.

"Nothing," she replied.

She had no time to form any further conclusions, as the woman snapped her white coat back around her body before she turned and quickly left the cell, stopping only to lock the door. After she had gone, O was surprised by her liberty and used it to get off the bed and reexamine the letters on the wall. There was no mistaking it. G.O.D.

D awoke from a nightmare, alone in her bed in the privately staffed hospital in New York where Kate had taken her. She no longer had any real conception of time, but had awoken in this way on several occasions since being snatched from the Power Company's club on Harrison Street in San Francisco. Each time she awoke, the physical pain was so bad that the nightmare she had just escaped from seemed preferable and she allowed herself to fall asleep again. From her snatched moments she had managed to piece together what had happened to her, and remembered Kate stroking her face and telling her everything would be okay.

D noticed a hooded figure standing by her bed. She was about to scream when the hooded figure raised a leather-gloved finger to her lips. "Shhh, D, it's okay, it's me."

"Kate?"

"Yes. Don't be frightened. I have to take you to the Power Company's headquarters."

"No," D squealed, "please, I'm so exhausted, my body's torn to ribbons."

"Relax," Kate said, "I won't let them hurt you. That's why I persuaded them to let me take you there. Some of the other people in Mr. Miller's employ are so hypersexual that you wouldn't be safe. I brought you this far, you just have to trust me a little longer."

"I can't move, Kate. It hurts so much." There were tears in her eyes.

"I know," she said, "it's okay. I'll carry you."

Kate came over to D's bed and pulled back the stiff white sheets. D's body was so bloody and damaged that it was impossible for her to wear any clothes, even pajamas, and she was naked except for the bandages that wrapped the worst cuts left by the whip. Kate lifted D into her arms, and D passed out.

Kate gently laid D's small, beautiful body across the backseat of the limousine and then squeezed in next to her, right by the door. She gently placed a gloved hand on D's thigh, thinking about how difficult it was to be good. She had made a promise to D, and she would keep it, but the woman was irresistible, especially in this weakened state. She thought that if she did suck her pussy now, here in the back of the limousine, she would almost be able to justify it to herself, as even if her attentions made D wriggle and hurt her wounds again, the orgasm would relieve some of the terrible pain she must still feel.

The only thing that stopped her was the kindness that various people had paid her in her life, at times when she needed it most. Of course, in a way it had been a series of tricks, the Order no more benign than the Power Company, and, it now seemed conclusively clear, the two groups were interlinked in ways she couldn't possibly imagine. She had allowed herself to become a pawn for both groups, at times, allowing Croy to tell that disgusting story about how her master made her mind snap with his coprophiliac games when it was no more true than the Power Company's myth that she had committed suicide at the Pavilion. The only thing that was true was that there was a room at the Pavilion named after her, but this wasn't because she had committed suicide there; rather, because it was there that she serviced hundreds of men and women. In any event, Croy had been there for her when she needed it, allowing her to fulfill a different role in Mr. Miller's grand plan.

She had no idea what awaited D at the Power Company's headquarters. She knew that Casanova and O would be involved, and she had already played her part in getting Casanova there. She allowed herself a small chuckle at how Casanova might react when he discovered Bellino's role in the game. Kate had always admired the way Mr. Miller gave his players such freedom to inhabit their roles, and one of his best jokes had been to take such a subservient role for himself. She couldn't imagine how he had coped having to spend so much time with Toby Faith, a man he evidently despised. Would she be allowed to witness the endgame? Would she be involved? She had no idea. Her instructions were often vague, but this had been the most brusque command yet: "D 2 PC HQ."

Kate looked up at the rearview mirror. She had been staring at D's pussy for several minutes, and if she looked at it any longer she knew she would be unable to resist. D had been shaved anew for her punishment at Harrison Street, and the sparse black stubble that had started to grow back only made her sex look even more edible. "Bad girl," she said to herself, slapping herself on the wrist. She could see the driver looking back at her and wondered if he could see D's body in the mirror. Somehow she doubted it, thinking that if he could, he would have an erection so stiff it would make driving somewhat of a challenge.

"How much longer?" she asked.

"With traffic this slow, about an hour," he said.

An hour? She doubted she would be able to resist that long. As a compromise to herself, she laid a gloved hand on D's thighs. D's eyes flickered open for a brief moment, and then closed again.

Chapter Seventeen

Casanova regained consciousness and stared groggily out of the car's tinted window. He was still bound, but at least his captors had removed the hood that had restricted his breath. "Enjoy the sights," Bellino said softly as she watched him stare out at the wonderful sprawl of the Metropolitan Museum, "for who knows when you will gaze upon them next?"

"Are we almost to the Power Company?" he asked, hoping against hope that he would get to see his beloved O, his Athena. He would accept all punishment without rancor if she were the prize.

"Close your eyes and make a wish," Bellino replied, her tone enigmatic as ever. He obeyed her and drifted into a deep sleep—and when he next opened his eyes they were drawing up outside one of the most magnificent buildings he had ever seen.

Two security men hurried out to meet the car, removed his shackles, and carried him into the center of an enormous ballroom. "Strip," one of them said.

He was clearly going to be the entertainment for the night—well, one of many lascivious entertainments. Casanova looked dazedly around as he undid his buttons, noticing the couples, threesomes, and quartets caressing in the room's numerous alcoves and antechambers. He, however, was on one of the dozens of raised plinths—in other words, he was center stage.

When he was completely naked, the security men left the arena carrying his clothes, and then a slim blonde approached holding a leather saddle. Slowly his eyes adjusted to the flickering candlelight and he realized that he knew her. "Cristiana!" he exclaimed, elated to see her sweet face and cute brown nipples, but alarmed by the horse whip protruding from her studded belt. Apart from the belt, boots, and a matching black wet-look thong, she was naked, as were a third of the men and women now gathering curiously around his plinth.

"Don't worry," she whispered as she urged him onto his hands and knees and fastened the saddle to his naked back. "It'll hurt, but I'll make sure that it's still erotic."

He nodded, remembering how she had become adept at S and M. Surely she would go easy on him, considering their shared history—yet here she was, attaching small spurs to her riding boots.

"I have to arouse you for this next bit," she said quietly, and slid his manhood between her pert breasts. Immediately he sprang to attention, and she laughed softly and slipped an unfamiliar leather restraint around his lengthening cock. Staring down, he saw that several straps were connected to the restrainer and that they were now being clipped to a harness that Cristiana was fastening under his belly and around his neck. The crowd broke into spontaneous applause, and a small man with a narrow jaw—could it possibly be Pierre Depuis?—shouted, "Ride him, girl."

"I intend to, but first he deserves a good whipping," Cristiana said, bowing to the crowd. She helped a tattooed girl onto the plinth and bade her to take hold of Casanova's harness, to hold him in place.

"Lilah," he gasped delightedly, recognizing her customized clitoral ring before he looked up into her equally familiar face.

"Bury your face in your hands, Jacques, and you'll be able to maintain the position," she said helpfully.

Casanova did what she said and quickly realized that she was right. If the whip were to bite into him while he was balanced on his hands and knees, he would jerk and flounder all over the place, and the whip could stripe his belly and thighs and perhaps even his manhood. But by resting his weight squarely on his elbows, he would be able to stay in place. Unfortunately, his new pose ensured that his haunches were especially elevated, a position that made him feel very vulnerable and ashamed. He took a deep breath and tried to think of Venice—why did so many people insist on thinking of England?—as Cristiana raised the whip.

The first blow fell low on his flanks and he bore it well, though its successor, placed slightly farther up, made him shudder. The third stroke was hard enough to make his tumescence shrink.

"Play with him for a while, Lilah," Cristiana said lightly, and Casanova groaned as the jeweled beauty tugged at his harness so that the leather restrainer buffed his most intimate flesh.

"Give him some eye candy, Cris," Lilah suggested, and Cristiana obligingly walked in front of Casanova and knelt down so that he could take one of her taut nipples in his mouth. He suckled greedily at the brown bud until Lilah said, "That's enough." He continued to tongue Cristiana's teat as Lilah continued. "We don't want to excite him too quickly when he has a whole night of teasing ahead."

"Teasing and torment," Cristiana corrected, removing her sweetness from his eager lips and picking up the whip again. Marching around to his nether quarters, she laid on three more strokes.

Despite his determination to take it like a man, Casanova cried out and jerked his punished haunches from side to side before getting back into position. "I'd go for a blitzkrieg approach if I were you," Lilah said. "That way the endorphins will kick in and he'll float."

Cristiana nodded, then bent down as if to tighten the harness around her naked lover's neck. "It'll burn for a few minutes, Giacomo, but then you'll go into trance pain and the pleasure will kick in," she whispered. "You have to trust me on this."

Casanova nodded mutely. Who else could he trust? He stared around the cavernous room and caught sight of an elfin girl, who looked enticingly like Croy, disappearing through a shadowy doorway. Breathing in the scent of *eau de mille fleurs,* he realized that Bellino must still be around. He thought that she had remained in the car that had brought them and been driven on to some other mysterious destination,—but now he suspected that she was staring at his tethered nakedness. Who else was feasting their eyes on his ignominy? It was impossible to tell, as many of the audience wore masks.

Before he had time to muse further, a hellish line of fire streaked its way across his proffered ass. It was soon followed by another and another. He tried to rise up, but immediately felt a girl straddle his back, holding him down. He realized that Lilah must have mounted him, and the sound of her jeweled clit rubbing against his leather saddle soon served to confirm this.

"It takes time to break in a pony," Cristiana informed the crowd while continuing to flog his buttocks. Beyond pride now, Casanova groaned and shifted the little he could under Lilah's weight. He could feel the saddle pressing into his back and the restrainer buffing against his manhood as she jerked experimentally at the harness straps.

He moaned softly at the mingled pain and pleasure, and the crowd whistled and stamped their collective feet. Again he tasted the whip on his exposed sore haunches, one cut underlining his sentient buttocks, and the next falling halfway up his flanks.

"I'm sorry," he muttered, though he was no longer sure what he was sorry for. Was it so wrong to wish to find his O, his chosen one?

"It's my duty to make you sorry," Cristiana whispered, and he wondered who was giving her such orders. But his thoughts were interrupted by the scourge of the flogger, which brought more and more heat to his tethered flesh.

The whipping went on and on, and just as he thought he couldn't take any more, the fire was superseded by a feeling of suspended animation and he became wonderfully contented, as if in the moments between sleep and waking. He wasn't even aware that he was still aroused until he felt Lilah tugging at the leather straps attached to his burgeoning root. The restrainer was tight enough to exquisitely rub him, yet not so tight that it stopped his erection from reaching its full circumference.

Rub, rub, rub went the leather against his shaft. He looked straight ahead, picturing Cristiana wielding the whip behind him, her clit pulsing as she took his pleasure to new heights and, indeed, to new depths. He could also envisage Lilah astride his back, bouncing up and down on her delightful oval buttocks and jeweled sex. Rub, rub, rub. He groaned again and stared hungrily down at the many nude and seminude women in the audience, enticed by their shaven quims, rouged nipples, and athletic bodies. Some caressed themselves as they gazed up at him, their expressions wantonly inviting and lewd. Rub, rub . . . he came loudly, crying out in unwilling abandon, wishing there weren't so many observers to this most private act.

"Time for a little riding lesson," Lilah said when he had recovered slightly. She clambered off him and took hold of one of the reins. Meanwhile, Cristiana clambered on and said, "Giddyap, horse." Casanova wondered why the two women had bothered to change places—then understood when he felt Cristiana's spurs graze lightly at his flesh.

He crawled carefully to the top of the stairs, and then Cristiana disembarked and helped him crawl down. When he reached the ground, she mounted him again and urged him forward, as did Lilah, the crowds moving aside to let them pass.

Now that he was on a level with the other revelers, he could make out more detail and focused briefly on a man with a ringed cock being pleasured by female triplets, one licking each of his nipples while the third attended to his straining sex. Another alcove was filled with women sitting on strangely shaped chairs, and it took Casanova a few seconds to see that the chairs were actually men, submissively offering their bodies as occasional furniture.

Cristiana spurred him on, and they passed a room in which six Japanese men and six Japanese women were seated around an ornate dining table. "They're having a *komba*," Lilah explained. "You know, communal dating?"

"But why here?" Casanova mumbled as she led him past another room where young women were playing an all-female version of strip poker.

"Why not?" Lilah answered. "The Power Company is all things to all people. Be all you can be, and all that."

"So what does it want with me?" he asked, as he crawled along yet another corridor, his buttocks blazing. He looked up at Lilah, his eyes pleading for an answer, but she simply tugged his reins harder and shook her head.

They slowly passed a large open chamber, and he saw D lying on a bed with bandages covering much of her café au lait body. Despite her wounds, she looked relaxed and self-assured. A man he didn't recognize was stroking her hair and whispering, "It'll be all right, Sarah." Overhearing this, Casanova felt absurdly pleased.

But his pleasure diminished as he was ridden into another of the main rooms and saw a huge black man seated on an overstuffed armless chair. He had a white youth over his knee and was spanking him soundly. As Casanova squinted up at the man, trying to make out his shadowy features, he heard the unmistakable strains of Orange Sky's barbarous but infectious music.

"I have to leave you now, Giacomo," Cristiana said softly, clambering from his saddled back. The tenderness in her voice transported him back to their first encounters in Venice, shortly after his "resurrection." Now he knew he had not encountered her by accident; she had been installed across his path, as his guide or nemesis. He looked up into her face, but she refused to meet his gaze and walked swiftly away.

"Me, too," Lilah added, holding out his reins to someone who was fast approaching. He stared upward, curious to see his new owner, but the person wore a leather mask.

This definitely wasn't a horse whisperer. Indeed, he or she said nothing, just tugged sharply at his harness. Breathing fast and hard, Casanova crawled forward and was steered into a large square anteroom where everyone was masked or hooded and many had metal handcuffs hanging from their belts.

For a moment he scanned the crowd that he was suddenly part of, then followed their collective gaze to the candlelit stage, and his heart began to beat faster. For O—wearing only a leather thong and what appeared to be nipple tassels—was being led up the stairs on a studded red collar and leash. Clearly adept at crawling in a previous life, she moved lithely, almost sensuously. The watchers cheered.

O's new owner—or whoever he was—led her to the center of the plinth and ordered her to bend over a sloping glass whipping stool. Obediently she got into place.

Casanova tried to stare into her face, but her blonde curls fell over her adored features. He longed to call out her name but feared that doing so would result in further punishment for both of them. As he watched in an agony of indecision, the man stepped forward and slowly pulled down her thong.

It was only then that Casanova became aware of the numerous looking glasses festooning the candlelit alcove. There was a huge magnification mirror under the glass stool, while others dominated the ceiling and the walls. They made it possible to see every angle of O's near naked body in incredible close-up, and to observe exactly what the masked man was doing to her.

Her skin had the pallor of milk, and Casanova quickly perceived that those were not tassels at the tip of her modest but perfectly formed breasts; they were small diamonds mounted on thin metal stems that savagely pierced her teats. The leather thong dropped to the ground and her genitalia were exposed. Casanova caught his breath: back on the occasion of his first sighting of her on the Venice Lido private beach, she'd had sequins sewn into her ash-blonde pubic thatch. She was adorned with minuscule sequins again, reflecting the prisms of light darting endlessly through the chamber, but it was clearly visible now that she had been depilated and the sequins had actually been sewn with metal-colored thread into her mound. This unusual decoration enhanced to maximum effect her outstretched labia, which had been colored dark scarlet and gaped open across the sea of light.

As Casanova and the others stared, mesmerized, a serving girl approached and handed the masked man four velvet scarves, which he used to bind each of O's limbs to the beautifully crafted see-through stool. She quivered slightly in her bondage but didn't utter a word. Casanova stared at her perfect alabaster bottom and longed to kiss both nether cheeks and lick playfully at her dark divide. He could see that her nipples were hard and long under the weight of the jewels and wondered if this was caused by dread or excitement. How had she fared in the Big Apple without him? Would she always be for-bidden fruit?

He was still musing on the event when another girl mounted the stage carrying a large jewel-encrusted bowl. Those closest to the stage, like him, looked directly at the vessel, while those with an obscured view stared into the tell-all mirrors and then grinned know-ingly and nudged their friends. As if sensing the newcomers' curiosity, a disembodied voice—presumably from the PA system—announced, "And now, for your delectation, we shall test the limits of female self-control."

A slight tremor worked its way through O's wholly displayed flesh, though Casanova suspected that he was the only one who saw it. He felt so close to her that he almost shared her mingled anticipation and shame. Once upon a time, back at Roissy, she had submitted in the knowledge that her captors cared for her, whereas here . . .

"We shall oil the entrance with warm lubricant," the voice pro-claimed. On cue, the masked man dipped his right hand into the bowl that the serving girl proffered. She then curtseyed deeply and put the bowl on the mirrored ground.

The masked man approached O's rear and reverently rimmed her anus several times with the warm oil before inserting one digit up to the knuckle. He nodded to himself then inserted a second digit and turned it around. A few of the watching women winced, but O remained immobile, though she clearly had freedom to flinch and squirm in her bonds.

Only I should be allowed to pleasure her in such a way, Casanova thought, then was jolted out of his reverie when the man, woman, or her-maphrodite holding his own reins pulled at the straps attached to his restrainer. To his chagrin, his manhood hardened so that it looked as if he was aroused by O's public shame. He was reassuring himself that her hair hid her eyes so that she couldn't see him, when the masked man walked to the front and gently smoothed her tresses back from her face, clasping them behind her head in an onyx barrette.

But his Athena kept her eyes downcast, either because she had been ordered to do so or because she didn't want to see her own ignominy reflected in the mirrors. Yet she was so much more than an ignoble offering, and Casanova stared at her greedily, noticing the outrageous puffiness of her labial lips. Those damn pubic sequins that had so captivated him when he first saw her glistened enticingly, while the heart-shaped emerald in her navel also reflected the light.

"Insert the vibrating anal plug," ordered the disembodied voice. A third serving wench—how many did the Power Company employ? or were some of them spies for the Order?—ascended the stage and handed the masked man a red velvet pillow with a black appliance displayed provocatively in the center. They had not had vibrating plugs during his last incarnation, Casanova mused.

He watched as the masked man took the penislike instrument and inserted it inch by exquisite inch into O's oiled rectum. Again she somehow refrained from moving a muscle, though her face flushed slightly and her lips parted for a moment before she gritted her teeth. When the crossed handle reached her flesh, he wound the instrument's straps around her buttocks and fastened them under her belly, holding the appliance firmly in place.

"Fetch the razor strop," the voice said. On cue, another girl arrived and placed a cushion holding a leather strop in front of O. Yet again she betrayed no sign of nervousness. But Casanova knew that she must be deeply ashamed of her tethered and held-open stance. He himself, while no stranger to control games, had felt ridiculous when Cristiana had ridden him like a donkey and Lilah had led him around as the crowd cheered. He felt less exposed now that he was no longer the center of attention, but he had no doubt that the audience hadn't seen the last of his reluctant nakedness.

"The vibrating plug will operate for ten minutes, during which the slave must not orgasm," explained the voice. "If she does, she will receive ten tastes of the strop and then the test will begin again."

"Ain't goin' to be easy, darlin,'" some callow youth shouted. Casanova thought that the voice sounded horribly like Toby Faith, but reminded himself that Faith had a very commonplace accent.

"This is a better high than I get from skydiving," another male voice said.

"She's so wet already," a tall woman in Gothic clothing murmured appreciatively.

"She'd do better to stay dry," her companion said wryly, warily eyeing the leather strop.

The murmurs of the crowd faded as the masked man stepped forward and switched on the anal plug. Immediately a low humming sound rent the air and O's rosebud puckered slightly. By looking in the mirror, Casanova could see that her nipples were being stretched by the diamond weights and that her artificially colored sex lips had begun to peel apart even wider. Her body was becoming beautifully receptive, and he wished once more that it was receiving him, alone, on a private beach.

"Nine minutes to go," said the disembodied voice. O inhaled hard and the watching crowd sighed with sympathy. But a few of the more sadistic ones began taking bets.

"She's got no chance," said one woman in a southern drawl. "I once had one of these things up me and lasted barely two minutes. The plug may be in your back hole, but the vibrations go straight to the clit."

"Here or at the San Francisco club?" the man next to her asked.

"Hell, no—at home, where I could wriggle about and change

positions. This poor bitch has no chance, all strapped down and splayed open like that."

She was proving to be right, Casanova thought sadly, as he watched his darling squirm and jerk in her velvet bonds. It was obvious that she was already nearing nirvana—her increasingly glossy quim and tensing thighs said it all.

"Eight minutes to go. I hope you won't fail us . . ." Everyone looked at the leather strop lying on the luxuriously overstuffed cushion; then they turned their collective attention to O's alabaster backside.

It was such a beautiful bottom, Casanova thought, full yet pert, curvy yet without an ounce of superfluous tissue. He longed to kiss her deep divide then nip playfully at each warm, silken cheek. These cheeks were now tightening and untightening to O's internal rhythm as the vibrations oscillated through her belly. She let out a breathy whimper, followed by another and another. Suddenly she went rigid on the whipping stool and howled, "Giacomo . . ."

So she had thought of him as the rapture rushed through her body. Again he felt an almost supernatural connection. They were meant to be together, so why had the fates kept them so cruelly apart?

For long moments after O's climax, nothing happened on the stage, though money changed hands between several people in the audience. Then the disembodied voice crackled into life again. "It seems fitting that she is punished by one of her own gender," it announced dispassionately, "someone who knows the feminine sweet spots best." The crowd broke into applause as a slim brunette in a black rubber dress mounted the stage and picked up the leather strop. It was strange to see the smaller girl preparing to beat the Amazonian O.

The dominatrix stepped back and seemed to weigh up her victim's buttocks, which flinched, as if aware of her scrutiny. Casanova observed belatedly that O was looking into the mirror and watching the other woman's every move. Did the two girls have a shared history at Roissy? After all, O had recruited other women there . . .

Crouched—naked except for his saddle and harness—on all fours, he was utterly helpless to intervene, and, given O's sporadically chosen submission, he wasn't even sure if she would want him to.

"Stroke one," said the brunette with obvious relish and laid the strop on hard, creating a blurred red band across the central swell of the waiting buttocks. O winced slightly but otherwise remained immobile on the whipping stool. She had taken much worse punishment in France and America, Casanova knew—the problem was that this one was to be cumulative. After all, a receptive body could orgasm numerous times, causing the lashes with the strop to build up and up.

"Stroke two." This one fell over the already punished flesh, and O flinched again but remained silent. She remained equally soundless when the strop landed slightly farther up, but she exhaled audibly when the fourth stroke hit the tender area where buttock meets thigh. "You're warming up nicely now," her tormentor said with obvious satisfaction, laying her hands on O's heated flesh.

It would have been an arousing image for him, Casanova thought, if O had been here of her own volition. Nevertheless, it was clearly highly stimulating to the audience; he looked around and saw that many of the men, and several of the women, were openly playing with themselves. "Beat her harder," one man urged and the dominatrix swiftly obliged.

Casanova watched as the raven-haired woman went on to deliver the remaining strokes to O's obscenely displayed buttocks. When she had finished, the disembodied voice said, "Reinsert the vibrating plug into her anus," and the test began again.

Suddenly Casanova felt a cruel tug on his harness and realized that he was being pulled away from the action. "Please, just a little longer," he said raggedly, desperate to remain close to O. But his new owner slapped twice with a gloved hand at his naked buttocks and tugged harder at his reins. Rather than cause trouble for himself and his lover, Casanova crawled obediently from the room and followed the masked creature up and down various corridors until they came to a chamber where speed dating seemed to be taking place.

"Now it's your turn to learn self-control," an auburn-haired matron in her fifties said, kneeling down to unfasten his saddle and harness. Divested of their heavy restrictions, he felt momentarily free. But his freedom lasted only a second as the woman led him to a glittering pole, removed the handcuffs from her belt, and cuffed his hands together behind his back and around the pole. Now he was naked and helpless, with his genitalia firmly on display.

And it did indeed become firm as, feasting his eyes on the numerous half-naked young women in the vicinity, Casanova immediately grew rampant. "Get used to it," the auburn-haired woman said in a mocking tone, "because each woman here gets to pleasure you for three minutes but won't let you come."

He would stare straight ahead and think of sheep gamboling in a field and of naked octogenarians. He wouldn't be bested. But, despite his intentions, Casanova's attention was drawn to a large screen overhead. To his surprise, he saw the image of O, who was still writhing over her whipping stool as the vibrations worked their magic, her excitement trickling down her thighs.

"I'm Candy," a seductive voice said, and he turned his attention to the statuesque nude temptress kneeling before him. "I like to suck sweets and lick lollypops." So saying, she took hold of his shaft and began to nibble at its mushroom head. "Mmmm . . . , it's getting very sticky," she continued, nibbling with increasing fervor. Casanova groaned lustfully.

Almost, almost . . . just as he was close to completion, a bell rang and Candy let go of his root. "See you," she said lightly. He looked longingly at her slender back and full buttocks as she hurried to a nearby table where more conventional speed dating seemed to be taking place.

"Next!" the auburn-haired woman said as if directing a post office queue. Casanova stared at the large black girl approaching him. Her breasts, topped with full, dark aureolas, were the roundest and most impressive that he had ever seen. He was flexing his cuffed arms and wishing he could take one breast in each hand when she bent down and placed his manhood in her ample cleavage, whispering, "I think he would enjoy a very special ride."

Holding her breasts together, she began to chafe them up and down, reexciting every sinew of his manhood. "Please," Casanova said desperately, "please let me . . ." But again, just as he was nearing his climax, she stopped and pulled away. "Why are you doing this?" he gasped as his phallus throbbed and jerked, all revved up with no place to go—at least, no place he was allowed to go. "Orders," the young woman said mysteriously.

"Whose?" he asked, but his thoughts were interrupted by the arrival of a small Asian beauty who jumped up and wound her legs around his waist so that her raven quim was brushing his wettening shaft. She kept her sex close so that he could see and smell her musky excitement, but not so close that he could penetrate and gain relief.

It was all about power . . . As he tried in vain to spear the prize, he kept musing on the words *The Power Company*. What if they weren't just about control games? What if they were literally using sexual power to provide the world with a new source of energy? It would explain why they were desperate to recruit young eroticized people— especially those in the first few weeks of a love affair—and bring them to this heavily charged place. Of course, it seemed fanciful, but the last few days had taught him to question everything and discount nothing. Very little in this brave new world was as it seemed.

He looked up at the overheard screen in time to see O shudder unwillingly to yet another multiple orgasm. Smiling grimly, the dominatrix took the leather strop and lined it up with her already scarlet ass. At the same time, Casanova's latest tormentor arrived and began to caress his testes so that he was instantly, and painfully, close to completion again.

Just how, Casanova wondered weakly as she kept him on the edge of satiation, was this all going to end? He had traveled through New Orleans, Seattle, and San Francisco during this extraordinary quest, and now he was being tethered and teased in New York City. Would he see his beloved Venice—or hold his darling O in his arms—ever again?

Chapter Eighteen

He tried to hold back the wave of pleasure savagely coursing through his body as his now shadowy tormentors kept edging him to the very limits, then holding him back, then provoking him again. All around him was a blur, apart from the shining image of O on the wide plasma screen ahead of him, now being mounted in succession by man after man as her own ordeal continued just a few rooms away.

Finally, Casanova closed his eyes, both repelled and nefariously excited by the spectacle of the young woman's abominable defilement at the hands of a large black man—was it Maurice? The man roughly took hold of her neck and flowing blonde hair to correct her position and have her raise her rump obscenely skyward to his level before he impaled her now scarlet anal opening with his monstrously thick cock. Sweat was pouring down from her body onto the sacrificial stage.

Even though Casanova was now in darkness, he could still picture O's agony on the screen of his brain. It would not go away. Inside his head, it was like a roar of sounds and emotions, a terrible soundtrack where his grief collided in fifth gear with his awful, compulsive uncontrollable lust. It was just too much. His body went limp and he came. And screamed. Just as he imagined her also reaching her ulti-mate, deathly orgasm as the dark, trunklike penis plunged even deeper into her innards and began literally tearing her flesh apart, ripping her sphincter, opening her up like never before in an unholy mess of semen, blood, shit, and torn skin.

He opened his eyes. Fearing all he might now see would be the broken, dead, and violated body of O. Fucked to death.

Why was he imagining such things? Why was his mind so diseased? he sighed. Nobody should wish such suffering on anyone.

But the screen was now dark. His shadow torturers were silently moving away from him. He sat on the cold floor, his cock detumescing, his come pitifully spent, drying across his thighs and stomach.

Casanova began to cry.

Morning came. Casanova wiped the sleep from his eyes. At first his vision was blurry as reality and vision filtered through his raised consciousness, his whole body sharp with awakened pain. He remembered yesterday evening and groaned. He was still in one piece physically, but his mind was still putting the pieces together all over again, and all of a sudden the bodily pain—in his joints, all across his flayed skin, in his genitals—encountered the mental pain in sheer overdrive and he slumped.

He could hear the muted sound of urban traffic through a nearby window. He opened his eyes fully. He was sprawled, still naked, across a gray, deep shag carpet in what appeared to be a hotel room. The furnishings were tasteful if unimaginative. A sliver of light timidly made its way into the room through the vertical gap in thick, light brown draperies.

He made it to his knees and crawled a few yards across the soft floor and finally raised himself fully, every fiber in his body still screaming silently. He found his bearings and realized he was in a suite of rooms, as there was no bed in this particular area. There were

doors on either side of the room. He tried one; it led to a large bathroom, clean white fluffy towels hanging still unused. He crossed the
room to the other door. It wasn't closed. He slipped his left foot in the
small gap and quietly pushed the door open. As he had expected, it led
into the bedroom.

It was in darkness, curtains carefully drawn to keep the nascent
daylight out. As his eyes accustomed to the penumbra, he made out
the shape of the bed in the center of the room. A king-size bed with
pale blankets, and an even paler body sprawled across it, lost in its
almost polar whiteness.

Casanova knew instantly it was O.

His heart skipped a beat.

Was she alive?

He nervously moved closer to the bed.

And heard her ever-so-gentle snore.

Just sleeping. He heaved a sigh of relief. No wonder, he reckoned,
after such a delirious and painful night.

He approached the bed and its sleeping beauty.

Her smell reached him, a familiar scent of dried sweat and sex,
with an underlying foundation of faraway flowers and subtle fra-
grances. It looked as if she had been brought here still unwashed from
her earlier sexual exertions.

His balls tightened and he realized he was still naked himself.

He felt a wave of shame wash over him. How could he have such
thoughts, such reactions? He was a fool for lust. Surely, his wonderful
O had endured enough for quite some time, but still . . .

Casanova moved to the window and pulled the curtains slightly
apart, allowing the gray morning light to illuminate the room. He
looked back at the bed.

O slept on her stomach. The pale alabaster skin of her back and ass was crisscrossed with red weals and stripes where she had been flayed. The sharp initials she had been branded with were now barely visible. Some appeared fierce, where the skin had visibly been broken, others were less intense. The spectacle was both awesome and compelling to Casanova.

Her legs were parted as she sought the solace of sleep and forgetfulness, and he could not avoid focusing on the puffy, reddened lips of her partly gaping cunt. She was leaking secretions, the thin liquid catching the light from the window as it pearled down across her inner thigh to the bed's surface. Casanova gulped. His mind just did not want to know the nature of this obscene flow. Surely, as she rested, she deserved a presumption of innocence? And then O moved in her sleep, a cushioned moan arising from her mouth, and she shifted her position slightly. Casanova's eyes caught sight of the dark star of her anal opening. Bruised, bloody, no doubt torn.

He rushed out of the room and made a beeline for the bathroom, where he was violently sick.

"Once I had a master . . ." O said.

Casanova had wrapped himself in one of the white robes hanging in the other room's closet and brought its smaller twin to the bedroom to await O's awakening. He sat in a chair by her side in silence for a few more hours, listening to the rhythm of her breath, watching quiet, nervous tremors surge through her resting skin as she clung to the solace of sleep. Maybe he even dozed off himself at times.

Finally O slowly opened her eyes, and she stretched her long, splendid limbs as she welcomed both consciousness and her body back again. It was afternoon, and outside the New York traffic busied itself, impervious to the alien couple in the hotel room.

There was no surprise in O's eyes when she turned on her side and noticed Casanova looking at her, with his dark brown eyes full of sadness and a raging desire he could not conceal for all his wishes of propriety. She sat up and glanced down at her nakedness, the marks on her body, the swollen scarlet pinkness of her pubic mound, where someone had mercifully unstitched yesterday's sequins, leaving just the trace of an almost invisible network of punctures scattered across her tortured and delicate skin. The Power Company female acolyte who had been assigned to her "decorations" had used a particularly thin needle, after bathing O's parts with a soothing liquid that had deadened the pain for a while. She would heal quickly, O knew. It wouldn't be the last time, she supposed.

Casanova offered her the robe.

She turned down his gallant offer. She was accustomed to nudity. She had been trained to accept it as her natural state, even with others present.

She looked up at Casanova.

"So . . . ," she said.

He sketched a thin smile.

"So . . . ," he answered.

"Just the two of us."

"Alone at last," he added. And briefly ran out of things to say, things to ask, as a strong sense of anticlimax settled upon him. As if being alone with O had not been what he was seeking since that first fortuitous vision on the Lido of Venice.

She smiled understandingly at him. "I don't have all the answers," she said. "Maybe I'm just too pragmatic at heart, but I'd long given up on them. I just live in the present, you know. It's just the way that I am, that I've always been."

Casanova came to his senses at long last. "Tell me who you really are," he asked her. "At first you appeared to me like a vision of Athena, then I discovered they called you O. Who is the real you?"

Her eyes looked down as she prepared to embark on her story. "It's long and complicated," she said.

"I suspect we have all the time in the world," Casanova replied, sensing wrongly that their ordeals were now over. "Do tell me all, O."

She took a deep breath, and then embarked on her tale.

"Once I had a master . . . ," O began as she revealed herself to Casanova. Her life in Paris, Sir Stephen, Roissy, the training, what she had willingly endured, how she understood the essence of her submissiveness, her understanding of those treacherous cravings inside the heart and body. The story of O and how she had embraced slavery in the name of love. It took a long time, and New York outside journeyed slowly into a new night. He listened to her, rapt with attention, at times amazed, at times shocked, but always fascinated, and by the time she had almost finished her tale, he loved and desired her more than ever before.

"This was in Paris in the 1950s," she said. "Now it seems such a long time ago," she wistfully added and shivered as the temperature inside the darkening hotel bedroom fell progressively lower. He offered her the bathrobe again. This time she accepted it and covered her partly scarred skin to the waist down, allowing the robe to still reveal her lower stomach and her legs held apart in obedience to her erstwhile training. Casanova's eyes were yet again drawn to her sexual parts, now somewhat less red and swollen, the tantalizing lips of her flowered cunt betraying the nacreous and moist insides of her sexual soul.

A thought occurred to him.

"But it's now 2005," he remarked. "How old are you, may I inquire, however ungallant that question might be?"

"I am as I was," O answered.

Which is when Casanova realized they were *both* newcomers to this world. Strangers. He probed.

"It was a year or so after my second stay in Roissy. I had unwittingly ignored a command from one of the masters then in charge of the grounds. For my punishment I was assigned to enforced servitude to a group of wealthy doms who required entertainment on a cruise in the Caribbean. I was not the only slave present and found it easy to endure their use and whims. I had been through much worse before.

"There was another youngster in our midst who somehow became the brunt of their cruelty. Her name was Isabella; she was Italian. They picked on her most unfairly, and she still hadn't the inner strength to find serenity in the acceptance of her condition. Her master, an older man who had been a professor of hers at university, didn't realize she was still not ready for this sort of training.

"One day, her resolve broke and she tried to drown herself. I threw myself into the water in an attempt to save her. This I managed, but as she was being dragged back onto the boat, I must have cramped and fell back into the sea. All I remember is the terrible weight in my lungs as the water filled me, and how my vision grew ever darker, and I could feel my body dropping like an anchor to the bottom of the ocean bed.

"I realized I was dying. My brain felt as if it were now floating inside my head, detached, indifferent. I did not fear death. So this was it, I thought, in those ultimate moments. Not the way I'd ever expected to go, but does one ever have a choice? I died, I think, because a moment later, I woke as if from a normal night's sleep. I was in my own bed in Paris, in the flat I had once lived in before Sir Stephen and Roissy. I was alive.

"The first thing I noticed as I looked down at my body was that the ring that had been pierced into my sex lips when I was fully accepted as a submissive in Roissy was no longer there. There was not even a minuscule hole in the delicate skin where it had been placed. Also, my bed sheets were damp, and when I licked them, looking for an answer, they tasted of seawater.

"It made no sense. For days, I thought I had fallen into madness, that I could no longer distinguish between dreams and reality. The memories of what I'd been and what had happened to me could surely not be a mirage; it was all too real, as was my inner sense of my condition. Finally, I became bold enough to leave my flat and wander the streets. And I found out that fifty years or so had passed. No one I once knew was still alive. Customs had changed. This new world was both alluring and scary."

Casanova nodded in understanding.

"Then, I don't recall how many days precisely it was after my return, there was an envelope in the mail. A train ticket to Venice, first class, and a summons to an address there a week later. The Roissy colophon was embossed on the paper on which I was being ordered to travel and obey. The rest you know, or at any rate, most of it," she paused.

"I don't know why I was brought back, why these adventures, why these ordeals, or why our paths always seem to cross. It's in my nature to accept these things, the Power Company and its hold on so many of us. As ever, there is an emptiness inside me, and I follow its path, wherever it takes me. There we are," she concluded.

"I also died," Casanova confessed to O. And then he related his story. She knew the early parts of it, having once browsed through his rambling book of memoirs, but she avidly listened to the tale of what had happened to him since his awakening that now faraway morning in modern-day Venice.

None of it appeared to surprise her.

Night came.

They were both strangers in a strange new world.

"Sleep?" she suggested.

Yes, they both had much sleep to catch up with.

She slid between the sheets and indicated he should join her.

They spooned together in a gesture of infinite tenderness after shedding the bulky robes, both too damaged emotionally and physically to even entertain the prospect of sex. All they sought now was silence and closeness, body warmth and softness.

Light had barely broken when Casanova awoke the next day. O still slept peacefully at his side, the steady rhythm of her breathing imperceptibly animating her bare, pale skin. The tribulations of the other night had evidently taken more out of her than she thought, and her present weariness was how her body was now recharging its batteries.

Casanova, on the other hand, felt all of his energy returned. He affectionately slipped a finger through her tangled hair, but O did not react and continued sleeping.

He moved out of the bed they had just chastely shared. He was hungry now. As he explored the suite, it quickly became evident there were no clothes in the closets or anywhere else. Signifying in all likelihood that whoever had left Casanova and O here had no wish for them to leave.

Escaping through the bustling streets of Manhattan in a bathrobe was not an ideal situation, he reckoned. They also had no money or access to any form of funds.

Apparently, the men (and women?) pulling their strings had just parked the two of them in this hotel room as a matter of convenience and would be back to claim them soon, for whatever nefarious use they could conjure. And Casanova had no doubt they had just that in mind, and worse.

He sensed that some terrible, ultimate purpose behind the Power Company, or some other occult entity with or without a name, was controlling their fate. They must have both been brought back for a reason. For an ultimate sacrifice?

All he could feel was despair and an abominable sense of helplessness. What had the beautiful O done to deserve this?

He, Casanova, had been a sinner, a man whose extreme love of women, and sex, had provoked unseemly debauchery, but never suffering on the scale she had experienced. Surely, he should be the one on whom punishment should be inflicted. But he also knew that justice seldom found its intended target.

"Giacomo," he heard O's cry from the bedroom.

He returned to her. She was sitting up on the bed, the lower half of her body still sheltered by the sheets and blanket. Her small, delicate breasts peered above the cover, her nipples pink and exquisite, the color of spring flowers.

She smiled at him.

Her strength had returned.

"How are you, my dear?" he asked.

"Better, much better," she replied as she looked into his eyes. "You appear sad. Why is this?" she queried.

"Because I believe the fact that we are now together in this room is what has been planned all along. It serves the purpose of these damn manipulators who have been covertly controlling our crossed destinies," Casanova said. "As much as I am pleased to now finally be here with you, it is also their victory . . ."

"Shhhh," she whispered, putting a finger to her lips. "Don't be so melodramatic."

She threw the sheets away and uncovered the rest of her regal body. The sight was almost enough to blind him, even after the many times he had contemplated her sensuous curves and softness before. Her open legs were a terrible invitation.

"Come to me, Giacomo. Let's just enjoy the moment . . . Make love to me. Have me, take me, enjoy me, open me up like I've never been opened before. I know you can. I know you want to."

And yes, he desired her with a passion that dwarfed all the cravings that had until now controlled his life.

But he held back from the welcome of her embrace.

"No, my love. We musn't."

"Why?"

He was about to attempt some clumsy form of explanation, to iron out the wrinkles in his paranoid intuition about their situation when the door to the suite opened and he heard the soft patter of footsteps making their way to the bedroom.

He turned to look in the direction of the door while O instinctively pulled the bedcovers back toward herself.

"Good morning."

It was none other than Cristiana, his erstwhile Venice companion. O also recognized her from her stay on the ship and elsewhere, although she had never been told the young woman's name. She wore a thick, brown leather coat that reached down to her knees, and beautifully polished black boots.

"Hello, Cristiana," Casanova said.

"Hi, Giacomo," Cristiana replied.

"Maybe I should have known it would be you," he said. "You were there from the beginning. No wonder you are here now. I do believe it was no accident I came across you, was it?"

"No, it was not, Giacomo. I was under orders to be your guide for those first steps in our world."

"You've always worked for them?" he asked.

"No, not always. I was also once an actress, so I am practiced at playing roles."

"You played yours well, Cristiana."

The young woman sighed deeply.

"Too well," she said. "Now I can't go back to the way things were. I know too much and I crave constantly what they make available to me. I have become one of their creatures. It's like signing a deal with the devil, sort of. They don't want your soul, just your mind and your body. Little did we know, Giacomo Casanova, that those little games we played were but a shadow of what already existed at the very core of ourselves. You contaminated me."

"I'm truly sorry," he said.

Cristiana glanced at O, who sat there silent.

"She is truly beautiful, Giacomo. She really is. How could anyone not desire her intensely?"

He nodded.

"And now?" he finally asked her.

Cristiana's eyes clouded.

"They will be coming for both of you tomorrow morning."

"And?" O interjected.

"I'm not sure exactly," Cristiana said. "I know a stage is being prepared, and all have been summoned to attend and participate, at every level of the company. It's something that has apparently been decades in the planning."

"And we are to be the centerpiece of the bacchanal?"

Cristiana lowered her face. "Yes."

"Will the two of us even still be alive at the conclusion of such a unique feast?" O asked, before Casanova could even formulate a similar question.

Cristiana bit her lips.

"I don't know," she answered.

But the look on her face said it all.

There was a heavy moment of silence.

"Why are you here?" Casanova asked Cristiana.

"To keep you company until then and see to your needs. I expect you've not eaten or drunk anything since you've been here. We can call room service. Whatever you desire."

"Just order enough for the three of us," Casanova asked her.

Cristiana walked over to the phone in the other room to arrange for food. Casanova took the opportunity to quickly explain to O the plan he had just formulated in his mind.

Her instant reaction was a negative one.

"You can't do that," she argued. "You just can't."

"It's necessary, my darling. We can't allow this to happen."

"I know, but is there just no other way?" she begged him.

"I can't see one. They badly need for both of us to participate. It's what all of this has been about. With one of us gone, the other is worth little to them. Don't you understand?"

"I do," O feebly protested. "But . . ."

Cristiana returned to the bedroom as Casanova silenced O.

"I've ordered champagne," Cristiana said in a semblance of cheerfulness. She slipped out of her leather coat. She wore just a thin white T-shirt and a short black skirt underneath, and looked almost like a schoolgirl, unmarked by all the excesses of the past few weeks.

"Where shall we eat? Here or in the main room?" she asked.

"Not the bedroom," O said, and buried herself between the sheets again. "I have no clothes, call me when room service has delivered the food. We don't want to arouse the staff unnecessarily, do we?"

Cristiana smiled and Casanova tied the sash of his bathrobe tighter across his waist.

The meal had been just adequate. The steaks were somewhat

overcooked and dry, but the champagne had been a decent Cartier vintage and duly warmed them inside.

"I'll sleep on the settee in the suite's main room; you can keep the bedroom," Cristiana had told them, and they had all retired for the night after switching the lights off.

Sitting on the bed, Casanova and O stayed silent for quite some time, almost holding their breath.

Finally, they estimated, it was time to move back to the other room, which they did stealthily. Cristiana was sleeping soundly, as they had expected. She had stripped to her white cotton panties, evoking some bittersweet memories to Casanova, which he quickly banished away from his mind.

While O silently straddled the dormant body of the young woman, Casanova quickly positioned himself on his knees between her outstretched legs and quickly seized her hands behind her back and tied them together with the belt from one of the bathrobes. Before Cristiana had regained enough consciousness to protest being manhandled, O had brutally stuffed the young Italian girl's crumpled T-shirt inside her mouth and muffled her screams.

Pulling her panties down and using one of the steak knives, they quickly cut the skirt and underwear into a series of strips with which they expertly tied Cristiana's now naked body to a chair, legs obscenely akimbo, arms pulled behind her to their utmost extent, ankles bound to the chair's wooden legs. To reinforce the bondage, O quickly discarded her own bathrobe and, stark naked herself one more time, patiently shredded the soft but resistant material into more strips to make absolutely certain Cristiana could not escape from the double set of bindings. To cap it all, she used the belt to hold the young woman's neck back at a sharp angle, which made it totally impossible to move her head. Casanova checked to make sure Cristiana could still breathe properly. It was all rather crude, but he was confident she would not evade these bonds.

Abandoning the helpless young woman, O and Casanova slowly walked back to the bedroom. O was about to say something, but he put his hands to her lips. Mere words were now superfluous.

They stood at the foot of the bed. Casanova shrugged his untied bathrobe off and it slid heavily to carpet. He looked O in the eyes and lost himself in the deep gray-blue sea of her infinite sadness. His hands extended in her direction, and he took her breasts into the cup of his hands, gliding across her softness, her nipples hardening under his fleeting touch. He bent over to kiss them, delicately, licking the nub of her tips, wetting them until he could almost chew on them. O moaned softly, affected by both pleasure and sharp pain as his teeth left a brief imprint within the puckered darker skin of her nipples. She dropped her hands and took hold of his cock. He was already hard.

Casanova took a step back and she had to let him go. He dropped to his knees, and his tongue began a thorough exploration of her cunt, his fingers holding her well open, splayed. He tasted her inner musk, his tongue digging deeper into her pink crevice, feeling with every moment within the beat of her heart as the emotions coursed through her veins, connecting heart and cunt in an insane Escher curve of lust.

O's legs felt weak, and Casanova helped her down onto the bed. With his head still buried between her thighs, he continued worshipping her cunt with science and application. O came a first time, and then another, her whole body erupting like a volcano, skin shivering with unseen tremors, a babel of words struggling to overcome the barrier of her throat. He tasted her strong secretions, and it felt better than alcohol or sugar. Finally, he moved away from her sex and forcibly raised her rump until his tongue could reach the darker crater of her anal opening. As he drilled her sphincter, tasting its slightly acrid flavor, she came a third time. She pulled him away from her by his hair, almost begging silently for him to now penetrate her.

But his resolve stood.

"No, that's what they would want," he said.

There were tears in her eyes. Casanova could feel his own well up inside and knew he was also perilously close to breaking down. He rose to his feet and pulled O toward him. Their bodies made contact. Sheer electricity. Her softness was exquisite, as if his own flesh just melted into hers until they were one. He closed his eyes.

"Kiss me," he whispered.

Their mouths met. He still had on his tongue the taste of both her cunt and her asshole. She licked him clean of herself, and then another welcoming taste poured into him as their tongues twisted in desperate intercourse and they were but a single breath.

The kiss lasted an eternity, and it was both too much and not enough as the world surrounding them disappeared. They stood joined at their mouths, in an unholy halo of desire and tenderness.

Still intimately wed to her lips, Casanova picked up the steak knife he had earlier dropped onto the bed and placed it gently inside her right hand.

Now, he intimated silently as they still kissed.

O hesitated.

Casanova's mouth dragged the air from her lungs until she thought she would scream in agony.

"Now."

She took careful aim, and with her lips still entangled with his, she stabbed him as hard as she could. Then she closed her eyes as he flinched, and she drew the knife out again and repeated the deadly movement several times, puncturing his flesh on each occasion. They were still entwined, and she could feel the blood now freely pouring from him and dripping down onto her own stomach, submerging her enflamed cunt, and then coursing down both their legs toward the bedroom floor.

She kept on dutifully assaulting his poor body until she felt him lose consciousness. Their lips were torn apart as his head moved to the side, but his whole body still adhered closely to her, supported by her, still refusing to leave the harbor of her warmth.

"You must let go, Giacomo," she said to her dead lover as she carefully took hold of his shoulders and lowered him onto the bed.

She looked at his face one last time, holding back a veritable flood of tears. He was at peace.

She rushed to the other room, where Cristiana's eyes could not help glaring at the spectacle of O's blood-covered nudity and the knife she still held in her hand. She quickly showered, then grabbed Cristiana's brown leather coat and put in on. It was too tight for her and barely came to her mid thigh, as the young Italian woman was so much shorter than her, but it would have to do.

She walked to the hotel suite's door, rushed through the anonymous corridor, and took the elevator down. The lobby was almost empty; just a night clerk dozing at the counter.

O walked into the Manhattan night.

Central Park was a half dozen blocks north. It was cold and the leather coat barely covered her. O shivered.

She did not know where she was going. She crossed Fifth Avenue and moved on to Park, in the direction of the Metropolitan Museum. It seemed the right thing to do. The streetlights felt harsh and unforgiving, so to evade the fierceness of the wind, she descended into the darkness of Central Park.

She was alone, she had no money, she was naked under the coat.

"On your own, you have a better chance of surviving," he had said when he had unveiled his terrible plan. "They might not need you any longer."

Time would tell.

O melted into the encroaching darkness of Central Park at night. The moon above was totally obscured by a lowflying bank of clouds

The sleeping man opened his eyes. At first disoriented, he took stock of the unfamiliar surroundings.

The air in the room felt rank, almost fetid.

He rose from the bed and walked hesitantly to the window and undid the wooden shutters that kept the light out.

He took in the view and inhaled.

He knew that smell all too well. The canals in summer were always so malodorous. It was a wonder the thousands of visitors who flocked here never objected. He stretched his neck and caught a glimpse of the Palazzo Grassi and, beyond, the muted shape of Santa Maria dei Frari.

Venice in summer. *Bella* Venezia.

He looked down at his body. He was unmarked.

And then he remembered Manhattan, the knife, and O.

So, he shrugged, *was death not enough?*

He needed no calendar or guide this time; he knew that the year was the wrong one and that he was separated from O by a bridge of centuries and would never see her again, unless in the sweetest of dreams.

He hoped she had managed to escape the clutches of the Power Company. Though without him, he assumed she was of little use to them. He prayed for this to be true.

That afternoon, he took a walk along the Grand Canal, all the way from the Palazzo Ducale to the Ponto di Rialto. His city would never change, a fact that comforted him deeply.

A crowd of foreign tourists were crossing the bridge, busy taking photographs and 3-D movies of themselves and all the classic vistas with newfangled pencil-thin cameras. Some spoke German, others English. A young woman with shocking, wild, untamed red hair and a tight green dress caught his attention. A thing of beauty; his eyes traveled down to her thin ankles and a strange feeling invaded his heart. They could have been O's ankles, delicate though solid, perfectly angled, pale, waiting to be caressed.

The crowd dispersed and the woman in green moved away in a small group of four. Casanova allowed himself a melancholy smile and began following them.

Old habits died hard, didn't they?

About the Authors

MAXIM JAKUBOWSKI is the well-known editor of the best-selling *Mammoth Book of Erotica* series, and himself one of today's most notable erotic writers. His latest books in the genre are *Fools for Lust*, a collection of his short fiction (Blue Moon), a trilogy of erotic thrillers *Skin in Darkness* and a novel, *Confessions of a Romantic Pornographer*. He also edits the Neon imprint. He lives in London, where he is a regular contributor to a variety of newspapers and magazines and a frequent radio and TV broadcaster, owns the famous Murder One bookshop and runs Crime Scene, London's annual Film and Literature Festival.

M. CHRISTIAN is a prolific San Francisco-based writer of erotica, whose short stories have graced most of the major anthologies. He has also edited many himself, including some with Sage Vivant, *The Mammoth Book of Future Cops* and *The Mammoth Book of on the Road* (both with Maxim Jakubowski), *Best S/M Erotica*, *The Burning Pen*, *Rough Stuff*, and *Blood Lust*. His short stories have been collected in *Dirty Words*, *Speaking Parts*, and *The Bachelor Machine*. His last novel is *Running Dry*.

MICHAEL CRAWLEY was born and bred in London's East End. He dropped out of grammar school at the age of 16 and began a career of beginning careers. After trying soldiering, the rag trade, mill work, shop work, demolition, construction, bartending, real estate, clerical serfdom, maitre d' and a couple of trades he'd rather not mention, he turned his attention to writing. So far about two million of his words in short stories have been published plus a score of books, including in the erotic field *The Watched And The Watched* and *The Persian Girl.*

CAROL ANNE DAVIS was born in Dundee, Scotland, but now lives in south-west England. Her true crime books include *Couples Who Kill,* *Children Who Kill,* and *Women Who Kill,* the latter profiling female serial killers. On a bad day she refuses to leave the house without a bullet-proof vest. She is also the author of the dark crime novels *Kiss It Away* (which deals with the true horror of male on male rape), *Noise Abatement* (killing the neighbors from hell), *Safe as Houses* (sexual sadism) and *Shrouded* (necrophilia) so you can always find her in the kitchen at parties as she's shunned by the shockable. Carol also enjoys writing erotic, humorous, historical (some would say hysterical) and psychological-horror-based short stories. Visit her disarmingly basic website at www.carolannedavis.co.uk.

STELLA DUFFY has written ten novels. *State of Happiness* was long listed for the 2004 Orange Prize and is in film development. With Lauren Henderson, she edited *Tart Noir,* from which her story "Martha Grace" won the 2002 CWA Short Story Dagger. She has also written many stories and articles and created the Saz Martin mystery series. With the National Youth Theatre, she adapted her novel *Immaculate Conceit* for the Lyric, Hammersmith, most recently writing and directing *Cell Sell* for the Soho theatre. She also writes and performs for theatre and radio. Born in South London, Stella grew up in New Zealand but has lived in the UK since 1986.

O'NEIL DE NOUX has published six novels, a true crime book and two short story collections. His over 200 short stories have been published in magazines and anthologies in nine countries. His latest books are *Mafia Aphrodite* and a short story collection of 1940s private eye stories, *New Orleans Confidential*. A native of New Orleans, where he lived until recently with his wife, he was exiled twice during the recent hurricane disaster and is soon moving back, although to higher ground.

SONIA FLORENS is the pseudonym for a well-known British author and translator in both the erotic and the science fiction and fantasy fields. She has published short stories in a variety of anthologies, as well as translations from the French and the Italian. She lives in London with her husband, with two children now having flown the nest.

JOHN GRANT is the author of over 60 books and winner of several international awards, including the Hugo and the World Fantasy Award. His non-fiction books include *Masters of Animation, The Chesley Awards,* and the *Encyclopedia of Fantasy* (co-edited with John Clute). His humor books include *The Alan Smithee Diaries, Earthdoom, Guts,* and *Sex Secrets of Ancient Atlantis.* His novels include *Dragonhenge* and *The Stardragons.* He has also edited many art and illustration titles. He lives in rural New Jersey with his wife and four cats.

MICHAEL HEMMINGSON lives in San Diego, California and has proven one of the most provocative and prolific erotic writers of his generation, with scores of unsettling and sexy books. He has also edited several anthologies and written crime novels. A playwright and theatre director, he has also written extensively for television. He is the co-editor of *Expelled from Eden,* a William T. Vollmann Reader (Thunder's Mouth Press). His most recent novel is *The Yacht People.*

VICKI HENDRICKS is the author of noir novels *Miami Purity, Iguana Love, Voluntary Madness,* and *Sky Blues.* Her short stories have appeared in many magazines and anthologies. She lives in Hollywood, Florida, and teaches writing at Broward Community College. Her work reflects her interest in adventure and sports, such as skydiving and scuba, and knowledge of the south Florida environment. Her latest novel of murder and obsession *Cruel Poetry,* is set in South Beach, Miami.

THOMAS S. ROCHE has written over 200 erotic short stories and countless articles, and contributed to all the major anthologies of the last decade. He has edited many anthologies, including three volumes of *Noirotica, Brothers of the Night, Graven Images, In the Shadow of the Gargoyle,* and *Hers and His* (both with Alison Tyler). He has published *Dark Matter,* a story collection and has completed a novel, *Violent Angel.* After a detour in New Orleans, he has now returned to San Francisco, where he is the editor of a major Internet project.

MITZI SZERETO is the author of *Erotic Fairy Tales, Highway,* the M.S. Valentine erotic novels, and editor of *Dying for It, The World's Best Sex Writing 2005, Wicked,* and *The Erotic Travel Tales* anthology series. She is also a pioneer of erotic writing workshops in the UK and Europe and has been profiled in a variety of publications and on radio and TV. Originally from the USA, she now lives in England.

LUCY TAYLOR is a full-time writer whose most recent novels include *Left To Die* by "Taylor Kincaid," *Saving Souls,* and *Nailed.* Her collection *The Silence Between the Screams* was recently published and her *The Safety of Unknown Cities* won the Bram Stoker Award for Best Horror Novel of the Year. She works as a hospice volunteer and enjoys tango and salsa and working out on the low-lying trapeze. She lives in Lyons, Colorado, with four wonderful cats and a Samoyed named Chloey.

MATT THORNE was born in Bristol, England. He is the author of six novels: *Tourist, Eight Minutes Idle* (Winner of the Encore Award, 1999), *Dreaming of Strangers, Pictures of You, Child Star,* and *Cherry* (long listed for the Booker Prize, 2005). He is also the author of the 39 Castles series of children's books and has co-edited two anthologies *All Hail the New Puritans* and *Croatian Nights.* He reviews books and restaurants for many leading British newspapers and lives in London with his wife, a literary agent.

MARK TIMLIN is the notorious British crime writer and creator of the hardboiled Nick Sharman series, which was adapted for television with Clive Owen playing the ambivalent and violent South London private eye. He is also the author of the acclaimed gangster saga *Answers from the Grave.* A controversial on the British mystery scene, he is also the crime reviewer for the Independent on Sunday. He lives on London's Isle of Dogs.

SAGE VIVANT operates Custom Erotica Source, where she crafts tailor-made erotic fiction for individual clients. She is the author of *Giving the Bride Away,* and the co-editor with M. Christian of *Confessions, Amazons,* and *Leather, Lace and Lust,* as well as several others. Her stories have appeared in dozens of anthologies. Visit her Web site at www.customeroticasource.com

MOLLY WEATHERFIELD is the author of the best-selling comic SM novels *Carrie's Story* and *Safe Word.* As Pam Rosenthal (her real name) she writes erotic historical romance novels: *The Bookseller's*

Daughter was named one of *Library Journal*'s best romances of 2004. Her next novel is *The Slightest Provocation*. She also reviews for Salon.com and the *San Francisco Chronicle* (both as Pam and Molly). She lives in San Francisco with her husband, bookseller Michael Rosenthal.